THE TRIDENT SERIES II

BRAVO TEAM

JOKER

Book 1

Jaime Lewis

This is a work of fiction. Names, characters, business, events, and incidents are the products of the author's imagination. Any resemblance to actual persons, living or dead, or actual events is purely coincidental.

The Trident Series - JOKER
Copyright © 2022 by Jaime Lewis

All rights reserved. No part of this book may be reproduced or transmitted in any form or by any means without written permission from the author.

ISBN:978-1-952734-29-8

TABLE OF CONTENTS

Prologue	1
Chapter 1	3
Chapter 2	14
Chapter 3	31
Chapter 4	52
Chapter 5	62
Chapter 6	68
Chapter 7	76
Chapter 8	93
Chapter 9	96
Chapter 10	116
Chapter 11	124
Chapter 12	138
Chapter 13	153
Chapter 14	166
Chapter 15	182
Chapter 16	191
Chapter 17	206
Chapter 18	236
Chapter 19	246
Chapter 20	257
Chapter 21	268
Chapter 22	280
Chapter 23	283
Chapter 24	294
Epilogue	307

PROLOGUE

Clover Walker submerged herself beneath the Caribbean Sea's warm, crystal blue waters. She kicked her feet, her fins propelling her through the serene marine life of colorful coral, tropical fish, and playful dolphins. The sea was her haven—a place where peace and beauty came together as one, creating an ambiance like no other.

Suddenly, from the depths of the blue sea, a grumpy-looking, yet, vibrant colored Splendid Toadfish appeared in front of her. Its mouth opened wide as if it were trying to speak to her, but all she got was an odd buzzing sound much like a cell phone's vibration. Before she knew it, her oasis transformed into a frightening scene, as a large school of toadfish soon surrounded her. With their mouths open and sharp little teeth visible, they closed in on her as the buzzing sound grew louder the closer they got. The sound soon became too much to bear, and she began to panic. She kicked her legs and moved her arms, trying desperately to propel her body toward the sea's surface to escape the scary fish. However, her freedom was short-lived as the school cut her off and began to swim in circles around her, creating a whirlpool effect and pulling her down. As the sea slowly swallowed her, the intense vibration returned, pulling all the air from her body until she could no longer breathe. Suddenly, everything went black and silent. Was she dead?

Buzz...buzz...buzz...

Clover's eyes popped open as she jolted awake, her heart pounding in her chest. She laid there for a moment, trying to calm her breathing. She looked around, trying to make sure she was indeed in her bedroom in San Diego, and not stuck in the abyss. The thought of ever encountering a Splendid Toadfish had her rethinking her scuba diving hobby.

The buzzing started again, and now that she was awake and alert, she realized it was just her cell phone. Blindly, she reached above her, searching for the phone on top of the headboard. Once she had it, she took one look at the screen and sighed in frustration. She was being called into work.

There had been only a handful of times that she damned her job. In truth, she loved her profession and wouldn't trade it for the world. Serving her country in a capacity meant to protect those she loved had long been a dream of hers since she was a little girl. But today was one of those rare occasions she wished she didn't have to jump when ordered.

She laid the phone down next to her and rolled onto her side. The soft snores coming from the pillow next to her brought a smile to her face. His dark hair was a stark contrast to the snow-white pillowcase his head rested on. She reached out and gently threaded her fingers through his thick hair. He stirred, shifting to his back, and threw one of his arms above his head. His movement caused the sheet covering his glorious body to slip down to his thick but solid waist, revealing that sexy V cut in his lower abdominals.

She lifted up, leaning on her elbow. Last night was unbelievable and very unexpected. Had she known years ago that the man lying next to her was filled with so much compassion, empathy, and understanding, she would have acted on her feelings sooner.

The sound of her phone buzzing again made her realize that her fairy-tale night had come to an end, and it was back to reality.

He appeared so content that she hated to wake him. Not knowing when she would have an opportunity to see him again, she grabbed the pen and small pad of paper she kept by the bed, jotted down her number, and left it on her pillow for him to find before she silently slipped out of bed.

As she headed out the door, she hoped Landon Davis knew he had been gifted a part of her that no other man would ever obtain.

CHAPTER ONE

Present Day – Eritrea: Two Years Later

"We're two minutes out from the extraction point. You ready for this, Lucky?" Major Brent Saunders asked Marine Captain Clover "Lucky" Walker.

Clover grinned, firmly gripping the cyclic stick to the modified stealth version of the sleek HH-60W Black Hawk helicopter she was piloting. She lived for flying, even more so while serving her country.

"When am I ever not ready?" She countered through the headset as she eyed the instrument panel, making sure her aircraft was prepared as they sped into hostile territory in the dead of night. It was in the wee hours of the morning local time in Eritrea, a country nestled in eastern Africa, bordered by the Red Sea to the east, Sudan to its north, Ethiopia to the west, and Djibouti to the south.

Clover and Major Saunders had a few potential obstacles on their hands. Not only did they have to contend with the enemy forces trying to pin down the Special Forces team they were assisting, but they also had to contend with the ongoing friction between militia groups in Eritrea and the neighboring countries. It wasn't uncommon for the groups to use military aircraft as target practice.

"We're going in hot. We have confirmation from the UAV team that the team is in place and standing by for our arrival. However, they did spot a few clusters of individuals assembling, and the team radioed in that they've got a crowd behind them approaching rapidly. I've called in for backup, but their ETA is four mikes."

Crap. Lucky knew she and the Major didn't have four minutes to circle and wait for backup. That team on the ground didn't have four extra minutes to spare. Four minutes was a lot of time, especially in a battle situation. If they waited for backup, there was a high probability that the rescue mission could become a recovery mission—not the outcome anyone was seeking, nor would Lucky ever accept.

"Copy. We don't have time to wait on reinforcements," she replied, glancing over at the Major, hoping he was in tune with her judgment call.

"I agree. We're going to have to go in." Calling back to the crew chief, Major Saunders asked, "Hollis, are we clear to go?"

"Cleared," Hollis' snappy response came back.

Lucky bit her tongue to prevent her from saying anything derogatory that could land her in hot water. She couldn't stand their crew chief, Sergeant Hollis, for various reasons. And it pained her that even though she and Major Saunders outranked him, it was the crew chief who, for the most part, was in command of the aircraft, though at times, the pilots had the authority to overrule the instructions of crew chief.

The role of crew chief for their squadron was a position of great responsibility, consisting of having the authority to dictate to anyone getting on the helicopter where they had to sit and what cargo they were allowed to bring on board. Crew chiefs also assisted in relaying intel from the ground communications to the pilots, operating weapons, and overseeing the aircraft's overall maintenance. In a nutshell, the selected individual had to be on their "A" game for every mission. And in Clover's opinion, that wasn't Hollis by any means.

"How many are we expecting for the ride?" She asked, looking through her night-vision goggles for any incoming projectiles.

"Team of eight and one rescue. Rescue is an injured American needing medical attention. I've already alerted medical back at the base. They're standing by for our arrival."

Lucky piloted the chopper with ease. Flying into enemy territory gave her an instant adrenaline rush, adding to the gratification of being in the sky while serving her country. Flying was her life. Being named to the Situational Combat Unit had been a huge deal for her. The squadron was a tight-knit group consisting of only ten teams. Each team comprised of two pilots, a crew chief, and a five-person ground crew. Out of the eighty team members appointed to the SCU by the President of the United States himself, she was currently the only female. Members of the SCU went through extensive background checks, and were given top security clearances that mirrored the Special Forces community. The identities of all SCU members were closely guarded because of their role in highly classified missions worldwide.

Nobody, not even her family, knew what her true profession was. Not that she was forbidden to tell them. It had been her personal decision not to. They were all under the impression that she was a helicopter mechanic stationed in San Diego, California. After she graduated from the NROTC program at Embry-Riddle Aeronautical University as a Second Lieutenant in the Marine Corps, she attended flight school before being recruited by the President to pilot one of the helicopters for his elite flying squadron. Keeping that sort of information under wraps from her family was challenging on so many levels.

The missions she and her team were called up for consisted of highly classified operations ordered by their Commander in Chief. The main task of the SCU was to provide insertions and extractions for many Special Forces teams, as well as some questionable black ops firms conducting high-level missions. Herein laid the issue of her family finding out what she was really up to. The Special Forces teams she flew were the same Special Forces teams her four older brothers were members of. Justin, Zach, and Ethan followed their dad's footsteps as enlisted Marines, and were assigned to the Raiders' elite unit. Then Tripp, a.k.a. Bear, a Naval Academy graduate, was assigned to SEAL Team 2, BRAVO team. She'd never brag because she was never one to seek attention, but her family was badass.

On several occasions, she piloted the aircraft that flew her brothers into action and had been the pilot to pull their asses out.

When she was informed of her appointment at the SCU, she decided she didn't want her gender to reflect on her career. Their unit was small, and not a typical air assault team that liked attention directed toward them. So, keeping her gender under wraps kept the media and others who dug for gossip away. That also included those within the rank and file. She had been the subject of a few slanderous comments when her name was floated around about joining the team, especially by those she ultimately beat out of the position. As far as she was concerned, the best man or woman in her case won. The less drama, the better, and it'd been that way.

"Who do we get the pleasure of chauffeuring on this lovely evening?" She called over to Major Saunders with a hint of sarcasm, though she kept her eyes focused on the ground below.

"Team 2, BRAVO."

"Shit," she muttered to herself, but loud enough that Major Saunders heard her because he snickered.

"Yeah, I figured you'd say that." He reached over and patted her hand in a teasing manner. "Don't worry. I'll handle the communication from the cockpit. You just do your magic and fly us the hell out of here, but stay alert for any engagement from across the border. We're still getting Intel reports stating tensions have been high between a few of the militia groups in the last few days, so even when we move on from this area, we've got a few hot spots along the route we're going to need to keep an eye on."

"Copy that," she responded and prepared her game face.

As they approached the extraction location, Major Saunders watched for any enemy forces engaging, while Clover guided the aircraft closer to the landing site. Once it was confirmed there was no direct enemy fire in the immediate area, she began the descent as Sergeant Hollis dropped two smoke grenades out the door marking the landing zone.

Clover took a deep breath, praying her brother and his team moved their asses.

"Let's do this," she uttered to herself.

Landon "Joker" Davis heard the unmistakable *chuff-chuff-chuff* sound of the incoming helo and knew it was their ride. The timing was impeccable, because he and his fellow SEAL team were pinned down and had a truckload of armed, pissed-off extremists on their tail.

"We need to get the hell out of here!" Bear, BRAVO's team leader, shouted in his mic.

Joker wasn't going to disagree. He and the team were sitting ducks out in the open. They were outnumbered and running out of time. As soon as the helicopter swooped in like a blackbird bringing positive energy, he glanced over at Bear, waiting for him to give the signal to move. A few seconds ticked by before the helo camouflaged its movement by dropping two smoke grenades. Seconds later, white and grey smoke began to spread into the darkness, blocking the light coming from the high moon.

"Now!" Bear ordered, raising his left hand in the air and waving it in a circular motion, signaling the team members to move out. Nails, one of the team members, lifted the injured American they were sent to rescue into a fireman's carry, then hurried toward the helicopter. They had recovered the guy from a secret underground facility thought to be run by a terrorist organization that was linked to the Iranian military. When they found him, he had been severely beaten, and suffered from a gunshot wound to his shoulder. Joker wasn't even sure if the guy would survive due to the amount of blood he had lost. His condition also complicated the mission, but they were trained to adapt and overcome any situation they found themselves in.

Joker stayed back with Bear to help provide cover for the team as they made their way to the approaching helicopter.

As Jay Bird, the last of the six, climbed on board, Joker and Bear took off, sprinting toward the waiting helicopter. Joker pumped his legs as he tried to avoid the flying debris and dust kicked up by the chopper's rotor wash. As the pair neared the opening of the helicopter, Joker took one look over his shoulder, and could see through the smoke the headlights of a vehicle speeding toward them. The truck skidded to a stop approximately fifty yards out from their position. Mere seconds later, the group huddled in the back of the old pick-up opened fire on them. The spray of bullets sent Joker and Bear diving into the chopper just as Jay Bird and Snow appeared in the gunner's window with their rifles, returning fire. As the transmission and engines began to whine, signaling their liftoff, Nails stepped up to the opening and lofted two grenades into the advancing angry mob.

Joker counted to himself as he took up a position against the wall behind the cockpit. *"One, two, three."* On three, two explosions rocked the area below.

"Go…Go…Go…!" Bear barked, but the chopper was already lifting into the air as the words flew out of his mouth.

As the aircraft reached treetop level, it came under heavy fire. Joker cringed as the fuselage was pelted with bullets. He was aware of how well-built military helicopters are, especially modified ones like the one he was in—but hearing the shots as they pinged off the side of the aircraft in rapid succession left him uneasy.

Seconds later, the crew chief shouted for everyone to hang on. Joker reached above his head, snagging the hand strap connected to the fuselage just as the helicopter banked hard to the left. Equipment and gear began to slide along the slick metal flooring. Wondering what had caused the dramatic directional change, Joker peered out the gunner's window just as the wide-open velvet sky erupted into a massive fireball, followed by a thunderous boom. Joker shielded his eyes from the spectacular light show of the yellow, red, and orange glow.

Realizing they had come within yards of being killed, Joker leaned his head back against the wall, closed his eyes, and tried to bring his speeding heart rate and breathing under control. *Jesus, that was close.*

He felt the helicopter begin to level out and assumed they were in the clear when another wave of gunfire hit them. Suddenly, the cockpit window on the pilot's side exploded. The sound of shattering glass was horrific. But not as scary as hearing one of the pilots shouting that they'd been hit. The seconds that followed were complete chaos, as everyone held on for dear life as the chopper began to rattle, shake and lose altitude. Joker and everyone else knew they were going down and they all began bracing for impact. From his position, he could see just inside the left side of the cockpit, and saw how the pilots were working vigorously to bring the damaged helicopter under control. He closed his eyes praying for a miracle. Just as he had lost all hope, he felt the Black Hawk gain forward motion and increase its speed. Within seconds, they had leveled off again.

The crew chief asked if everyone was good, and they all gave a thumbs up. Though, Joker was pretty sure some if not all of them needed a change of underwear. Never in his eleven-year career had he ever experienced something so terrifying that was out of his control. Sure, he had a few close calls while in combat, but there was always a way to deal with it. This experience left him shaken. For the first time in a long time, he felt helpless because there was nothing he could have done. He was pretty sure the others shared his take on the situation. He wasn't troubled by flying by any means. However, if he had a choice, he'd rather have his feet planted firmly on the ground, especially during combat.

Joker's attention shifted to the crew chief assisting Duke with the injured American. After making sure that Duke was good, the guy grabbed a medical kit and hurried to the cockpit. Joker couldn't see or hear much, but he was concerned about the pilot who'd been on the receiving end of whatever projectile crashed through the window.

Joker shot a look at Bear, who shared the same concerned expression as the others on board.

A few minutes later, the crew chief returned without the medical kit and took an empty seat. Joker could only see the guy's eyes because of the facemask he wore, but judging from his body language and rigid posture, he didn't appear pleased with how the situation in the cockpit went. But Joker was genuinely worried about the pilot, and wanted to make sure the guy was okay.

"Everything okay up there?" Joker shouted to him over the loudness, giving his head a nod in the direction of the cockpit.

"Fine." The guy spat out. His tone clearly indicated that things weren't fine, but it wasn't any of Joker's business to get involved.

"Sorry about earlier." One of the pilots called back. "The rest of the ride should be uneventful."

Joker couldn't hide the small smile that appeared on his face when he recognized the deep, gravelly voice, and he looked at the crew chief, who still looked as if someone had pissed in his cornflakes.

"Is that Lucky?"

The crew chief didn't give a verbal answer. He just nodded.

Knowing Lucky was their pilot explained how they escaped death.

In Joker's opinion, Lucky was the best damn helicopter pilot around. Hearing his voice and knowing he was at the controls helped ease his nervousness.

His first interaction with the death-defying pilot was still etched in his brain. A few years ago, during a mission, the team had been sent to an undisclosed location in the western mountain region in Pakistan to rescue a group of medical professionals who the Taliban had taken hostage. But they hit a snag when their extraction route became blocked by another wave of extremists. The only other way off the mountain was an air rescue. That was where Lucky came into the picture. Where they were stranded offered no solid landing site for any type of aircraft, meaning that the pilot had to get a little creative to extract the hostages and the team.

As the helo crew communicated the plan, the entire team, including himself, doubted that the pilot could pull off such a daring and risky maneuver. But the crazy bastard surprised them when the helicopter's two front wheels touched down along the ridgeline while keeping the aircraft steady and level as the hostages and the team quickly jumped on board.

The pilot was a legend and was often talked about amongst the special operations community. Everyone hoped Lucky was behind the controls whenever a mission involved SCU support. Joker hoped that one day he'd get the opportunity to meet him personally and maybe buy him a beer, considering he'd saved their asses more than a few times.

As the helicopter sped through the darkness of the night, and they weren't facing a life-or-death situation, Joker relaxed and let his mind wander.

Leaning his head back, he closed his eyes. Of course, one person instantly popped into his thoughts, and it shouldn't have come as a surprise. Anytime Joker rode in or even saw a Black Hawk, he was reminded of a certain woman—Clover Walker.

Clover was a force to be reckoned with; not to mention, she was Bear's younger sister. No matter how hard he tried, he couldn't shake her from his mind. It just wasn't possible. Not after the wild but passionate night they had spent together. The night Bear knew nothing about. In fact, no one, at least he was aware of, knew about his and Clover's private after-party. Not that it mattered because he and Clover were both consenting adults, and he would never hurt her by revealing what occurred between them, even though she had wounded his heart. After two years and no direct contact with her, he still felt jilted. How fucked up was that? He had no trouble moving on when any of his previous relationships ended. And that was what had confused him, considering he and Clover never even established a relationship. However, he'd definitely entertain one if given a second chance. He couldn't put his finger on it, but something about Clover had a hold on him that refused to let go.

He'd known Clover for about eight years, but their paths didn't cross often. It was usually at one of their family get-togethers or a holiday, when he'd tag along with Bear. They always got along, and he enjoyed her company, but he never once thought of them being together as a couple. At least, not until two years ago, when he and the team were in San Diego for training.

It had been their last night in town, and since Clover was stationed there, she invited the team to dinner at a Hibachi restaurant just down the road from her apartment. It had been an enjoyable evening for everyone. After dinner and a few rounds of drinks, the rest of the team had called it a night. Joker hadn't been ready to head back to the base, and Clover wasn't ready to go home either, so they hit up a few bars together.

He remembered vividly how her presence turned heads every place they stopped. That was when he started to pay more attention to her, and he wasn't talking about her looks. Clover was a beautiful woman with long, wavy blonde hair and hazel eyes that would change colors depending on her mood. But there was more to her beauty—a lot more.

Spending time around Clover that night reminded him of a statement his grandmother always used to make—*it wasn't the beauty on the outside that mattered; it was the beauty offered on the inside.*

As the night went on, and they spoke more about their lives, he became more intrigued by her. He discovered more about her in a few hours than he had over eight years of knowing her. By the end of the night, he learned that she wasn't just Bear's little sister who got overshadowed by her older brothers. Clover Walker was all woman with a good, strong head on her shoulders. He admired her for several reasons, but more so for her honesty, courage, and hearing her talk about the things she valued in life—her family, friends, community, and health.

She had surprised him when she talked about the time when she informed her family that she was joining the Marines. Joker knew from talking with Bear that even though her family had been supportive, they hadn't been thrilled with her decision to follow in her dad and brothers' footsteps. Not because they thought she couldn't handle it, but they were just overly protective of her—something they still were today.

Joker's fatal mistake when he walked her home that night was walking her up to her door. He should have just made sure she safely got into the elevator, then turned and left.

As he stood at her door, waiting for her to unlock it, all it had taken was one look into her bright eyes as she peered up at him over her shoulder. Her windblown hair from their walk on the beach added to her sexiness and radiance. He remembered it all like it was yesterday. She had made the first move when she rose on her tiptoes and kissed him on the cheek. Her soft lips lingered against his skin. As she snuggled closer, her body's warmth made his heart pound in his chest. All he did was slightly turn his face, and their lips met. It was a slow burn as he covered her soft, pillowy lips, and his hands threaded into her silky golden locks. He felt corny for even thinking it, but that first kiss with Clover had been magical. Before his brain could register a coherent thought warning him that he was making a mistake, the two of them were inside her apartment, naked and engaged in the most explosive and spectacular sex he'd ever experienced. That night, Clover Walker had turned his world completely upside down.

Here he sat, two years later, and she still got under his skin. There was just something special about her that he couldn't let go of, even though she had made it clear that night hadn't meant a damn thing to her. Waking up alone in her bed with her nowhere to be found confirmed that.

Joker was still lost in the memories when he felt a nudge on his shoulder. His eyes popped open, and he found Bear staring at him. He looked around and realized they had arrived at the base.

"Have a nice nap?" Bear teased.

Damn, had he zoned out for forty-five minutes? He grabbed his gear and exited the aircraft behind Bear. He needed a shower—a cold one to scrub away any reminders of Clover Walker.

CHAPTER TWO

As soon as the wheels of the crippled Black Hawk touched down, Lucky began powering down the machine but didn't dare remove her helmet until the SEAL team had disembarked and were out of sight. Those guys never stuck around anyway, and that was fine with her.

The medical staff had met the helicopter and carted off the injured man the team had rescued. From what she could see out of the busted window as the medical staff tended to him, it wasn't looking good.

She loosened the belts around her shoulders and immediately felt the pain in her right upper arm, where the shards of the heavy, thick glass struck her when the window exploded from the direct hit they took.

Initially, when it happened, it scared the ever-living shit out of her, but at the time of the impact, the adrenalin surge in her body prevented her from feeling the pain. Now that she was coming off the high and beginning to relax, she started to feel the throbbing and ache begin to materialize, and feared the injury was worse than she initially thought.

She closed her eyes, leaning her head back against the seat. She needed a moment to process the situation. Quickly, she realized how close they came to crashing. That alone sent a shiver through her body that was already trembling.

The sound of her door opening and pieces of broken glass hitting the pavement below had her opening her eyes, only to meet the intense gaze of Major Saunders. He was giving her his concerned fatherly look—the one where his eyebrows were drawn inward, and his lips pressed firmly together. For a brief moment, she thought he'd call the medical team back, just so they can look at her. Hopefully, the slight shake of her head had him rethinking. He knew that if she felt she needed immediate medical attention, she'd say so.

"How bad is it?" He asked.

She tried to lift her arm but bit down on her lip when the sharp pain traveled through her bicep. *Shit!* The last thing she needed with her brother roaming around the base was for her to be spotted receiving medical attention. That would surely make for an awkward reunion and conversation.

Brent leaned inside and helped remove the belts still wrapped around her arms before he unzipped her flight suit and assisted in maneuvering her injured arm from the ripped sleeve.

She honestly didn't want to look at it because she feared it was bad. She normally had a high threshold for pain, but she was nearing an eleven on a scale of one to ten.

"Shit, Clover! You need to have this looked at."

Now visibly worried, she peeked for herself and cringed at the amount of blood seeping from the large wound. The sleeve of her undershirt was already soaked with bloodstains.

She grabbed a towel from her bag and pressed it against her arm, again breathing through the pain, hoping the pressure would ease the bleeding. She went to slide out of her seat when Brent put his hand on her leg, stopping her.

"Don't move. You're covered in glass," he informed her. When she glanced down, her lap was littered with pieces ranging in all sizes. It was a wonder she hadn't been sliced up more than she was. Or worse, the bullet that struck the window could have hit her. Now, that was a shock to her system.

She sat still while Brent used his gloved hands to free her from most of the glass, especially the larger pieces. He then assisted her out of the helicopter, and to a nearby chair inside the hangar.

He appeared to be biting his cheek when she looked up at him, and she could tell he was pissed—not at her, but with the situation. She and Brent went way back to when she first joined the SCU. He was older and a seasoned member of the unit. He had taken her under his wing when nobody else elected to. Since then, they had both formed a great friendship and working relationship. Aware that she didn't have family in the area, he and his wife would always extend an invitation to their house for any holidays that she couldn't make it home for or just go over to their house to hang out. She considered them an extended part of her family.

"I'm sure a few butterfly band-aids will do the trick," she told him as she looked at the damage to her skin. *Shit, on second thought, maybe he is right, and I do need to get this looked at,* she thought.

Brent cocked one of his eyebrows as he peered down at her. "Uh, I think stitches are more like it. That wound is deep, and that little towel isn't helping anything. The bleeding isn't slowing down. Plus, it needs to be flushed out. Think about all that dirt, grime, and whatever else was on that glass. If you leave it untreated, you could be facing a serious infection, and that's not happening on my watch because you're being stubborn."

She squinted her eyes. "But the routine post-flight checklists need to be performed. I'll get it looked at afterward."

"The checklists can wait. Your health and well-being are far more important."

She moved the towel, looked again, and saw the two-inch gash and one hell of a bruise that started near the top of her shoulder and stopped midway down her bicep. It was already turning a purplish-blue color. *Lovely!*

She looked back at Brent, who was standing in front of her with his hands on his hips, looking ready to argue with her if she tried to finagle her way out of a trip to medical. Her gaze then traveled toward the left, where the damaged helicopter sat. Focusing on the shattered window, she realized how lucky she was to walk away with just a few stitches.

Brent followed her eyes and ran his hand over his high and tight haircut.

"We were damn fortunate. I never thought I'd say this, but that wayward RPG saved our ass up there."

She pressed the towel back to her arm and glanced in his direction.

"How so?"

"Think about it. If you hadn't banked us hard to the left to avoid the RPG, those shells that hit the window most likely would've hit you chest level." He chuckled while giving his head a slight shake. "Hot damn woman, you're one badass pilot," he exclaimed, giving her a congratulatory slap on her good shoulder.

She gave her co-pilot a coy smile. "Yeah, well, don't say that too loud around here. Never know when there could be listening ears nearby."

Major Saunders shook his head in annoyance. "Your family still has no clue what you do, do they?"

"Nope, and it needs to stay that way."

She stood up and walked back over to the helicopter to retrieve her bag.

Major Saunders called over her shoulder. "Damn, Clover, your old man would be proud knowing what you do. But on the other hand, your brothers would probably find a way to get you discharged from the Marine Corps."

She turned around and pointed at him. "Exactly! It's bad enough I hide my identity during missions, let alone the missions where I've had to swoop in and rescue my brothers and their teammates." Thank goodness there hadn't been too many of those occasions.

"Well, I'm damn glad I know the real Lucky. You're one of the best helicopter pilots in the service."

She gave him a pointed look, telling him not to blow smoke up her ass.

He chuckled but then got serious. "Jesus, Lucky. You really don't know how talented you are. I've been around a lot longer than you. I know many men—pilots who have double the years and experience on you, and they couldn't fly this bird like you do. You make it look effortless. Hell, use this incident as an example. A fucking bullet penetrated the cockpit window, injuring you and causing us to lose altitude. It was you who kept calm throughout the whole ordeal and maneuvered us out of the dire situation. The keyword here is *you*. You did that."

She may look cool as a cucumber on the outside, but people couldn't see how twisted her insides got when things got a little hairy during missions. They couldn't see the fear ripping through her, or feel how fast her heart was pounding in her chest. There were times when she'd been so worked up during a mission that she'd puke afterward.

"Thanks, Major. But it takes a team up there in the air."

He shook his head at her lack of taking due credit.

"Are you going to avoid your brother?" He asked, moving on to a different subject and referring to Tripp, or Bear as he was known in the teams. The identical brother she just pulled out of the line of fire.

She ran her hand over the metal where they had taken on fire. She was amazed at how well the material used to build those things held up. With all the top-secret modifications made to the standard Black Hawk, this particular version was one of a kind. *Too bad the windows weren't*, she thought.

She looked at the Major and thought about his question. She'd love to see Bear, considering it'd been almost a year since she last saw him. However, running into him here at Camp Lemonnier would generate questions about her presence in Djibouti, especially since her family thought her mechanic job kept her stateside.

"I honestly don't know. It'd be nice to see and talk with him, but on the other hand, I just want to keep my head down for the next eighteen hours before we head home."

"Well, I'm going to give you my opinion. If it were me, and considering the type of careers you both have, I'd spend some time with him because you don't know when the next opportunity could be, or if you'll even get that chance."

She nodded in understanding. She knew what he was getting at. And, as grim as it sounded, he was right. They all worked in dangerous professions, and there was always a possibility they may never make it back home.

The Major squeezed her non-injured shoulder. "Give your family a chance to form their own opinion about your career."

She wouldn't lie. She missed her family, and if an opportunity presented itself, she wouldn't want to waste it. And perhaps it was time to come clean with them. She'd been harboring her secret for four long years, and it was getting harder and harder every time she saw her parents or brothers.

"I'll see if he's around once I finish here."

She started to walk toward the tool chest to pick up the clipboard when Brent called after her.

"Not so fast, slick." He was next to her before she could turn back, giving her a sideways look. "Are you forgetting something?"

"What?"

His eyes traveled to her arm, and she inwardly rolled her eyes. She had hoped he had forgotten. Not many people knew, but she hated needles. He started laughing as he guided her toward the door.

"Come on. I'll go with you and hold your hand if it helps."

Fresh out of the shower, Joker stepped into one of the vacant containerized housing units the team had taken over and threw his dirty clothes into his bag.

With SEAL Team 10 having a steady presence at Camp Lemonnier, it helped logistically when other teams in the area needed a place to crash, or in Joker and his team's case, it offered them a spot to chill while they waited for their ride out.

Bear was across the room, putting his things in his bag. Now that they had all showered, they were getting ready to head to the chow hall. Since they'd been living off MREs and protein bars for the last two weeks, everyone was looking forward to some real food.

Joker glanced over just as Bear was pulling on his shirt.

"Any word on our American friend's condition?"

Bear shook his head. "No, nothing yet. I'm not very optimistic. He was in pretty bad shape. I spoke with Derek, and he said they still don't know who he is, or what he was doing in that facility."

Joker raised his eyebrows. That wasn't good.

"Duke said he'd go over and talk with the medical staff to get an update."

The door behind them opened, and they both turned, thinking it might be one of the other guys.

Joker grinned and gave a chin lift when he saw their friend, Fins. Fins was a member of Team 10. The three of them had gone through BUD/S training together.

"Wow! They let you guys run loose around here?" Joker teased and shook Fins' hand, followed by Bear.

Fins smiled. "Yeah, well, someone has to control the kids on this base."

"How long are you over here for?" Joker asked.

"Probably another four months or so, unless things across the water settle down, which I don't see ever happening."

Fins was referring to ongoing conflicts within Yemen. The United States had upped its threat level for American interests in the immediate area due to some chatter and activity that had recently taken place in the terrorist haven.

"Well, when you get back stateside, let us know, and we'll plan to get together. Maybe Ace and the guys from Alpha team will be around as well. It could be like one big reunion."

Fins smiled. "I'd like that. Speaking of Ace, how's his fiancé Alex doing? We heard about what happened in California during that earthquake."

"She's getting better every day. You know she and Ace are expecting a baby, right?"

Fins' eyes grew wide, a slow smile spreading across his face. "Really?"

Joker nodded. "Yeah, but that's a secret. They haven't told many people. After everything they've been through, it's a perfect ending."

"Don't forget the big surprise Ace has planned in a few weeks," Bear interjected.

"What's that?" Fins inquired.

"He's taking Alex down to the islands for a vacation. It's where they were planning to go for their honeymoon."

"I thought they postponed the wedding."

"They did, but Ace is throwing a surprise wedding for her at the resort."

"That's awesome. Are you guys going?"

"We plan to. Unless we get called out."

"Well, when you see them, please tell them congratulations from Team 10. We'll all be thinking about them. Where are you guys headed now?"

"Chow," Joker answered, rubbing his stomach.

"Yeah. Some real food would be great right now." Bear commented.

A smile broke out on Fins' face. "You guys might be in luck," he said, giving his eyebrows a playful wiggle.

"What's so lucky about chow? Did they put in a Bob's Big Boy or something?" Joker asked.

Fins leaned in and kept his voice down as if he was telling them a secret. "Around this time is when *she* has breakfast."

"Who's 'she'?" Joker asked, a bit amused by Fins' code talk.

"*She,* is one of the most stunning women I have ever had the pleasure of meeting. I can't remember her last name, but damn, let me tell you that she is easy on the eyes and extremely intelligent. She makes a lot of the men around here look stupid. Oh, and she's a tough one too. I've seen her put a few guys in their places."

Joker was a little curious because Fins was very particular about the type of woman he dated. He wasn't one to mess around. He took relationships and sex seriously.

"What does she look like?" Joker asked, wanting to hear more about the mystery woman who caught Fins' attention.

"Long wavy golden hair, piercing hazel eyes that reel you in, and a dazzling smile that blows you away."

As Fins ticked off the woman's qualities, Joker immediately pictured Clover. He clenched his jaw in frustration at how easily she affected him. *Dammit, why can't I get her out of my head?*

Fins crossed his arms across his chest, tapping his index finger against his lips as if he was thinking.

"Give me a minute, and her name will come to me. It's a unique one." A few seconds passed before he held up his finger. "Clover! That's it—like a four-leaf clover."

Joker almost choked on his own air when he heard her name roll off Fins' tongue. Talk about a punch to the gut. He was floored and left utterly speechless. His eyes traveled over to Bear, and one glance told him that Bear shared a similar reaction, except Bear appeared more heated. Joker even found himself putting a little distance between himself and his friend.

"Clover? Are you sure that's her name?" Bear questioned Fins in a none too pleased tone.

Fins, oblivious that he was talking about Bear's sister, just smiled. "Positive. She's a helicopter mechanic. She spends the majority of her time over at the hangars. It's funny to watch some of the guys around here try to sneak over there to get a look at her."

Bear turned toward Joker, and Joker saw the fire burning in his eyes. The vein by his temple was even visible, which was an indicator Bear was pissed.

"What the fuck is Clover doing here?" Bear growled.

Joker shrugged his shoulders, though he'd be interested in knowing the answer, seeing as everyone, including her family, was under the impression that she was in San Diego.

Hearing that she was in Djibouti concerned him as well. Overall, Camp Lemonnier was a safe base and well-guarded. Still, many bordering countries were of concern because of their lack of stability due to the hostile environments and their dislike of the United States. Clover didn't need to be anywhere near that type of shit.

Bear grabbed his ID off the top of his bag. "I'm going to go find her. You coming?" Bear asked Joker, but Joker shook his head. As much as he was interested in hearing her story, he wasn't ready to see her just yet. Because seeing her and being blown off would only add to his misery. He needed a little bit of time to prepare himself before facing her.

"I'm good. I'll let you handle that interrogation."

Bear turned and stomped out the door. In a way, Joker felt sorry for Clover. She was cheated out on the career she wanted to pursue. She wanted to fly helicopters but settled for being a mechanic to appease her family's wishes. *Shit.* Bear was going to ream her a new ass. On second thought, maybe he should go. Then he thought about it again. *Nah. Best I stay out of their family drama.*

After Bear left the room, a shocked Fins looked at Joker. "What in the hell was that all about? I haven't seen Bear that upset since that mission three years ago in Syria when that spy chick almost tricked him into following her to that compound rigged with explosives."

Joker rubbed the back of his neck. "Well, the woman you were talking about—Clover. That's Bear's little sister."

Fins' jaw dropped. "Oh shit!"

"Yeah." *Oh, shit is right.*

Clover wiped the droplets of sweat from her forehead with the back of her hand. It was only mid-morning, and the temperature was already well into the nineties.

She was looking forward to leaving tomorrow and having some time to relax in San Diego before heading home for her parents' anniversary party. When she spoke to her mom a few weeks ago, her mom told her that Justin, Tripp, Ethan, and Zach were supposed to be there. That news brought a smile to her face. She couldn't remember the last time she had joined the service, when she and all her brothers were home at the same time. It would be a nice reunion.

She looked down at her arm and the white bandage wrapped around her bicep. She was now the not-so-proud owner of twelve stitches.

Luckily for her, when she arrived at medical, the doctor she knew, Captain Mickens, was on duty, and he was able to stitch her up pretty quickly. He had lectured her on the importance of making sure wounds were cleaned out. She could thank Major Saunders for that because he was the one who told the captain about her plans to slap on a few band-aids.

Before she left, he had given her a few over-the-counter pain relievers to help with the pain. And, since she wasn't on the flight rotation, she took four of the pills—the maximum dosage he told her she could take.

She hoped that the stitches all dissolved before she traveled home. Even if they did, she'd still have a bruise and scar to contend with, and her astute family would most definitely notice because nothing ever got past them. She could opt to wear long sleeves, but that would only draw more attention to her since it was the middle of summer, and she was a tank top girl, and her family knew that. *Damn!*

She let out a frustrated sigh. This was just another sign that it was time to come clean with the truth. Keeping them in the dark was becoming a burden. Major Saunders and Captain Mickens spoke to her about it, and they both offered valid points. She was supposed to be proud of what she'd accomplished, and be able to share her successes with her family. But it was guaranteed that she'd get an ear full from her brothers. The one she was more worried about was her dad and how he would take the news. Her dad was a quiet and reserved man. He would listen to the whole story before giving judgment. She'd have to make sure she swung by the liquor store before she got to her parents' house because if she was going to do this, she would need some liquid courage.

She refocused on the paperwork lying on the desk in front of her. Since Sergeant Hollis was nowhere to be found, she took the liberty and had gone through all the maintenance checklists twice and completed all the necessary paperwork. She needed to speak to Major Saunders about Hollis. This marked the third time he'd pulled a disappearing act and neglected his duties. His *Houdini* act was becoming a habit, which was unfair to the rest of the team, especially those like herself who had to pick up the slack and make sure their job was complete.

Just as she stood, her stomach growled, and she placed her hand on her belly. She was starving. She had skipped dinner last night but managed to scarf down a protein bar before she left to pick up her brother and his friends. The sound of that made her giggle a little bit.

She scanned the hangar seeing what else needed to be done before they pulled out. While she and Major Saunders were over at the medical facility, the ground crew had packed most of their gear. She found a few tools lying out. Again, that should have been Hollis' responsibility to make sure everything was stowed and ready for transport. She reached for the tools on the table and placed them in the tool chest before securing all the crates with the locks.

She took one final look around, ensuring everything was cleaned up and stowed. She walked over to her helicopter, reached inside, and removed her helmet that was still there from when she had taken it off.

She stepped down and started toward the exit when a sharp whistle pierced the air. She knew right away that it was Major Saunders. She turned around and saw him walking briskly towards her.

"Hey, have you seen Hollis?" She asked him as he approached.

"I saw him over by the CHUs a little while ago. Why?"

"I'll give you one guess."

He ran his hand over his head before he sighed. "He didn't complete his post-mission tasks, did he?"

"Nope." She turned and grabbed the folder off the table and handed it to him. "I completed it. Would you mind submitting it?"

He took it from her, and she could tell he wasn't happy. Nobody had been happy with Hollis' work ethic lately.

"I'll take care of it," he told her in an annoyed tone.

"What brings you back over here?" She last saw him when they parted ways after she left medical.

"I came to warn you," he told her, but the playful smile on his lips had her a little worried.

"Warn me? About what?"

"If you don't want to be caught red-handed, you better hand over your gear. Your brother is walking across the tarmac, and he doesn't look too happy. I think someone outed you."

Her jaw dropped, and as soon as she wanted to question him, she heard Bear's strong, resounding voice echo through the giant hangar.

"Clover!"

Her eyes widened, and she began to panic as she threw her gear at the Major, and removed her flight suit in record time. Thank goodness she always wore an underlayer and was grateful for the clean t-shirt Captain Mickens found for her at the hospital.

She could hear Bear's heavy footsteps approaching quickly. "Oh shit! How did he find out?"

"I don't know, but act cool and natural, not like you just saved an entire team of SEALs by pulling off some amazing maneuvers in midair. Remember, you're just a mechanic." He pulled a screwdriver off the tool cart of another team and handed it to her. He then took his finger and rubbed it on a grease rag before wiping it on her cheek. She looked at him as if he were crazy.

"What the hell was that for?"

Amused, Saunders said, "You're a mechanic. You need to look the part. A little grease down the cheek will make it more believable. Oh, and throw this on if you don't want him to see your new arm bracelet." He tossed her a long-sleeved t-shirt, and she threw it over her head quickly, pulling the sleeves down to conceal the large bandage around her arm.

She shook her head as the Major grinned before turning and walking in the opposite direction. She was glad someone found amusement in her turmoil. But she'd owe him a drink for the heads up.

As soon as she turned back around, she caught sight of her brother coming around the front of one of the helicopters. Judging from the scowl on his face, the Major wasn't exaggerating. Shit. He looked downright pissed off. However, at least he had cleaned up.

She dug deep and gathered herself together to play the part of the shocked little sister, who was excited to see her big brother. She walked toward him, meeting him halfway. She'd love nothing more than a big hug from him, especially after the day she'd had.

Bear halted his stride, and since they weren't in uniform, she ran over and threw her arms around him. He lifted her into the air and swung her around before giving her another good squeeze.

"God, I missed you," he told her as he hugged her tight.

She closed her eyes and smiled to herself as she hugged him back. "I missed you too."

He released her, and she tilted her head back to look up at him. His unique grey eyes held hers, and they were full of questions.

"What in the hell are you doing here?" He bluntly asked.

She took a step back and swallowed hard. She was nervous and began to twist her fingers. She tried to convince herself that now would be the perfect time to tell him the truth, but she chickened out.

"You're mad."

"I'd say more shocked than mad, considering I heard about your visit here from a friend of mine."

"I was getting bored of the same routine every day. Plus, I've been itching to see more of the world. So, when a temporary spot here opened, I jumped at the opportunity."

"Clover. There are better places to see than Djibouti."

"I know, but at least I can say I was here, and it's not San Diego," she said, trying to reason with him. She even threw him that bright, cheery smile that always worked on her brothers.

He shook his head, knowing what she was doing.

"Do Mom and Dad know?"

She dropped her smile. "No. And I'd prefer to keep it that way." He went to interrupt, but she held her hand up, letting him know she wasn't finished. "I'd like to tell them myself. I planned on doing it when I see them in a couple of weeks." She planned on telling them a hell of a lot more.

He pointed his finger at her. "You better tell them."

"You have my word."

He held her gaze, and just when she thought he would press her further, he relented, and the side of his mouth lifted, almost resulting in a smile. Anyone who knew Bear knew his smiles were far and in between.

"How are you doing otherwise? How long is your deployment?"

How was she doing? Now that was a loaded question.

"I'm holding my own and staying busy. At least trying to. I'm actually heading home tomorrow. What about you? Are you hanging around here long, or is this just a pit stop?"

"I'll be around for a few hours. We're waiting on a ride."

"Oh. Is the whole team here?" She inquired, trying to act as if she didn't know.

"Yep. All here. In fact, we were all headed over to grab a bite to eat. You up for joining us?"

She nibbled her lip and knew she was showing her cards. Her brother knew she chewed her lip when she was nervous or anxious. She looked down at the oversized long-sleeved t-shirt and black Adidas compression pants she wore. Tie that in with how sweaty and tired she was, and she could only imagine what she looked like.

"Do I have time for a quick shower?"

He grinned. "You do look like you could clean up a bit."

She playfully punched him in the arm. "That wasn't nice."

He rubbed his shoulder and laughed before ushering her toward the exit.

"Come on. I'll walk with you, and we can catch up more."

As she and Bear walked from the hangars to the CHUs, she tried to pay attention to what Bear was telling her, but it was difficult because she was mentally preparing herself for when she would see Joker. She could already feel the anxiety building within her. She just hoped it didn't turn out to be an awkward reunion, considering what he'd done to her.

"Just so you know, Joker was with me when I found out you were here, and I don't think he was happy either."

She gulped at the mention of Joker's name. A few weeks after she had slept with him and he never called, she tried to tell herself that it was probably for the best, considering she was an officer, and he was enlisted. That was a big no, no in the military. However, her heart didn't agree.

Joker had all the qualities she looked for in a guy. Having grown up as a military brat, she was accustomed to being around men in uniform. So, it wasn't his military status that snagged her attention. Joker had always been a respectful, friendly, and funny guy. But that night in San Diego, he showed a side of himself she'd never seen before—a side she felt that he kept guarded and didn't let many people see. He was very open when they talked about their families. She knew he didn't have the greatest relationship with his family, but she never knew why until he shared a bit of his past with her. She found it very easy to talk with him and speak her mind without any judgment from him. He was attentive and understanding. Not that she craved attention, but when she spoke, he listened. He would give his opinion at some points in their conversation, which she appreciated.

She had no idea what had come over her when he walked her to her door, and she kissed him on the cheek, which led to—.

"Clover?" Bear barked, interrupting her thoughts.

She gave her head a quick shake before glancing up at him. "Huh?"

"Did you hear anything I just said?"

She bit down on her lip. "Sorry. I've got a lot on my mind."

He stopped walking and reached for her hand.

"Are you sure everything's okay?"

As she stood there staring at her brother, the voice inside her head shouted for her to tell him. After a moment of an internal battle with herself, she decided to come clean with him. She took a deep breath to ready herself.

"There's something I need to tell you. And before you interrupt, I need you to let me finish everything I need to say."

Looking concerned, he squinted his eyes. "Clover, you can tell me anything."

Her heart started to beat faster, and her stomach felt like it was twisted into one big knot. Why was this so hard? The words were there. Just as she opened her mouth, Bear's phone rang. He held his finger up, telling her to wait as he pulled the phone from his pocket.

"Crap. I'm sorry, but I need to take this. Where's your CHU?"

Feeling a bit of a reprieve, she forced a small smile. "No worries. I'm two rows down, on the very end. It's number nine."

He nodded. "Give me about fifteen to twenty minutes, and I'll meet you there."

As he answered the call, she turned and continued walking. Before she made it to her CHU, the battle within her re-ignited, and she started having second thoughts. Maybe it was best to let things be for now, and then when she got to Tennessee, she'd lay it all out for everyone to hear all at once. Besides, she had another issue on her hands—seeing Joker. But then again, it was just a meal. How bad could it be?

CHAPTER THREE

Clover walked out of the small bathroom with her yellow towel wrapped around her. She was already chilly from the lukewarm shower, so when the cool air blowing from the small air conditioning unit hit her damp skin, it sent goosebumps scattering along her flesh. On the upside, she was at least clean and a little refreshed, though she'd kill for just a few minutes to rest her eyes. She was feeling the effects of being up for twenty-four hours, coupled with the side effects of the pain medicine she took earlier.

She walked to the small dresser sitting against the wall and pulled a pair of jeans and a long-sleeved t-shirt from the drawer. As she was closing the drawer, she saw the t-shirt her mom had given her for her birthday a few years ago. It was Clover's all-time favorite t-shirt. Her mom, bless her heart, hadn't fully understood the meaning of the words printed on the shirt when she'd bought it. Everyone had laughed when she opened the box and held the shirt up. It was a black t-shirt, and in white print, it read, *"I SCREW, I NUT, I BOLT, It's tough being a mechanic."* Her mom had been mortified when Zach explained the saying. At first, her mom was adamant on returning the shirt, but Clover refused to hand it over. In fact, she wore it all the time—in the right setting and company, of course.

Clover looked around the place she had called home for the last few weeks. She was thankful she'd been allotted one of the newer and more accommodating CHUs on base with a bathroom attached. The rest of her team had been assigned to CHUs with shared facilities. All in all, she couldn't complain. It was much better than other places she'd stayed in before.

She sat down on her cot and reached for the clear plastic bag Captain Mickens had given her. It contained an antibiotic ointment and extra bandages to wrap her arm. She peeled the plastic covering off her arm that prevented the stitches from getting wet and tossed it into the small wastebasket sitting on the floor next to her.

After dabbing a bit of ointment on the wound and wrapping it in a fresh bandage, she slipped into her matching yellow bra and panties, making her feel sexy and womanly. Yellow was one of her favorite colors because it reminded her of happiness and sunshine. During working hours and deployments in uniform, she usually opted for more generic moisture-wicking undergarments for comfort. Her tradition was to pack a cute bra and panty set to wear home. Some may call her weird or a dork, but at least she was a happy, weird dork.

As she pulled the jeans and t-shirt on, she realized she would sweat her ass off. But she wasn't taking any chances with Bear or one of the others seeing her arm.

Knowing she was pushing it on time, she looked at her watch. *Shit!* Bear would be there any minute, and he was and always would be a stickler on time.

Not bothering to mess with her hair, she quickly threw the damp tresses up into a messy bun before slipping on a pair of flip flops. It wasn't the most suitable footwear for the location, but it'd do. She grabbed her ID, key, and sunglasses off the table next to the bed and slid them into her back pocket.

In a rush to get out the door, she flung the heavy door open but hadn't realized someone was walking by, and she struck the person with it. She gasped, covering her mouth in shock as soon as she heard the thump of the man hitting the ground. She knew it was a guy because he was cursing up a storm.

"Motherfucker! What are you stupid? Why don't you fucking watch what you're doing!" The person ranted on, but she ignored his insults and rushed to his side as he lay sprawled out on the ground.

"Oh my God! I'm so sorry."

When he turned his head in her direction, she jerked backward, surprised to see the dude she took out with the door was Hollis, her crew chief. Suddenly, she wasn't as sorry as she felt. He deserved that and a lot more. *Karma!*

She stood up and backed away. "Sorry." She apologized again. "It's not like I could see you through a solid metal door, or that I hit you on purpose."

He picked himself up and dusted off his dark dress slacks. She wondered where he was headed off to, looking all important.

She saw a small black bag on the ground he had dropped when he fell. She went to reach for it, but he barked for her to leave it alone before bending down and picking it up himself.

"For God's sake, I'm just trying to help. You don't have to bite my head off."

"Well, I don't need your help," he retorted harshly.

She backed away and was in complete shock at his attitude toward her.

She placed her hands on her hips. She felt insulted at his admission, but at the same time, she felt that his statement was inaccurate.

"I'm sorry, but considering you abandoned your duties back at the hangar, and I had to finish your tasks, I think you need all the help you can get."

He leveled an evil, nasty gaze, in a bid to intimidate her, but she didn't flinch. He didn't scare her one bit.

"Yeah, that's right, buddy. I just called your ass out." She wanted to say it out loud but chose not to.

She looked him over. "Where you headed anyway?" Not that she cared, but she was curious since he couldn't be bothered with his actual job.

He hesitated, and she took that as a sign he wasn't going to say, or he was trying to think of something to tell her other than the truth.

Before he did either, she held her hands up in front of her. "You know what? Forget it. It's your business. I've got other things to do before we leave tomorrow."

She turned to walk away before she said something she shouldn't. Plus, she didn't have room for that kind of pettiness in her life. Once she got back to San Diego, she'd bring up her concerns with their CO, Colonel Jenkins, and get his thoughts on Sergeant Hollis' recent behavior and how to either rectify it or move forward with a new crew chief. She hoped for the latter, because she was tired of his shit.

Before she was able to take five steps, he shouted at her.

"You know, you think you hold some higher power than the rest of us. You think you're the princess of the SCU."

Now, he struck a nerve. That right there was a prime example of why she kept quiet about her involvement within the SCU. She didn't want to be singled out because of her gender. She turned around and took a few steps toward him.

"Are you delusional?" She asked him. "Did that door hit you in the head? Because the accusations you're lobbing at me are completely false. I'm treated no differently than any of the men I serve with. I come to work every damn day and give it my best. If I'm treated any differently, it's because I fucking earned it. And if anyone has a problem with it, then they can be a man and come talk to me."

"Maybe that's the issue. You try too hard to fit in and act like one of the guys." He curled his lip up at her as his eyes raked over her body.

"Just because, in your opinion, I may act or dress like a dude at times doesn't mean I have a dick in my pants."

"No, but I got one that I can stuff into your mouth to shut you up."

"In your dreams, assh—."

She was cut off mid-sentence by the roar of what sounded like a bear coming from behind her. Even the jerk, Hollis, appeared alarmed and had begun to retreat backward. She spun around, and the moment she laid eyes on her brother, moving in on Hollis with a killer expression, she knew the situation was about to get a whole lot worse.

"What the fuck did you just say, asshole?" Bear laid into Hollis, who appeared frightened and was holding his little bag in front of him as if a piece of fabric would fend off a six-foot-two, two-hundred-pound Navy SEAL.

Clover hadn't realized that her brother had been standing nearby, and she started to panic. Had he heard their whole conversation? Obviously, he heard Hollis' last sentence, but the most critical question was, had he heard that she worked in the SCU?

She stood back as Bear gave Hollis a good tongue lashing. She didn't think she'd ever seen Bear that pissed off. But she now understood where his call sign came from. Jesus, he was like a grizzly bear when they stood up on their hind legs, roaring aloud, and looking ferocious.

When Bear grabbed Hollis by the collar of his shirt, she knew it was time to end the fiasco before her brother did something to get himself in trouble and cause a major scene. She hurried toward the two men, forced herself between them, and pushed them apart.

"Enough!" She shouted, and they both stopped speaking and looked at her.

She addressed Hollis first. His face was bright red, as he breathed heavily, and she could tell he was pissed. "Go. Get the hell out of here right now!"

Her brother went to say something, and she shot him a glare.

She waited to see if Hollis would respond, but all she got was a disdainful snarl. Before he turned and walked away, he leveled a look at her. She recognized the vile expression on his face and knew she hadn't heard the last from him. *Just fucking great!*

Bear grabbed her shoulder and spun her around. He was still seething.

"What the fuck, Clover! Are you kidding me? Are you just gonna let him go scot-free? What he said to you was very disrespectful, not to mention, sexual harassment."

Before she could respond, someone behind her spoke.

"What's going on here?"

Clover didn't need to look back to know who was standing behind her. She'd recognize his smooth, deep voice anywhere. She turned around, and she nearly lost her breath when she saw those raw emerald green eyes staring back at her.

The sight of him caused an instant reaction within her body, causing her heart to beat faster and her body temperature to skyrocket. She wiped her sweaty palms on her jeans as he approached.

He stopped in front of her, and she fought back the moan trying to escape through her lips as she met his penetrating gaze.

Oh damn! She said to herself. He looked good—like, really good. She was a sucker for men with five o'clock shadows, and Joker's black whiskers didn't disappoint. She remembered all too well how his scruff chafed her smooth skin as he made love to her.

The dark wash jeans he wore, paired with the plain grey t-shirt, boots, and dark hair that stood on ends in a sexy way, made him look rugged and delicious.

He didn't say anything, and neither did she as they stared at one another. Even if she wanted to, she couldn't because her voice had suddenly disappeared.

"What was that all about?" One of the other guys asked, repeating Joker's question.

She was so caught up in the moment and seeing Joker that she tuned out her brother's detailed explanation of why he was about to pummel Hollis' ass.

"Sexual harassment?" She heard one of the others ask, which shook her from the spell Joker had on her. Bear was still carrying on about the incident when she tore her eyes from Joker, spun around, and stuck her finger into her brother's chest.

"Just stop it!" She pleaded with him, and he gave her an angry look. "I don't need, nor did I ask you to step in and fight my battles. While I really do appreciate your concern, I'm afraid that your barbaric tirade has only made me more of an enemy."

Bear balked at her comment. "Doubtful. Do you deal with this kind of shit often?"

She shrugged her shoulders. She wasn't about to tell him that she'd heard worse comments, though they were never directed at her as Hollis had done.

"Look around, Bear. I work with predominantly all men. I don't let comments like Hollis' bother me. My beef with him was about something entirely different. You just happened to walk up at the wrong time when he made that comment."

Over the years, she learned to take it with a grain of salt and knew who to stay away from. If things ever got to the point where she felt threatened or comments like the one Hollis made were directed at her, she'd take the appropriate action. Until then, she'd just ignore their childish behavior.

Staring down at her, his grey eyes locked with hers. He placed his hands on her shoulders, thankfully, not near the stitches.

"Clover, that's not the point. He shouldn't be doing that, period. Has he ever tried to hurt you?"

"What? No! Bear, please just drop it."

"No. I won't just drop it. Dammit, I worry about you, even more so that I now know you're here."

She grabbed her brother's hands and squeezed them tight. "I get what you're saying, but I'm a big girl now. You need to realize that. The same goes for Justin, Ethan, and Zach."

He brushed off her comment, "Who was that guy anyway?"

Oh shit! How was she going to explain that?

"Umm. I know him from San Diego. He's stationed there."

Her slight hesitation was apparent because Bear squinted his eyes as he held her gaze.

"Really? So, you work with him?"

Oh, man. She was digging a hole, and it would get a lot deeper and harder for her to claw her way out unless she put this thing to bed. But she had her own questions. Did Bear know that Hollis was a member of the SCU? He'd been on the flight earlier, but Hollis wore a face mask.

"Our paths cross once in a while at the base."

"I see." He replied, still holding her gaze with his scrutinizing eyes.

Wanting to move on from the situation, she asked, "Are we still getting food? Because I'm starving."

"I'm with Clover. I'm fucking famished," Playboy commented.

Dismissing her brother, Clover threw her sunglasses on and started walking. She walked right past the others, who were all staring at her, but never said a word. If they wanted to join her, then by all means, but the conversation about what just happened was over.

☙

Joker watched in shock as Clover stormed off, kicking up a dust storm behind her. She was fired up. But damn, did she look good! He glanced at Bear, who was doing a horrible job trying to calm himself down. He kept running his fingers through his hair in frustration.

"I take it your reunion didn't go over well," Joker stated. He was curious as to what Bear found out.

Bear shook his head, clearly still miffed.

"That fucking asshole is lucky he's still able to walk." He took a deep breath, running his hands down his face. "Clover shouldn't be here, let alone around people like him. I don't even want to imagine what could have happened to her."

Aussie spoke up. "I understand your concern, man. But as she said, she's a big girl. You're going to have to trust that she knows her boundaries. Plus, you and your brothers taught her a lot, and she *is* a Marine herself."

Joker agreed with Aussie's comment, but he also saw where Bear was coming from. He was a bit alarmed when Fins mentioned her being in Djibouti. Just because he held a grudge against her didn't mean he wasn't worried about her. He wasn't that big of an asshole. And feeling how his body reacted to seeing her proved that he still cared deeply for her.

"Come on," Bear told them, and they all followed.

Clover was walking at a snail's pace, so it didn't take long for them to catch up to her. She still had her sunglasses on, but Joker could tell by her body language and facial expression that she was still upset. He just hoped Bear dropped the topic and they could all have a nice meal, though it would be hard to sit near her, listening to her sweet voice and breathing in the scent of her apple-scented lotion. He quit eating apples for a while because it reminded him of her every time he bit into one.

He took in her appearance from behind and couldn't help but admire her ass as she walked directly in front of him. The jeans she wore hugged her ass perfectly. Watching it twitch with each step she took drove him bonkers.

Someone cleared their throat, and when he looked up, Jay Bird was looking at him with one of his eyebrows raised as if asking what the hell he was doing.

Knowing he was caught red-handed staring at Clover's ass, he tried playing it off to just being a guy admiring a nice view. He gave his shoulder a slight shrug in a silent reply. He couldn't help it, because he knew firsthand how those soft globes felt beneath his fingers. He felt his cock harden beneath his jeans as an image of Clover from that night popped into his head.

She was naked and laid out on her bed like a work of art. He had taken his time exploring every inch of her glorious body with his hands and mouth. She'd been a shy but amazing lover—full of passion and affection and enjoyed giving pleasure as much as she enjoyed receiving it. Watching her ignite into a sex goddess had turned him on, and the moment they fell into each other's arms in the wee hours of the morning after hours of lovemaking, he knew there would be no other woman who could measure up to what Clover had to offer. She had taken hold of his heart that night, and embedded herself so deep he'd be left with a piece of her for the rest of his life.

Seeing her now brought a wave of emotions he hadn't expected to feel, which confused him. The moment their eyes locked, he felt the attraction that still burned between them. No matter how hard she tried to deny it, her eyes told a different story. Her luminous hazel eyes showed her emotions.

He had no clue where to go from here. Maybe he should use this unexpected opportunity to his advantage and find a way to talk to her alone—even if it was just to find out why she left that morning with no further contact. It was either now, or wait another two weeks when they'd meet up at her parent's house. He wondered if she knew he was coming with Bear to spend the weekend with her family. He didn't care because either now or later, he'd get an answer.

※

By the time Clover got to the chow hall, her temper had cooled. The walk gave her time to think, and she actually felt terrible for jumping Bear's shit. She knew his intentions were good, but she was serious when she told him she could handle most of her battles. Sure, there'd be times when she'd welcome the backup, but the incident with Hollis wasn't one of them. Hollis was an asshole, and honestly, his words weren't enough to hurt her feelings because she knew well enough that others on the team had her back.

She was rethinking her strategy for telling her family about her involvement in the SCU. If Bear's earlier outburst was any indication of how things might go, then it might be best to sit her parents down first to break the news to them, and if that discussion went in the right direction, she'd at least have her mom and dad in her corner when she told her brothers.

She sensed Bear and the others behind her. She was glad they decided to join her. Besides her brother, she hadn't seen any of the guys since dinner in San Diego.

Before she opened the door, she spun around to face them. She looked at Bear first.

"I'm sorry for snapping at you." She tried to say more, but Bear cut her off and stepped toward her.

"No, Clover. I should be the one apologizing, and I get it now. You're right. I need to get past that you're all grown up, and don't need your big brothers meddling in your business."

He offered a small smile, and she closed the gap between them and hugged him.

"I know you'll always have my back. I love you," she whispered to him.

"Just so you know, we did a little convincing ourselves. He knows you're not a little girl anymore. I mean, look at you, gorgeous. You're anything but little," Nails said jokingly, and pulled her into a hug as soon as Bear released her.

"Watch it, Nails," Bear warned. Clover knew Nails was only kidding, but she also knew about his reputation with the ladies. He was a love them and leave them type of guy.

When Nails released her, she looked at the others and felt embarrassed. "I'm so sorry. I was so busy busting my brother's chops that I didn't even say hello to you guys." She hugged them, starting with Jay Bird, then Aussie, Playboy, and Snow. The further she made her way down the line, the more nervous she felt, knowing that Joker stood at the end. Just as Snow released her, she realized Duke wasn't around. Buying herself a little more time, she looked to her brother. "Where's Duke?"

"He'll be here shortly. He had something he needed to check on," Bear told her before he and the rest of the guys headed inside, leaving Clover and Joker standing outside.

There was nobody else left to throw her a lifeline. This was it. She tilted her head back to look up at Joker. The moment she met his deep green eyes, she felt the tightness in her chest. Thank goodness she still wore her sunglasses because she couldn't resist giving his body another once over as he stood before her with his arms crossed, putting his biceps on display as they flexed under his cotton t-shirt. His nostrils flared, his jaw was firm and clenched, and she wondered what was going through his mind.

"Hello, Landon," she greeted him using his real name, which surprised him, and he quirked his eyebrow at her.

"Clover," he acknowledged with a slight nod of his head.

Surprising her, he dropped his arms and pulled her into a hug. His large arms swallowed her frame, and before she knew it, her arms wound around his neck. She closed her eyes as her traitorous body relished in the moment of being held by him again.

"We need to talk," he whispered, his warm breath tickling her ear.

Her eyes popped open, and she slowly pulled away at the same time Joker released her.

"Do we?" She probed, wondering if this was where he'd tell her that what happened between them had been a mistake. She didn't think she could handle hearing those words—at least not right now, when she would have to go in and sit with her brother and the others acting as if everything was okay when she'd be devastated.

She started to walk backward as she shook her head.

"I don't think now is the right time for us to talk about—"

She was interrupted by Playboy as he popped his head out the door.

"Hey! Bear's getting impatient. Are you guys coming in or what?"

Joker gave her an annoyed look before giving Playboy a short reply. "We're coming."

Before she could entertain another thought or word, she was ushered inside with Joker's hand flush against her back.

It wasn't very crowded inside, so they found the group right away at a table off to the side, away from the others. She took the empty seat next to Bear while Joker took the seat directly across from her.

Don't show him how much his presence affects you, she calmly told herself. *And definitely don't act nervous.* She didn't need Bear picking up on that weakness and calling her out. He was notorious for doing that.

Bear turned toward her. "I know I said I'd let things go, but after talking with the guys, we as a team have one last request we want to make, and then I promise we'll never talk about it again."

She tilted her head sideways and narrowed her eyes. "Yeah? What's that?"

"We say this only because we care about you. Can you please think twice before you *volunteer* for deployment? We get it if you're given orders to go somewhere. But there are plenty of other places—safer places for you to go and 'see the world.'"

She wrinkled her nose up at him. "Maybe I'm here on some super-secret operation that I can't talk about," she replied, giving him a cheeky grin.

He snorted a laugh, and a few of the others snickered. "Yeah, okay," he quipped.

She gave him a shit-eating grin. *Only if you knew, big brother.*

Moments later, they were talking and laughing as if the drama earlier hadn't ever happened, though she could feel Joker's eyes on her the whole time.

"So, Bear said you're leaving tomorrow. Does that mean you're heading back to San Diego?" Nails asked her.

"That's the plan." She hoped that was still the plan, and they didn't have to take a detour somewhere else. She was ready to go home and relax. Maybe she'd even hit the beach for a bit of fun in the sun before heading to her parents' house, although she had to consider the injury to her arm. She definitely couldn't go swimming until the stitches dissolved.

"Speaking of home, you're going to make it to Mom and Dad's in two weeks, right?" Bear asked her.

She smiled as she popped a French fry smothered in ketchup into her mouth. "Absolutely. I wouldn't miss it. I already got my leave approved."

"Joker. Aren't you going with Bear?" Playboy asked.

That newsflash caught Clover's attention, and she swung her head around toward Joker.

"You're going to my parents' anniversary party?"

Joker nodded, but before he could say anything, Bear butted in. "Mom was adamant that he come."

*Oh, for heaven's sake, s*he thought to herself. She would have to spend an entire weekend with the man who brushed her off after having sex with him. She looked over at Joker again and could tell there was something he wanted to say to her. Honestly, she wasn't sure if she wanted to know.

She was still looking at Joker when Bear called to someone over her shoulder.

"Hey, man. I was wondering if you were ever going to make it."

Before she peeled her eyes away from Joker, she thought he mouthed the word "later" to her.

When Clover looked over her shoulder, she saw Duke. She smiled, and when he got to the table, she stood up and hugged him.

"I was hoping I'd get to see you," she told him, avoiding the glare Joker threw her way. Was he jealous?

"Likewise," he said in that smooth southern Georgia drawl of his.

"What'd you find out?" Bear asked him. Duke shook his head and gave Bear a grim look.

"Duke was over at medical checking up on someone," Bear explained to her, and it dawned on her they were most likely talking about the guy they rescued. Judging from Duke's dismal expression, she wondered if the guy hadn't made it.

Clover picked up her bottle of water just as Aussie spoke up.

"Speaking of medical, does anyone know whatever happened to our pilot?"

Clover couldn't control her reflexes and spewed the mouthful of water all over the table before she started coughing uncontrollably.

"Shit!" Bear slapped her on the back a few times, and she coughed a few more times before getting herself under control, and everyone asked if she was okay.

"Sorry, water went down the wrong pipe."

She wiped her mouth and the mess she made on the table. She listened as Duke answered Aussie's question.

"No. I asked, but they said the guy never came through medical. But I did manage to meet up with a buddy of mine." Duke said, making her a little more relaxed, knowing her cover hadn't been blown.

"Really? Who was that?" Bear questioned.

Duke glanced at Clover. His eyes suddenly appeared to be full of questions before he answered Bear.

"Captain Mickens. He and I had a nice chat." He looked at her again, raising an eyebrow. Her gut clenched, and she wondered what exactly Duke and the doctor had chatted about.

"I've talked with Captain Mickens several times since I arrived. He seems like a nice man and a good doctor," Clover stated, trying to get a little more out of Duke and where he was going with his dialogue.

"I'm sure you have. He's a master when it comes to *stitches*." As he emphasized the word stitches, his eyes traveled to her arm, and she knew she was busted. But what exactly did he know?

Acting as if his comment hadn't affected her, she picked up her drink and took another sip before offering a rebuttal to Duke.

"Well, it can get dangerous around here. I've seen many incidents requiring medical attention, especially the Seabees. With the kind of work they do, someone's always getting injured."

"MmmHmm…" Duke uttered but then changed the subject—sort of.

"So, what brings you to Djibouti? This is a long way from San Diego."

Clover rolled her eyes and heard several of the others snicker.

"Let's just say my little sister wanted to get out and see the world," Bear told Duke.

Duke swung his eyes back to her. "You do know there are a lot of nicer and *safer* places to see in the world, right?"

"That's what we told her," Bear said, giving her a stern look, but he winked.

Clover knew it would take a while for Bear to accept her being there. Maybe one day, when she and her brothers were old, they could compare notes on where they had been. That made her laugh a little.

"So, what exciting sites have you gotten to see so far?" Joker asked her, surprising her by even speaking to her. Since they spoke outside, he hadn't uttered a single word to her. He just watched her, which made her feel a little uneasy.

She looked at him. "What do you mean?"

"I mean, you said you wanted to see the world. What has Djibouti shown or offered you?"

For some reason, it seemed as if he was testing her. Besides, all military personnel knew leaving the base in Djibouti wasn't allowed unless permission was granted. And you needed a solid reason to even ask.

"Well, let's see..." She began to name places or things she'd seen on the base. "The hangars are a pretty cool place to go, if I say so myself. The different types of aircraft just blow you away, literally." She grinned. "Though I tend to favor the helos." Her eyes went wide. "I also got to see a group of Seabees erect a building firsthand. And I've gotten to hang out at the little pub and play some pool and ping pong. Oh! I can't forget the recreational building. That place is off the charts. I mean, who doesn't like shuffleboard and checkers?"

She heard Bear laughing beside her at her sarcasm, but she never took her eyes off Joker. He didn't appear to find any amusement in her comments as he continued to stare at her. Then he fired off another question.

"How long have you been here?"

"About three months." She wouldn't tell him a portion of that time was spent in other Middle Eastern countries.

"What exactly are you working on here?"

She gave him a sideways glance. "What do you mean what am I working on? I'm a helicopter mechanic, and there are three hangars full of helicopters. I think that's pretty much self-explanatory." What was he trying to get at? Did they all know her secret, and she was being punked? Just the thought of that had her going on the defensive. "What's next? Do you want to know what I eat every day, or maybe when I go to bed?"

When Joker glanced at Bear, Clover became even more suspicious. It was like they were communicating telepathically, and she hated that. Growing up, her brothers did that, and it drove her nuts. She suddenly became uncomfortable with the line of questioning.

Just when she thought they would press her further, she spotted a group of Seabees she had gotten to know a little bit. She gave them a wave, and the one guy in the front, Andrews, waved back and started walking toward her.

Andrews was a nice guy, but he was a total flirt and had been hitting on her since she arrived. *Crap!* Maybe she shouldn't have acknowledged him. Perhaps the wave was enough, and he and his friends would just keep walking. But judging from the gleam in his eyes, that wasn't going to happen.

"Clover, we missed you last night," Andrews said, stopping next to her.

She smirked. "Sorry, Andrews. I had other plans." *Like saving my brother's ass,* she felt like saying.

"No worries. You're coming to the show later, right?"

She forgot about the country band that flew in to perform for the troops on the base.

"I might stop by. I'm leaving tomorrow, and I have things I need to get done before then."

Andrews nodded, then scanned the table.

"You guys new around here?" He asked, and Bear shot him an annoyed look.

"No," he told him flatly.

"Huh. I don't remember ever seeing you around. I've been here for nearly a year, and believe me; I remember faces."

"That's because you're not meant to see me. However, I can say that I've seen you." Bear stated in a low-toned badass way before throwing Andrews a smartass smirk.

Clover covered her mouth to try and hide her smile. Andrews was known to be a hothead who had a set of balls the size of King Kong. He was sort of the leader of the pack, but he had no clue who he was messing with this time, and the need to intervene before Andrews got his ass kicked was imminent.

She stood up and placed herself between Andrews and Bear. She put her hand on Andrews' forearm and shot him a warning look, telling him to cool it.

Thankfully, he heeded her warning as she saw his shoulders relax. But then he caught her completely off guard when he wrapped his arm around her waist and pulled her close.

Stunned by the daring move, she looked up at him. He flashed her a flirty grin, winking before he kissed her cheek.

"See ya later, doll. I'll save you a seat next to me," he said before releasing her and walking away.

Clover stood there for a moment, wondering what in the hell just happened. Then it dawned on her. He made that move to make her brother and the others think she and him were an item.

She nibbled her lip as she sat back down. She felt like crawling under the table with all the eyes on her. Especially the icy glare Joker was throwing her way.

"Who the fuck was that?" Bear barked in a commanding tone she was becoming accustomed to.

She rolled her eyes, hoping he didn't start his shit again.

"Just a guy, and he's harmless."

Joker snorted. "Harmless, my ass. He was practically undressing you with his eyes, not to mention his hand was practically on your ass. You aren't really going to meet him later, are you?"

She gave him a sideways look, clearly taken aback by his mini outburst.

"Does that upset you?" She asked with a bit of snark. She knew she was poking the bear, but she'd had enough of his snide remarks. It was starting to piss her off.

Joker pinned her with his bold green eyes. She would've cowered under the intensity of his fierce gaze if she didn't know him.

"All I'm saying is to be careful, sweetheart, because just when you think you know someone, they can do a complete one-eighty, surprising the hell out of you." He huffed, grabbing his water bottle off the table and taking a big gulp.

She was stunned by his hostility toward her. She felt as if his statement was directed toward her, which hurt her deeply, especially after what they had shared. But if that were the case, then he needed to look in a mirror and repeat those words because if anyone had done a one-eighty, it had been him.

Feeling the tension thicken between her and Joker, she felt now would be a good time to say goodbye. Plus, she was feeling a little emotional from everything that had happened in the past few hours. She gathered her trash and stood up. Bear stood up next to her.

"Where are you going?"

"I think it's time for me to go. Plus, I have things to settle around here before I leave." She said, leaning in to hug him. "I'll see you in two weeks," her voice cracking as she spoke.

When Bear released her, she stepped back and avoided eye contact with him. She felt fragile, and all it would take was one worried look from her brother, and she'd shatter.

She gave a slight wave to the others. "It was nice seeing you guys. Be safe."

As she turned to head out, her eyes fell on Joker one last time, but she quickly made her exit before he could say anything else. Feeling the tears burning her eyes, she threw on her sunglasses as soon as she was outside. Damn her emotions.

જે

Joker stared at Clover's back as she stormed out. He'd pissed her off and probably hurt her. He felt like a complete asshole. *Christ! What had he been thinking?* He knew better than to engage in a confrontation with her. The worst part was that he'd exposed himself in front of the others, including her brother. *Fuck!*

Ever since hearing her name fly out of Fins' mouth, he'd been wound up and feeling anxious. Maybe a bit jealous as well. Hearing Fins describe Clover had struck a nerve. Everything Fins said about her was true, but he didn't like hearing it coming from another man, especially when he was in love with the woman in question.

But what also bothered him was hearing how that guy she knew from home had treated her. Then having a front-row seat while that last douche bag hit on her, and Clover insisting he was harmless. It all just came to a boil, and he reacted.

Who knew? Maybe the guy was harmless, but she didn't know that. And this wasn't Joker's first rodeo. He'd been to many bases worldwide and had seen a lot of bad shit go down involving female military personnel being sexually harassed and even assaulted by their fellow soldiers—the same soldiers that some of those women initially thought were harmless.

Running a hand through his hair in frustration, he knew he would have to answer for his actions—not just to Clover, to whom he owed an apology, but also to Bear.

When he turned his head and met Bear's glare, he knew an ass reaming was coming his way.

"Do you want to explain what the fuck that was all about?"

Joker shook his head in defeat and offered the only thing he could—an apology.

"I'm sorry, man. I was just pissed off at how she gave everyone a free pass or the benefit of the doubt. She deserves better—a lot better." He wanted to say that she deserved a man like him who'd respect and care for her. But wasn't that the pot calling the kettle black? Instead of being an ass, he should have chosen his words more wisely.

Bear continued to stare at him, and Joker vowed that he wouldn't break. He wasn't going to show his cards—what he was feeling. He wasn't saying anything until he spoke with Clover and settled whatever was happening between them—if there was anything left. Finally, after a few tense and eerily quiet moments, Bear nodded.

"It pisses me off too. I just hope everyone's right, and she knows what she's doing."

Joker stood up and held his hand out. Bear looked at it, then reached out and shook it.

"We good, man?" Joker asked, and Bear smirked.

"Yeah, we're good."

Joker grabbed his drink from the table. He needed to make things right with Clover.

"Where are you going?" Snow asked.

"I'm going to find Clover and apologize. It's the least I can do."

As Joker turned to head out the door, Bear called after him.

"Thank you," Bear told him, and the gesture caught Joker by surprise.

"No need to thank me. I fucked up, and I tend to rectify my mistakes."

Bear shook his head. "No. I'm not talking about you making an ass of yourself and needing to apologize. I'm saying thank you for caring about my sister."

Joker didn't know how to respond, so he just nodded and went on his way.

CHAPTER FOUR

Clover took her time walking back to her CHU. She needed time to cool off and get her emotions under control. She was upset with herself for letting Joker and his assholeness get the better of her. She chuckled and asked herself, *"Is assholeness even a word?"* She didn't care. It sounded good to her.

For the life of her, she couldn't figure out what had triggered the abruptness in Joker's attitude toward her. He went from hugging her to attacking her. Her only thought was jealousy. But why? He had nothing to be jealous of. He's the one who chose not to acknowledge what occurred between them. She left him her number, and he decided not to use it—end of the story.

For two years, she kept the hope alive that there would be a day when Joker walked back into her life and swept her off her feet. Sure, they'd be skirting the military rules, but she was coming up on the final year of her enlistment contract, and she would have given up military life just to be with him. In the last two years, she'd turned down several suitable prospects. But Joker's behavior in the mess hall confirmed he was finished, and it was time for her to move on. There were greener pastures, with many stallions waiting for a mare.

She promised herself that she'd take the next couple of weeks back home and focus on herself, her career, and her family. Only then would she consider jumping back into the dating pool. She faced an uphill battle to eliminate Joker from her life, but it was the right thing for her to do.

She made the last turn down the row that her CHU was in. She was so deep in thought that she never saw the other person until they collided.

◆

Joker walked through the maze of tents and container buildings, hoping to spot Clover along the way. When he couldn't find her, he finally stopped and asked someone where number nine was, and they directed him toward the last few rows of CHUs.

Dammit! Maybe this wasn't a good idea. He should just wait two weeks until he sees her at her mom and dad's house. That way, they'd have uninterrupted time to talk. But it was killing him. He needed to know why she walked away.

Making up his mind, he made a one-eighty turn and toppled the person in his path. They hit so hard that the other person bounced off him and fell to the ground. When Joker glanced down, he saw a mass of blonde waves, and his gut tightened.

"Clover?"

"Son of a bitch," she muttered as she brushed her hair from her face. As soon as she peered up at him with those hazel eyes he fell in love with, his gut clenched. A dull sadness had replaced the brightness that normally shined in her eyes. The redness around her eyes told him she'd been crying, which made him feel even worse. He regretted every single negative word he said to her earlier.

He bent over to help her up, but she swatted his hand away. It pissed him off, but he deserved her brush-off. However, he wasn't that much of an asshole to leave her on the ground. He ignored her attempt to keep her distance from him, and he gripped her biceps, helping her stand. As he put a little pressure on her arms, she yelped and tried to pull away. His quick reflexes saved her from tumbling back onto her ass.

She placed her left hand on her right arm and cringed as she appeared to breathe through the pain. Realizing that she was injured, he was by her side in a flash.

"You're hurt," he said, taking her hand.

"I'm fine," she told him. But the pained look etched on her face told him different story.

"You're not fine," he retorted, and she pinned him with a look that warned him to back off.

"Why do you care?"

"Clover..."

She held her hand up. "You know what? I don't want to know."

"Clover, please." He pleaded, hoping she'd let him talk to her.

She pulled her hand from his and took a few steps back, crossing her arms in front of her chest and putting some space between them. It was a standard defensive move. However, he noticed she was still favoring her arm, and he was concerned.

"How did you hurt your arm?"

She didn't answer. She just stared at him. He took a few steps toward her. She never moved.

"Clover, don't lie to me. Are you hurt?"

Sighing, she slowly dropped her arms to her side. "If I say yes, will you stop asking?"

He raised his eyebrows at her snarkiness.

"Maybe," he replied.

She huffed in annoyance. "Fine. Yes. I cut myself this morning and had to get a few stitches."

"What happened?"

"It was an accident in the hangar," she told him before redirecting the conversation—another defense mechanism. Not to mention, it was a vague answer.

"Joker, why are you here?" She asked in a softer tone, and it broke his heart because he could hear the pain in her voice. And it wasn't the pain from her arm. It was coming from the pain that he caused.

"I came to apologize. I was pissed off and took it out on you. I'm so sorry, Clover."

"Apology accepted," she voiced quickly and turned to walk away, but he wasn't finished. He had her undivided attention, and he wasn't going to waste the opportunity.

"Clover, please don't walk away."

She spun around quickly and laughed sarcastically. "That's a funny request, coming from you."

"Can we just talk for a minute? Please?"

"I only have a few minutes. I have things I need to do before I meet up with some friends."

The image of the asswipe who had his hands on her popped into his head. "Not that Andrews guy, I hope."

Her eyes narrowed, and she flashed him a grin that the Cheshire Cat couldn't have done any better before giving her shoulder a quick, short shrug.

"Maybe."

She was baiting him. If she wanted to play games, he was certainly up for it. She just didn't know he always played to win.

Oh, sweetheart, your ass is mine. He glanced around, making sure nobody was around before placing his hand on her hip and walking her backward.

Hearing her gasp as her back hit the wall of a nearby building brought a small smile to his lips. She was caged in between his arms and legs. He towered over her five-feet-five stature, but to her credit, she never broke eye contact as he stared into her eyes.

"Are you trying to piss me off intentionally?" He growled, and she vehemently shook her head, offering no words. "Because if that's what this is, it's working," his voice was low but commanding, and he moved his face closer to hers.

The desire to taste her again was growing. Her tongue flicked out and slid across her bottom lip, taunting him. Before he convinced himself he was making a big mistake, he closed the distance, pressing his body snugly against hers and taking her lips in a searing kiss that would leave them both thinking about it until they met again.

Her small, delicate hands moved to his waist, which fed his hunger for more. He wanted all of her. He took her face between the palms of his hands, tilting her head back further so he could deepen the kiss. He tried not to devour her as he tasted the sweet essence of her coconut lip balm.

The hot sun beating down on his back had nothing to do with the heat ravishing his body as he pulled her closer. She moaned softly, gripping his shirt tighter. Thankfully the kiss muffled her soft purr. He hadn't really thought his plan out too well as the thought that someone could walk upon them any moment came barreling into his mind. He was forced to pump the brakes. He didn't want the moment to end, but he knew it had to. He released her lips but not before leaving a trail of kisses along her cheek, jaw, and neck. They were both breathing heavily, and he could feel the hammering of her heart. He opened his eyes and smiled when he saw that Clover still had her eyes closed. There was no way she could deny the attraction between them. She looked beautiful, and he kissed her forehead, letting his lips linger against her heated flesh. He knew deep down that they were meant for each other. He just had to make her see it.

As the seconds passed and she slowly opened her eyes, he could see some of the brightness had returned to her eyes, making him smile. However, that smile faded as the intensity and fire hiding in the shadows came forefront.

"Clover?" He questioned as tears suddenly began to fill her eyes. She covered her mouth before giving her head a shake. She stepped from his hold, and he instantly felt the loss.

"Why did you do that? I can't—no, I won't go through what I did again," she said to him as tears rolled down her cheeks.

He didn't understand. What had she gone through? Before he could question her any further, someone came walking down the road.

"I need to go," she said hoarsely, wiping the tears from her face.

Joker reached for her arm as she turned to leave, and he held her in place. He whispered in her ear with his chest pressed against her back and his arms securely wrapped around her.

"This isn't over between us. I've waited two long years to feel you in my arms again, and I'm not giving up on us. You have two weeks to really think about what you want. But I promise, as soon we get to your parents' house, you and I will be having a long-overdue conversation and work out whatever the hell happened between us."

He kissed her cheek before she pulled away and walked away from him.

Joker didn't take his eyes off her. He watched her until she made it to her CHU and opened the door. Before she stepped inside, she looked back over her shoulder at him. That one glance was all he needed. She still had feelings for him. He just hoped his caveman tactics hadn't ruined his second chance. The thought of losing her for good didn't sit well with him, and he spun around in frustration and hit the side of the building with his fist.

"Fuck!"

Suddenly, a sharp whistle pierced the humid, gritty air, and Joker looked toward the intersection where the main road met the CHUs, and he found Duke standing there.

Shit. He wondered if Duke had seen him and Clover kissing. He told himself to play it cool, even though he felt anything but cool.

Quickly, he pulled himself together as Duke approached.

"What's up?" Joker asked, ignoring Duke's curious glance.

"Bear sent me to find you. Our ride's here."

"Good."

As they walked to their meet-up location, it gave Joker some time to think, and boy did he have a lot to process. But one particular thought came to the forefront as he recalled something Duke mentioned earlier. It had to do with Clover's injury.

"That doctor you talked about earlier…"

"Captain Mickens?"

"Yeah. I couldn't help but notice you seemed focused on Clover while talking about Captain Mickens having a busy day stitching up people. Were you implying that Captain Mickens stitched up Clover?"

Duke stopped walking and turned to face Joker. Duke was a straightforward guy. Judging from the serious expression on his face, Joker was pretty sure he knew something.

"Why do you ask?"

"Because Clover told me she cut herself earlier today and needed stitches."

Duke was hesitant at first to answer. But then he nodded. "Yeah. But he wouldn't say how she sustained the injury. He said it was a pretty nasty cut, and that she had a lot of bruising to go along with it."

"Did you tell Bear?"

Duke shook his head. "Nope. Not my place. If Clover wanted him to know, she'd tell him herself."

Fair enough, Joker thought to himself, and they continued walking.

"So, I take it you and she kissed and made up," Duke stated nonchalantly.

Joker swung his head around. "What?"

Duke gave him a funny look and appeared like he wanted to say something, but then changed his mind before he answered.

"It was just a metaphor."

Joker felt instant relief and laughed off Duke's comment. He slipped his hands into his pockets. "Clover and I are good." God, he prayed that statement was true.

"That's good," Duke replied, smiling.

Yep, it sure was, Joker thought to himself as the two of them walked the rest of the way in silence.

ॐ

A few hours later, Clover was trying really hard to enjoy the country music playing, but it was turning out to be extremely difficult. No thanks to Joker and her wandering mind. Her earlier encounter with him had totally flipped her world upside down.

But isn't that what you wanted—him? The little devil inside her head asked. And the answer was yes! She longed to be given a second chance with him. But the question that remained was, why now? Why did he suddenly seem interested in her, especially when he never tried contacting her after the night they shared together?

That doozy of a kiss he had left her with earlier was impactful. She touched her lips, still feeling the remnants of his warm, alluring lips pressed against hers. There was a meaning behind the kiss, and she had felt the emotion he poured into it. She wouldn't dare deny the attraction between them, no matter how upset she was at him.

She had no idea what to do. She was so confused. Thank goodness her deployment was coming to an end, because the way her brain was wired, she had no business flying a helicopter.

The nudge to her arm brought her back to the present. When she looked up, Andrews and a few of the other guys she was sitting with were staring at her.

"What?" She asked cautiously, feeling a little timid by the attention she was receiving.

"I asked if you were okay," Andrews said, his eyebrows furrowed.

"Why wouldn't I be?"

"I don't know, maybe because the show ended a few minutes ago, and you're still sitting here completely zoned out. You weren't even paying attention through most of the show."

She noticed the hangar was primarily empty except for a few stragglers. *Dang, it!* Had she really zoned out for that long? She rubbed her forehead before she looked back up at Andrews. Even though they could be immature and inappropriate at times, they all seemed genuinely concerned.

"Sorry. I've just got a lot on my mind right now."

She started to get up, but Andrews touched her arm, and she sat back down.

"This doesn't have anything to do with those guys you were with earlier, does it?"

She took a deep breath. There was no way she would get into her issues with these guys. She shook her head.

"It's nothing."

Apparently, Andrews wasn't getting the message that the subject was off-limits, as he continued to press further.

"Who were they? They didn't seem like people you'd hang out with. Did they do or say something to upset you?"

Her first reaction was to laugh. Since the day she arrived in Djibouti, Andrews had wanted in her pants for a quick roll in the hay, and now to see him acting so protective was a switch she hadn't expected, nor did she think he even had a caring and compassionate bone in his body.

"They're harmless. Plus, I know them. Very well, might I add."

"When you say you know them very well, did you date one of them? That one dude with the freaky grey eyes seemed awfully protective."

She chuckled. "That dude with the freaky grey eyes is my brother."

Andrews' eyes widened. "Your brother?"

"Yeah. The others were his teammates."

"Teammates?" He questioned, but then his eyebrows slowly rose dramatically, and she knew then that he'd understood. "Your brother is a SEAL?"

She just stared at him, neither agreeing nor denying his inquiry.

"Dude, you're lucky you didn't get your ass kicked," Jones, one of the other guys, said to Andrews.

"I was joking!" Andrews exclaimed, then glanced around before turning his attention back to Clover. "Are they still here?"

She snorted a laugh. She didn't want to tell him they had already left, just to make him sweat a little. But that would be mean, and she had dealt with enough drama and meanness for one day.

"You don't have to worry. They left out on a transport a few hours ago. At least, that's what Bear told me."

"Bear! Your brother's name is Bear?"

"It's his call sign."

Andrews ran his hand through his hair nervously, and she couldn't help but chuckle.

"Hey, don't worry about him. I told him you were a good guy."

Her compliment must have surprised him because he raised his eyebrows and flashed his flirty smile her way, which caused another laugh from her.

"So, you think I'm a good guy?" He lifted his arm and looked down at his watch before looking back at her. "You said you leave in the morning. Going by my watch means I have eight hours to show you how good of a guy I can really be."

She laughed even harder when he scooted closer and draped his arm over her shoulders. Even his friends were laughing at his nonsense. They were calling him desperate and ridiculous for even thinking he had a shot with her. She knew it was all innocent, and he was just playing around.

She looked up at him and smiled. "How about a hug? Would a hug suffice?"

She must've surprised him because he looked totally caught off guard. "Seriously?"

"Yeah. I hug many of my friends, and I have to say, Andrews, you've grown on me over the last few weeks. So, yes, I consider you a friend."

After giving Andrews his one hug, she hopped down off the bleachers. The guys followed, and they all said their goodbyes. A few exchanged numbers with her to keep in touch. Andrews even finagled another hug out of her before she left, which she found funny.

On her walk back to the CHU, she began to think about her and Joker again. Maybe it was best they got a chance to talk before they met up at her parents' house. It would be a shame if their differences ruined what was supposed to be a happy and enjoyable occasion. As soon as she got home, she'd call her brother and get Joker's number.

CHAPTER FIVE

Hoping to find an empty table, Sergeant Anthony Hollis weaved through the crowded swanky café as soft Somali Balwo music blasted from the speakers. Just when he thought he was out of luck, a woman he assumed was a waitress waved her hand in the air, getting his attention. As he started to walk toward her, she pointed to a small two-person table next to a window near the back that he hadn't seen. He offered the woman a pleasant smile when he arrived at the table.

"Mahadsanid," he said, thanking her in the Somali language, one of the two main languages spoken in Djibouti. He wasn't fluent but he knew enough to get him around.

The waitress offered a warm smile in return.

"I speak a little English." The woman admitted, catching him by surprise.

He looked closer at the name tag pinned to her t-shirt—*Asma*.

"Well, Asma, we're both alike as I speak a little Somali."

The young woman's smile widened upon hearing that.

"May I offer you a drink?"

"Yes, a drink would be lovely. How about a cup of kafeega."

She nodded, jotting it down on her notepad. When she left to retrieve his coffee, Hollis glanced around the café, taking in the eclectic atmosphere. The café was adjacent to the University of Djibouti, so, most patrons were primarily young college students. He noted a few older individuals, and it made him wonder if any of them were the contact he was supposed to meet. He glanced at his watch. It was a few minutes past the agreed meeting time. He could thank that bitch, Clover Walker for causing him to miss his ride into the city. If it weren't for her carelessness, he would have never gotten into the altercation with that guy who came to her rescue. She seemed to know him personally, and

Hollis wondered who he was. A boyfriend, maybe? What did he care, though? He only had a few more months left on his enlistment contract, and then he was gone. With enough money stashed away, and nothing keeping him in the continental U.S., he planned on using his hard-earned money to travel the world under a new alias. That was to ensure his identity would be covered should his name wind up on a list when the organization he was doing work for was busted. However, if everything went according to plan, he'd be long gone before that ever happened.

He looked at his watch again. His contact's tardiness wasn't sitting well with him, and he began to feel a bit uneasy. He could feel the sweat trickling down his back. He half wondered if this meeting was a set-up, and he was already made.

The unsettled feeling made him recall the day he had been unexpectedly approached by the CIA Director, Clayton Perkins, and was sucked into the web of deceit and destruction.

Nearly a year ago, he'd been in line at a small coffee shop near his mom's house in Chula Vista on an early Sunday morning. One minute, he was ordering coffee, and the next, he was being ushered to a table in the back of the shop by the Director and a woman named Rose. He'd never met either one, but they knew everything about him.

A year earlier, his dad had left his mom with no warning. His dad was a salesman, and traveled the country for business. One day, his dad came home and told his wife he was leaving her. The bastard didn't just leave her, though. He also left her with all their financial burdens. He had begged his mom to fight his dad during the divorce proceedings since it had been him who had taken out several loans, opened numerous credit cards, and maxed them out. But his mom was too nice and just wanted to move on. She had been swimming in debt.

Two months later, she was diagnosed with stage three pancreatic cancer. It had already spread to her lymph nodes. Even with the odds stacked against her, she was determined to fight. Of course, that meant taking on more debt. After a few months, she couldn't stay afloat with the mounting hospital bills and other financial obligations. He had tried to convince her to file for bankruptcy, but she had too much pride and refused. He tried to help where he could, but the Navy didn't pay that much, and he had his own bills he was responsible for.

So, when Director Perkins invited him into a twisted world that promised to free him and his mom of all their financial woes, even going as far as assuring that his mom's entire cancer treatment would be paid in full, he really didn't have a choice; he was desperate, and Perkins knew it.

His gut warned him that it was an offer too good to be true, but it had been difficult to say no with the amount of money that was being dangled in front of him. However, what Perkins failed to tell him before he had accepted their offer, was that once he committed himself, there was no way out, and he was sworn to secrecy. In other words, he was at the mercy of an organization filled with high-level government officials who had no qualms about selling out their country for greed and power. He was as good as dead if they found out that he uttered a single word about anything relating to the organization.

Hollis knew he had been targeted because of his job. Being a crew chief for the SCU meant that he was able to travel all over the world, giving him easy access to make the drops as he was instructed to do.

He had no idea what was in the small, black, poly bubbled envelopes that he'd receive in the mail a week before he left for any deployment. He was provided a burner phone used to receive the instructions on what to do with each envelope. Usually, it was quite simple, like going into a particular grocery store and placing the envelope on a certain shelf behind a specific product. The last drop was done at a library, where he had to leave the envelope in a specific book. Or, like now, in a restaurant, though this was the first time he'd actually be handing over an envelope to an actual person.

Of course, he wasn't privileged to know exactly who the organization's mastermind was. The only person he knew involved was Perkins.

Perkins wasn't someone he wanted to cross. Hollis had heard stories about Perkins and how ruthless he was during his military career. The only person he knew who wasn't involved was his boss, The President of the United States, which meant President Evans had no idea he had traitors within his administration.

The woman, Rose, who had accompanied Perkins during the initial visit, was a mystery. She had been quiet for most of the conversation, but she had a strong posh British accent when she spoke. Even though she identified herself as Rose, he wasn't born yesterday, and knew that wasn't her real name.

Even though he knew what he was partaking in was wrong in so many ways, he couldn't complain because the organization had kept its word. He'd been involved with them for close to a year and had amassed just shy of one million dollars. Today's deal would push him over that threshold, officially making him a millionaire. The best part was that it was untraceable, as all payments were made with cryptocurrency. He didn't know how it all worked, and he never asked. As long as his money showed up in his crypto wallet a week after every drop he completed, he didn't care who or where it came from.

Over the last two months, he had become a bit apprehensive. There had been several occasions where he'd gotten that tingly and uneasy feeling that he was being watched. The first time, he let it go, chalking it up to just him being paranoid. But when it happened a second time when he was at the grocery store near his apartment, he used the burner phone and texted the number he was given to contact if he had any issues. Nonetheless, the response he got back didn't ease his worries. Even though they vehemently dismissed his concern, telling him their operation was constructed to be untraceable, he'd been extra vigilant while engaging in any transaction.

Asma returned with his coffee, and he thanked her. When she set a plate down in front of him, he looked at her. "This isn't mine. I didn't order any food."

"It's compliments of the chef," she told him, then tore off the ticket she had written his drink order on and placed it on the table face down before she disappeared into the kitchen.

That was strange, he thought to himself. He glanced down at the plate in front of him. He recognized the food. It was samosas; a tasty appetizer compiled of dough, stuffed with meat and onions, then fried and served with an African red sauce.

He picked up the ticket the waitress left and flipped it over. His gut clenched when he saw the writing on it.

Eyes are upon you. So you don't appear suspicious, eat the food. Once you're finished, place the envelope under the plate, then leave through the back exit. Follow the instructions exactly as stated. The note was signed *"E."*

"E" was who would send his instructions. The "eyes upon him" warning left him feeling edgy and vulnerable. Maybe he hadn't been overreacting, and he was actually being watched.

He was at an impasse. He wondered if those behind the operation would use him as the scapegoat. He wanted to roll his eyes at himself. Of course, they'd use him and anybody else who had been stupid enough to get involved in the first place. Even if he pleaded guilty and went to prison, he was sure those involved would find a way to have him murdered on the inside. He would be a dead man either way.

The more he thought about that, the more he quickly realized that his only option to be free and alive was to go into hiding. Once he left the military, he wasn't of any use to the organization. Again, there was no other option for him. He made his mind up right there on the spot. He'd finish whatever other jobs he had between now and his discharge date, and after that, he was gone.

He grabbed his fork and knife and cut into the first delicious treat. The steam rose from the piping hot meat and other fillings as the piece separated. He took a bite and closed his eyes, savoring the taste.

After taking the last bite, he wiped his mouth before reaching into the black bag he carried and pulling out both the envelope and his wallet.

He pulled some cash from his wallet and placed it along with the envelope under the plate as instructed. He then picked up the note, tore it into small pieces, and threw it into his coffee cup that was still half full. He swirled the paper around using a spoon until it had softened and broke apart into even smaller pieces. He hated to do it because it was gross, but he wasn't taking any chances. He picked up the cup and drank what was left in the cup, swallowing all the evidence.

Before he stood up, he glanced around the café one last time, making sure nobody seemed to be watching. When the coast seemed clear, he quietly exited through the back entrance.

As he stepped out into the dark alley behind the café, he grinned, knowing that he'd be a millionaire once his pay hit his account next week. That called for a celebration. As he stood in the alleyway, he dug through his bag, looking for the cigar he put in there earlier. He didn't hear the footsteps until it was too late. Before he could react, he felt the gun's barrel against the side of his head. Then everything went black.

CHAPTER SIX

Rick Evans' black Oxfords heel clicked on the dark marble flooring as he made his way down the narrow corridor leading to the Situation Room complex beneath the West Wing of the White House.

His mind was flooded with agenda items. Life as the President of the United States could be inundating at times, but nobody said it was an easy job. If that were the case, there'd be a slew of people lined up to snag it.

On a day when he should have been prepping for a teleconference scheduled with European leaders, he was instead playing hide and seek with the FBI Director. Eddie Caruso was a good friend and an outstanding public servant in heading up the FBI, but Evans wasn't sure what could be so significant that Eddie requested to meet in one of the smaller conference rooms in the secured complex. Usually, those rooms were reserved for when classified intel was being discussed.

As Evans passed by intelligence staff members handling computers and television screens, he was amazed by the complexity of the space and how it operated. Many people attributed the Situation Room to be just a large, secured conference room where the president and his most trusted advisors gathered to discuss highly classified information. But it was more than that. It was a complete intelligence management center built with several rooms, that was run by the National Security Council.

He made a right turn down another hallway and spotted Eddie standing outside the conference room, speaking with one of the Secret Service Agents.

When Eddie saw him, he excused himself from the conversation and met Evans by the door.

"Mr. President," Eddie greeted and shook his hand.

"Director," Evans responded and motioned Eddie to follow him into the conference room.

Evans knew that the moment the door closed and Eddie's expression turned cold, he wasn't going to like the news that was about to be delivered. He walked around the table and took his seat at the head of the table.

"What's going on?"

"Always to the point." Eddie said pulling a yellow file folder from his bag, and sliding it across the table. "I wish I didn't have to deliver this."

Evans eyed the folder before taking it and flipping it open. As soon as he saw the word microchip in the first sentence, he knew why Eddie was adamant they met in a secure setting.

A foreign intelligence agency had intercepted another microchip containing what appeared to be some sort of an inventory consisting of various unmanned aerial vehicles used by the U.S. military. It included The Reaper MQ-9, which could carry a variety of deadly weapons, RQ-21 Blackjack, Switchblade, and a few others.

Evans was thankful it had been an ally of the U.S., and immediately turned over.

Visibly upset, Evans looked up from the report. "Please tell me this isn't real."

Eddie shook his head, his grim expression holding firm. "Believe me. I wish it weren't."

Evans ran his hand through his hair. Before taking office as the President, he had served two terms as a congressman representing his home state of Tennessee. He served on several committees, including the House Intelligence Committee. Only once was there an incident involving a civilian who had been leaking information about the intelligence community. Between the Department of Justice and several intelligence agencies, the situation had been handled quickly and quietly. He never imagined he'd have to deal with corruption inside his own government during his own presidency.

Disgusted, he closed the file and slid it back across the table before leaning back in the chair.

"That's the third one in what? Six, seven months?" Evans asked Eddie. It was the FBI's Counterespionage Section that was responsible for the findings.

"Seven. And those are just the ones that we know exist. And it's damn scary knowing there could be others like it out there."

Evans wasn't happy, because they weren't just lists of weapons. Next to each weapon on the spreadsheets was a quantity as well as a low and high price.

The first microchip was discovered in Bern, Switzerland, and included a list featuring MK19 machine guns, M3 Carl Gustafs, M2 machine guns, and M240H machine guns. The second chip was turned over in Pretoria, South Africa. It, too, contained a list of military equipment comprising of anti-tank weapons, anti-fortification weapons, and body armor systems.

"We need to find the bastard behind this," Evans implied and slid the folder back across the table.

The way the spreadsheets were laid out made Evans and Caruso believe that the American weapons listed were being auctioned off to the highest bidder.

Someone with close ties to the government had to be providing the information. But the question was, who? Whoever it was had to have significant security clearance to access the sensitive data. Evans initially thought it would be easy to pinpoint where it was coming from since only a handful of individuals held top security clearance. But so far, he and the FBI had come up empty-handed. The person responsible definitely knew their way around a computer and how to mask their identity, because they always left no traces.

Shortly after the first chip was discovered, Evans had gathered his Cabinet and agency heads to brief them on the severity of the situation. Most of the members in attendance were just as concerned as Evans was, but a few seemed to downplay it.

Now, with the discovery of the third chip, Evans knew that they had a serious problem—one of their own was committing treason. He hated where his mind was wandering, but they had to look at all avenues.

If foreign intelligence agencies discovered the chips, why hadn't the CIA? If it was one chip, he could let that slide, but now three? It was a legitimate question, considering that the CIA was one of the most advanced intelligence agencies globally. It made him wonder if someone within the intelligence community could be intercepting intel before it reached who it was intended for.

On the other hand, he had to consider who was at the agency's helm—Clayton Perkins. He was a nasty son of a bitch who didn't like to play by the rules. He didn't like Evans, but the feeling was mutual because Evans didn't care much for Perkins.

He and Perkins had clashed during their military careers. Perkins had been appointed to the Director's position a few months before Evans had taken office. He was still in the position, because folks in the agency had seemed to like working for Perkins, and until recently, he'd been doing a fine job running it. As the old saying went, "why fix something that's not broken?"

However, two complaints had been filed against him in the last few months. One was for sexual harassment, which was dismissed because the woman withdrew the complaint—though, Evans had his suspicions that she was coerced into withdrawing it. The other complaint, filed by two former clandestine intelligence officers, was still actively being investigated, and was one that Evans was watching closely. The two men accused Perkins and several other higher-ranking officials at the agency of Intentional Tort. The complaint stated that the accused knowingly and willing omitted crucial intel, which resulted in a botched executed operation that ultimately caused the deaths of four CIOs and critically wounded two complainants, both of whom were no longer with the agency due to their injuries.

Evans had no qualms in firing Perkins. He already decided that once the investigation into the complaint was wrapped up, he would let

Perkins go. There was too much controversy around the agency, and Evans wouldn't let it happen on his watch.

That was also why Evans decided he wasn't taking any chances and called his good friend Eddie at the bureau, enlisting his team to lead the investigation into the microchips. Even though the FBI mainly worked within the United States, it still had worldwide teams and offices.

Eddie's team had delivered a treasure trove of information in just a few weeks of being on the case, starting with who had access to the military's weapons inventory and future purchases, as well as how the microchips were being moved around the world. The latter was a tedious job that involved linking any government employee, including military personnel, to where the microchips had been found.

Sadly, his elite flying squadron, the SCU, had been flagged as a potential source. For Evans, that was a tough pill to swallow, and he hoped it wasn't the case, but the evidence that Eddie's team had uncovered proved otherwise.

Two of the microchips recovered were handed over in countries where SCU teams had operated weeks prior. As the agents narrowed down their list, one particular team had initially drawn more scrutiny—TS-13. However, after a deeper dive into each team member's background, including family connections, finances, social media, phone records, computer records, and even interviews with their direct supervisors, it wasn't so much the team they were concentrating on but a specific person. Sergeant Anthony Hollis had plenty of motives, starting with his mom's massive debt in medical bills. The government wasn't out to judge or make assumptions based on an individual's finances. However, it seemed very suspicious that an unemployed woman, on the verge of losing her house, suddenly gained access to a little over six hundred thousand dollars to pay off the mortgage, credit cards, loans, and all her medical bills she had racked up, undergoing treatments for her cancer.

Tracing the money should have been easy, but in Hollis' case, it was difficult. When they looked into his finances, as well as his mom's, all it showed were cash deposits. Accountant Forensics couldn't trace where the cash came from, forcing the belief that Hollis could have been paid using cryptocurrency.

The money situation wasn't the only factor for pushing Hollis front and center of the investigation. His access and movements while abroad during deployments contributed to the decision.

Through interviews with Colonel Jenkins, who headed up the SCU, several of Hollis' team members weren't happy with his job performance. He'd disappear during critical times when he should have been tending to his duties as crew chief.

Two of his disappearances occurred while he was in Switzerland and South Africa—exactly where two microchips were located. Could it be a coincidence? It was possible. But Evans' always trusted his gut, and his gut was telling him that Hollis was the key to breaking the case wide open.

If Hollis was involved, then there was no way he was acting alone. Hollis didn't possess the proper clearance to access the information found on the microchips. And second, it took someone with a lot of smarts to organize a scheme as such, and Hollis was one of those brilliant people who lacked common sense. There was no way he could have masterminded a scheme on this level.

The burning question now was, who was the person behind the curtain making the deals and giving the orders? If the person or persons weren't identified soon, it could spell disaster for the United States and other countries.

"Who knows about this one?" Evans asked Eddie, referring to the newest chip found.

"Besides you and I, only the team who it was turned over to."

"Can they be trusted to keep this quiet?"

Eddie nodded. "Yes, sir. If they weren't loyal agents, they never would've brought it to my attention. I've already explained the severity and confidentiality surrounding the situation."

"Alright. I trust your judgment. And you haven't steered us wrong yet." Evans stated with a wry grin.

"Rick, this frustrates me just as I know it does you, because we both like to think that the people working for this country are loyal to its citizens."

"What are you trying to say, Eddie?"

"You know me well, and how I hate to throw out accusations, but I think it may be time to start looking into certain individuals within your administration."

Evans met Eddie's gaze. It was ironic that he'd been thinking the same thing just a minute ago.

"It's unfortunate. However, I think you may be right. But the questions are who, why, and how?"

Eddie ran his hand through his short brown hair. "Now that we've ruled out the majority of the SCU and now have our focus on Hollis, I say we start with the obvious—those with access to the information. I'll pull out the list you gave me a few weeks ago and start going down the list."

Evans took a deep breath, exhaling in frustration. He hated to think someone within his inner circle was involved, but he understood the need for a thorough investigation. Nobody could be given a free pass, not even his most trusted confidants.

"Alright."

"You've spoken to Colonel Jenkins, correct?" Eddie asked.

"I did. Once you confirmed that Jenkins was in the clear, I spoke with him and told him that all SCU members had been cleared except Hollis. He assured me that we have the full cooperation of the SCU." Evans then asked, "Have you heard from the team in Djibouti?"

"I did while I was on my way here. The team said Hollis did leave the base, but he only stopped at a café to get a bite to eat. After he ate, he left through the back exit. By the time the team was able to leave without being obvious, Hollis was already gone."

"He didn't meet anyone at the café?"

"Nope. He sat by himself and ordered a coffee with a small plate of food. As soon as he was done eating, he left."

"Hmmm…" Evans was thinking. There had to be something they were missing. "Do you think Hollis suspects that we're on to him?"

"It's possible. Scooter, the agent overseeing the surveillance, said Hollis did appear a little skittish. He was constantly looking around."

"Still nothing on his phone or email?"

"They're clean. If he's involved, he's using untraceable accounts."

Evans pounded his fist against the table. "I'd love to know the coward who's orchestrating this."

"As would I."

"Well, at least we have a plan. How soon can your team start filtering through the list of individuals?"

"Tonight. I'll call in a few of my top agents and get them started."

"Alright. In the meantime, I'm going to update Vice President Torres since he offered to assist. Keep me posted if you run across anything else."

"Yes, sir."

Eddie grabbed his bag and turned to leave when Evans called after him.

"Hey, Eddie?"

"Sir?"

"Thank you."

"No need. It's what we do. And believe me when I say this. Those responsible will be caught, and they'll pay for their actions."

"I have no doubt. I'm reiterating what I've told you before. You have unlimited resources. If you run into a wall, let me know, and I'll have that wall taken down."

CHAPTER SEVEN

Two Weeks Later – San Diego, California

Clover took her time climbing the stairs to the second floor of the team's building. She wasn't in that much of a hurry to meet with Colonel Jenkins, especially not with the sour mood he'd been in over the last two weeks. However, in his defense, she understood why. The sudden disappearance of Sergeant Hollis in Djibouti had rocked the entire unit.

Sure, Hollis had a habit of vanishing when he was supposed to be working, but after he failed to show up for the flight home, everyone became suspicious that something was wrong.

After checking his CHU and determining that Hollis never slept in his bed the night before, the Military Police began investigating and searching the entire base, which was placed on lockdown. Finally, after several hours, it was discovered by security cameras that Hollis had left the base in the early evening, but it never showed him returning. That would also explain why he had been dressed in nicer clothes when she had run into him, which she disclosed to the MPs when she spoke with them.

Clover and the rest of the team had flown home the next day. The vibe on the plane had been unsettling as everyone was concerned. Sure, Hollis could be an asshole and wasn't everyone's favorite person, but that didn't mean they weren't worried about his well-being.

Everyone was being tight-lipped about the circumstances of the disappearance. A few days after she returned to San Diego, Colonel Jenkins had held a meeting with the entire unit to address the situation. He hadn't shared much more than what everyone already knew—that Hollis was indeed missing and that the FBI was now involved. The vagueness in the details only left more questions. Did they think he left on his own will, like he went AWOL, or did they suspect foul play? There was so much that the imagination could spin up. Clover had a feeling there was a lot more to the story than what they were being told.

By the time the team returned to the base, Hollis' equipment and computers had been removed from the hangar, his locker, and his office. Every day, it was a revolving door of law enforcement inside their building, although it seemed to be the same team of men and women coming and going. On a few occasions, she had spotted the FBI Director entering the building. If he was personally overseeing the investigation, then things had to be dire.

When Jenkins had spoken with the team, he mentioned there was a possibility that the FBI would want to interview certain individuals, and he asked that everyone cooperate. She had yet to be interviewed by anyone but knew it was just a matter of time before they came knocking on her door. After all, she and Major Saunders were the two people who spent the most time around Hollis. Who knew? Maybe today was that day, since Jenkins asked to meet with her.

She prayed that Hollis' disappearance wasn't a case of foul play. She would never wish that on anyone. However, if he went AWOL, that was a different story, and he needed to be held responsible for his actions.

It made her wonder if Hollis knew the team was getting fed up with his lackadaisical attitude, and he bolted. It was upsetting that the situation had evolved this far, but his latest stunt in Djibouti left her no choice but to report him. It wasn't fair to the rest of the team.

The other day, she overheard a couple of guys from another team talking about how they heard that Hollis had been planning to leave the Corps once his enlistment period expired in the coming months. Hearing that made her rethink the AWOL scenario. If it were true, why would he throw away his entire career when an honorable discharge was just months away? Unfortunately, those were questions that only Hollis himself could answer.

Since life in the SCU had to go on, even with an investigation looming, Colonel Jenkins had notified Clover and Major Saunders that they would be assigned a new crew chief sometime within the next week or two. Clover hoped it was Darnold. Darnold was a crew chief who rotated between teams. Clover and the Major had heard many good things about the guy, so she was anxious for the decision to be announced.

As she made it to the last step, two of her colleagues—pilots themselves—came out of the Colonel's office.

"Hey," she greeted them, and they both offered her a warm smile.

"Are you meeting with the CO?" Rust, the crazy ginger, asked, and she nodded. Rust had the reddest natural hair she'd ever seen.

"I am. How's his mood?" Jenkins was a hard man to read most of the time, and he wasn't one to just sit around and chit-chat. He was a straight to the point kind of guy, and he expected his direct reports to follow his lead, at least when engaged in a conversation with him.

The other pilot, Quinn, answered. "We weren't in there long, just enough for him to answer a question we had about the upcoming training up in Washington next month. But he did seem a little preoccupied. In my opinion, if you don't have anything pressing to talk to him about, I'd consider rescheduling."

"Oh, I didn't ask for the meeting. I was summoned."

They both scrunched their face up, making a painful gesture.

"That sucks," Quinn said, and she couldn't disagree. She liked keeping her head down and staying out of the drama.

"Well, we won't keep you since he's probably waiting for you," Rust commented.

She thanked them for the heads up, and in return, they wished her good luck. She walked down to the end of the hall until she got to the closed door. She felt like she was heading into her old high school principal's office instead of her boss'. There was no reason for her to be nervous.

She raised her hand to knock on the dark wooden door, and she could feel how sweaty her hands were, making her realize just how nervous she was.

"Get a grip," she whispered to herself, before wrapping her knuckles against the door.

She didn't have to wait long before the colonel's gravelly voice shook the door. "Come in."

Clover took a deep breath. *His bark is bigger than his bite. Remember that.* She tried convincing herself.

She pushed open the door and saw Jenkins standing behind his desk, reading over a paper.

"Have a seat Captain Walker," he ordered without even looking up.

She shut the door behind her before walking in and taking a seat in one of the two ugly olive-green plastic chairs that the Colonel kept in front of his desk for visitors. She shifted in the seat to get her butt comfortable on the hard, unforgiving plastic. She swore he picked those chairs with a purpose in mind—so people wouldn't stay long.

Clover used the few seconds of awkward silence to look around the surprisingly nicely decorated office. Those who knew Jenkins would expect his office décor to be nil to none, maybe dark like a cave. But instead of doom and gloom, it was full of pictures from his flying days and numerous awards and accolades. In contrast, it was bright and cheery—well, except for the older, five-foot-ten, stocky man standing behind the desk with a frown on his face. But then again, Jenkins always had a frown.

Colonel Jenkins let the paper fall to the desk before he leveled a scrutinizing look her way, making her swallow hard. *Damn, was he intimidating!*

"How's it going, Captain?" He asked, taking a seat in his old squeaky chair. She swore he had to have found that chair in an old storage closet from the days of World War II. It actually made her smile because it fit him.

"I guess, as good as it can be, Sir, considering the circumstances."

At first, he didn't say anything. He just stared at her with his curious, hawk-like eyes. He then leaned forward, and placed his elbows on the desk, before folding his hands together and resting his steepled pointer fingers against his lips.

"Clover, our discussion from this moment on doesn't leave this room. Is that understood?"

She sat up straighter when she heard the seriousness in his tone.

"Yes, sir."

"I had hoped to speak with you and Major Saunders sooner; however, with everything surrounding Hollis' case, I just haven't had the time. So, I apologize," he told her, running a hand over his thinning grey hair.

It wasn't often that the Colonel showed his cards, but Clover could clearly see the frustration consuming him.

"There's no reason to apologize, Sir. Hollis' disappearance has affected us all in some way, shape, or fashion. I can only begin to imagine the position you're in."

"You have no idea. Anyway, I spoke with Major Saunders yesterday."

That surprised her. The Major hadn't mentioned it.

"You did?"

"I did. He told me about what happened in Djibouti after the last mission."

Clover raised her eyebrows as it dawned on her. Major Saunders must have told Jenkins about what went down between her and Hollis. *Crap!*

"Sir, if this is about the little scuffle between Hollis and me—"

"Scuffle?" Jenkins interrupted, and he squinted his eyes.

Oh shit! She bit down on her lip. "Apparently, that wasn't it."

Jenkins leaned back in his chair, crossing his arms in front of his chest and holding her gaze.

"No. But I'd like to hear more about this *scuffle*."

"It really wasn't an actual scuffle per se. I sort of nailed him with a CHU door—accidentally, that is, and he lost his cool."

Jenkins cringed as if he knew firsthand what that must have felt like.

"So, the two of you didn't get into a physical fight?"

"Him and I?" She shook her head. "No."

His eyes narrowed further, rich in scrutiny. Shit, there was no way she was telling him about her brother.

"Let's just say others were around who helped settle the situation with no further injuries."

"I see," he told her, but it was apparent that she hadn't sold him on her version. She hoped that incident wouldn't bring the FBI snooping around her. He reached for a stack of folders sitting on his desk, pulled one of them out, and flipped it open. He looked over the page sitting on top before turning his attention back to her. "I see here in the notes where you told the MPs you saw Hollis before he left the base."

She nodded. "Yes, Sir. That was the same time I hit him with the door."

"And you never saw him after that?"

"No, Sir. I spent the rest of the day getting everything packed up, and then later that evening, I attended the concert over at the hangar."

"How did Hollis seem when you saw him?"

"Besides being pissed off? Maybe anxious or eager to move on. His clothes made me think that he was heading to a meeting or something. When I asked him where he was off to, he hesitated to answer."

"Did he say where he was going?"

"No."

"In the last six or so months, besides his lack of dependability and teamwork, have you noticed any other changes in him?"

"That was around the timeframe he started to become withdrawn from the team, and even short-tempered. My first thought was that it was caused by his mom's cancer diagnosis and the toll it was taking on him. But any time one of the other team members or I would try to talk to him, he'd snap at us. After a while, we stopped trying and just dealt with his piss poor attitude."

Something passed in the Colonel's eyes, and she wondered what it was. He tapped his finger against his lips, appearing as if he was torn on whether or not to say something.

"Were you aware that Hollis' mom passed away two months ago?"

Clover couldn't conceal her shock.

"No. I had no idea. He never said anything." She then thought back to when Hollis had taken a week of leave around that time.

"Apparently, he didn't tell anyone. We found out when the FBI tried to get in touch with her."

*Hmmm...*Clover thought. Why had the FBI tried to notify Hollis's mom and not Casualty Assistance? It created even more questions she needed answers to.

"Sir, if you don't mind me asking, why wasn't Casualty Assistance tasked with notifying his next of kin?"

Jenkins stared at her. His bushy eyebrows were drawn inward. When he didn't say anything, she thought maybe she had stepped over the line and should have just kept her mouth shut. But then, seconds later, she saw Jenkins's lips twitch upward.

"Nothing gets past you, does it?"

She felt her cheeks get warm from embarrassment.

Jenkins chuckled. "Lucky, I didn't mean that in a bad way. You're a very observant person, and that's a good thing." He then exhaled. "As for your question, let's just say that there are many moving pieces with Hollis' situation."

"Yes, Sir."

"If you can think of anything else, please let me know. That's all I had. Thank you, Captain. You're dismissed."

Clover stood up. "Thank you, sir."

She turned to leave when Jenkins called after her.

"Captain Walker, one more thing."

She spun on heel, turning back to face him.

"Yes, sir?"

A small smile graced his lips. "Enjoy the long weekend with your family. You've certainly earned it."

She smiled back. "Thank you, sir. I'm looking forward to it."

As Clover was leaving Jenkins' office, she felt her cell phone vibrate and pulled it from her pocket. She saw it was Bear. He responded to the text she had sent him last week, asking him for Joker's phone number.

In the blink of an eye, thoughts of Joker flooded her mind like a raging river. She'd be lying if she said she wasn't eager to see him.

She had spent the last few nights in the company of a big glass of wine, having some serious discussions with herself. His show of affection in Djibouti had left her in a confused state. She couldn't stop thinking about him. Her heart won out even as she tried to convince herself that she should just cut her losses and move on. So, last week, she mustered up enough courage to text her brother and ask for Joker's number. She expected to get a response from him with a million questions about why she needed it. But instead, she got nothing—until now, that is. That led her to believe that he was busy with his team. She had spoken with her mom the other day, and she even said she hadn't been able to get a hold of him. It made Clover wonder if he and Joker were even going to make it to the celebration this weekend.

She held her breath as she read through his text, waiting for the big rejection. However, to her surprise, it never came. She felt the giddiness spread within her as she saw the ten digits on the screen.

With a little more pep in her step, she descended the stairs, then took a right toward the women's locker room to start packing up. She only had one hour to go before she was officially on leave. A weekend in the Tennessee mountains surrounded by her family sounded wonderful, and exactly what she needed.

She pushed the door to the locker room open, and went straight to her locker. She had several things she needed to take home. Reaching into her locker, she pulled out the white mesh laundry bag containing her dirty uniforms. She'd drop those off at the cleaners on her way home.

That way, she wouldn't have to worry about them until she got back from her parents.

She took a seat on the wooden bench in front of the locker and pulled her phone out, immediately clicking on her brother's text. She looked at her watch. It would be close to ten in Virginia Beach with the time difference. Her finger hovered above the number. She shook her head and decided to send him a text. With their crazy schedules, she never knew if they were working or not.

Her fingers moved over the screen.

Clover: *Hey you. Do you have some time to talk tonight?*

She hit send and nervously waited. She waited another minute or two, staring at the phone. When it was apparent that he wasn't going to answer, she pulled her backpack open to throw the phone inside. But then she heard the ping. As she opened the message, her heart beat faster.

Joker: *Who's this?*

Seriously? He was going to play that game? She thought to herself.

Clover: *Clover*

Joker: *I thought you didn't have my number*

She scrunched her nose up. That wasn't the response nor the greeting she had been expecting.

Clover: *I didn't. Bear gave it to me.*

Joker: *When?*

Clover: *When what?*

Joker: *When did he give you my number?*

Clover: *Does it matter?*

Joker: *Yes.*

What the hell was his problem? Either he wanted to talk to her, or he didn't. When she didn't respond right away, he sent another text.

Joker: *Clover?*

Clover: *Yes?*

Joker: *So?*

Clover: *So, what?*

Joker: *When did Bear give you my number?*

Were they really doing this?

Clover: *About 15 minutes ago.*

Joker: *I'm on my way to Bayside. Now that I have your number, can I give you a call later?*

She read his response and scrunched her eyebrows together. What did he mean by *now that I have your number*? God, he could be so frustrating!

She'd never been to Bayside, but she'd heard stories about it. It was a local bar and restaurant right on the beach where her brother and his team liked to hang out. Apparently, it was a haven for military personnel in that area. Not many tourists knew about it. From Bear's description, it sounded like a pretty cool place, but another thought came to her. Who was Joker meeting there this late at night?

Clover: *That works.*

Joker: *Later*

Clover: *Bye*

She slid her phone into her backpack and began to gather all her things to take out to her car when there was a knock on the door, which was followed by the voice of Major Saunders.

"Hey, Lucky. You in there?"

"Yep. Come on in."

"Are you sure?"

She rolled her eyes. What was it with these guys? Even though she told them it was okay to come in, they still never wanted to. Because she was the only female on the team, she was the only person who used the small room. It wasn't like they were going to see something they shouldn't.

"Positive," she called back.

The door pushed open, and he poked his head in.

"Hey."

"Hey, yourself. What's up?" She asked with her back to him, bending over to pick up all her bags.

"Uhm, you might want to put that stuff back in your locker sans the flight suit. Then grab the rest of your gear."

She spun around quicker than she meant to and almost fell over. She eyed the papers in the Major's hand.

"Please tell me those aren't what I think they are," she said, pointing at the papers.

"I could. But then I'd be lying."

She stomped her foot like a toddler when they didn't get their way.

"Brent! No!"

He chuckled. "Sorry, kiddo. This order comes from the top."

She crossed her arms in front of her chest. "All our orders come from the top," she reminded him.

He laughed again. She reached for the papers and read through them. "Humanitarian?"

"I know. I thought the same thing. But Cooper said we're the only available team. Everyone else is gone."

"Ugh! I was so close."

"Oh, come on. It'll be a relaxing flight. Two hours over and two hours back. You'll be back and in your own bed before you know it."

"Fine!" She tried to give him her best-annoyed smirk, but it only made him laugh. "When do we leave?"

"The ground crew just started loading the crates now. So, probably in about an hour."

"Alright. I'll meet you out there."

Once the Major left, she turned back toward her locker and grabbed her flight suit and gear before stuffing everything else back into her locker. As she was doing that, she remembered Joker. *Shoot!* It would be between 0300-0400, his time on the East Coast when she got back. She grabbed her phone and sent him another text.

Clover: *Something came up at work. It may be pretty late by the time I'm able to talk. Please don't think I'm ignoring you if I don't answer.*

Joker: *No worries. Call when you can. I've waited two years. I think I can wait a few more hours. Be safe.*

She cracked a smile, then closed her eyes and took a deep breath, reminding herself that no matter what, tomorrow morning at 0730, she'd be on a plane headed to Tennessee. That was what she had to look forward to.

&

Joker sat in his vehicle, grinning like a fool. He had just pulled into Bayside's parking lot a few minutes ago when he got Clover's text. To say he was surprised was an understatement. When Clover walked away from him in Djibouti, he thought the next time he'd talk to her was when he got to Tennessee, and even then, he wasn't sure what kind of reception to expect from her.

He shoved his phone in his pocket and got out. He hadn't planned on going out, but Jay Bird and Nails invited him to have a drink, and since they had just arrived back in the states earlier in the day, and he thought, *what the heck, a drink sounded pretty good.* Plus, he was starving and was looking forward to sinking his teeth into Bayside's famous seasoned prime rib. Paul, the owner, made the best prime rib around. His mouth watered just thinking about it.

Bayside was a cool hangout. What made it special, though, was the atmosphere within it. From the outside, the place looked like a dump. But that was the way Paul, the owner, had designed it. Being a former Special Forces operative himself, Paul wanted a place off the beaten path. Knowing how Special Forces soldiers could gain the public's attention, he wanted to create an environment where they could relax and have a good time without being hounded. It was the kind of place where everyone knew everybody, and all drama was left at the door.

As soon as Joker walked inside, he spotted Jay Bird and Nails sitting at the bar. Nails turned just as he approached and raised his beer bottle in greeting.

"You look like you're in a better mood. The way you were snapping at people earlier today, I thought you'd be home taking some Midol and resting."

Joker felt bad for being a prick earlier, but it wasn't because of work or the guys. It was knowing that he had to leave tomorrow morning Bear's parents' anniversary party, which meant that tomorrow, he'd see Clover.

He was a little hurt and upset because he thought she might have called after the kiss he left her with in Djibouti. But instead, he got nothing. He didn't try to reach out either because he had told her that he'd give her two weeks to think about them. But after receiving the text from her wanting to talk, he wondered if she'd made her decision. Damn! Now the anticipation was going to drive him crazy. Maybe he should have just called her.

"Funny. Sorry about that," he shot back at Nails as he walked past him and took the seat next to Jay Bird.

"No skin off our backs. We all have days where we want to bite someone's head off."

Arianna, the bartender, approached and smiled. She was married to his buddy Dino from Alpha team. Arianna was also Paul's daughter.

"Hey, Joker," she greeted, placing a coaster down in front of him.

He glanced around. "No Dino tonight?" He asked, knowing that Dino usually hung out at the bar when Arianna worked nights so she wouldn't be alone while walking out in the dark. He couldn't blame him, considering Arianna's situation that almost got her and her dad killed last year.

She gave him a bright smile. "Nope. He's home with Nigel tonight. Poor guy got clipped today," she told him, making a scissors gesture with her fingers. Nigel was her beast of a dog. He was a mix—Great Dane and Lab.

Joker winced, and Arianna giggled. "Nails and Jay Bird each had the same reaction when they asked."

She pointed to the cooler behind her. "Beer?" He debated, but shook his head. With his current state of mind, if he drank one, that would lead to another and possibly more. He didn't want to show up at Bear's parents' house with a hangover. Plus, he wanted to be sober when Clover called him later.

"Give me a club soda with lime, please."

Arianna's eyebrows shot upward in shock, and Jay Bird nearly choked on the sip of beer he had just taken.

"You alright there, man?" Joker asked, trying to hide his amusement.

Wiping his mouth with a napkin that Arianna handed him, Jay Bird, with his eyebrows furrowed and a look of total dismay, asked, "Yeah, I'm good, but the question is, are you alright? Club soda?"

Joker nonchalantly lifted his right shoulder. "I figure I'd better behave since I have a flight in the morning."

"Oh, that's right. You're heading to Tennessee with Bear."

Arianna placed the club soda in front of him, and he thanked her.

"Yep. It'll be nice to get away for a few days."

"And to see Clover, right?"

Joker slowly turned his head in Jay Bird's direction with his drink in his hand. As far as he knew, nobody knew about him and Clover and what happened between them. So, he brushed off Jay Bird's comment.

"I assume she'll be there. At least that's what she said in Djibouti."

"She looked good." Jay Bird commented, and Joker suspected that Jay Bird was trying to get a reaction out of him deliberately.

He brought his drink to his lips and took a mouthful while thinking of a comeback statement. Not to appear guilty, he figured he'd state the obvious.

"She did. She seems to be handling herself just fine."

Jesus! Had that been difficult to say because he was still pissed off at how that guy, Andrews, had hit on her right in front of him. He took another drink to wash down the bad taste the words left in his mouth. Thankfully, Nails popped his head over and broke up the uncomfortable conversation.

"Hey. Did y'all see the two women Cruz and a few buddies from his team just walked in with?"

Joker turned to look and noticed the tall, short-haired blonde woman right away. She was a Coastie stationed just down the road. She was also the woman his teammate Playboy had been eyeing for a while. He thought her name was Gabby.

"I can't stand that asshole," Jay Bird bit out, referring to Cruz, and both Joker and Nails agreed. Cruz was one of those guys who boasted about his SEAL status to empower himself. Of course, many women ate it up.

Nails' grin turned feral, and Joker knew the hot-tempered SEAL would do something. Hopefully, it was nothing too over the top.

"Why don't we go save the two women before they get pulled into Cruz's web of destruction and lies."

Joker looked over his shoulder and saw that Gabby had already moved on from Cruz, but her friend was getting sucked in, and it appeared she was hanging on to his every word.

"I think Gabby can hold her own, but her friend looks like she needs rescuing," Joker said.

"Well, if you think she's cute, why don't you go rescue her?" Nails fired back, but Joker shook his head. He had no interest.

"Not tonight."

"Nope. Joker has a big trip ahead of him tomorrow," Jay Bird stated calmly before taking a slug of his beer.

Nails took a drink of his beer before setting it down on the bar. "That's right, you and Bear head out tomorrow."

Joker nodded, but he was still fixed on Jay Bird, and how it appeared that he was speaking in code. It was starting to drive him crazy.

"Well, I'm going to go stir up trouble, and if I play my cards right, I'll have a little reward to take home with me tonight."

Joker wanted to roll his eyes at Nails. He was always causing some sort of ruckus, whether intentionally or not. He was also the guy on the team who had no trouble taking a woman home for the night. In fact, in the many years he'd known Nails, he'd never seen a steady girlfriend on his arm. And that was okay because that was his cup of tea. A lot of guys in Special Forces didn't have a significant other. Joker, however, wasn't like a lot of guys. He wanted a woman to love and grow old with. And if he had any say, that woman would be Clover Walker.

He saw Arianna pass by and asked her if he could still order food.

She grinned. "Anything for you guys. What did you want?"

He opened his mouth to give her his order, but she held up her hand.

"Wait, let me guess. Prime rib, mashed potatoes, and green beans. Did I get it right?"

He gave her a crooked smile. "Are we that predictable?"

Tilting her head sideways, she replied, "Predictable? No. But you're all consistent. I'd say nine times out of ten when you guys come back from wherever, you order the prime rib." She turned her eyes on Jay Bird, and he actually grinned—barely, but it was a grin.

Jay Bird lifted his shoulder. "She's got a point."

"See!" She winked. "Give me ten minutes, and I'll have it out to ya."

Joker picked up his glass and took another drink. He and Jay Bird sat there for a bit, watching the baseball game on the TV above the bar.

"So, what exactly is going on between you and Clover?" Jay Bird blurted out, and Joker swung his head around to meet his gaze.

"I don't understand."

"Come on, man. The tension between you two in Djibouti was so thick you could have cut it with a knife. Plus, you couldn't take your eyes off her."

Joker didn't know what to say. But then he didn't have to because Jay Bird's eyes widened. "Oh, shit. You like her."

Fuck, fuck, fuck! He couldn't lie. He exhaled.

"It's worse," he admitted.

Jay Bird leaned in closer and spoke in a low tone. "Did you sleep with her?" Joker continued to stare, neither confirming nor denying. Nonetheless, Jay Bird knew. "Are you fucking crazy?"

Joker turned back toward the TV. "Apparently, I am."

"Who else knows?"

"Nobody. At least I don't think there's anyone else."

Joker explained how it all transpired in minimal detail—all the way to when he woke up the following day alone in her bed.

"Wait. She left you, and you didn't even notice? Hot damn! It must have been an exhausting night."

Joker didn't respond verbally, though Jay Bird found it amusing because he chuckled before taking a drink, then shook his head.

"Dude. I don't know what to tell you. You both haven't spoken in two years?"

"No, and it wasn't like I could ask Bear for her number without getting interrogated by him."

Joker ran his hand through his hair as Jay Bird watched him.

"You really like her, don't you?" Joker could hear the seriousness in Jay Bird's question.

He nodded. "I don't just like her—I care about her. I know it sounds crazy, but she and I just connected. She's someone I can see myself settling down with."

"But what about those other women I've seen you with since your little rendezvous with Clover?"

"Nothing," he stated firmly. "I may have kissed them or fooled around a bit, but I never had sex with them. I couldn't. No matter what I did to try and get her out of my mind, I couldn't and can't."

Jay Bird nodded in understanding. "Damn. Well, I hope like hell things work out for you both." He started to laugh. "Now I'm wishing I would've told Bear I could go with y'all."

Joker shook his head, picking up his drink. It was going to be a trip of a lifetime.

CHAPTER EIGHT

"You're positive everything is set for this evening?" Vice President Torres asked Rose as he worriedly paced the pool deck outside his Washington, D.C. home.

Under normal circumstances, he wasn't one to panic. However, after attending an earlier meeting at the White House with the President, he was beginning to feel the squeeze on his operation that had gone under the radar. At least he thought it had gone undetected, but it seemed that somewhere in the last few months, some slip-ups resulted in several microchips being recovered and handed over to the FBI.

Because of the sensitive information on the microchips, it was a no-brainer that someone from inside the government was responsible. How else would lists of weapons and other military equipment that the U.S. had in its inventory make their way onto a microchip, uploaded to a host site on the dark web, and sold to the highest bidder?

With the FBI launching a full investigation, which extended to high-ranking government officials, it was time to close shop, which Torres was fine with. He had accomplished what he had set out to do. In just over a year, he had amassed over fifteen million dollars from arms trafficking, guaranteeing him an early retirement. All he had to do was serve out the last two years of his term, and then he'd be free.

However, with the FBI closing in, Torres felt it was time to sever *all* ties with those who'd partook in his operation.

"Yes. Everything is ready. Blanyard has three men ready to move the weapons when they arrive."

Blanyard was a rogue operative. Eight years ago, he parted ways with the CIA after the agency tried to frame him for a hit job that he had nothing to do with. Rose was another operative who separated herself from the agency for similar reasons. Both Blanyard and Rose were freelancers and worked for the highest payer. Torres first met Blanyard through the CIA Director, Clayton Perkins. Then Blanyard had introduced Rose to Torres.

The four of them were the leading players to ensuring that the deals went down. Then there was Sergeant Hollis, a member of the President's elite helicopter unit. Hollis was easy to manipulate. His mom's illness played right into their hands. However, there was that saying, *"all good things must come to an end."* After the FBI discovered the microchips, Hollis became a liability and a top suspect in the FBI's investigation. Perkins was tasked with taking care of Hollis and seeing to it that he was eliminated.

"What about Perkins? Has he arrived yet?" Torres asked.

Perkins played an integral role, as he could intercept and destroy any Intel that should pass through intelligence channels, which could jeopardize the operation. However, with the FBI's investigation gaining steam, it seemed that Perkins hadn't been on top of his game.

"He called about twenty minutes ago and said he was about forty minutes away."

"Very good. Make sure you and Blanyard stick to the plan we discussed. No screw-ups."

"Yes, Sir."

Tonight's shipment would be the last arms deal before Torres shut down the operation. Once the drop was complete, he'd rake in a little over three million dollars.

Having another source inside the White House who could alter documents was a huge benefit.

"It should be seamless. I received notification that the shipment arrived in San Diego and was transported to the base. It shouldn't take Blanyard's guys long to transfer the weapons from the helicopter to the plane. After that is complete, you know what needs to happen."

"Yes, Sir. Trust me. Everything will go as planned."

"It better. A lot is riding on this deal. Call me when the swap is complete, and the items are en route to Miami."

Torres disconnected the call and set his phone on the table. He sat back in the patio chair, propping his feet on the matching floral ottoman. He looked out beyond the sprawling pool deck to his home's vast acreage. Even late at night, the property glowed from the many outdoor light fixtures scattered throughout.

He closed his eyes as he listened to the sounds created by the cicadas and crickets that called home in the foliage around the land. Most people couldn't stand the overwhelming relentless whining sound of the cicadas or the shrill chirp of the crickets. But for Torres, the sounds played like a song, and before long, he was smiling as he got lost in the tranquil melody.

His life couldn't be any more perfect.

CHAPTER NINE

Clover pulled herself up into the helicopter and began performing her preflight checks. She grabbed the logbook and signed it, taking control of the aircraft.

Major Saunders joined her a few minutes later and commenced his preflight routine, checking the weather and filing their flight plan.

"Have you heard anything new on the Hollis situation?" The Major asked.

She shook her head. "No, although when I met with Jenkins earlier. He asked me about something, and I thought he was referring to the incident with Hollis in Djibouti. I thought you had told him."

"Oh, shit. No. I told you I'd stay out of it."

She was surprised he'd kept quiet because while they were on the plane traveling home, she had told him what went down, and he'd been pissed. He wanted to tell Jenkins, but she asked him not to.

"Did you tell Jenkins what happened?"

"Not everything. I told him that Hollis and I had a slight scuffle, but we settled it."

Saunders looked at her with one of his eyebrows raised. "And he was good with that?"

She shrugged her shoulder. "Yeah. He seemed to be."

"Hmmm."

"Why?"

"I don't know. The last month or two, Jenkins has seemed preoccupied with something."

"You think?" Clover wondered if it had anything to do with the questioning she got from Jenkins regarding Hollis.

"I don't know. Maybe it's just me."

"He has a stressful job. Then add on Hollis' disappearance. How did he seem when you and he met yesterday?"

"His usual—straight to the point. How about you?" Saunders asked.

"Same," she replied. She wasn't comfortable with the conversation, since Jenkins asked her not to talk about anything they discussed. She excused herself and got out to do the inspection.

She walked around the helicopter, lifting every cover panel, looking for any fluid leaks, broken wires or hoses, structural cracks, or anything that could compromise their safety during flight.

She was still a little annoyed that she had to make the trip, but she knew how dire the situation was in Haiti, and how the country's citizens depended on the food and supplies; and if she could help in any way, she would.

Telling Major Saunders they were clear, she climbed back inside the cockpit and fired up the bird. She turned in her seat, glancing into the belly of the chopper. She eyed the three large wooden crates. It brought a smile to her face, knowing they were doing a good deed.

She put on her headset and buckled herself in. "How does the weather look?" She asked Saunders.

"There's a weather system down in Mexico pushing northward. Radar indicates that it's producing significant rainfall, wind, and dangerous lightning, especially in the low-lying areas of the desert. If we stay on schedule, we should arrive at the airstrip and have enough time to unload the cargo before the storm reaches the area."

"Can we depart before it arrives?"

"I think so. Let's get moving, Captain."

Clover smiled, trying to brighten up the mood. "Yes, sir."

Major Saunders radioed to control for clearance to take off.

"TS-13 to control. Requesting clearance to lift."

"Control to TS-13. Clearance granted. You're clear for lift off."

Upon hearing those words, Clover opened the throttle to increase the speed of the rotor, then slowly pulled up on the collective as she depressed the left foot pedal. As soon as the Black Hawk began to hover and the cyclic became sensitive, she took a firm grip on it, nudging the helicopter forward and upward.

Ignoring the bright, colorful city lights of San Diego below, Clover focused on climbing to the blanket of twinkling stars, lining the night sky.

"It's a beautiful night," Major Saunders said, and she couldn't agree more as she gazed out into the wide-open sky. She'd never get tired of the views from her vantage point in the air, especially on a night like this where she wasn't facing hostile actions, and she could just relax and take in the sights. It was mesmeric. Flying was something she would never get tired of or give up, even after her military career.

The longer they flew, the more her mind spoke to her. She spent a good chunk of the time reflecting on her and Joker, and what the upcoming weekend could mean for them. Could it lead to the second chance she'd been waiting for? If his actions in Djibouti were of any indication, she felt it could be promising. And that made her feel giddy inside. That kiss he left her with had brought back wonderful memories of that night in San Diego. It also had her craving more of his kisses. Soon she thought to herself.

"You're pretty quiet over there, Lucky," Major Saunders called over to her, and she grinned.

"Just enjoying this incredible view."

"I bet you are. What time does your flight leave tomorrow?"

"0730. I'll probably have enough time to make it home, shower, and pack before I need to leave for the airport."

"Sorry about that."

"It's not your fault." She snorted a light laugh. "It's not like I've never pulled an all-nighter before. At least it's a four-and-a-half-hour flight, so I can get some shut-eye then."

"Are you looking forward to it?"

She smiled even though the major couldn't see it. "I am." *For several reasons*, she thought to herself.

"Have you thought about whether or not you'll have that talk with your family?"

She scrunched her nose up, knowing what *talk* he was referring to. And she had indeed thought about it—a lot, weighing the pros and cons. Surprisingly, the pros won in a landslide.

"I have."

"And?" She could hear the eagerness in his tone. Ever since she joined the SCU and he had taken her under his wing, he'd been advocating for her to tell her family what her true profession was.

"I've decided that it's time. I took your words to heart, pondered over them for a few days, and concluded that you're right, and that my family deserves to know. Plus, I think telling them may reduce some of my stress." She chuckled. "I don't think I can go through another run-in with one of my brothers and have a repeat of Djibouti."

The Major laughed. "I'm sure your anxiety level was through the roof when your brother got a hold of you. Remember, no matter your family's reaction, I'm damn proud of you. But, if your family is anything like you say they are, I'm quite sure they'll understand why you chose not to tell them, and I'm confident they'll be proud of you too."

God, she hoped so.

They spent the next hour in silence except for the few instances they briefly communicated with the control towers.

They were about thirty minutes out, hugging the U.S. and Mexico border when they were contacted over the radio by Corporal Porter back at the base, informing them that forecasters updated the storm's path moving in. Now it was expected to move more northward, putting their drop location in its path.

Clover rechecked the radar. The green indicated that the storm's precipitation was moving faster, and was already closing in on Douglas.

The Major pointed at the radar indicator.

"That's a doozy of a storm. I'm not comfortable with all the lighting and the wind speeds. Let's change our course now, head north, and then back to the east. Once we get there, we may be grounded for a bit until it clears."

Clover glanced toward the south, saw lightning in the far distance, and agreed with the Major's decision. Lightning and strong winds weren't a good mix with helicopters. The drawback was how long they'd be grounded. She wouldn't be happy if she didn't make it back to San Diego in time for her flight.

"Are you familiar with this airstrip?" She asked the Major, trying to ignore her previous negative thought.

"There's actually quite a few of them out here. It's not uncommon for small businesses to utilize them. We use them for training exercises as well. We're heading to the one about midway between Route 80 and the New Mexico border. I've done pickups there before during training exercises."

Clover didn't even have to look at the radar to see they were entering the desert, as the darkness of the remote desert slowly swallowed the bright lights on the ground below. A few moments later, Major Saunders pointed out the lone lights on the ground just ahead as they started to descend.

"That's it," Saunders called to Clover.

"It's tiny."

"It is. But at least there's a building connected to the hangar where we can hang out."

She circled and guided the Black Hawk to an area adjacent to a small Cessna airplane. She assumed it belonged to the organization.

As Clover powered down the helicopter, four grungy-looking men emerged from the small building connected to the hangar that appeared big enough to house maybe one small airplane. She noticed the men caught the Major's eye as well.

"They look a little rough around the edges if you ask me," the Major admitted, and Clover agreed.

Clover unbuckled her belts and told the Major she was going to find the restroom before she started her walk-around inspection.

"You're armed, right?" He asked her, and she squinted her eyes at him.

He grinned. "Humor me."

She smiled and patted her right thigh. She had a spare strapped to her ankle that was concealed by her pant leg. Not many people knew she carried a backup. Her dad taught her that it never hurt to have a backup weapon.

He winked. "Good." He then nodded toward the four men standing near the helicopter with some equipment to offload the cargo. "I'll talk with these guys and get them started. Hopefully, they can get everything off before the storm arrives."

Clover nodded as she walked toward the hangar. The crunching of gravel beneath her booted feet echoed in the thick air. It was a quiet night, but what did she expect for a place smack dab in the middle of the desert. If she had to guess, the closest town with civilization was probably over a hundred miles away.

She saw the clouds moving in, cloaking the moon's light. The wind rustling through the desert's dry shrubbery and low thunder rumbling could be heard. She could tell the pressure in the air had dropped by the slight discomfort in her sinuses. There was no way they would get the crates offloaded before the storm hit, meaning she would just have to suck it up and hope it was a quick-moving system.

She took in the area's surroundings. The Major wasn't kidding when he told her the place was in the middle of nowhere. From what she could see in the dark and minimal lighting, one dirt road led in and out of the small compound. A small pavilion-type structure stood to the left of the building about thirty yards out. The more she looked at it, the more it reminded her of a hitching post to secure a horse. *Weird*, she thought. But maybe the landowners rode a horse instead of driving, though she did catch a glimpse of two vehicles. One was a smaller SUV, and the other was an old late model truck that looked like it had seen its last day on the road. Besides that, it was just the typical desert—full of dry brush, rocks, and dirt.

Just as she reached for the door's handle, a sudden chill raced down her spine, followed by a sensation that caused the hairs on her neck to stand up. Call it intuition or whatever, but it was a feeling her dad and brothers warned her never to ignore. She glanced over her shoulder and found one of the men, a large bald guy casting an evil glare her way. His dark, suspicious gaze put her on edge. His large stature was enough to intimidate her, but what caught her eye was the handgun he had slipped into the back of his dirt-covered jeans. The way he stood with his chest puffed out and arms folded across his chest led her to believe he was probably a supervisor of the other three men. His sketchy behavior had her sliding her hand down her outer thigh to the handle of the pistol she had holstered there. She waited a few moments to see what he'd do. When he broke eye contact with her and started talking to one of the other guys, she pushed the warning bells aside and stepped inside.

The heavy door slammed closed behind her, making her jump. Damn, she felt twitchy. She could also feel how tense her body was. She needed to relax. What would be even better was a soothing deep tissue massage. Maybe that was something she and her mom could do sometime over the weekend. She missed doing those sorts of things with her mom. She smiled, remembering how they used to get manicures and pedicures together.

Closing her eyes, she reached for the back of her neck, trying to rub away some of the tension. It didn't feel as good as a professional massage, but it helped. As she slowly blinked her eyes open, she saw the small sign indicating that the restrooms were to the right. As she walked the hallways, she realized the inside was actually a lot larger than she thought. Its size was deceiving from the outside. It also smelled like fresh paint.

Once she found the restroom, she didn't waste any time. She wasn't comfortable leaving Major Saunders by himself, nor was she comfortable being inside alone and unaware if others were lurking around. The place, in general, gave off a bad vibe.

After washing her hands, she splashed some water on her face hoping the coldness would give her a little jolt, though what she could really use was a cup of steaming black coffee. She tore off a sheet from the paper towel machine and dried her face and hands.

A loud thud resonated through the empty hallway as she pulled open the door. It sounded like someone had slammed a book down on a hard surface. It made her pause for a few seconds, but she chalked it up to her imagination when she didn't hear anything else. As she started down the long, dimly lit hallway leading back to the hangar, the sound of a man's deep, stern voice caught her attention and made her stop. She definitely hadn't imagined that. It was crystal clear, and the sound came from the opposite end of the hall. She told herself it wasn't any of her business, but as she placed her hand on the door's push bar, she heard another voice and swore she heard him mention Sergeant Hollis' name. Of course, that captured her interest, and she pressed forward toward the only room with a light on. The voices grew louder as she approached. The door sat ajar, just enough to where she could see two men standing a few feet from one another.

The man facing more toward the door, dressed in tan tactical pants and a black polo shirt that stretched across his broad chest and shoulders, appeared angry as he stood with his feet, shoulders width apart, and his arms folded across his chest. His dark crew-cut hair was sprinkled with grey. He looked badass, like someone she certainly never wanted to cross.

"Look, I don't know what the hell happened. This is the first time I'm even hearing about this," the guy with his back to her dressed more conservatively in dark dress pants and a white button-up dress shirt.

"Well, the Skipper isn't happy, and he's ready to pull the plug on the entire operation."

"What? He can't do that."

The badass guy snorted a sarcastic laugh. "Are you forgetting that he's the one who calls the shots? He can do whatever the hell he wants to."

"Look. I don't know how the microchips ended up in the wrong hands before they were turned over to the FBI, but I already told the Skipper I'd handle it, and I did. Hollis isn't a problem for us anymore. I made sure of that."

"What did you do?"

"I made sure Hollis was eliminated."

"You did that?"

"He was being closely monitored, and the Skipper felt he could become a problem for us. He had already become a weak link. The Skipper also found out that he was planning to bolt, and he didn't want to take any chances. So, I stepped in and began the clean-up process."

Clover's eyes widened in shock. At the same time, she felt as if someone had sucked all the air from her body.

Hollis was dead?

Suddenly, the nicely dressed man turned more toward the right, revealing his face, and Clover had to do a double-take. She couldn't believe it. The man who just admitted to murdering Sergeant Hollis was Clayton Perkins, the CIA Director.

The badass guy glanced to his right and smirked, making Clover think a third person was in the room. But that was beside the point. She drew in her brows as she began to think. What in the hell had Hollis been involved in?

Clover's gut warned her to get out of there, but her curiosity got the better of her. What had Hollis been involved in with the CIA Director?

"Look, the Skipper said that I could pick up the money that I'm owed for tonight's drop."

The badass guy pointed to a black duffel bag sitting on a chair. "It's there. But it's only half."

"Half? Why only half?"

The guy shrugged his shoulders as if he didn't have any care in the world. "Once the drop is complete tomorrow, the Skipper will ensure you get the other half."

"That's not what I was promised, and I'm not leaving here without the full amount."

"Well, Director, I hate to break it to you, but that's not gonna happen. What's in that bag over there is all you're getting. End of story."

"Well, maybe I'll go outside and take back half of what's in those crates," Perkins fired back, and the badass guy took a giant, threatening step forward and was now nearly nose-to-nose with Perkins. The guy oozed confidence and strength. She wasn't even inside the room with them, and she could feel the hostility. It was apparent from the man's heated expression that Perkins had pushed the guy too far.

"You've got a set of balls on you, Perkins. I'll give you credit for that. But I don't take too kindly to threats, and neither does the Skipper. So, here's the deal, you can take it or leave it. You made sure the weapons were delivered. Now I'm offering you two-hundred-fifty thousand dollars. As I said before, the other two-hundred-fifty thousand will be handed over as long as everything checks out tomorrow."

Whoa! Clover gave her head a slight shake. Had she heard that right? Weapons? She was rooted in place as she listened to the guy explain what had been hidden in the three crates *she* transported. Her eyes got bigger by the second as he ticked off an array of weapons—submachine guns, assault rifles, semi-automatic pistols, mortars, and grenade launchers. He continued to talk, but Clover had difficulty staying engaged because her mind was still stuck on the word weapons. Weapons that someone close to the President had arranged to be delivered on her helicopter.

Weapons! What in the hell was going on here? She couldn't wrap her head around what she was witnessing. Had she been placed in the middle of an arms trafficking deal?

Her instincts told her to get out and find Major Saunders, but she couldn't peel her eyes from the event unfolding in front of her. The head of the CIA, a member of the United States government who took an oath to defend their country, was involved in an illegal arms deal. How in the hell had this been able to happen?

Suddenly, a mountain of questions formed in her head. Was the President a part of it? His signature was on the orders. She saw it with her own eyes. Oh, God! And Jenkins too. Were they all playing some sick twisted game? It even made her wonder if the Major was involved as well. Clover suddenly felt like she was going to be sick.

"So, what's it going to be, Director?"

"It seems I don't have a choice."

"Actually, you do." The guy gave Perkins a mock sympathy expression before pulling a pistol from his waistband. Seeing the move as a threat, Perkins took a retreating step backward.

"Look, man. I'll do whatever. There's no need to escalate this."

"I think otherwise. You see, the boss wants to tie up loose ends."

"Loose ends?"

Perkins' eyes widened, and so did Clover's.

"I...I mean, I—" Perkins stammered, but the guy interrupted him.

"Save the excuses, Director. The Skipper feels like he can't trust you anymore."

"Trust me? I was the playmaker behind the scene. I'm the one with the contacts. I'm the one who made him millions of dollars. I kept the Feds off his ass. All he did was gain access to some information and download it onto microchips. I made sure that the President never found out."

"Yeah. The Skipper has his own infiltrator in Evans' inner circle feeding him information."

Clover's heart was pounding as she took all of it in.

Suddenly, a tall woman appeared next to the guy, confirming that someone else was in the room. She was tall, very muscular, and just like the guy, she carried herself as if she was former military or had extensive military training.

The woman made a sound with her mouth as if she was bored with the situation. She turned toward the Director with a gun and aimed at him.

"Let me make this easy for you, Director. Your contract has been terminated."

Perkins opened his mouth to speak when she pulled the trigger.

The sound of the gunshot was deafening, and Clover covered her mouth, stumbling backward as if she had been the one who was shot. She turned away, shielding her eyes as Perkins' body hit the floor with a thud. She leaned against the wall for support as her chest tightened to the point where she felt like she couldn't breathe.

Suddenly, an earsplitting crack of thunder sounded as if the gates of hell had just exploded, sending her racing heart into overdrive.

"Get Ramon on the line and find out the status of the transfer. I need to get moving as soon as this storm clears out."

"What do we do with him?" The woman asked.

"Leave him. There won't be any traces of him once this place goes up in flames."

A radio attached to the guy squawked just before another man's voice came over it.

"Boss. Everything's loaded. What else do you need us to do?"

"Did you take care of the two pilots?"

"The guy has been taken care of. We loaded him onto the helicopter and set the explosives."

"And the other pilot?"

"She disappeared inside the building a while ago. We thought you took care of her."

"We haven't seen her. She must be around here somewhere. Find her now!"

"Yes, sir."

Clover couldn't stop the tears from flooding her eyes. They killed Major Saunders, too. She was in shock and despair. These people had planned it all out. They were ruthless and would do whatever it took to achieve their goal, including eliminating any threats they deemed valid. She and the Major were on a suicide mission and never knew it. Now that the Major was dead, she was alone.

She needed a few minutes to focus and think, but she barely had seconds before she could become the next victim. She needed a place to hide and then find a way to get help. But where and how? She couldn't stay inside the building since the guy planned on burning it down. She thought about the helicopter. If she could make it to the helo, she only needed about two minutes to get it into the air. But hearing it was rigged with explosives, that idea was thrown out the window.

Clover heard the woman tell the man she was leaving and for him to call her once the drop was complete. The sound of footsteps approaching the door had Clover panicking. Pushing all the wild emotions she was experiencing to the side, she quickly pulled herself together and frantically looked around for a place to take cover until she could figure out what to do.

She saw three doors and tried them, but they were locked. Trying to be as light on her feet as she could to avoid being heard, she followed the hallway back toward the restroom and found a small breakroom. It held a small table with four chairs, with a few cabinets lining the back wall and a sink. Running out of time and options, she eyed the cabinets. It would be tight, but she'd make herself fit.

The door to the hangar slammed shut, followed by heavy footsteps of not just one person but multiple people. They were searching for her. Staying calm, she quickly opened the bottom cabinet to the left of the sink, pushed a few rolls of paper towels to the side, and squeezed her body in.

She drew her pistol, holding it ready if she needed to use it. She was determined she wasn't going down without a fight.

She could hear the men pacing up and down the hallway, the sound of opening and closing doors echoing as they combed the building looking for her.

The storm outside continued to lash out as the thunder rumbled and the torrential rainfall dinged furiously off the tin roof of the building.

She needed help. But even if she had backup, it was probably hours away, especially with the storm raging outside.

She rested her head on her knees and thought about what to do. Where was she going to go? She was in the middle of nowhere. Even if she did escape, she'd probably die somewhere out in the desert. Just when she was about to lose all hope, her eyes lit up—her phone. She could get a text out if there was a strong enough signal.

She slipped her hand into her pocket but cursed when she found it empty. She remembered putting it into her backpack after texting Joker and putting the backpack into her locker.

"Shit! Think, Clover." She mumbled to herself. But she didn't have to mull over it long because she remembered they had an emergency satellite phone. The only problem was that the phone was on the helicopter. She had to find a way to get to that helicopter without being seen before they blew it up.

The men's footsteps grew louder. They were close, either inside the room or right outside it. She held her breath, praying they wouldn't look around.

"She ain't in here, you idiot," she heard one of the guys say. He had a strong Hispanic accent.

"The boss said to check everywhere."

"Well, I'm telling you she ain't in here. Come on, let's check outside. Ramon and Pascual checked the hangar. She ain't there either."

"When we leaving?"

"Boss said in twenty minutes. He needed to finish up some things in the office."

"When do the fireworks start?"

Clover assumed the guy was talking about the bombs they planned to detonate.

"In about forty-five minutes, but we'll be long gone before then."

Clover glanced at her watch and noted the time. At least now she had a timeline to make sure she was far enough away.

She heard one of them curse. "Damn! We just lost power."

"What? You scared the boogeyman will get you?" The guy teased.

They started to walk again, and she listened closely, determining which way they went. The heavy door slamming, followed by silence, made her believe they had gone back to the hangar. At least, she hoped that was the case.

With the main guy preoccupied in the office, now was her opportunity to start making her way back outside.

She pushed the cabinet door open just a smidge to peek out, making sure the coast was clear. They weren't lying. The power really had gone out. She could tell because there was an emergency light right outside the breakroom, and it was lit.

She used the sound of the rain tapping against the building to her advantage. Unfolding herself, she slipped out of the cabinet and got to her feet. She stepped up to the doorway with her pistol at the ready and executed a turkey peek. Seeing that the hallway was clear, she moved quickly to the left, following another hallway that wrapped around to the other side of the hangar—opposite where she came in.

She stepped into the wide-open space and hugged the wall with her back while walking as lightly as possible. She spotted a table just inside the hangar door littered with tools and what looked like engine parts. Her eyes inventoried the items on the table, searching for anything she could use as additional weapons. Seeing nothing that would benefit her, she moved on. Just feet from the hangar's large opening, she saw a box. Quietly, she unfolded the top and took a peek inside. When she spotted several hand grenades lying on top, a smile formed on her lips. She didn't hesitate and reached in, grabbing two and shoving them into the pockets of her flight suit. Those could come in handy.

As she neared the hangar's opening, she could hear the men talking. She popped her head out, and of course, they were huddled near the helicopter, where she needed to get. The rain had died down to a steady drizzle, though the thunder and lightning lingered.

As she watched the men waiting to see what they were going to do, one of them glanced in her direction. She reacted by hauling her body back inside the structure. In her haste to avoid being caught, she knocked over a broom resting against the wall. She tried to reach for the handle before it hit the floor, but it was like one of those moments that felt like it all happened in slow motion. Yet, she didn't get the intended outcome when the handle smacked the concrete floor, creating a loud echo that was probably heard miles across the quiet desert.

Fuck, fuck, fuck!

"What the hell was that?" She heard one of the guys say.

"Go find out." Another instructed.

She saw a utility closet to the right of her. She tried the knob, found it unlocked, and slipped inside. It was pitch black. She couldn't even see her hands in front of her. She heard the footsteps approach, and then they stopped. He was standing right on the other side of the door. She raised her gun and prepared to defend herself. She waited, anticipating his move.

One second…

Two seconds…

Three seconds…

Clover held her breath. Suddenly, the door flung open. As soon as Clover saw the man, she pulled the trigger once, twice, striking him in the chest. His body crumpled to the ground. She leaped over him, taking off in a dead sprint out into the open toward the old truck she had seen. She channeled her track days back in high school as she pumped her legs as fast as they could go. She didn't even look to see where the others were. Her only focus was finding cover.

Her freedom was short-lived when gunfire erupted behind her. As bullets flew past her, nearly hitting her, she dove to the ground. She rolled across the wet desert floor as more bullets sprayed the earth surrounding her. She quickly got back to her feet and continued to run.

A strong gust of wind blew in, bringing the rain again and sending the sheets of rain smacking violently against her face. She was halfway to the truck when a burst of lightning lit up the murky sky. The colorful spectacle illuminated the area, revealing a large white propane tank about thirty yards to the west of her position. She pulled one of the grenades from her pocket, pulled the pin, and chucked it toward the tank. In mere seconds the tank exploded, sending a fireball upward into the sky.

She didn't bother to stop and watch the fireworks. Her feet continued to move at a fast pace until she reached the old truck. She ducked down and slithered underneath the rusted frame. With her body flattened to the ground, she waited and listened.

The men were shouting in Spanish, and she mentally chastised herself for not heeding her brothers' advice and taking Spanish back in high school. She chose to take French because that was the class her high school crush was in. *Stupid!*

She was trapped in a nightmare that she didn't know if she'd survive. So many things ran through her mind—mostly about her family. Would she ever see them again? Then there was Joker. Would she ever get the chance to tell him that she loved him? An unexpected sob bubbled up her throat, and she slapped her hand over her mouth to keep quiet.

With the rain pelting the truck's metal, she never saw or heard the footsteps behind her until it was too late, and a set of hands latched onto her ankles, yanking her out from beneath the vehicle. She screamed as her body scraped against the rough terrain and was pulled out into the open. Amid the chaos, she lost her gun somewhere under the truck.

The giant hulking man reached down, grabbing her shirt's front, and lifting her off the ground. Before she could get her footing, he slammed her into the side of the truck. The impact to her chest and stomach caused the air inside of her to whoosh out of her body. She was momentarily stunned. He pulled her arms behind her back to restrain her, but her instinct to fight roared back when her brain finally kicked in gear. She lifted her leg and stomped on his foot. His grip loosened, and she twisted out of his grasp and then elbowed him in the ribs. As he was bent over holding his gut, she delivered another blow to his face. She drew the gun from her ankle holster when he fell to the ground and fired a shot into his body, killing him.

Her ears were still ringing from the gunshot when suddenly, she was hit in the back from behind. She fell to the ground, and the third guy pounced on her. He was smaller than the others, but he held his own as they rolled around on the ground, delivering blows to each other. He was screaming at her and calling her a whore. She got in a few punches before he knocked her in her head, wrapped his hands around her neck, and squeezed, cutting off her air supply. Her chest and lungs began to burn, and fear instantly gripped her as she thought this was it. She was going to die. But she didn't want to die. She still had too much to live for. She was a soldier—a goddamn Marine. Images of her family flipped through her head. They were telling her to fight.

The guy lowered his face and screamed. "I kill you!"

Not today, she thought to herself.

She gritted her teeth and gathered the strength to throw the guy off her. She was coughing and trying to suck in air when he charged at her again. She attempted to roll away, but he snagged her foot and yanked her back. She felt the rocks and debris dig into her back. She kicked him in the chest using her free leg, and he fell backward. She had trouble catching her breath, but the adrenaline flowing through her gave her the push to keep her in the game. She spotted one of her guns on the ground and reached for it. She flipped back over onto her back just as her attacker lunged at her. She screamed as she pulled the trigger.

She scrambled to her feet, pushing aside the pain in her body. She needed to get to that helicopter. Thankfully, the rain had once again slowed, leaving behind a nighttime chill in the air.

She had no clue where the main guy was, which frightened her. She grabbed the rifle lying next to one of the men.

As she was checking the rifle to see if it was loaded, she heard the whine of an aircraft engine in the distance. She looked up and saw the small Cessna starting to roll toward the small airstrip. Through the cockpit window, she saw it was the badass dude. He was going to escape with all the weapons.

"Not if I can help it," She said aloud and dropped to the ground with the rifle. Like her dad had taught her, settling on her stomach, she prepared to take the shot. With her shoulder pressed firmly against the rifle's stock, she extended her index finger just above the trigger. She aligned her eye directly through the targeting sight. Once she had her target in the crosshair, she relaxed her body, took a deep breath, counted to five, and exhaled as her finger tapped the trigger. The gun fired, giving her a kickback and making her ears ring. But she never took her eye off the target until she knew the 7.62mm caliber bullet had done its intended job. She couldn't fully describe the feeling that came over her when she saw the man behind the control column slumped over with a hole in his forehead. However, the sight did leave her with the feeling of hope—hope that she would make it out of the horrific situation and get to live another day.

She glanced down at her watch and realized she needed to hurry. If that guy was telling the truth, then she only had five minutes, give or take, until the bombs detonated.

She hobbled over to the chopper and slid the side door open. She covered her mouth and her eyes filled with tears upon seeing the Major's body lying inside. He was bleeding from his head and his leg. She assumed the injury to his head was what killed him. She made a quick decision that she wouldn't leave him behind. She'd make sure his body was respectfully returned to his family.

She spotted the bag attached to the fuselage, holding the satellite phone. She'd have to climb over the Major to reach it. As she extended her arm to reach for the bag, she accidentally bumped the Major's body. She was met with an unexpected low, moaning sound. She shrieked and fell backward upon hearing the eerie sound. Luckily she caught herself on a hand strap before tumbling out the door.

She sat there shaken for a few seconds. Her eyes were wide as saucers, her body trembled, and her heart pounded in her chest. She stared in shock at the Major's body, wondering if the sound had actually come from him.

The events that unfolded had been traumatic for her, and she was exhausted, so maybe it was a case where her mind was playing tricks on her, though it would be cruel and malicious. But as she continued staring, she saw his chest rise and realized it was no joke. She burst into tears as she crawled over to him.

She felt his neck for a pulse and was overcome with joy as she felt the thrumming of his heartbeat under her fingertips.

With time running out, she quickly grabbed the phone bag and slipped it over her shoulders. She then maneuvered Major Saunders into a position where she could lift him into a fireman's carry. She gritted her teeth, feeling her muscles strain as she lifted his large frame over her shoulder. She panted through her body's burning pain as she walked the Major and herself to safety.

Signaling that the storm hadn't finished its assault, a streak of lightning cut through the black sky, followed by a loud thunderous roar that split the air and shook the area as if an earthquake had struck. It was so close that the atmosphere around her felt electric.

Her focus was on getting them as far away as possible from the helicopter and the building. The issue was where in the hell were they supposed to go. The desert didn't offer any options for cover. The rain started to pick up again, and she frantically looked around for a place to take shelter. Just when she had about given up, she spotted the little pavilion that looked like the hitching post. It was the only option available. She just prayed it was far enough away to shield them from the blast.

She was about halfway when her back couldn't take the weight anymore. She gently placed the Major on the ground and dragged him the rest of the way. Just as she got the two of them under the covered structure, the world around her exploded.

CHAPTER TEN

Colonel Jenkins resignedly walked into the SCU control room to check in with the overnight crew before he headed home.

He was looking forward to the weekend, although he doubted he'd have any time to relax with the Hollis situation looming over the SCU.

Hollis' disappearance alone was a significant blow to the SCU, but then add on the FBI investigation into Hollis' possible involvement in arms trafficking, and Jenkins felt ready to throw in the towel.

The situation nagged him, and he'd been running back through his mind everything that the FBI and President Evans had presented to him. Even though there was substantial evidence pointing to Hollis' involvement, there was one thing they all agreed on—Hollis wasn't operating alone. He definitely had inside help.

It was a crying shame because Hollis had the skills and intelligence to make one hell of a crew chief. He knew the job inside and out. And that was probably what had attracted him to those operating behind the scenes. Jenkins still hoped Hollis would be found, so that he could explain his actions.

Jenkins glanced around the room and spotted Corporal Porter studying something on the computer monitor.

"What's got you looking constipated, Corporal?" Jenkins asked with a wry grin on his face. He loved messing with Porter innocently, of course. Porter was an Aircrew Readiness Manager, which was a rigorous job. ARMs were integral staff members who many operational commands and squadrons relied on. However, Porter's primary responsibility were the SCU teams. His responsibilities included anything related to missions, training, and administration. In a nutshell, Jenkins and the rest of the SCU would be lost without individuals such as Porter.

Corporal Porter shook his head and appeared to be biting his tongue, even though he too sported a slight grin, which amused Jenkins even more.

Porter then scrunched his eyebrows together and became serious.

"That's odd," he stated out loud, and Jenkins looked up from one of the monitors he was looking at.

"What's wrong?" Jenkins asked.

"It's TS-13."

"What about them?"

"They radioed in over forty-five minutes ago when they landed. Major Saunders said they were grounded because of the weather system moving through the area. I haven't heard from them since, but their transponder signal just went out."

Confused, Jenkins walked closer and peered over the Corporal's shoulder at the bank of computer monitors he was studying. As far as Jenkins was aware, no current missions were being conducted by SCU teams. Again, anything could go haywire, and a team was called in, but he was always notified.

"What in the hell are you talking about? On the way back from where?"

Porter flinched at the Colonel's bark but then scrunched his eyebrows together, flustered by Jenkins' response.

As Porter explained TS-13's current situation, Jenkins was literally dumbfounded and outraged. He had no clue what the hell was going on. At least that he was aware of, this supposed mission was never on the books. Suddenly, a feeling of doom settled in his gut.

"Who the hell authorized this?"

Porter stared at Jenkins as if he had just asked the dumbest question.

"The President, sir."

"When? And how come I wasn't made aware of it?"

Porter's fingers flew across the keyboard.

"The order came through around 1600." Porter then shook his head, glancing up over his shoulder at Jenkins. "Wait. You didn't know about it?" He questioned, appearing confused.

Jenkins' patience was wearing thin. He wanted answers, and he wanted them now.

"If I'm asking you, I believe that would insinuate that I wasn't aware." He wanted to roll his eyes at the young Marine.

"But, sir. Don't you have to sign off on all flights?"

"Last time I checked, I did. Don't all flights have to check in with the ARM on duty and provide the completed orders?"

Porter flipped the logbook from the prior on-duty ARM.

"They did." He pointed to the log entry at the bottom of the page. "Sergeant Cooper logged it."

Jenkins took the binder and examined the entry before looking at Porter.

"Douglas, Arizona, to drop supplies to a nonprofit?"

Porter pulled up several documents onto the screen.

"According to the documents scanned into the system, it's a humanitarian supply drop. The items are being dropped to a non-profit organization called Hope 2 Smiles."

Still looking over Porter's shoulder, Jenkins examined the document on the screen. There, written in blue ink at the bottom of the first page was President Evans' signature. However, the record lacked another required signature—his. Well, at least his authentic signature. The signature scribbled on the line above his typed name was definitely not his signature. He swallowed hard as questions and scenarios began to race through his mind. What in the hell was going on? Who had forged his signature? And one that stuck out like a sore thumb. Why would the President request TS-13, the SCU's top team, to serve as the transport for a supply drop?

"Something's not right," Jenkins told Porter. "That's not my signature."

Porter's eyes widened. "It's not?"

Jenkins shook his head. "No. Get TS-13 on the radio."

Porter didn't hesitate. "Command to TS-13. Do you copy?"

The pair waited a few moments but received no response.

Jenkins took the radio from Porter. "Captain Walker, this is Colonel Jenkins. Do you copy?" Jenkins asked, feeling a wee bit panicked with no reply coming from any team member. Typically, Jenkins was a man who kept his cool, but he knew without a doubt that something was wrong. Suddenly, a vital question popped into his mind.

"Who submitted the orders to Sergeant Cooper?" Jenkins asked Porter.

Porter clicked to a different screen. "Uh...this can't be right."

"What is it?" Jenkins asked.

"According to the system, the orders came through an email sent from Sergeant Hollis' account."

As soon as Jenkins heard Hollis' name, his gut twisted into a ball of knots as a dark cloud of uncertainty formed. There was no way this was any coincidence.

"Son of a bitch! Get me the President on the phone now!"

෴

President Evans removed his reading glasses and placed them on the monstrous but beautiful wooden desk. Every time he stepped into the Oval Office, he couldn't help but stop to admire the magnificent piece of art, even if it was just for a quick second. Most would say it was just a desk, but The Resolute desk, or the Hayes desk as some would call it, was a nineteenth-century desk, dating back to 1880. It was a gift from Queen Victoria to President Rutherford B. Hayes. The one-thousand-three-hundred-pound desk was constructed from oak timbers of the British Arctic exploration ship, the HMS *Resolute*.

He rubbed his tired eyes and fell into the comfort of his plush leather chair before glancing at the clock on the phone. He couldn't believe it was nearing one in the morning.

His back-to-back schedule had been grueling. He knew it was going to be one heck of a day when his scheduler, Monika, jokingly asked him if he wanted her to block off a few minutes in the day for him to use the restroom.

The day started with a tough meeting on Capitol Hill as he went back and forth with congressional leaders and staff on a new veterans bill that, if agreed upon, would open up more funding to implement more crisis centers for veterans to turn to for help. Being a military veteran himself and having lost friends to suicide, he was fully committed to seeing that this bill passed. Thankfully, both parties put aside their political differences and agreed unanimously to move the bill forward when Congress resumed after the summer recess.

By the time he arrived back at the White House, he had just enough time to shower and change before escorting the First Lady to her first fundraiser for the Global Clean Water initiative she was spearheading. Her focus was on securing clean water for impoverished nations.

He pulled open the top left drawer and placed his pen and notebook inside as he did each night before leaving the office. Just as he stood from his chair, one of the two phones on his desk rang. When he saw it was the secured phone, the one furthest to the left, he instantly felt a twitch in his gut. Calls on that line, especially late at night, typically weren't good.

He reached for it and answered.

"This is Evans."

"Mr. President, I've got Colonel Jenkins on the line for you," a White House phone operator stated. Evans was a little caught off guard. He anticipated the call to be from one of his advisors.

"Thank you. Put him through."

As soon as Evans heard the familiar click signaling the call was accepted, he responded.

"Colonel Jenkins. What can I do for you, considering how late it is?"

"Apologies for the late call, Mr. President." Jenkins' booming voice came over the line. "But, sir, we've got a major problem."

Evans knew from working with Jenkins during his military career that Jenkins would never use the words "major problem" unless the situation was dire. Just like that, the sleepiness Evans felt a few minutes ago had vanished. He retook his seat in the chair and leaned back.

"What kind of problem?"

"We've lost contact with TS-13."

Evans thought his heart had stopped beating for a moment, and he immediately leaned forward to brace himself on the desk. TS-13 was Clover Walker's team. He ran his hand down his face. Not only was Captain Walker his top pilot, but she was also a family friend. The Walker and Evans families had been friends for years, having lived in the same Tennessee town.

"Jesus. Where?"

"Northeast of Douglas, Arizona. Their last location was an airstrip between Route 80 and the New Mexico border."

"Were they part of a training exercise?"

There was a pause, and Evans thought he'd lost the connection, but then Jenkins responded.

"Sir, I mean no disrespect, but if you're asking me that question, then I'm afraid our issue is more complex than a missing helicopter."

"I'm don't understand. What are you not saying, Colonel?"

"I'm going to get straight to the point. Did you order TS-13 to partake in a supply drop that would include humanitarian supplies for a non-profit group Hope 2 Smiles?"

Supply drop? Evans thought to himself. He'd been juggling a few situations over the last few days, but a supply drop hadn't been one of them.

"Colonel, I have no idea what you're talking about. I never ordered a supply drop. And even if I had, I certainly wouldn't have requested Captain Walker and Major Saunders."

Evans then began to second guess himself. Had he signed off on something and just didn't remember? He swiveled his chair around and slid open the bottom drawer of the credenza where he kept working files and started flipping through the color-coded file folders marked for non-classified SCU operations. When he got to the end, he went back and did one more pass-through to ensure he hadn't overlooked it. But again, he got the same outcome—there was no file.

"I just double-checked to make sure. I've got nothing."

Evans heard the long sigh that Jenkins released.

"Sir, I believe the orders presented to Captain Walker and Major Saunders were fraudulently endorsed. I can assure you that I did not sign those orders, and considering your reaction, I assume you never signed the order."

Evans rubbed his forehead. He couldn't believe this was actually happening.

"Was there a manifest included in the orders?"

"All it states is blankets, clothing, and non-perishable food."

Evans wanted to roll his eyes. How fucking convenient!

"You haven't had any contact with the team since they left San Diego?"

"Corporal Porter, the ARM on duty, last spoke with them approximately forty-five minutes to an hour ago when they landed at the airstrip. They radioed in, stating that a storm was moving into the area and their return would be delayed. Now that we've lost the signal to the transponder, we have no idea where they are."

Evans felt his insides twist. With the ongoing investigation, he had reason to believe that this incident was well planned and possibly executed. But what he really needed to know exactly, were the contents of those crates.

"What about satellites? Have you checked those to see if you can get an aerial view?"

"Can't see a damn thing right now because of the weather and cloud cover. I'm very concerned about my team."

So was Evans. He didn't want to wait; he needed boots on the ground.

"I need to make a call. Give me a few minutes, and I'll call you back with a plan. In the meantime, can you please forward to me the orders you have?"

After hanging up with Jenkins, Evans pulled up a number in his contacts. On the second ring, a man with a gruff-sounding voice picked up.

"Lawrence."

"Lawrence, it's Evans. I need some assistance."

"Name it."

"I need a Unit for an in-country operation ASAP."

"Done," Lawrence answered without hesitation.

Evans grinned before rattling off the specifics that Lawrence's team would need. It wasn't the first time Evans had made a call in the middle of the night asking for Delta Force's top unit's assistance.

CHAPTER ELEVEN

Feeling physically and mentally exhausted, Clover sat on the ground, shivering. Her clothes were soaked, and the cover she found wasn't big enough to shield both her and the Major from the storm's elements, so she sacrificed herself to make sure the Major stayed warm and dry. Luckily, she was able to find a few dry blankets inside the Cessna. She had two tucked around the Major and the other one wrapped around her. She had forgotten how low the temperature could drop in the desert at night, especially after a rainstorm.

She was so tired, and she fought to keep her eyes open, even though she wanted to close them for just a few minutes. But she was afraid that she'd fall asleep and not hear if someone approached. She was still on guard, knowing that there was still one person unaccounted for, though she believed they were long gone considering the small SUV she had seen when they arrived was no longer at the airstrip. That didn't mean she didn't jump at every noise she heard.

A strong gust of wind hit her, and she felt the coldness to her bones, and her teeth began to chatter again. She looked at her watch. About an hour had passed since the world around her had literally gone up in flames. Unfortunately, the satellite phone hadn't been in the bag, leaving her with no communication channels. Now that the storm had moved through, she hoped that those in charge of monitoring the movements of the aircraft would realize something was wrong when the transponder on the Black Hawk quit sending its signal.

She glanced down at Major Saunders. She hoped he made it through this. Thankfully, the bag she grabbed contained a medical kit. She'd done everything she could for him, using the available items. She kept her hand on his chest to make sure he was still breathing. A few minutes ago, she thought he would wake up when he had moved his body a little. But nothing materialized, and he lay still ever since. She cleaned out the gunshot wound to his leg as best as possible and applied some QuikClot gauze to help stop the bleeding. Her biggest fear was the extent of his head injury. You never knew what you were dealing with when it came to those kinds of injuries.

The air still reeked of smoke and aviation fuel. Fortunately, a lingering rain shower extinguished the fires, leaving behind a pile of twisted metal and smoldering ash. Had that rain not come through when it did, Clover wasn't sure if she'd be alive right now. The way the wind shifted would've fanned the fire directly into her path, causing a massive wildfire that she could never have escaped, especially with having to carry the Major.

She was riddled with emotions—anger, fear, and sadness as she sat and thought about the situation. She couldn't believe how she and the others missed the signs of Hollis' treasonous behavior. But then again, many of the signs coincided with his emotions and actions in dealing with his mom's illness. Then to find out that the CIA Director had played a major role in the illegal activities was a blow to her confidence where government agencies were concerned. The whole situation just sucked.

As she let her mind wander, a dark aura suddenly settled upon her as reality set in. In the four years she'd flown for the SCU, she was never affected mentally by having to fire weapons from the air at enemy combatants on the ground. This was the first time she was face-to-face with her enemy, where the decision she made would determine if she lived or died. She kept telling herself that she had done the right thing. It was the only choice she had. She had been protecting herself, so she couldn't understand why the guilt was laying heavily inside her. The multitude of questions kept coming. Would the government think she was part of the operation and was just trying to cover her own ass? Was her career ruined? Then she had her family to think about. What would they think once they found out?

It was too much, and she finally gave in and closed her eyes, but swore she wouldn't fall asleep. The risk was too high. Even if she tried to get some shut-eye, she couldn't. Not with the way her mind kept spinning, wondering who else was involved in putting weapons in the enemy's hands.

She felt the anger growing deep inside her, knowing that the same individuals who took an oath to defend their country were also aiding known adversaries. She couldn't fathom how a person could be so ruthless. Her eyes popped open, and she glanced at the black duffel bag she had retrieved from the airplane filled with stacks of cash. Her answer was right there—greed. Her biggest hurdle now was who she could trust.

Funny how her brothers immediately popped into her head. She could sure use their help right now. She shook her head and almost laughed at the thought, considering she had scolded Bear a few weeks ago about her being a big girl who could take care of herself. But then again, sometimes even the strongest needed help once in a while.

She was already dozing off when she was jolted awake by a faint sound in the distance that traveled across the stillness of the desert. She strained her ears, listening as the sound grew louder. Soon, she recognized the low thrumming sound coming from a helicopter. She kept her eyes peeled on the sky, waiting for a glimpse of what she hoped was her ride out of the hell hole she was stuck in.

Moments later, two Black Hawks appeared above, instilling hope inside her.

She stood up just as the first helicopter landed, followed by the second one. Three men in full gear jumped out of the first one, followed by four more exiting the second. They headed straight toward her. Even though she assumed they were the good guys, she wasn't taking any chances and she kept her hand near her weapon.

"Captain Walker?" The tall guy leading the pack called out in a deep voice over the sound of the whirling rotors.

She nodded as she took in his appearance. He was easily over six feet and had mysterious dark eyes that were both fascinating and instilled a bit of fear. He was lean, but that didn't mean a damn thing knowing his capabilities. He stuck his hand out. "I'm Oz."

She firmly shook his hand. "Clover Walker, but it seems you already know that."

"Looks like you've got one hell of a mess here, Captain."

No shit, Clover thought to herself.

"You have no idea. The situation here gives FUBAR a whole new meaning," she mumbled and was surprised when Oz appeared to crack a small smile.

"We're getting Colonel Jenkins on the line for you. It is just you?" One of the other guys called out to her.

"No. My co-pilot, Major Saunders, he's over there." She said, pointing at the covered pavilion. "He's in pretty bad shape and needs medical attention." She motioned for the group to follow her. As they walked, she went over the Major's injuries. Oz also introduced her to the other guys.

When they reached the Major, an Army medic and two of the men dressed similar to Oz started assessing and tending to the Major's injuries. As she looked on, a thought suddenly hit her. None of the guys identified their rank when they were introduced. Instead, they went by what seemed to be nicknames or callsigns. Having four brothers in the Special Forces, she wondered who exactly these guys were. But before she could dwell on that thought, she felt a tap on her shoulder. When she looked over, she found one of the guys, Cheeto, holding a phone out for her.

"I've got Colonel Jenkins for you," he informed her as he handed over the phone.

She took a deep breath and drummed up some strength before bringing the phone to her ear.

"Colonel?" She spoke, and even she could hear the fragility in her voice.

"Jesus, am I happy to hear your voice, Lucky," Jenkins roared, forcing Clover to pull the phone away from her ear because he was so loud. She stepped away from the rest of the group.

"I can say the same, sir."

"What the fuck happened? One of the pilots I spoke to said it looked like a war zone."

Clover scanned the property, surveying the damage to what was left of the building and her helicopter. The pilot wasn't lying. It looked worse than some war zones she'd been in.

"I won't sugarcoat it. It's bad, Colonel. And I'm afraid what occurred here tonight is just the tip of the iceberg. It's a small part of an operation that extends beyond our borders and threatens the safety of our country. The President has a major problem on his hands."

"What kind of problem?"

"For starters, treason and murder."

She started at the beginning and explained everything that went down from when she and the Major arrived at the airstrip until now. Clover was grateful that Jenkins let her speak with minimal interruptions. However, he did emit a few expletives. By the time she was finished, her head was spinning, and she felt sick. She just wanted to put all of this behind her, but she had a feeling the events here were going to haunt her for days to come.

"Jesus, Lucky. I'm so sorry," Jenkins told her.

She grunted. "I don't know why you're sorry. It's not like you were aware."

"Just so you know, the orders that you received were forged. I never signed them and neither did the president. I wasn't even aware that you and the Major had taken off."

"Yeah, I kinda figured that out when I overheard Perkins talking."

"Are the weapons still there, or were they destroyed in the blast?"

"They're in the Cessna."

"What about you?"

"What about me, sir?"

"How are you holding up? Are you injured?"

"I'm holding my own. It's Major Saunders I'm worried about."

"What a clusterfuck," Jenkins said, releasing a long sigh. "I've spoken with President Evans. In fact, he's the one to thank for getting a team out there so quickly."

"Speaking of the men here. Who are they?" She asked.

"A Unit."

"I figured they were somewhere along those lines."

Clover knew what the "Unit" was. To most people, they were known as Delta Force. They were the most lethal group of soldiers the Army had to offer. They were just as badass as her brothers, if not more, though she'd never say that in front of them.

"They're the good guys, Lucky. Trust them."

"Trusting anyone is hard for me right now, but I trust you, Sir, so I'll take your word for it."

She heard someone in the background talking to the Colonel.

"Hang on a minute, Lucky. I've got another call coming in," he told her.

As she waited for the Colonel to come back on the line, she wandered back over to the group to get an update on the Major.

She stood back and watched as the two Deltas: Tums and Moon and the Army medic, were still working on the Major.

Tums glanced up at her. "You did a good job with this wound," he complimented, referring to the Major's leg.

"I did what I could with what I had to work with."

"Considering how long it took us to get out here, you most likely saved his life," the medic told her as he and Moon loaded the Major onto the stretcher.

She wouldn't admit it to these guys, but she was still nervous about his condition. And she couldn't help but feel partially responsible for him being injured. If she hadn't used the restroom, he wouldn't have been on his own to deal with those men. Before she got too far inside her own head, the Colonel returned to the line.

"Lucky, are you still there?"

"Yes, sir."

"Here's the plan. Oz, who I assume you met, and a few members of his unit will bring you to D.C."

Her eyes widened in surprise. "D.C.?" She questioned.

"President's orders."

Okay then. Who was she to question the President? But it also still left other questions and concerns she had.

"What about Major Saunders and the weapons still here?"

"The remainder of Oz's team will accompany Major Saunders to a medical facility. Concerning the weapons and everything else on the ground there, a team from the FBI's Counterintelligence office is en route and will take control of the area to sort through the mess. They're all operating on President's orders. Do you have any questions?"

She was nodding her head even though he couldn't see her. She had numerous questions, but her priority was herself and Major Saunders' safety.

"What facility will Major Saunders be taken to?"

"I don't know, but I'll let you know as soon as I find out. I know this is difficult for you, Lucky. But believe me when I say he'll be taken care of."

While he had eased her concern for the Major, she wasn't sold on her fate, and she felt her chest tighten as multiple scenarios whirled through her mind, starting with the guys who were sent to "escort" her to Washington. She knew their capabilities, and that alone added to the questions in her head. Were they taking her to D.C. because they thought she could be involved in the weapons deal? Were they planning to interrogate her? Jesus, just the thought of that made her sick to her stomach. How could Evans think she was involved in something so traitorous? Hell, he and his family were good friends with her family.

"When will I talk to you again?" She asked Jenkins.

"I'll see you in D.C. And, Lucky?"

"Yes, sir?"

"I know it wasn't easy, and probably isn't what you want to hear—but well done, soldier."

"Thank you, sir." She replied, her voice cracking at the end. She tried to be strong, but the emotion from everything was taking a toll on her. More so now that she knew she was safe for the time being.

Once she disconnected the call, she handed the phone back to Cheeto. Tums and Moon were already heading toward one of the waiting helicopters with Major Saunders.

Oz looked at her. "You ready?" He asked, and she nodded.

One of the other guys, Pad, she believed his name was, reached for the duffel bag sitting by her feet, but she beat him to it, placing her hands on it.

When he eyed her curiously with a cocked eyebrow, she said to him, "That bag doesn't go anywhere unless it's in my hands."

She couldn't get a read on the guy. Out of the six Deltas, he was the most closed-off, wearing the same blank expression he had when he first arrived.

Like her opinion didn't matter, he looked at Oz as if asking if that was okay. She didn't give two shits what Oz thought. That bag stayed in her possession until she got to D.C. and handed it over to the President.

Oz gave a slight nod, and Pad backed away, making room for her to bend down and pick up the bag.

"You know you can trust us," Oz asserted.

Standing up straight with the bag in her hand, she locked gazes with the Delta leader.

"I thought I could trust my teammate too, but look where that got me."

With his hands on his hips and his rifle slung across his chest, he gave her a slight nod as if understanding, but he wasn't finished.

"Understood. But we're here now, and we're helping you."

She swallowed hard and knew he was right. She would have to trust these guys if she wanted out of here.

She walked toward the two awaiting helicopters powered up and ready to go. She stopped at the first one where the medic was getting the Major situated inside. She glanced at Tums, Moon, and Hutch, the three

Deltas accompanying the Major. She had tears in her eyes. "Please take care of him," she told them, and they each nodded their head.

She then looked up at Oz and took a deep breath. Oz held her by the shoulders and stared down into her eyes, sensing her worry.

"Captain, you have my word that my guys will take care of him."

She searched his eyes, looking for any sign of distrust. Her dad had always preached that the eyes held the truth. She found herself relaxing her shoulders.

"I believe you. And, Oz…"

"Yeah?"

"Thank you."

He gave her a curt smile before she turned and walked to the second Black Hawk. As she, Oz, Pad, and Cheeto all took their seats and buckled in, the helicopter lifted off. As they ascended, they passed the aircraft carrying the FBI team.

Once up in the air, Clover glanced out the window, and in the distance, the first rays of the early morning sun began to rise over the mountains. It was a welcoming sight compared to the smoldering remnants of her burned-out Black Hawk helicopter, the scene of a nightmare she didn't think she'd ever recover from.

ತಾ

Clover's eyes popped open as the wheels of the Learjet made contact with the runway. With a quick glance out the window, she saw they had arrived in Washington, D.C. She leaned back against the seat as the plane taxied to their destination. She was utterly exhausted, and her brain felt like mush.

Once she and the Delta team arrived at Fort Huachuca Army Installation in southern Arizona, she was given about thirty minutes to clean up before boarding a plane and whisked off to D.C.

The only positive factor was that they flew private versus commercial, which lessened her anxiety about having to be around crowds. Oz, Cheeto, and Pad were still with her.

For most of the plane ride, she kept to herself, claiming the furthest seat in the back of the plane. The three Deltas sat near the front as if knowing she needed the space, and she appreciated that.

She tried to sleep, but her mind wouldn't shut off. No sooner would her eyes close than the flashbacks flooded her mind, producing graphic images of death and destruction she wished that she could scrub from her memory.

As the plane rolled to a stop, she glanced out the window and saw the light grey sedan with heavily tinted windows parked near the jet's stairs. Knowing that her life was about to change when she stepped off the plane, a part of her deep down didn't want to move. She felt secure and protected where she sat. What would happen when she was out in the open? As the Deltas stood and gathered their belongings, she realized she didn't have a choice but to go. There were so many unknowns at this point. Without any contact with her family, she felt lost and alone.

"Clover?"

She looked up and met Oz's gaze.

"You ready?"

"Umm...yeah. Sure."

She unbuckled her seatbelt and moved to stand when her legs began to shake so bad she almost fell. However, she caught herself on the seatback. She closed her eyes, thinking about how she would get through this?

Fifteen minutes later, they pulled into an underground parking garage of a large hotel in downtown D.C.

Clover looked around. "Why are we here?"

"This is your stop," Oz quipped.

"A hotel?" She questioned curiously. Colonel Jenkins never mentioned a hotel. President Evans requested that she be brought to D.C., so she expected to be taken to the White House, not a hotel.

Pad, who sat next to her in the back seat, turned toward her. He still hadn't said a word to her since she snapped at him about the bag. But then again, she hadn't heard him utter a word to anyone since they left the airstrip. She knew how guarded and reserved Special Forces soldiers could be, but there was more to this guy's story. Maybe if she weren't up to her ass in alligators with her own problems, she wouldn't mind trying to get him to talk. After all, she did minor in psychology.

She held Pad's penetrating gaze.

"You are one of the bravest and most courageous soldiers I've ever met. Don't ever change who you are or what you represent."

Clover just stared at the brooding Delta. She wasn't sure how to respond to his compliment, and she didn't have to because moments later, a door leading into the hotel opened, and a man dressed in a pair of dark dress pants and a light blue button-up dress shirt with the sleeves rolled to his elbows appeared. Oz got out of the car and opened her door for her. As she got out, the man approached and held out his hand.

"Captain Walker. My name is Eddie Caruso with the FBI."

Clover knew who Director Caruso was, and she shook his hand while offering a small smile.

"It's nice to meet you, Director Caruso."

The Director then turned to Oz and shook his hand as well, thanking him and his team for their assistance. It was funny to watch because, just like her brothers, Oz didn't seem to like being called out. Special Forces guys were a rare breed. They were humble and resilient, and they were deadly.

Caruso then turned his attention back to her.

"Are you all set, Captain?"

She gave him a nod and then turned to reach into the car to grab the duffel bag but was shocked and amused when Pad was holding it out for her.

"See? I'm trustworthy," he told her, then winked.

She thanked both him and Cheeto. Before she headed inside, she turned to face Oz.

"Thank you for everything, Oz. It was nice meeting you and your team, though it would've been nicer had it been under better circumstances."

"It was to meet you face-to-face as well, and I'm pretty sure you haven't seen the last of us."

She cocked her head and squinted her eyes. "I haven't?"

Oz gave her what she could only think was a grin.

"We only ride with the best pilots. Catch ya later, *Lucky*. Oh, and by the way. Tell your brother Bear I'm still waiting on that beer he owes me. He'll understand."

She stared at his back with her mouth agape as he folded himself into the front seat. Once he was in and closed the door, he looked at her and offered a mock salute as the car drove off. She smiled as she shook her head. They were a unique group of guys for sure.

"Captain Walker?"

When she turned and met the eyes of Director Caruso, she took a deep, cleansing breath because she had a feeling the next few hours were going to be anything but calm.

෴

Clover changed out of the oversized men's clothing the Delta team lent her and stepped into a pair of baby blue comfy cotton joggers. She grabbed one of the three bags of clothing off the floor and placed it on the vanity counter.

When she first arrived at the penthouse, she wasn't sure what to expect. But when the President met her at the door with open arms, she almost lost her composure. Yeah, it wasn't professional, and she tried to tell him that, but he blew off her concerns telling her in his words *"to screw the formalities."* And boy, had she needed that hug. President Evans and his family were very close with her family. She may be a Marine and a kickass pilot, but deep down, she was still a daddy's girl, and if she couldn't have a hug from her dad, she'd accept one from the next closest person.

Although, Joker chose to pop in her head right then. She'd love nothing more than to snuggle close to him and feel his strong, muscular arms wrapped around her body, giving her the security she desired. Then to help occupy her mind, he'd whisper into her ear all the naughty things he'd do to her before whisking her off to the bedroom.

She squeezed her thighs together as the memories of their night together seeped into her mind. Not that she had anything to compare him to, but Joker was a man who took great care in loving his woman, making sure that no part of her body went untouched. He kissed, licked, stroked, and caressed her skin, starting with her toes all the way up, leaving her body feeling all tingly under his warm muscled flesh.

Clover's eyes popped open, and she leaned against the vanity in the bathroom, trying to control her libido. Joker rocked her world, throwing her into another universe.

Now that she had come back to reality, it was definitely not the time to be having those thoughts. She just hoped that Joker didn't think she blew him off last night.

First, she needed to finish getting dressed before going in front of Evans and Caruso. She'd been surprised when Evans had handed her three large shopping bags full of clothes and other necessities she might need. It also made her think about how long she'd been there.

She smiled as she looked through some of the clothing that Jocelyn had picked out for her. Jocelyn Thompson worked on the First Lady's staff, and she was also a good friend of the family. Evans told her that Jocelyn didn't know that the clothes she had bought were for Clover.

Jocelyn was the same age as Bear. Jocelyn and Bear had been best friends all through childhood. But shortly after Bear earned his Trident Pin, Clover hadn't seen or heard much from Jocelyn. She was always tempted to ask Bear what happened between them, but anytime their mom brought her name up, he got that mean, annoyed look, so Clover chose to mind her business. Maybe one day, she'd ask him.

Clover reached into the bag, searching for a bra. She couldn't stand not wearing a bra. She liked to keep her *girls* supported and tucked in. Just when she thought Jocelyn had forgotten that tiny detail, she spotted two at the bottom of the bag—a white one and a pretty pink one. Of course, she went for the cotton-candy-colored one. She pulled it from the bag and held it up. That's when she saw the matching thong attached to the plastic hanger. "Son of a bitch," she mumbled to herself. Clover hated thongs. In fact, she'd rather go commando than wear a piece of dental floss up her ass. She had worn one once back in high school on a date, and she swore all night she kept trying to pick the never-ending wedgie from her ass. She shook her head. The bra she'd keep, but the thong had to go.

As much as she wanted to wear the pink lacy one, she opted for the plain white one since she planned on wearing a white tank top. She pulled the tags off and slipped it on gingerly to avoid the bruises. She was definitely starting to feel the effects of last night's ordeal. She pulled on the tank top and a zip-up hoodie that matched the joggers.

She turned toward the large mirror and was shaken by the reflection of the woman staring back at her. The usual blonde, bubbly, and charismatic woman was almost unrecognizable. Her normal bright hazel eyes were shadowed by dullness and dark half-moons beneath her lower eyelids. The large bruise covering most of her right cheek, and the crusted scab on her bottom lip, added to the haunting look. Christ, she was a mess.

"What's next?" She asked the stranger staring back at her, wondering where she went from here. There was only one way to find out what that answer was.

She was aware that the President and God knew who else was itching to speak with her. She was grateful that he gave her some time to change and get squared away before the interrogations began.

Knowing she was stalling, she inhaled a deep breath and exhaled. Like every mission she'd ever taken flight in, she squared her shoulders and gave herself a little reassurance.

"Let's do this."

CHAPTER TWELVE

Clover opened the bathroom door and walked into the living room. She was prepared for the onslaught of questions she knew were coming, but the smell of food caught her attention first. As if right on cue, her stomach rumbled, which wasn't a surprise considering she hadn't had anything to eat since lunch the day before. Oz had offered her a breakfast sandwich on the plane, but she wasn't interested in food at the time. She walked over to the large glass dining table covered with silver serving platters.

"I had some food brought up." The man's voice from behind her said, startling her and causing her to jump. She spun around and found President Evans standing by the floor-to-ceiling windows watching her.

He offered her a warm smile. "I thought you'd be hungry." He rubbed his hand against his forehead. "However, I wasn't sure what you'd want, so I ordered several items off the menu." He motioned with his hand toward the table. "Please help yourself."

"Thank you." She responded as she eyed the spread of dishes, deciding which one to check first. She lifted the lid to the first plate and nearly gagged from the smell of the fish. She had never been a fan of seafood. The second plate offered a more appealing choice of grilled chicken breast marinated in a Hawaiian pineapple sauce with vegetables and steamed rice. Though it looked and smelled divine, it still wasn't quite what her stomach was seeking, so she moved to the third plate. When she lifted the lid, she nearly moaned in bliss at the sight of the bacon cheeseburger with all the toppings, and a side of French fries. She picked up the plate and turned to sit when she noticed another man had joined the President and the Director.

Looking polished, dressed in a dark gray suit and wearing an earpiece, she wondered if he was part of the President's secret service detail.

Evans stepped forward. "Captain Walker, I'd like to introduce you to Special Agent Merrick. Merrick is head of the Presidential Protection Detail, and an old friend of mine."

But could he be trusted? She thought to herself.

"He's someone you can trust," Evans said as if reading Clover's mind.

Damn. Was it that obvious she had trust issues?

She managed to greet him with a small smile and placed her food down on the table so she could shake his hand.

"It's nice to meet you. And please call me Clover."

"It's nice to meet you, Clover," he replied smoothly.

"Come have a seat, and you can eat while we talk," Evans told her.

She took a seat on the sofa directly across from where Evans sat down. Merrick followed, sitting in the chair to her right. Caruso was already seated at the other end of the sofa.

"First and foremost, how are you doing?" Evans asked her. Even though his question seemed simple to answer, it was a loaded one. There was a lot she needed to think about and process. Answering now would be premature, considering how she felt now compared to what she may feel tomorrow.

She shrugged her shoulder and gave an honest answer. "Right at this moment, I guess I'm okay."

He tilted his head slightly to the side. "Just okay?"

"I feel like I'm riding a rollercoaster. One minute I'm up, and the next, I'm sliding down. I'm tired, on edge, a little sore, and just wondering what tomorrow will bring."

He squinted his eyes, appearing concerned. "Did the doctor give you anything for the pain?"

"He did, but I haven't taken it yet. Earlier I felt fine. I'm just bruised up a bit. My main concern is Major Saunders. Have you heard anything about him yet?" The last time she asked was before they left Arizona, and at that time, they didn't have an update on his condition.

"Thanks to your quick thinking and actions, the doctors say he'll make a full recovery. But it might be a little while before he's up in the air again."

Hearing that brought a smile to her face. "I'm happy with that. Flying is a significant part of the Major's life."

Evans grinned. "As it is yours if I'm not mistaken. I remember your dad telling me all about your fascination with helicopters." He paused for a moment. "Clover, I know you went over some things with the Colonel, which he relayed to us. But if you're up for it, we'd like to ask you a few follow-up questions."

She leaned back into the cushions. She looked down at the plate of food on her lap, and suddenly she didn't feel all that hungry anymore. She leaned forward and set the plate on the coffee table.

She swallowed the large lump that suddenly formed in her throat. She had prepared herself for this. She didn't want to talk about it anymore and just wanted to put it behind her. Even so, she knew she had to do it. It was her duty and responsibility to make sure those who broke the law and were trying to endanger the citizens of this country were brought to justice.

"Alright."

She glanced to her right at Merrick, unsure of what to say in front of him.

As if sensing her concern Evans spoke up. "Merrick is aware of the situation and accusations against Sergeant Hollis and Director Perkins. He also has top security clearance because of his job, so you can speak freely."

Accusations? The use of that word caught her off guard. She, without a doubt, wasn't spewing accusations. She leveled her gaze at Evans.

"They aren't accusations, sir. It's the truth. Both Sergeant Hollis and Director Perkins were involved. They were selling out their own country for profit. They were both traitors."

The anger she had hidden inside her started to show. Did they not believe her? For heaven's sake, she knew Evans. He, of all people, should know she wouldn't lie or throw a comrade under a moving bus unless she had a damn good reason for doing so.

"Nobody is saying you're lying. I'm trying to be dutiful and collect all the facts before the President of the United States goes slandering someone, especially individuals like Perkins and Hollis."

She understood what he was saying, but he wasn't there. He didn't go through the horrendous ordeal. He wasn't the one who was put into a position and forced to make a split-second decision to either live or die. Nor was he the one to endure an assault that could've resulted in being raped or killed. That was all her. She was the one who fought to survive to the point of taking the lives of other human beings.

Suddenly, she closed her eyes and lowered her head as that silent admission hit her square in the gut. As she opened her eyes, she stared at her hands folded in her lap. She had the blood of four men on those hands. What would people think of her? She blinked back tears as she thought about the ramifications and how people would judge her.

"Clover?"

Her name being called steered her back to the conversation. She looked up, seeing the three men staring at her with concerned expressions.

"What happened there?" Evans asked.

"What do you mean?"

"You completely blanked out for a moment."

She wouldn't admit her weakness. It would be challenging, but eventually, she'd come to grips with what she'd done and could only hope that others forgave her.

"I'm fine," she quipped, and Evans looked as if he wasn't going to accept her answer. He narrowed his eyes, ready to argue when a knock at the door interrupted him.

Merrick stood and went to see who it was. Moments later, she heard Colonel Jenkins's booming voice. When the hulking Colonel strode into the room, she stood up from the couch to greet him because even though she wasn't in uniform, she still respected him enough to give him a proper welcome.

"Sir," she greeted him.

To her astonishment, instead of responding verbally, he pulled her into one of the biggest hugs she'd ever received. Caught off guard by his gesture, she wasn't sure how to respond. In the four years she'd worked under his direction, he'd never shown affection toward any team member. In fact, many on the team were afraid of him because of his burly and no-nonsense demeanor.

When he released her, she took a step back and looked up at him, still taken aback by his uncharacteristic behavior.

"If you ever mention that I have a soft spot, I'll deny it," he told her. But she saw the corner of one side of his mouth lift slightly, revealing a hidden smile behind his stern and demanding disguise.

She offered a small smile in return. "Your secret is safe with me, Colonel."

Jenkins took a seat in the empty chair to her left. She was surrounded, and even though she knew she could trust the four men, she still felt anxious and distrusting. But that was to be suspected, right?

Evans cleared his throat and glanced in Jenkins' direction. "Before you arrived, we were just speaking with Clover regarding Sergeant Hollis and Director Perkins' involvement."

Clover decided to bring up the trust issue wreaking havoc on her. "Hearing what I did last night about what's been taking place, I don't know who to trust. And, that's a tough statement for me to admit, because I'm supposed to say that we all should trust every individual who takes an oath to protect and honor our nation." She ran her hand down her face, trying to find the words she was seeking. "I'm not naïve. I know backdoor deals occur probably more often than I think they do. But the problem I'm having a hard time dealing with is that I never imagined something like that would ever occur within my own team or even with people I know."

"I agree with you. We all should instill trust in our teammates and colleagues. Unfortunately, there are a few rotten eggs," Jenkins commented.

"Clover, so that you know, Sergeant Hollis has been under investigation for the last few months. But based on what you overheard, we know now that it was true. That it was him who was helping move the microchips."

Clover appeared shocked at that admission. She wondered if her name ever surfaced as being an accomplice. The thought of that didn't settle well in her stomach.

"Am I under investigation?" She thought to ask.

President Evans wanted to answer, but Jenkins held his hand up. "Sir, if you don't mind, I'd like to answer that, considering Captain Walker is under my directive, and I prefer she hears the truth from me."

Evans nodded for Jenkins to go ahead.

"Clover, when it comes to an issue of national security, know that everyone is scrutinized." He pointed at himself. "Even me. So, in short, yes, you and every other member of the SCU were investigated at some time or another over the last few months."

Evans followed up on Jenkins' comment. "But as of last night, you have my word that you are no longer part of the inquiry."

She exhaled, feeling the weight of an elephant being lifted off her shoulders.

In another show of his unusual compassion, Jenkins pointed to her plate of food on the coffee table.

"You haven't eaten?" He asked with a bit of fatherly concern.

"I'll eat after we talk."

"Be sure that you do," he advised before President Evans took back the conversation.

"Clover, I know this is hard for you to rehash, considering what you went through. And let me state right now, and I'm speaking on behalf of everyone in this room—that none of us can begin to understand what you endured last night. That being said, we're all in agreement with how damn proud of you we are. Your courage and act of bravery are to be commended. Your actions demonstrated the true meaning of a patriot."

She felt a tad bit awkward as she had never been comfortable with praise in a public environment. She was good with the Colonel saying "well done," but coming from the President in front of others embarrassed her. Most people would probably think she was foolish for feeling that way, but that's just who she was.

"Thank you, sir."

"If you're good, we'd like to ask you a few questions about last night. Again, this is just to clarify a few things."

She sat up straighter and tucked a strand of hair behind her ear. "Alright."

"You mentioned you saw a woman who left later on," Evans said.

"Yes. She's the one who shot Perkins."

"Were you able to catch a name, or can you give a description of her?"

"No. I don't recall anyone calling her by name. I only saw her for a brief moment. She was very tall, though, and appeared physically fit. Maybe brownish hair. Again, she was wearing a ball cap, so it was hard to tell."

Evans nodded as Caruso was jotting down something in a small notebook he had.

"Captain Walker, before any gunfire was exchanged, did you hear any mention of names or organizations?" Caruso asked.

She sat back, trying to remember what had caught her attention when she first came out of the restroom and heard the voices across the hall.

"Hollis' name being mentioned was what had caught my attention. Perkins and the other guy did mention someone named Skipper. In fact, they cited his name a few times. And how they used his name made me believe that Skipper was the person calling the shots."

She then turned her head and looked directly at Evans. "There was another reference to an individual, but no name was given. But one of them mentioned that there was someone in your inner circle feeding them information."

From the angry expression on his face, she could tell that Evans was trying to rein in his temper, but she couldn't blame him for being angry. Whoever was behind the sick and twisted plan needed to be stopped.

"Is there anything else you can think of?" Caruso asked.

She shook her head. "No. I'm sorry. That's all I heard before...."

She lowered her eyes to where her hands rested in her lap. She swallowed hard, recalling the hell she went through trying to survive the ordeal. As if sensing her uneasiness, President Evans got up and moved to sit next to her. He placed his hands over hers, and she looked up at him with her glistening eyes.

"You don't have to say any more, Clover. The pained expression on your face says it all. We get the gist of what happened."

She tried to smile at him, but it was weak. She appreciated his concern and compassion. And honestly, she wouldn't have expected anything less coming from him.

Just then, Caruso's phone rang, and he excused himself and walked into one of the other rooms.

While they waited for Caruso to return, Clover looked at Evans.

"What happens now?" She asked.

Evans sighed. "Well, to start, I have to make a public statement about Director Perkins. After that, we start digging into my inner circle for suspects."

"What about me?"

Evans sighed, and Clover didn't take it as a good sigh. "The main priority for you is keeping you safe."

"Safe? I don't understand."

"Clover, you're our only eyewitness. We don't know who's driving this operation. If they find out you're a witness, you could be targeted. Obviously, the person in charge of this sick operation has no problem eliminating people."

"I understand. But when you say to ensure my safety, what does that entail?"

"Clover, you need protection."

Protection? She reached for the water bottle on the table in front of her and took a drink. She needed more information on this protection thing.

"I can protect myself."

Evans shook his head. "No. I'm not putting your life at risk. We'll make some arrangements."

"Arrangements? You mean I can't go home?"

"Not until we know that you'll be safe."

"So what then? Do I stay here?"

Evans peered over at Merrick, and the regrettable look Merrick passed to Evans didn't sit well with Clover.

"The best bet right now is to place you in protective custody until we can sort this out."

Protective custody? Hearing that was like being punched in the gut. Would she have to go into hiding? Like a Witness Protection detail? *Oh, no.* There was no way she was entering a program like that, especially if government officials were involved in this operation and were the same people who could be searching for her. *No, thank you.* She'd rather take the chance at staying alive by isolating herself somewhere off the beaten path.

"I see the concern etched on your face. What are your thoughts about that?" Evans asked.

"Well, sir. Maybe I've watched too many shows and movies over the years, but inserting myself into WITSEC doesn't make me feel all warm and fuzzy. Plus, if I had to have protection, I'd rather it be with someone who I knew I could trust and was comfortable around."

"Like whom? It can't be anyone related to you."

Darn it! She had hoped to use one of her brothers. Who did she know well enough that she could trust her life with? Only one other man came to mind.

"Landon Davis. He's a Navy SEAL."

"Not a boyfriend or ex-boyfriend that someone can tie back to you?"

She shook her head. "No." She wasn't lying. Sleeping together one night didn't constitute dating. "He does serve with my brother Tripp Walker, and he knows my family. But he's someone I can trust to keep me safe."

Evans raised his eyebrows and looked to Merrick and Colonel Jenkins, asking for their input on her suggestion. Merrick nodded in agreement, and Colonel Jenkins gave his shoulder a slight shrug indicating he didn't have a problem with it.

"Okay, then. It's settled. We'll make the call and get Mr. Davis here."

"What about my family? Am I at least able to call them? My parents' anniversary is this weekend, and I'm supposed to be there." She looked toward Colonel Jenkins. "Remember, I had leave scheduled."

Evans gave her a pitying look, and she braced herself for his response.

"I'm sorry, Clover, but until we can unravel this mess, you're cut off from any communication with family, friends, and colleagues, except for those in this room."

"What does that mean?" She was starting to become a little flustered.

"It means we've placed your military status as MIA stemming from last night's incident. Unfortunately, your parents will be notified this afternoon."

Clover covered her mouth in shock as the words sunk in. "You mean my family will think I'm missing? Or that I could be dead?"

"I'm sorry, Clover, but this is the way it has to be until we know you're not a target."

This wasn't fair. She was just an innocent victim in the ordeal, so why should she have to sacrifice everything?

Caruso rejoined the group and sat back down. Clover didn't like the angry look on his face. Jesus, she couldn't bear any more troubling news.

"Judging from your angry expression, I guess that wasn't a good call," Evans said to Caruso.

"My team did find human remains inside what was left of the building at the airstrip. They've been sent to the FBI's forensic unit for identification. However, a partial ID was recovered near the body."

"An ID?"

"The name wasn't on it, but it was definitely one issued by the CIA."

"How long before they'd get the identification?"

"Not too long. They've already pulled dental records."

The talk about bodies and identification made Clover think about Sergeant Hollis. She turned toward Jenkins.

"Are they going to try and locate Hollis' body?" She asked him.

"We'll have a team investigate and try to locate it. But considering the area he disappeared, it could be challenging."

Caruso then spoke up and directed his comment at Evans. "My IT team also gained access to Hollis' email. We found the email with the orders from last night. It came through at exactly 1236 yesterday afternoon."

"What was the sender's email address?"

Evans licked his lip. "It came from your office."

Evans' eyebrows shot upward. "My office?"

"That's what they told me."

Evans ran his hand through his hair, clearly frustrated and caught off guard by Caruso's revelation.

"Well, it's pretty clear that it wasn't me, considering I knew nothing about this until I got the call from you, Colonel." Evans then pulled out his phone and flipped to his calendar. "At 1236, I was still at the Capital having lunch with several Senators and members of Congress." Evans glanced over at Merrick, who had been quiet up until now. "Merrick, you were there, and you had a visual on me the entire time. He can vouch for my whereabouts."

Merrick nodded. "He's telling the truth. The White House logbook can confirm when he arrived back at the White House."

"Mr. President, nobody here believes you're involved," Caruso admitted, and everyone agreed, including Clover, who was still trying to wrap her head around it.

A sudden wave of exhaustion came over Clover. She didn't want to hear anything else. All she wanted to do was lay down and be alone for a while. She even wanted to cry, and that was saying something because she hated crying. She hated feeling weak. And weak was how she felt at the moment.

She looked at the men. "If you all don't mind, I'd like to lay down for a while."

Evans nodded, and so did the others. As she stood, she grabbed her bottle of water because she was going to need that to wash down the pain pill that the doctor had given her. Without that, she feared sleep wouldn't come easily.

ے

President Evans watched as Clover somberly left the room. He felt terrible, seeing how defeated she looked. He kept telling himself that they were only doing what was best for her. He could never live with himself if something happened to her when he could've done something to protect her.

As soon as he heard the bedroom door close and she was out of earshot, he turned toward the other three men still sitting.

"I don't know about the three of you, but I'm so pissed off right now that I could spit fucking nails. The audacity of someone to undermine this administration and their own country just to benefit themselves monetarily is unbecoming."

All three agreed. How could they not?

"What's the statement being given to the families?" Jenkins asked Evans.

"Eddie and I have agreed that we need to keep the details to a minimum. We will play this by the book and act like this were a classified mission. The statement will be short, saying that their helicopter is believed to have suffered mechanical failure, based on the communications with the crew prior to the control tower losing contact with them. We will not provide a location, but assure them that we are doing everything possible to locate the aircraft and crew." Evans was aware that Clover's family didn't know about her work with the SCU, and this was certainly a shitty way for them to find out. He'd try his best to keep her secret, but her dad and brothers were smart, and he knew it would only take them a short time to figure out something was up.

"What about Perkins?" Jenkins asked.

"I'll wait until we get a positive ID from forensics. Then I'll make a statement to everyone."

"Everyone?" Caruso asked, his eyebrows raised.

"At least the cabinet and senior advisors to start with. Sooner or later, the CIA Director's absence will be noticed. Plus, maybe we use this to our advantage."

"How so?" Caruso asked.

"According to what Clover overheard, we know there's at least one more person involved, possibly two who are deep in my inner circle. If we get everyone lumped into one room and disclose some details about the situation, we might be able to get a read on some people."

Merrick nodded. "I like it. But there are only four of us. How are we supposed to keep an eye on twenty-five other people?"

Turning toward Merrick, Evans said, "We'll need some reinforcements." And Evans knew just who to call.

"I recognize that look. Who did you have in mind?"

"An old friend," Evans said with a sly grin.

Merrick's eyes widened with clarity. "Tink?"

Evans nodded. "He's the best in the business. His company Rockwell Inc. receives almost half of the government contracts that require skills like this, amongst other qualities."

Tink was a former SEAL. When he retired from the SEALs, he formed his own elite security company in Virginia Beach. They did a variety of work ranging from personal security to classified black ops for the government. His staff was extremely skilled and deadly.

Colonel Jenkins scrunched his bushy brows together. "I've heard of Rockwell, but I'm not familiar with them."

"Tink and his team are one badass group. They take jobs the government doesn't want to dip its feet into. Tink's a former SEAL, and many of his employees are former military and law enforcement. If anyone can sniff out a traitor, it's Tink."

Evans stood up. "I'll give the SECNAV a call in a few minutes. I'll need his help in getting in touch with Mr. Davis' commander."

"What are you going to tell him since we're trying to be limited in the information we're giving out?" Jenkins asked.

"That Mr. Davis is needed for an assignment. I'll have Monika look at my schedule for either Sunday late afternoon or Monday morning and get a meeting on the books. I'll send her a list of who I want there. I'll also get with Gale in the press office to get a statement prepared to release after I brief the Cabinet."

At that moment, Caruso's phone chimed with an incoming text. Evans waited as Caruso read the message. When he finished, he looked at Evans.

"The main guy Captain Walker heard talking with Perkins is a rogue CIA operative."

"What?" Evans blurted out.

"His name is Roy Blanyard. At least, that was the name he used when he worked for the agency eight years ago. During a covert operation in the Middle East, some heavy shit went down, and Blanyard went missing. My team found several passports in the plane with Blanyard."

"Holy shit! And what about the other guys? Was your team able to identify any of them?"

"Not yet, but they're working on it. They're running faces and fingerprints through databases as we speak. If they were involved in something this big, then I'm sure they've had previous run-ins with law enforcement on some scale. I'm confident we'll get a match."

With all the information coming together, maybe they'd be able to wrap this up faster than Evans thought.

CHAPTER THIRTEEN

Joker sat in the passenger seat as Bear drove them to his parents' house from the airport. He looked out the side window as they passed through the small downtown area. He loved coming up here with Bear and enjoyed spending time with the Walkers. He felt as if he was a part of their family, and they treated him that way.

He was an only child, and his parents were jet-setters. Eleven months out of the year, they spent traveling. So, if he ever wanted to see them, he had to plan around their schedule, which was difficult since his schedule was constantly revolving. He never knew when the government would send him out. In fact, it had been almost two years since he'd seen his parents in person. His mom would FaceTime now and then when convenient for her. His dad, on the other hand, was a different story. He didn't have a great relationship with him. All through high school, his dad had pushed for him to follow in his footsteps and attend MIT to pursue a degree in nuclear engineering. Joker wasn't interested in college life. Since his pre-teen years, after a field trip to Patriot's Point near Charleston, South Carolina, he knew he wanted to join the Navy. He never considered the SEALs until he was pulled aside during recruit training at Great Lakes and asked if he was interested in seeing if he had what it took. And now, here he was. He wouldn't trade the teams for anything.

"God, I miss this place," Bear spoke aloud as he drove.

Joker looked around, enjoying the country landscape. "It's a nice change of scenery, not to mention peaceful."

Joker loved Virginia Beach and what it all had to offer, but sometimes it was nice to just get away with nature. And, this part of Tennessee certainly wasn't lacking nature.

"Hey, I've been meaning to ask you. Did my sister get a hold of you?" Bear asked out of the blue, catching Joker off guard.

He wasn't going to lie. "She texted me last night."

Bear glanced his way with a questionable look in his eyes. "What did she want?"

Errr... "She didn't say. She wanted to know if I could talk, but I was getting ready to walk into Bayside to meet Jay Bird and Nails. I asked her if I could call her later, and she said sure. But then, a few minutes later, I got another text from her saying that something came up at work and that she'd probably be late."

Bear wrinkled his forehead. "That's weird. What did you say to that?"

"I told her if it was important to call when she could."

"And did she?"

Joker bit the inside of his cheek so he wouldn't express his disappointment. He had waited up all night for her call. And when she didn't, he couldn't help but think she had blown him off once again. But, she had said something unexpected had come up, so he'd give her the benefit of the doubt and let her explain when he saw her before making any judgment.

"No. She never called."

Bear snorted and shook his head. "Sometimes, that girl scares me." Then he grinned. "I can't wait until my brothers find out she was in Djibouti."

Joker winced. Again, he felt bad for Clover. Having four brothers in the Special Forces had to be hard, especially the Walkers. They were all hard men, but damn good soldiers.

He entertained himself the rest of the way, thinking about Clover and what the weekend would hold for them. He loved that she was an outdoors type of woman. He knew her favorites were scuba diving and hiking. Maybe they could drive to one of the nearby hiking trails and spend one of the days hiking to one of the hidden waterfalls the

Tennessee mountains held. At least there in the woods, she couldn't run from him. And honestly, they needed to talk.

He was going to be thirty-three this year, and he wasn't getting younger. He always imagined having a family of his own, but knew the difficulties in finding the right woman because of his career.

Like most guys in his shoes, early in his career, he fooled around and had his fair share of hook-ups, but over time he realized he wanted more than just casual sex with someone he'd probably never see again. He'd been waiting for the day when he'd meet that certain woman and just know she was meant for him. That day had been two years ago when Clover nestled her way into his heart.

If things worked out in his favor, Joker knew he and Clover would have to break the news to Bear. Hopefully, he'd be okay with it and be happy for them. If not, they would have a problem because once he had Clover in his grasp, he wouldn't let her slip away again.

The car began to slow as Bear made the turn onto the gravel road where the Walkers lived. Joker's nervousness increased the closer they got to the gray two-story farmhouse.

Seeing Clover and kissing her in Djibouti dug up many emotions that he had hoped to keep buried. But the moment he held her in his arms again, he realized those feelings were spot-on. He and Clover were meant for each other. Even though she tried to deny it, she felt the powerful bond between them. When she gripped his waist and held on as he made love to her mouth, it had taken all his willpower not to throw her over his shoulder and take her back to her CHU and love her the way she deserved to be.

As they made the turn into the driveway, Joker saw the white sedan parked in front of the house before Bear did.

"Are those government plates on that car?"

Bear pulled up alongside the vehicle and looked.

"Looks like it. It's probably one of Dad's buddies. They come out now and then to say hi."

"Your dad knows everyone."

Bear gave him an annoyed smirk. "I know. Sometimes that's a good thing, and other times not so much."

They both exited the car and grabbed their bags from the back seat. As they walked up the sidewalk to the large wraparound porch, Joker noticed a bunch of other vehicles parked in the driveway along the side of the house, but assumed they belonged to Bear's brothers and Clover.

As soon as Bear pushed open the front door, the aroma of Bear's mom's secret barbeque sauce poured out, hitting Joker's nose and making his mouth water. He loved his barbeque, especially when it was smothered in Jenelle's tangy secret sauce, which she made from scratch. He had tried to bribe her once for the recipe, but she wouldn't cave.

They both set their bags down in the entryway, and Bear called out to his parents.

"Mom, Dad, we're here."

The house had an open floor plan, with the large open modular kitchen as the focal point. Jenelle loved to cook while entertaining, but she hated being secluded in the kitchen. So, when the Walkers decided to remodel their home a few years ago, her one wish was for the kitchen to be open so she could be a part of the conversations when they were entertaining.

Just as they got to the kitchen, they were met by Zach, Bear's youngest brother. Out of the four Walker brothers, Zach was the most content one. He wore a smile on his face wherever he went. So, Joker knew immediately that something was up when Zach met them, appearing somewhat panicked but subdued. Whatever it was, it was out of character for Zach.

"Tripp, we've been trying to call you," Zach stated, using Bear's given name and not his callsign.

Bear pulled out his cell phone from his pocket. "Shit, I forgot to turn it back on when we got off the plane. What's going on?"

Zach swallowed hard as he ran his hand over his buzz cut.

"It's Clover."

Bear squinted his eyes. "What about Clover?"

Ethan, Bear's second youngest brother, appeared and waved them into the family room just before Zach answered. Joker didn't miss the dismal look on Ethan's face, and he started to wonder what was going on and what it had to do with Clover.

As they stepped into the family room, Joker saw Jenelle sitting on the couch being consoled by Ray, Bear's dad, while Justin, Bear's older brother, stood behind the sofa with his arms crossed. His expression didn't fare well either.

As he continued his peruse of the room, his eyes landed on a stranger dressed in Marine Corps dress blues, sitting in the chair adjacent to Jenelle, and he was holding her hand.

The only person missing was Clover. Right at that moment, Jenelle looked up, and as soon as Joker saw the grief and pain etched on her face, along with her red and puffy eyes, he understood what was unfolding. His heart shattered into a million pieces in a blink of an eye.

There was no way that Clover was gone.

Joker tried to blink back the tears, flooding his eyes, but it was useless to try because he couldn't stop them. As soon as he'd wipe one away, another one would fall.

Ray stood up. "Tripp, Joker, this is Sergeant Franklin from the Casualty Assistance Office."

The Sergeant stood and shook Bear and Joker's hands.

"I wish I was here with better news."

Watching Bear and seeing the fear in his eyes as he took in the Sergeant's words nearly brought Joker to his knees. Joker kept trying to gulp down the lump lodged in his throat, but it wouldn't budge. He was too choked up.

Bear looked at his dad, his eyes full of sadness, anger, and questions.

"Is she...I mean, did she...." It tore at Joker's heart listening to Bear struggle to even say the words everyone feared.

"We don't have confirmation yet. All we know is that the control tower lost all communication with the helicopter and crew. They believe it went down when they encountered bad weather," Ray calmly explained, and Joker wondered how Ray was still keeping his shit together. Joker knew the father and daughter dynamic between Ray and Clover was powerful. Even though Clover was a Marine, she was still the apple of her daddy's eye. Anyone could see the bond between them when they were together.

Bear reared his head back as if someone had slapped him. His brows were knitted in a frown.

"Helicopter? Where did it happen? Have they found the wreckage?" He fired off the questions faster than Joker could double-tap his rifle.

The Sergeant stepped forward. "Due to the sensitivity surrounding the flight operation, we cannot disclose the location. I know this is hard for you and your family, but know that the government is doing all they can to locate and bring the crew home."

Joker stood back and listened carefully. If what he heard was correct, then they hadn't found a body. Maybe there was still hope that she was alive. *She had to be.*

Bear scrunched his face up in anger, and he responded to the Sergeant's comment.

"Are you saying that my sister was involved in a classified flight operation? She's a goddamn mechanic. Why the fuck was she even up in the air?" His voice grew louder, and then he paused, covering his eyes with his hand. A few seconds later, he looked at his family. "I just saw her two weeks ago," he said in a much softer tone, appearing to be at his wit's end. It was a side of Bear that Joker had never seen. He sensed Bear was about to lose his shit, and that wasn't what the family needed right now. They all needed to stay positive and be strong—for Clover's sake.

"I am sorry, but I have no further details. I'll leave you my card, and if any information comes in concerning Captain Walker, I'll be in contact," Sergeant Franklin said to Ray and handed him the business card.

Bear moved to question the Sergeant again, but Joker stepped forward and placed his hand on Bear's shoulder. Bear glared at him, and when Joker saw the unshed tears in Bear's eyes, he felt his pain and grief. He just felt it differently. Whereas they were her family, Clover was the love of Joker's life.

After the Sergeant left, the house became eerily quiet until Bear looked at his dad and brothers before taking a deep breath.

"Something's not right. Don't ask me why or how, but I can feel it. What would Clover be involved in that she'd be on a classified flight? She fixes helicopters, for Christ's sake."

Joker could sense the frustration and fear in everyone in the room, including himself.

Ray shrugged his shoulders. "Your guess is as good as mine, son. I don't know, but I agree with you. They know more than they're saying."

"So, what do we do?" Ethan asked.

"I can try and make a few calls, but if they're being tight-lipped, I don't know what else to do but wait for answers."

Justin huffed out an annoyed grunt. "This is bullshit. Our sister is considered MIA, but the government won't tell us where?"

"I understand your frustration, Justin. But we all know how this works." Ray stated.

Ethan turned toward Bear.

"You said you saw her two weeks ago. How did she seem? Between all of us, we know many people in San Diego. Maybe we can ask around."

Bear shot Joker a look. He wasn't sure what to say. He gave Bear a pointed look, telling him it was his call whether or not to tell them about Africa.

Bear cleared his throat before looking at his dad. "When was the last time you spoke with Clover?"

Ray looked at Jenelle. "Maybe four or five weeks ago?" He turned back at Bear. "Why?"

"Did she ever mention that she was being deployed?"

From the initial reaction of Ray's widened eyes and gaping mouth with no words, it was clear that the answer was no.

"Deployed? No. She never mentioned anything about being deployed to me." He looked at Jenelle again. "Did she say anything to you?"

Jenelle shook her head as she continued to sniffle. "No. When I asked her how work was, she said that everything was fine, except for the many late nights she was having to work."

Bear threw another look at Joker out of the corner of his eye before turning back to his family.

"Joker and I saw Clover two weeks ago." Joker saw Bear biting the inside of his cheek. He was still pissed that Clover had volunteered herself to go to Africa. "She was in Djibouti."

Everyone was silent as Bear's admission sunk in. Until Justin shouted, making Jenelle flinch.

"Djibouti?! As in Djibouti? Africa?"

Bear nodded. "To say we were shocked when one of our buddies mentioned that a certain blonde hair, hazel-eyed helicopter mechanic with a unique name had caught the attention of many men on the base was an understatement."

"Clover?" Zach asked, sounding like he couldn't believe she'd gone there.

"I wasn't happy for several reasons. Once I found her by the hangars, she and I talked for a few minutes, and then about an hour later, we had breakfast together with the rest of the team. We didn't have a lot of time to catch up." Bear glanced at Joker. "What—about an hour if that?"

Joker nodded, backing up Bear's claim.

"How did she seem?" Justin questioned.

"She looked okay. Maybe a little tired, but I don't know the hours she works."

Okay? Joker thought to himself as he listened to Bear. In his opinion, Clover never looked better. But then again, he saw her differently.

"She told me she was tired of the repetitiveness in San Diego, and when the opportunity arose, and her CO asked for volunteers to help at a few of the forward operating bases because of staff shortages, she raised her hand. I believe her exact words were, 'I wanted to see the world.'"

"What the fuck! I can think of many other places I'd rather see than Djibouti," Ethan said, annoyed at his sister's stubbornness.

Joker grunted and added his comment. "That's what we told her."

"Dad, did the Sergeant say how many other crew members were on board?" Bear asked.

Ray thought about it, then shook his head. "No. I don't believe I heard him say. Why?"

"Just curious."

Joker began to think about the situation more in-depthly. He thought about the media. In this day and age, the media had ways of getting the scoop on almost anything. How was it that a military helicopter goes down with a crew uncounted for, but nobody has reported on it? Then another thought hit him. Clover was in San Diego last night. She had texted him telling him that something at work had come up. The Sergeant did say that the helicopter went down in bad weather. Joker thought about the timing of everything, taking into account Clover's location, and a scenario started to form.

"Joker, I see you thinking over there. What's on your mind?" Ray asked.

"I got a text from Clover last night around 2200 East Coast time, which would've been 1900 West Coast time." Joker ignored the raised eyebrows he got from Justin, Zach, and Ethan.

"What did she text you about?" Ray asked.

"She wanted to see if I was available to talk, but I was at Bayside with Jay Bird and Nails, so I texted her back and asked if I could call her when I was finished. She told me no problem. But a few minutes later, she texted again, saying that something came up at work and she'd be late getting home. I told her it was fine and to call when she could."

"Did she?" Justin probed.

"Nope. But that's not all. If she was in San Diego and even late getting home, she still couldn't have traveled that far. The weather could give us a clue as to where she could have been."

"I'm not following," Ethan stated.

"Last night, while I was at Bayside, the news station on TV showed a nasty weather system moving up through Mexico and into the Arizona and New Mexico area. Sergeant Franklin said the helicopter went down in bad weather."

"Alright. What else ya got?" Ray stated.

"I find it hard to believe that there have been no reports in the news about a helicopter going down, especially when a crew is missing. Even if it was classified, the media has a way of sniffing out a story, even if it's just a sliver of something for them to report on. But in this case, there's been nothing. Not even a blip."

Bear looked at his dad and brothers. "He's got a point. It does seem odd that there's been no media attention drawn to it."

Jenelle stood from the couch, grabbing her husband's arm. "All I care about right now is finding my baby. She's out there somewhere."

Joker agreed wholeheartedly with Jenelle. Clover was out there somewhere. He just hoped that she was alive.

As Ray took Jenelle into the kitchen, Bear motioned to Joker and his brothers to follow him outside. Joker felt his phone vibrate as they made their way onto the back porch. He pulled it from his pocket, and as soon as he saw it was Derek, his CO, his gut clenched. He excused himself and walked further out into the yard to take it.

"Commander?"

"Joker, I tried to catch you before you and Bear took off. Have you guys settled at his parents' place yet?"

"Yeah, we arrived a little while ago, but we walked into a shit show."

"What happened?" Derek asked, sounding concerned.

Joker ran his hand through his thick hair. Jesus, even saying it was hard.

"Clover, Bear's sister. She's been listed as MIA. The Casualty Assistance Officer was just here to notify the family."

"Oh fuck! What did they say?"

Joker explained what they knew, and even the commander sounded perplexed by the situation.

"I thought she was a mechanic?"

"She is. That's what everyone's trying to wrap their brain around. That and the fact that she may have been involved in something classified."

"Shit…Tell the family that if there's anything we can do, we're just a phone call away. I'll let the others know, and Ace and his team."

"Thank you, sir. Since you weren't aware of Clover's situation, I'm guessing you called me for another reason."

"I am, and I hate to make matters worse there, but I need you on a plane to Washington."

Joker had started to walk back toward the others, but stopped short upon hearing that.

"Washington?"

"I just got off the phone with the SECNAV. The President has specifically requested your presence."

"Me? For what?"

"Beats the fuck out of me. The SECNAV called, gave me the orders, and when I asked about it, he said it was need to know, and apparently, I'm not in the know." Joker heard the frustration in Derek's voice, and he understood. If he were in charge and someone requested a member of his team, he'd probably want to know why.

"What about the team? We were due back Monday for rotation."

"Your spot will be covered in your absence. Don't worry about that."

"Alright. When do I need to be in Washington?"

"The SECNAV's office chartered a plane for you out of Tri-Cities Regional. It's on standby, ready to leave as soon as you show up."

Joker looked at his watch. Shit, it would take about an hour to get to the airport. He hated to ask Bear for a ride, but he didn't have any other choice since they rode together.

"I guess I can't say no to the Commander in Chief."

"No. Unless you want to lose your job. Send me the address of the Walkers, and I'll arrange for a car to pick you up. With this Clover situation, I don't want to burden the family."

"Alright. I'll be waiting."

"Joker?"

"Yeah?"

"As I said, I don't know what in the hell is going on, but know that if you need anything, you call me. Got it?"

"Yes, sir."

"Call me when you can."

"Will do, sir."

Joker disconnected the call and ran his hand through his hair again. Jesus, if he kept doing that, he was going to pull all his hair out before he was forty. He glanced toward the porch where Bear and his brothers stood talking.

Fuck. He wished he didn't have to leave, but he had no choice. And to add fuel to the fire, he didn't have a single clue what the President wanted him for.

He walked back and climbed the steps. Bear looked at him.

"Everything good?"

Joker shook his head. "That was the commander. Apparently, I'm being summoned to Washington."

Bear's forehead wrinkled. "Washington? For what?"

Joker threw his hands in the air. "I have no idea, and neither does Derek. The SECNAV called him and told him that the president requested my presence."

"That's odd," Justin stated as he crossed his arms and leaned back against the railing.

"You aren't kidding."

"When do you need to be there?" Bear asked.

"The SECNAV's office chartered a plane for me out of Tri-Cities. I let Derek know what was going on here, and he said they would send a car so you don't have to leave. He said to keep him in the loop on the situation and that if you need anything, let him know."

Bear nodded his head.

Joker felt bad. He cared for Clover. Hell, he cared for the whole family, and the last thing he wanted to do was leave them when they needed the support.

"Bear, I'm sorry."

Bear shook his head. "Don't be sorry. You can't ignore an order from the President." He motioned toward his brothers. "We were talking and thinking about what you said. We're going to call some people we know out in San Diego and see if they've heard anything."

"Let me know if you find out anything."

"Of course."

A horn honked out front about ten minutes later, indicating the ride was there. *Damn, that was fast,* he thought.

After grabbing his bags and saying bye to Jenelle and Ray, he climbed into the back seat of the sedan, closed his eyes, and prayed that by the time he made it to Washington, Clover would be found.

CHAPTER FOURTEEN

Upon Joker's arrival at Ronald Regan Washington National Airport, he was met on the tarmac by a car agency sent by the White House.

Clover's situation was still weighing heavily on his mind. However, he was a little skeptical about this trip. Something big had to be going down for the SECNAV not to tell Derek. And why would they want him?

He pulled out his phone and texted Bear.

Joker: *Any news?*

Bear: *No. Made some calls and waiting to hear back. Are you in D.C.?*

Joker: *Just got here. I'll give you a call later tonight once I find out what's happening here.*

Bear: *Copy that.*

Joker took in the sights of the city as the car drove past the Capitol and House and Senate buildings. He loved visiting D.C. and taking in all it offered, from the monuments to the museums.

The car drove a few more blocks downtown before turning into a large swanky hotel parking lot. Instead of pulling up to the main entrance, the car entered an underground parking garage connected to the hotel. That was when Joker became a bit leery. As the vehicle slowed to a stop, a gentleman dressed in a dark suit and tie emerged from the hotel and opened his door.

"Senior Chief Davis, welcome. I'm Special Agent Merrick. I oversee the President's protection detail."

Joker was caught off guard by the greeting but played off the shock as he extended his hand out in greeting.

"Pleasure to meet you."

"If you'll follow me, I'll show you up to your room."

His room? Joker grabbed his bag and exited the vehicle, following Merrick through the hotel's back door. By now, his brain was on overload. He had no idea what in the hell was going on, but he'd go along with it, considering he was here on the President's orders.

The entrance they used took them through the hotel's staff areas, passing the large laundry facility and the stock room where they kept all the complimentary toiletries for the rooms. At the end of the long hallway, they came to an elevator with a sign that read "Hotel Staff Only." When the doors opened, Merrick motioned for Joker to enter.

Joker wouldn't admit it out loud, but he wasn't a fan of elevators. Taking the stairs held a better appeal to him. At least if something went wrong in a stairwell, there were more options of getting out.

Special Agent Merrick joined him, then withdrew a room key card from his inside jacket pocket and inserted it into the narrow slot above the floor buttons. When the green light appeared, he pressed the button labeled PH, which Joker assumed was the floor for the penthouse. That piqued his curiosity even more so. Why were they taking him to the freaking penthouse of a five-star hotel?

As the elevator ascended, it gave a bit of time to study the Agent sharing the small space with him. He was thankful for the various forms of training that he endured in the SEALs that many people would consider boring—one of those times being now. Having the ability to read body language gave him an advantage over his enemies. Not that he considered Special Agent Merrick an enemy, but judging from his demeanor to the power behind his speech made Joker wonder if the Agent had previous military training himself.

He couldn't explain it, but something deep within Merrick's dark eyes added to his mystery. He'd seen the familiar hollowness and blankness in many of his teammates' eyes and expressions. But in Merrick's eyes, there laid a hawk with keen eyesight that kept watch over everything.

Joker took his eyes off Merrick to glance at the panel as it flashed the number twenty and chimed, indicating they had reached their intended floor.

As the elevator doors opened to what Joker would describe as a foyer, his eyes couldn't help but travel beyond the entryway to the penthouse's welcoming, bright, and airy open floor plan. The Art Deco-inspired design and décor were not only eye-catching but exquisite.

As he walked further into the space, he took in more of what the penthouse offered. From the expensive crystal and marble, along with the whimsical artworks adorning the walls to the soaring views out of the floor to ceiling windows reaching the Potomac River, proved that the penthouse was the hotel's crown jewel.

Walking into the heart of the living space, he set his bag down next to the sofa before moving over to the windows to take in the amazing view of D.C.'s nightlife. He whistled under his breath in amazement.

He heard a door close on the other side of the penthouse, followed by men's voices. Heavy footsteps approaching had him turning around, waiting to see who it was. Moments later, Merrick returned alongside President Evans. *Holy shit!* Derek hadn't been joking when he said the President specifically requested him.

President Evans approached with his hand out. "Senior Chief Davis, I'm Rick Evans."

Joker reached out and shook his hand. "Mr. President, it's an honor to meet you."

Evans offered a small smile. "Likewise. May I call you Joker? The SECNAV said it was your callsign." He gestured toward the sofa. "Come on over and have a seat. I appreciate you dropping everything and coming out here on such short notice."

Joker found a seat on the sofa. "Yes, Sir. Joker's fine. And it's not every day I get a call from my commander telling me I'm wanted in Washington."

Evans chuckled. "Technically, it wasn't me who summoned you. I mean, I made the call to the SECNAV, but it was someone else who asked for you."

Joker tilted his head. He couldn't think of anyone who would've asked for him to travel to D.C.

Evans' expression grew grim as if a switch was flipped.

"I understand from the SECNAV that you were at Ray and Jenelle Walker's house when you received the call from your CO."

Joker pressed his lips firmly together. It didn't surprise him that the President knew about Clover. He was the Commander in Chief. It was his job to know those things.

"Yes, Sir."

"The Walkers are very good friends of mine. I haven't had the opportunity to reach out to them yet. I'm sure they're beside themselves with the news they were dealt with today."

And just like that, that damn annoying lump in his throat had returned. *It wasn't just her family who was distraught;* he wanted to say.

"Her dad and brothers are taking it better than her mom," Joker expressed.

Evans took a deep breath before releasing it, and Joker braced himself for the worse news. *Jesus, don't let that be it. Don't let Clover be dead.*

"Joker, what's about to be said here goes no further than the individuals in this room."

"I understand, Sir."

"I can tell you're also upset with the news about Captain Walker."

Joker nodded.

"The Walkers are like family to me. So, yeah, I'm just as upset as they are." Not to mention Clover was the woman he loved. "I'll be honest with you, her dad, brothers, and I are a little curious why a helicopter mechanic was on a classified flight."

Evans' eyes widened, and Joker could tell he'd caught him by surprise. It also told Joker that there was definitely more to the story than they were letting on.

"Who said she was on a classified flight?" Evans asked, trying to play it cool. But Joker wasn't born yesterday.

"Sir, we're all Special Forces, and we know the protocols. When a family is notified that their loved one is MIA and the Casualty Assistance Officer can't provide a lot of details, including where the incident took place, it tends to raise a lot of questions."

Evans ran his hand through his hair nervously, or maybe it was just frustration.

"I never thought about that," he admitted. "Look, Captain Walker's incident is a very delicate situation."

Joker found it interesting that Evans didn't deny that it was a classified mission. But he was also curious as to how Clover was even involved.

"How so?" Joker asked.

"It disgusts me to even say this, but it's come to light that a group of individuals—government employees,, might I add, have been using their power and government resources to traffic weapons and sell them to the highest bidder."

Evans went on to explain in detail how with the help of the FBI, they quietly launched an investigation and found a possible connection to the SCU, which then prompted a full probe of the entire unit—ultimately leading to one particular soldier who the FBI had been tracking.

As Joker listened, he couldn't help but feel angry and disgusted. Treason was a serious crime, not to mention just plain wrong. But what pissed Joker off even more was learning that a member of the United States military was involved, and even worse, they were putting weapons into the hands of their known enemies. Joker wondered how many of their own had been killed from the weapons sold. It also made him wonder how any of this had to do with Clover.

As Evans continued to speak about a shipment of weapons delivered last night to a small airstrip in the Arizona desert, Joker began to put two and two together. Was Evans insinuating that Clover was involved in arms trafficking? *No fucking way!*

His expression must have shown what he had been thinking because just as Joker wanted to speak in Clover's defense, Evans spoke up again.

"That didn't come out correctly. Yes, Clover was involved in the incident last night. But she wasn't a willing participant in the deal going down. I chalk it up to one of those times of being at the wrong place at the wrong time. However, I have to say that if it weren't for her, we wouldn't have as much to go on as we do now."

Hearing Evans talk about Clover in the past tense was upsetting. He was biting his lip to keep his emotions in check, but it was difficult. Joker wanted to get to the part about Clover's involvement, but he needed to clarify some information because his head was spinning with everything Evans just threw at him.

"So, the guy that was moving the microchips is a member of the SCU?"

"He *was* a member of the SCU," Evans clarified.

"Was?"

"He went missing a few weeks ago. Initially, we thought he went AWOL. However, with the help of an eyewitness, evidence points to him being murdered."

"Jesus Christ. So, you have the suspect in custody then?"

"Not exactly."

"Why the hell not?"

"Because he's dead, too."

Joker stared at Evans, appearing dumbfounded. Then he started to wonder where this was even going and his purpose for being there.

"Sir, I mean no disrespect, but how does my presence factor into this situation?"

Evans chuckled, which surprised Joker, considering the seriousness of the situation.

"You're going to see to it that our star witness is protected for a few days, or until we can get a better handle on the investigation and hopefully smoke out the individuals running the show."

Personal protection duty? Joker had to hold back the urge to cringe. He despised personal protection duty. And maybe that was because the few times he was tasked with the role, it had been a nightmare. It was hard to offer protection when the person you were trying to protect didn't want to listen, or complained all the time.

"Before you tell me who the lucky person is, can you provide a little more information on Clover's situation? I'd just like to get a better understanding of what happened. We were told that the helicopter she was in lost contact with the control tower when they encountered bad weather and was believed to have gone down. As I said before, we weren't given any location or any explanation on why she was in the helicopter in the first place."

"I could, but I promised Clover that I'd let her explain the details to you."

Joker was looking down at his hands, but his head snapped up upon hearing Evans' words.

"What did you just say?"

Evans grinned. "I said that I promised Clover I'd let her explain everything."

"I'm not following," Joker expressed, looking at Evans for answers.

"Clover is alive, Joker. You're here because she specifically asked for you."

It was good that Joker was already sitting down, or he may have had to pick himself up off the floor after Evans delivered that bombshell. He wasn't sure what to think or how to react, considering just a few hours ago, he was told that the woman he loved was MIA, only to hear now that she was alive and safe.

Joker looked at Evans, a smile hanging on his lips. He couldn't hide his happiness. "Clover's alive? You're serious?" He asked again, making sure he heard Evans correctly.

"I wouldn't joke about something like that. Yes, Clover is alive."

Joker blew out a big breath. "I don't understand. Why tell her family she's MIA?"

"We had to. For her protection. She's the only eyewitness we have."

Joker was almost afraid to ask what she had witnessed. It had to have been something pretty significant for Evans to shield her from the public eye.

"What did she witness?"

"Arms trafficking, admission to murder, and murder."

"Holy shit," Joker uttered before raking his fingers through his hair.

"She witnessed the murder of Clayton Perkins."

Joker gave his head a small shake before addressing Evans. "Are you talking about CIA Director Clayton Perkins?"

Evans nodded. "Yeah. He was a guilty party in the arms trafficking. And, according to Clover, he's also responsible for the murder of another involved party we were tracking."

Joker wouldn't put anything past Clayton Perkins. Many people didn't like him, more so the Special Forces community, because he was known to take matters into his own hands, which usually resulted in botched missions. He was also a nasty son of a bitch, who would probably throw his own mother under a bus just to save face.

"Where exactly did this happen?"

"At an airstrip in the Arizona desert." Evans also explained Hollis' role in the situation.

Joker ran his hands down his face. Everything that Evans had thrown at him was a lot to take in. But the most important news, which was the best news, was that Clover was alive.

"Now you see why Clover's safety is a priority. If the person in charge catches wind that Clover's testimony could put them in jail, there's a good possibility she'd be hunted down."

Joker hadn't thought about that. He hadn't thought about much in the last few hours because he was only focused on Clover's situation.

Evans paused for a moment. "We gave her a choice. Either she went into WITSEC until we smoked out the culprits, or she had the option to choose a non-relative who she felt comfortable with and could protect her." Evans smiled. "She chose you."

Joker thought his heart would burst. To hear that she was given a choice to pick who she wanted to protect her, and she had chosen him, offered him hope.

"What about her family? How long before they'll find out that she's okay?"

"It all depends on where the investigation takes us. You must know that it's killing me to have them think that their daughter and sister is missing. The sooner I can give them the good news, the better."

Joker agreed. But now, knowing a little more of the story, he understood the reasoning.

"Where is she now?" Joker asked. He was anxious to see her and confirm that was she really okay.

"She's asleep in the bedroom. I'll warn you now. She's a little banged up, though she'd tell you she was feeling like a champ if you ask her. She saw and went through a lot last night, though I do think she held back on some things she talked about."

Joker wasn't surprised by that. Clover was never one to fuss over herself. It was one of the things he loved about her.

"She's exhausted but was fighting to fall asleep. I think she may have taken the pain pill that the doctor gave her." Evans paused a moment before he continued. "Joker. Your credentials speak for themselves. I trust she'll be in good hands until we figure this out."

"What if that information doesn't pan out?"

Evans smirked. "Oh, believe me. I'm confident it will. Someone will cave, and the dominos will start to fall when that happens."

A few minutes later, Evans walked Joker down the hall leading to the bedroom. Christ, he was nervous. His palms were even sweaty. It was so unlike him. But he was anxious to see her. He needed to see her with his own two eyes.

Evans opened the door, and as they entered the room, Clover's small frame came into view, and Joker could feel his knees buckle. Hearing she was alive was one thing, but physically seeing her was another.

He couldn't peel his eyes away from her as she lay curled up in a protective ball, as if trying to shield herself. She was out cold. When his eyes landed on the large bruise on her cheek, he had to fight back the anger.

"She's a special woman," Joker openly admitted as he stared down at her.

"She's special, alright. She's a secret weapon."

Joker glanced at Evans, thrown for a loop by his statement.

"Secret weapon?" He asked.

Evans shook his head while grinning. "I promised Clover I'd let her tell you. So, I'm keeping my word."

Now Joker was very curious. What was Clover up to?

Merrick knocked on the door. "We need to move her in three minutes," he stated, and Joker wondered what was happening. Were they not staying there at the penthouse?

Evans tried to wake Clover, but she wasn't budging. Obviously, the pill had done its job.

Joker then leaned over her and gently shook her shoulder, trying to wake her.

When she gave no response, Evans looked at Joker. "You're going to have to carry her."

Evans turned to Merrick. "Did you work things out with the hotel?"

Merrick nodded. "But we need to move now."

Joker could sense from Merrick's tone that it was essential to stay on whatever schedule they were working with.

Being as gentle as he could, Joker bent down and scooped Clover up in his arms. The only part of her body that moved was her head, resting snugly against his chest. Evans met them by the door and gently brushed her hair away from her face before he laid a small throw blanket over her.

"Merrick is working with the hotel security to have all the cameras switched off while we get her to the car."

"Car?" Joker questioned.

"There's a car parked right outside the door you'll exit from. Merrick will accompany you down, and then he'll get into a separate car that you'll follow to your destination."

"What's our final destination?" Joker asked.

"Merrick has all the details."

Joker cocked his head sideways. "You aren't going to tell me?"

Evans shook his head. "Not here," he stated and glanced around the suite. Joker understood the message Evans was delivering. There could be ears listening.

"Understood."

As Joker walked toward the door, Evans called out.

"Keep her safe, Joker."

Joker nodded at Evans, then followed Merrick out the door and the elevator. They didn't even have to wait. As soon as Merrick pressed the down button, the elevator doors opened, and they walked in. When the doors closed, Merrick turned toward Joker.

"As the President mentioned, hotel security has agreed to shut off the cameras to the hallway of the top floor, this elevator, the hall to the staff entrance, and the one right outside the door. They were giving us five minutes." He looked at his watch. "Now, we have approximately three and half minutes. Once we reach the basement level, we'll have to walk fast."

"I'm following your lead."

Merrick nodded just as the elevator pinged, signaling they had reached their stopping point. As soon as the doors opened, they hightailed it through the empty halls, and Joker wondered if Merrick had the security team clear the floor.

Merrick pushed open the door leading to the parking garage, and sitting idle in front of the door with the passenger door open was a tan Chevrolet Malibu with tinted windows.

"This is your car," Merrick told him and helped get Clover situated in the front seat. She was still asleep. Once they got her buckled in, Joker shut the door and went to the driver's side.

"Just stay close to me," Merrick instructed before heading to a dark grey Chevrolet Tahoe.

Joker jumped into the car and adjusted the seat. He took a quick glance over at Clover. Waves of hair were strung across her face. He reached over, brushed them back behind her shoulder, then gently caressed her cheek, careful to avoid the ugly bruise along her cheekbone. He was proud of her. She fought hard, and she won the battle. He couldn't ask for anything else. She was alive and under his protection now. There was no way he'd let anyone else get their hands on her.

ଈ

Joker followed closely behind Merrick's car as they approached the entrance to Camp David. Joker had to admit that it was a perfect place to lay low. Mountains and trees surrounded it, and it was guarded.

The drive had been uneventful and quiet, which was a good thing. Clover was still zonked out. She had barely moved during the drive.

Both cars came to a stop at the main gate. Joker watched as Merrick handed over some papers to the Marine on duty. After a few minutes, both Merrick and Joker were waved through.

Not many people knew that Camp David was actually a Naval Military base.

They drove the winding roads for what seemed like miles. They passed the main lodge where the President stayed, continuing down a gravel side road. About a mile further north, they turned right on a tree-lined driveway and drove back another fifty yards until the brake lights of Merrick's car glowed ahead of him, signaling that they were coming to a stop. Joker pulled up next to him and rolled the window down.

Merrick pointed to a newly built small cottage-type house that sat nestled against the trees. "This is it. You guys pull into the garage."

Joker nodded and went to pull forward when he noticed there wasn't a garage. There wasn't even a detached garage or a covered parking area. When he turned back to ask Merrick about it, he found Merrick grinning.

"I wanted to see if you saw it," Merrick said before tapping a button on his visor. Suddenly a magic show began right before Joker's eyes, as the siding on the right side of the house started to retract, revealing a single car garage door that lifted to allow Joker pull inside. Joker's jaw dropped. He'd seen some pretty creative shit during his career, but that right there topped it all.

"Go on and pull inside. I'll meet you there," Merrick called over to him. He still had a grin on his face.

Joker slowly rolled the car forward. Merrick parked his vehicle directly in front of the small porch leading to the front door.

Once they were inside the 007 garage, Joker turned the engine off, then reached over and gently rubbed Clover's shoulder. He hated to wake her, knowing she was exhausted. But the sooner he had her behind locked doors, the faster he'd feel better.

Her soft snores brought a small smile to his face. He softly ran his knuckles down her cheek. She stirred a bit and tried to turn onto her side, but the seat belt prevented her. He watched as her eyelids slowly started to open, revealing her gorgeous hazel eyes. Yes, this was a job first and foremost, but it was also an opportunity for him and Clover to have some uninterrupted time alone, and he was looking forward to it.

"We're here," Joker told her in a whispered voice.

He saw her wince as she tried to sit up, which upset him, knowing she was injured. She looked around, and her forehead wrinkled. When she looked at him, her eyes must've focused, and she realized who she was looking at because a tear slipped out of her eye and rolled down her cheek.

"You came," she said as her voice cracked.

He cupped her non bruised cheek with his palm and used his thumb to brush away the lone tear.

"I didn't really have a choice," he told her honestly. "When the President orders you to go, you go." Then he smiled. "But if I had known I was coming because of you, I still wouldn't have hesitated. I'll always be there for you, Clover."

She closed her eyes and leaned into his palm as if drawing warmth from his touch. When her eyes opened and met his, he could feel the energy bouncing between them. Her tongue slipped out as she held his gaze, giving her bottom lip a little swipe. He started to lean in, chasing the kiss he desired. He was inches away from sealing his lips to hers when suddenly, Merrick appeared in the doorway, putting his actions on hold.

Joker gave her a wink before he released her cheek and got out of the car. He went around to her side, helping her out while grabbing their bags.

"Where are we?" She asked.

"Camp David," he told her, pressing his hand firmly against her lower back and guiding her inside.

Once inside, Merrick showed them around the small, quaint, one-bedroom, one-bathroom guest cottage. The pantry, along with the refrigerator and freezer were stocked full of food.

Joker had kept his eye on Clover the entire time as Merrick walked them around. He became concerned by how quiet she was. She hadn't said a peep since they walked into the house.

Before Merrick left, he gave Joker a burner phone and a list of phone numbers in case they needed to contact anyone. Hopefully, they wouldn't have to hide out in the woods for too long.

Joker pulled back the heavy curtain in the front window and watched as Merrick drove away. Once he was out of sight, Joker let the curtain fall and double-checked that the door was secured.

When he turned around, he met Clover's gaze as she stood in the doorway between the kitchen and living room. Even with her earlier nap, she still appeared tired, and he could tell she was in pain from the pinched look on her face. She thought she was hiding it from him, but she couldn't fool him.

He walked over to where she was standing. She continued to stare at him. Seeing that damn bruise on her face and the busted lip enraged him. He could only imagine what she went through, and his imagination was running wild.

He ran his knuckles gently down her cheek. He couldn't help it. He loved touching her. He loved the feel of her smooth skin. He loved everything about her.

"You still look tired."

"I feel tired," she admitted.

"Why don't you go ahead to bed."

"What about you?"

"What about me?"

"You'll be by yourself."

"I think I'll be okay for tonight. Come on, let's get you tucked in." He took her hand and led her into the bedroom.

She dug through one of the shopping bags and found some pajamas. While she went into the bathroom to change, Joker found the sheets and blankets and made up her bed for her.

Clover returned a few minutes later wearing dark grey lounge pants and a matching tank top. She had thrown her blonde hair up into a messy bun on top of her head.

Joker couldn't hide his smile when he saw her bright yellow toenails peeking out from under the hem of her pants. He knew yellow was one of her favorite colors.

He pulled the covers back and motioned for her to hop in, but she hesitated.

"What's wrong?" He asked.

"It doesn't seem fair that I get the bed, and you have to sleep on the couch."

He waved her off. The couch in the living room was probably more comfortable than most places he'd slept when he was deployed.

"I'll be fine," he assured her, but he could see that she wanted to argue.

"Are you sure?"

He grinned. "Positive. Now, get in."

She walked closer to the bed but stopped next to him. He could smell that damn apple lotion or body spray she wore, and it tickled his nose. He sensed her nervousness by the way she stood there wringing her fingers.

"You okay?"

"I don't know," she told him, rubbing her forehead and looking away from him towards the window.

It seemed to Joker that she wanted to say something but internally, she wasn't sure. He gave her hand a light squeeze, and she turned back toward him.

"Listen. I know there's a lot that I need to tell you, but I'm struggling with how to do that." She sucked in a big breath. "I need you to be patient with me as I work through everything that happened."

He clutched her chin. "Clover, look at me." When she did, he looked deep into her eyes. "I'm not going anywhere. When you're ready to talk, I'll be ready to listen."

He bent his head and pressed his lips against her forehead.

"Do you need anything?" He asked her.

She gave him a quick nod of her head.

"What do you need?"

"It may sound silly, but can I have a hug? Tonight, I just need a hug. That's all. Just a simple hug."

He smiled. "I think I can help with that. Come here, sweetheart," he told her as he opened his arms, and she walked into them.

She rested her cheek against his t-shirt and sighed as his muscular arms enveloped her, providing her the security she was seeking.

With a bit of time and patience, Joker was confident she'd conquer her demons, especially with him by her side to support and guide her.

CHAPTER FIFTEEN

"What do you mean the President is unavailable? I have his schedule, remember?" Miles, the President's Chief of Staff, spat out, holding up a copy of the President's schedule as he spoke to Monika, the President's scheduler. He'd been trying to meet with Evans all day and was still getting the runaround. Something was up. It was now evening, and he still wasn't answering any of his messages.

Monica turned in her chair and gave him a pointed look from behind her wire-rimmed glasses.

"You of all people should know that his schedule can change at the drop of a hat."

Annoyed, he shot her a frustrated look.

"But I'm notified of those changes, and I wasn't made aware of any updates. How do you expect me to do my job if I don't know where he is?" *Especially if he doesn't answer his phone*, he thought to himself. He glanced at his watch. It was almost eight o'clock.

"I'm sorry, Miles," she said apologetically and started to turn back toward her computer as if telling him the discussion was over. But Miles wasn't going to accept her blow-off.

"You're not going to tell me?" He pressed, hoping for a miracle, and she would cave. "I'm his Chief of Staff."

Appearing exasperated, Monika turned back to face him, placing her elbows on the desk and resting her chin on her hands.

"Look, Miles. All I can tell you is that he asked me to block most of his day for personal reasons."

Miles drew back, confused. "Personal reasons? I hold a Yankee White security clearance—the highest level of clearance in the U.S. government. If something is going on with the President, I should know."

She stared over her glasses, and he could tell from the fire in her eyes that he had pushed the issue too far.

"Throwing around your clearance level won't impress me, nor will it get the answer you're looking for."

Taking a deep breath, she lifted her hands in the air and said, "I'm just the scheduler. I do what he asks, and I don't question him unless I feel it warrants it, and this isn't one of those times. I can assure you if there was a national security issue, I know how to get a hold of him."

He forgot that Monika was a stickler for the rules. She operated in black and white—there was no gray area for her. Even if she did know where he was, she wouldn't give it up. The woman was like a vault. But then that made her good at her job, and why Evans trusted her loyalty. Miles knew all too well that loyalty was hard to come by in the government social circle in Washington.

He glanced at his watch again. *Damn!* He really needed to talk to Evans. They had an opportunity to score big time with a potential donor that would kick-start their campaign.

Seeing that Monika had already moved on to her next task that obviously didn't pertain to him, he began his walk back to his office down the hall. When he entered his office, he was surprised to see someone sitting in one of the two chairs across from his desk. His glasses slipped down his nose, and he pushed them back up. Once his eyes focused, he recognized the auburn waves that fell across the woman's back.

He grinned as his head tilted to one side, and he walked around his desk to take a seat.

"Carrie. To what do I owe this visit?"

"I wanted to see if you've had dinner yet," she told him before glancing to the table next to her, where the two bags from the deli down the street sat.

She gave him a bright cheerleader smile. "I know that the *White House Deli* is your favorite. I picked up a turkey and cheese on rye for you. Oh, and no mayonnaise, but add mustard."

He felt his mouth start to water. Since he moved to the D.C. area, the mom-and-pop deli had been his go-to place. Over the years, he had gotten to know the owners well. He looked at Carrie and grinned.

"That was nice of you. Thank you. And I'm starving."

He moved the mouse cursor for his laptop, and his computer screen came to life.

"Let me just check my calendar and make sure I don't have anything else scheduled. It's been a crazy day around here."

He looked up and grinned, and Carrie flashed a beaming smile back at him.

"I hear you. The First Lady is booking appearances right and left. The country loves her."

"Well, she just announced her new initiative geared towards clean water in impoverished nations. I've heard that many leaders of other countries have already commended her efforts."

"Yeah. Thank goodness Jocelyn is heading up that initiative. In fact, sometime next month, she and the First Lady are scheduled to embark on a tour of African nations to promote the project."

"You're not going?" He asked, surprised she wasn't accompanying the First Lady.

Carrie curled her lip up in disgust. "Not my cup of tea. That's what Jocelyn's for. She's the professional 'water girl.'"

The sour reaction from Carrie concerning Jocelyn surprised Miles, as he'd ever only known Jocelyn to be friendly when he'd seen her around the White House. It could be that Carrie felt a little jealous, being that Jocelyn knew the Evans family before they entered the political scene. He usually wasn't a fan of politicians hiring friends just because of their association. But in Jocelyn's case, she was good at what she did and was a hard and dependable employee. He saw nothing wrong with her. But what did he know? Perhaps the two women disagreed on something, and Carrie held it against her. It wasn't his problem. He had more important issues to deal with than worry about a spat between the two.

Brushing off Carrie's response, he focused on what was at hand—dinner with Carrie. He quickly entered his login credentials and pulled up his calendar. He smiled to himself before looking across the desk at the woman he had lusted after for the last three years since they first met during a campaign stop.

"You're in luck. Looks like I'm free for the rest of the evening, unless Evans reemerges from his disappearing act. I need to speak with him."

Miles walked back around the desk, picked the bags up off the table, and motioned for Carrie to follow him over to the couch sitting against the north wall. The taupe leather couch had served as a bed for him when he'd had to work late. But having Carrie this close to him where he could smell her shampoo every time her auburn locks swayed when she moved her head aroused him, bringing several sexual ideas to mind on what he wanted to do to her on that couch. Couches made for some creative positions. He shook his head, trying to erase the erotic image in his head of her bent over the arm of the sofa as he sunk his cock into her from behind.

"Miles?"

He snapped his head up and realized he had been totally lost in his thoughts.

"Is everything okay?" She questioned, and he cleared his throat.

"Yeah. Why wouldn't it be?"

"Because you seemed a little lost there for a moment."

He stuck his hand inside the bag, pulled out her grilled chicken salad, and handed it to her.

"Sorry. I just have a lot on my mind." He offered a small smile with an apology.

"It's okay. Does it have to do with not being able to speak with President Evans?"

He opened the wrapper of his sandwich and took a bite before wiping his mouth with a napkin.

"A little." He didn't dare admit to her what he'd really been fantasizing about. She would be out the door faster than a speeding bullet if she knew.

She set her fork down and wiped her mouth.

"You really don't know where he is?"

He shook his head. "No. He's been MIA for most of the day. He's not answering any calls, and I tried talking to Monika, but she said she didn't know, and even if she did, she wouldn't say."

Carrie chuckled. "Monika can be like that. I could ask Lana if you want. I'm sure she knows where he is."

He thought about her offer, and at first, it sounded like a good idea, but on a second thought, he nixed the idea.

"No. That's okay. But thanks."

"Are you sure? It seems like it's really bothering you."

"It does bother me. I should know where he is—always. It's part of my responsibility."

"True. But he does have a private life as well."

"He's the President of the United States—his life is far from private."

"You know what I meant."

He set his sandwich down. He wasn't sure if he should talk about an incident that occurred last night when Evans called him in the middle of the night asking about an order sent to the SCU. It was a strange call, and Evans was very vague with Miles when he tried to push for more information.

Carrie reached out and touched his hand. "What is it, Miles? I can tell it's not just being unable to reach Evans. There's something else on your mind."

"I can't put my finger on it. He called me late last night, but he acted as if he wasn't giving me the full story. And then today, he pulls this out of character disappearing act."

She kept her hand over his but scooted closer to him. Their thighs now pressed against each other's.

He looked her over as if scrutinizing her, determining if she could be trusted. But then again, she was the COS for the First Lady. And it wasn't like he was secretly passing her classified information.

"This doesn't go any further than this room. But maybe after what I tell you, you can keep your ears and eyes open and let me know if you hear any rumblings making their way through the White House."

"You have my word, Miles. But now you have me thinking whatever has you concerned is scandalous."

A sarcastic laugh escaped him. "Scandalous. I hadn't thought of that word, but it's possible." He ran his hand down his face in frustration. "Last night, the president called me asking about a document he supposedly signed, but was adamant he never did."

"Hmmm. Did he show you the document?"

"No, because we were on the phone. But he said it looked like his signature. What's strange is that we can't find the original document. What he had was a scanned copy. So, you know, sometimes they can be a bit distorted."

She nodded her head. "Maybe he just forgot. I'm sure he signs his name many times a day."

He shook his head. "No. There's more to it. The signature line had a slight discrepancy."

"Like what?"

"There's a certain way President Evans signs his name when he physically signs and doesn't use the autopen."

Her mouth formed an "O," and Miles knew she understood how dire the situation could be.

"Now you see the problem."

She cleared her throat, pulling her hand away. He immediately felt her loss. But she suddenly appeared troubled.

"Let me do some digging for you. I have ways of finding out stuff," she admitted, and he had no doubt she could do it. Carrie was a resource he'd never want to lose.

Rose pulled into the one-car garage attached to her townhome she rented in Rockville, Maryland. As soon as the door closed behind her, she reached up and pulled off the wig she wore. The auburn-colored wig was beautiful. She just hated wearing wigs. But her current assignment, acting as Carrie Westerfield, the First Lady's Chief of Staff, required one. She also wore brown-colored contacts to conceal her blue eyes.

After her dinner date with Miles, she couldn't care less about the color of her wig or her eyes. She was more concerned about the document Miles told her about that had a discrepancy on the President's signature line.

One of the benefits of her job was that it gave her access to most parts of the White House, including the press room where the autopen machine was kept. Being COS for the First Lady, she was required to work some late nights. Most of the nights, the rest of the White Offices were quiet and vacant, giving her access to the machine to sign off on documents needed for Torres' operation.

With Miles' admission, she wondered if the document in question could've been one of theirs.

She pulled her phone out and hit the first name in her contacts. Torres answered on the second ring.

"I've been waiting for your call. We've got a problem," he told her.

"Well, we might have two if your problem is different from mine."

"Why, what happened?" Torres asked, his voice rising.

She went over the dinner conversation she had with Miles. She told him about the signature discrepancy, and she also mentioned how the president was absent from the White House and how Miles didn't even know where he was.

She heard the frustrated sigh on the other end of the line, and she knew that Torres wasn't happy. Torres liked things in order and organized. That was why their little secret operation had been so successful.

"You said that Miles didn't have a copy of the document in question?"

"No. But I'm assuming Evans does."

"This concerns me. It's possible your problem could be related to my problem."

"What is your problem?"

"I got a call from Joel in Miami. Blanyard never showed up this morning with the shipment, and when I tried calling him, it disconnected."

That definitely surprised Rose.

"I don't know why he wouldn't have. Before I left the building last night, everything was on schedule. After we got rid of Perkins, Blanyard confirmed that the weapons transfer was complete. I headed out when Blanyard was setting the detonators." She then remembered one of Blanyard's guys saying something over the radio about one of the pilots. "Oh shit!"

"What?" Torres barked.

"There was another pilot—a female pilot. When I was leaving the building, Raul said she was missing. They thought she had gone inside to use the bathroom. Blanyard told them to find her."

"So you don't know if they found her?"

"No. As I said, I left."

"So, you're saying that this pilot could've discovered what was going down and stopped it?"

She thought about it for a minute. There was only one of her, and there were four others. Surely, they had found her—or they left without seeing her. But then why hadn't Blanyard made the drop?

"I guess it's possible, but doubtful."

"Dammit. Without Perkins, I can't get a hold of any satellite pictures."

"Well, you still could. You are the Vice President."

"Yeah, but it would draw attention."

"So, what do you want to do?"

"If it's the case that the pilot discovered the shipment, then the government is hiding her. We need to find the little bitch and make sure she doesn't talk."

"How do we do that?"

"I'll call Evans tomorrow morning and see if he has any updates on the FBI's investigation into Hollis' disappearance. His answer or reaction to that question should determine if he knows more."

"Okay. I'll keep my eyes and ears open as well."

"If she's in hiding, then someone in the White House knows where. Don't fuck this up, Rose. Find out where that bitch is."

CHAPTER SIXTEEN

Clover leaned back in the chair next to the window as she took in the gorgeous nighttime view of the backyard. She couldn't wait until morning to see what it looked like in the daylight. With bright floodlights lighting up the area, she could see that it was a charming, rustic deck space. She loved big wooden decks, and the one she was looking at didn't disappoint. It was filled with all types and sizes of planters stuffed with vibrant, colorful flowers and foliage. It even had a cozy little fire pit area tucked into the corner. Directly in front of her was a little dining table that could seat six. It had an intimate feeling to it.

Of course, Joker immediately popped into her head. She'd love to sit with him and snuggle by the fire and even make smores. Mmm...she loved smores. When she was younger, she and her brothers would always sit out by the bonfire they would build in their backyard and eat smores in the summertime. There wasn't anything better than gooey marshmallows and melted chocolate smushed between two crunchy graham crackers.

She took another look around the bedroom, and a picture hanging on the wall near the closet caught her eye. It was a log cabin on a lake with a row of beautiful snowcapped mountains in the background. It made her tear up as it reminded her of home; her mom, dad, and brothers and what they must be going through, not knowing if she was dead or alive. She wished there was a way to communicate with them. Or at the least let them know she was alive. She couldn't wait to see them and hug them. One thing she'd already learned from this awful situation was to never take anything for granted.

She glanced over her shoulder toward the bedroom door. When she hadn't been able to sleep, she thought about going out into the living room to see if Joker was still up, but then nixed the idea when she saw the light coming from under the door go off. He deserved some sleep too.

Knowing Joker was just steps from her warmed her heart. She needed him more than she realized. She needed someone to talk to, and he said he would listen. She knew it wasn't healthy to keep feelings and thoughts bottled up. But how do you tell someone that you took the life of another human? Even though those men were terrible people and had bad intentions, she still felt guilty. It wasn't something she could just push to the side and forget. The images from that night would always haunt her.

A big yawn escaped her, and she looked at her watch and sighed. It was almost two in the morning. She should try to get some sleep. She stood up and turned from the window. Before climbing into bed, she arranged the pillows to form a barrier around her. It might seem silly to some, but it provided a sense of security for her peace of mind. Once she crawled into bed, she let her body sink into the soft mattress before pulling the blanket over her. She snuggled against the pillows and closed her eyes, hoping that tomorrow would bring some happiness back into her life.

☙

Joker settled into his spot on the sofa and stretched out. Since he put Clover to bed, he'd been doing some of his own research. It never hurt to be proactive in studying up on potential enemies, especially those who could be after the woman he loved.

He came across a few names that piqued his interest and who could be likely suspects, but it was something he would discuss with Evans the next time he calls.

He flipped over onto his side. Surprisingly the couch was quite comfortable, though he'd be even more comfortable lying beside Clover in the bedroom.

Under normal circumstances getting sleep wasn't an issue because his mind and body were trained to sleep on demand. It was his consciousness that was preventing him from sleeping. He couldn't shut it off. Not with all the thoughts he had running through it.

He'd admit that he was worried about Clover's mental being. He didn't know the specifics of what went down, but it was clear that she was struggling.

Overall he was a patient guy, except where it was warranted during missions. But in Clover's situation, he figured he'd need to give her a little push. He understood that all people deal with traumatic events differently. He recognized the lost look in her eyes—eyes that were once full of brightness, happiness, and sometimes mischief. There was always some sort of a spark there. But all that was gone, and he was determined to give it back to her even if it took baby steps.

Slowly, his mind shut down, and sleep was on the horizon when he was jolted awake by a terrifying scream that ripped through the small house. He didn't hesitate and grabbed his SIG off the table before bolting to the bedroom.

He burst through the bedroom door, ready to kick someone's ass. His first look was to the bed, but it was empty, and panic hit him at full force. The room was in total disarray. Lamps and chairs were knocked over, and the blankets and pillows littered the floor. But the most important thing missing was Clover. He didn't see her anywhere. He took a few steps toward the closet but stopped short when he heard her low, pleading voice.

"Please stop...It hurts...No...." Her voice sounded helpless and broken, but there was pain that melded in there too. Her voice sounded almost childlike.

Joker slowly walked around the bed, and in the corner behind the flipped-over chair was Clover, her body curled into a tight protective ball, clutching a small blanket with tears streaming down her cheeks.

Knowing she was caught in a nightmare, Joker didn't want to frighten her anymore than she already was. He got onto his knees and crawled over to her. She was mumbling something incoherent, but he could see the pained look on her face as her body trembled.

Joker knew whatever she had gone through had recreated itself into a nightmare terrorizing her.

Slowly and cautiously, he wrapped his arms around her, pulling her gently into his chest. He could feel her heart beating a mile a minute as she continued to sob. Suddenly she cried out and became combative. She began to swing her arms violently, trying to pull away. He reached for one of her hands, but she slapped him away.

Before she hurt herself or him, he wrapped his arms around her in a firm bear hug and held her against his chest. She continued to fight him until he finally had enough and shouted at her.

"Clover!" His voice was deep and loud, and he knew she heard him because she immediately went still in his arms.

He waited until he felt her tense muscles start to relax before loosening his hold. Moments later, he felt her arms come up and loop around his neck as her face stayed buried in his chest. When he felt her body start to shake and her silent tears soaked through his t-shirt, he knew she had let go, and he just held onto her and consoled her as she wept. It was gut-wrenching, but he was glad he had been there for her to lean on.

He buried his face in her hair as she burrowed further into his body. Every once in a while, he would hear a slight sniffle.

Once she seemed to be all cried out, Joker gently placed his hands on her shoulders, and she tilted her head back to look upward. Even with red, puffy eyes and a little red nose, she was a keeper.

"I got you, sweetheart," he told her repeatedly as he brushed some of the tears away.

❧

Clover was coming down from what she considered the most horrific nightmare she'd ever experienced. It felt like she was back in the desert fighting for life.

She felt utterly exhausted—like someone had ripped the wind right out of her sails. Her breathing was rapid, her heart pounded, and her body ached terribly.

But one thing she knew was that she was in the safety of Joker's strong, comforting arms. She didn't even need to look to make sure it was him. She could sense it. And it wasn't just the scent of his fresh-smelling deodorant or the feel of his soft t-shirt under her cheek. It was much more. It was an energy between them that was seated deep in her heart, bonding her to him. She couldn't explain it to anyone else because it wasn't something they could see. It was something you felt. It was a feeling she never wanted to let go of.

She wanted to be honest with him, but embarrassment washed over her. She took a deep breath.

"I'm sorry," she told him, His eyes narrowed into tiny slits, and at first, she thought she might have upset him.

"Don't ever apologize for something you have no control over."

She covered her mouth as a tear escaped her eye and rolled down her cheek. She couldn't go on like this. Maybe if she would just admit her fear, she'd feel more grounded—in control.

She wasn't sure why she did, but she placed her hands on his cheeks.

Honesty, she told herself.

"I'm scared, Joker. I'm so damn scared that I'm not going to make it out of this alive, and I'm scared of what people will think of me."

She started to lower her head, but he clutched her chin, stopping her.

"Hey. It's okay to be scared," he spoke soothingly.

"Is it?" She asked him, and he nodded. "Have you ever been scared?"

"Everyone's been scared at one time or another." He offered her a smile. "Even Bear, though he'd never admit it. But I can vouch for it."

She gave him a wet, sappy smile as she wiped her eyes. And she'd give him credit for trying to make light of a crappy situation.

"I'm just afraid that people will judge me differently once I tell my story."

"Then those people don't really care about you, and they can fuck off as far as I'm concerned," he said bluntly before taking her face between the palms of his large hands and staring deeply into her eyes. "If it's me you're worried about, don't be. You don't have to hide who you are with me."

He squeezed her tighter and stood with her cradled against his chest without saying another word. She cringed at the mess when she looked at the room.

"Please tell me I didn't do that." She felt mortified.

He shrugged his shoulder. "Okay. I won't," he replied with a bit of humor.

He set her down on the bed and then picked up the lamp and chair, setting them back in their rightful place. Thinking that she should help too since she was the one who caused the mess, she started to get up when he glared at her and pointed.

"Stay. I've got this," he told her, or more so, ordered. She wondered if she barked at him if he'd find that funny too.

He picked up the blankets and put them back on the bed. As he bent down to pick up six pillows, she heard him chuckle.

"What's with all the pillows? I thought you hated sleeping on pillows. In fact, I believe it was you who whacked me with one in your sleep."

Clover peered up at him, her eyes a little larger than usual. She was surprised he spoke about *that* night. She was torn on whether to respond directly or if it was wise to avoid any talk of that night, at least for tonight, because she was sure as shit wasn't in the right mindset to discuss the aftermath of that spectacular night, or the kiss he left her with in Djibouti.

She went for the wise decision. "I feel like the pillows offer a layer of protection. Sort of like a security blanket. I pile them up all around me."

He threw all but two pillows back on the floor and then plopped in the spot she was planning to sleep in, the side closest to the door.

"What are you doing?" She asked, staring at him.

He winked. "I'm going to stay right here, and we're both going to get some sleep—real sleep."

She gulped, then started to shake her head, but he stopped her.

"Clover…We're just sleeping. At least for tonight." He winked again and then laughed when her eyes went wide. He patted the space next to him. "Come on. Pretend I'm those pillows. Let me be your security blanket, Clover. I promise you. I won't leave your side."

Clover crawled over and laid down on the pillow beside him. She turned over onto her side with her back to him. She could still feel her body shaking, although some of it could be blamed on Joker lying next to her. She was embarrassed and scared.

Moments later, the small light by the table clicked off, plunging the room into darkness. The beat of her heart kicked up a notch. She had a feeling it was going to take some time to get used to being in the dark and not feeling scared.

She felt Joker moving around when suddenly he draped his arm over her hip. She flinched at first but soon relaxed into his hold. She could feel his warm breath against the back of her neck.

She peered over her shoulder and met Joker's intense but worried gaze.

"You're okay, sweetheart," he softly spoke, looking into her eyes.

"I can't show weakness, but I'm so scared right now," she admitted in a shaky tone.

"Come here," he told her, helping her flip over to face him. He pulled her close, and Clover closed her eyes as she rested her head against his shoulder.

They laid there for a few minutes, neither saying a word. Clover knew she wasn't going to be able to fall asleep. At least not right away. Not with the way her mind was racing.

Having Joker next to her and holding her helped ease some of her anxiety and mental anguish. But she knew the only way to free herself was to talk.

"I killed people, Landon. My two hands literally killed people."

She pried open the dam, and it all started to flow out. She told him everything from the moment she witnessed Perkins getting shot to the struggle she endured trying to stay alive, and to find out that Major Saunders was still alive and keeping him alive until help arrived.

When she was finished, she was a blubbering mess. She was crying so hard that she was hiccuping, and at one point, she even felt like she was going to be sick and had to stop for a few minutes to get herself under control.

When she finally dared to look up into Joker's eyes, she was surprised to find no judgment in his expression. It was like he knew what she was experiencing, and maybe he did since he was a SEAL and had experienced similar occurrences.

He helped her wipe her tears away and handed her a tissue from the side table so she could blow her nose.

Once she felt like she had emptied her soul, Joker spoke only then.

ふ

Joker was trying his damnedest to keep his cool as Clover detailed her ordeal in the desert. Even though he'd been in similar situations as a SEAL, he had never been alone. He always had at least one of the other guys to assist him. But poor Clover. Jesus, she had been all alone and outnumbered to fend for herself. Now he understood her fear of being scared of what people would think about her because she had to kill someone, even though it was self-defense.

That was one thing Joker didn't have to worry about, being that their missions were classified, and only a few select people were briefed on the entirety of the operation. But Clover's case was unique. Because of the high-profile investigation, Clover's name would come to the forefront and most likely be made public. The government can try to seal documents and mask identities, but the media were bloodhounds, and when they saw a good story, they never stopped sniffing until they found that bone.

Joker would do whatever he could to shield her from those seeking to harm her, including the media. He knew that once her story made its way through her family and the military, Clover would have a lot of allies in her corner.

He pulled her close, already forming that imaginary shield around her.

"I'm so sorry you had to go about that all alone. And, just so you know, it's natural for someone to have the thoughts you do, especially considering what you went through."

"But I'm trained. I shouldn't feel this way, should I?"

Joker immediately thought about Alex, Ace's fiancé. She had a similar experience where she was put into a situation that came down to her wanting to live or die. Alex would be a great person for Clover to talk to once this was all over and she was free to live a normal life.

"Every time I close my eyes, I see one of those guys, or worse, I see Perkins laying on the floor with a hole in his forehead." She looked up at him, and the sadness in her eyes broke his heart. "How do I forget it? How can I wipe my mind from those events? Explain that to me. Because I can't." She took a deep breath and exhaled.

He gave her a slight squeeze. "I wish it were that easy, Clover. Unfortunately, you never forget. But you do learn to deal with it."

"Is that what you do? You just deal with it?"

"I do. We all do. What we see and do has the potential to change us."

"How do you deal with it, though?"

"I talk to people."

"Like a counselor?"

He nodded. "That's one. Fortunately, we have access to resources. But we also have each other. I find it more helpful to talk to the guys, or in some cases, I'll meet Derek, our commander, for a beer, and we'll talk."

"I think it's wonderful you guys can lean on each other."

"What about your fellow soldiers? I'm sure you have friends on the base that you're close to. You have access to the same resources we do. There are professionals you can speak to."

"I know, but...." Her whispered voice trailed off as she started to lower her head, but Joker used his pointer and thumb to clutch her chin, tilting her face upward.

"But what, Clover? If the resources are offered, you need to take advantage of them."

"I don't know. It just seems weird opening up my mind to a complete stranger, especially a doctor of some sort. I don't want someone judging me and telling me what to think."

Again, Alex popped into his head, and even though the moment didn't call for laughter, Joker couldn't help the small snort as he thought about Alex's visit to a shrink shortly after her ordeal in Afghanistan. He could easily see Clover going off on a shrink if they said something to upset her.

"I have a very good friend who might be the perfect person for you to talk to. Would you consider meeting with her? Of course, once this is all over with and you're allowed to?"

She stared at him for a moment. At first, Joker thought she might say no, but she slowly nodded her head.

"If she's someone you trust, I'd consider it."

"I trust her completely, and so should you."

Clover laid her head down. "Is this woman special to you?"

Joker smirked. "She's extraordinary, but not how you're thinking. I can't get into specifics because it's classified, but Alex went through a similar ordeal. When she returned home, she felt defeated and lost, kind of like how you're feeling."

Clover lifted onto her elbow. "If you don't mind me asking. How did she get rid of the demons chasing her?"

Joker took her hand. "Friends and family. Derek, my CO, is her dad. She's also married to Ace, the team leader for Alpha team. That's what's so great about our tight-knit community. Everyone is there to support each other—in the good times and the bad. And I know for a fact that your family and friends will be there for you as well, including me. But a lot of it depends on you. You have to be the one to admit that you need help. Speaking solely for myself, once you get past that hurdle, it's all downhill."

She smiled. "I think I might like to meet this Alex."

He returned the smile. "You'll really like her, and I know she'll love you." They stared deep into each other's eyes until Clover surprised him by lifting herself higher and kissing his cheek. He closed his eyes, pushing away the urge to return the gesture by kissing her on the lips. It wasn't the time. However, he'd take her action as a sign that they were moving in the right direction. She just needed some time.

"Come on. Let's get you settled so you can get some sleep."

They both laid back down.

"Joker?"

"Yeah?"

"I didn't even think to ask. How was my family?"

Joker exhaled. "As you might think, they were pretty torn up. The COA was there delivering the news when Bear and I arrived. I won't sugarcoat it. Your mom took it really hard."

"On the other hand, your dad and brothers know that the government isn't telling them everything. You know how suspicious they can be. And I agreed with them. But we can talk more about it tomorrow. Right now, you need to get some rest."

As Clover fell into a deep sleep, Joker lay there thinking about the whole situation and how it affected Clover. There was still one question that nagged at him. What was she doing on that helicopter?

ಎ

Joker stirred the following day, then lifted his head to sniff the air. *Cookies?* Eyes still closed, he sniffed again. It was definitely cookies.

He turned over, expecting to find Clover still in bed, but when he opened his eyes, all he found was a pillow and rumpled sheets.

Instantly, he had a flashback from two years ago when he woke up in her apartment, and she was gone. But instead of panicking, he thought about it logically. Considering he smelled cookies meant she was still in the house. It was either that, or she invited the *Keebler Elves* to bake him cookies as a parting gift before she took off.

He glanced at his watch. Damn. He must have been tired. It was almost 0900. His usual wake-up time was 0430. He looked toward the window and saw the morning sun filtering through the sheer curtains. It looked like a perfect day for a workout outside.

He pulled himself out of bed and stretched his arms over his head. *Ahhh...that felt good.* Now for some coffee. Before he sought out some java, he spent a few minutes tidying up the room, making sure the bed was made and picking up a few items that had fallen on the floor during Clover's ordeal.

When he left the room and was halfway down the short hallway, he stopped when he heard Clover's voice. She was singing along to a song on the radio. It sounded like a *Miranda Lambert* song. He leaned against the wall, closing his eyes as he listened to her angelic voice. It had been so long since he'd heard her sing that he'd forgotten how good she was.

As the song ended and another began, he stepped around the corner. He had only made it two steps before he came to a complete stop, and his lips formed a smile. He leaned his shoulder against the doorway and just watched in amazement.

The entire kitchen was covered in what he could only describe as a cookie mess, from floor to ceiling. And in the middle of it all was Clover, barefooted and dressed in a t-shirt and cotton shorts, shaking her booty to the song on the radio as she bounced between tasks of mixing and shuffling trays of cookies.

He had to hold his hand over his mouth to keep from laughing aloud when she picked up a whisk and used it as a microphone.

There had to be dozens of cookies already baked and cooling on the breakfast bar. It was pretty impressive, minus the mess. But that was okay because it wasn't a big deal. What was important was the big joyous smile gracing her beautiful face. That right there was priceless. He thought his heart would burst when she turned around and saw him standing there, and that smile of hers grew even wider. It was like she woke this morning with a whole new outlook on life.

She reached for the radio and turned the volume down. She looked fucking adorable with all the flour stuck to her cheeks and nose.

"What's going on in here?" He asked with a slight grin as he pushed off the wall and walked further in.

Appearing nervous, she bit her lip and glanced away for a quick second. "Uhm...I'm baking."

He glanced around the space, still chuckling at the mess. "I see that."

She grabbed a big green mixing bowl off the counter and turned her back to him as she started stirring the batter. He could tell she was embarrassed. It was cute, but she had nothing to be embarrassed about. It was nice to see her relaxed and carefree while doing something she enjoyed.

He moved closer and crowded behind her as she stood at the counter. Her shoulders lifted as he heard the big breath she took, and the swirling of her hand slowed.

She let go of the whisk, slowly twirling to face him. There was probably only one to two feet between them. Her head leaned back against her shoulders as she looked upward. She brought her hand up as if she was going to place it on his chest, but at the last second, she pulled it back, and he felt a little disappointed because he'd wanted nothing more than to feel her hands on his body.

"My mom taught me to bake. I love to bake, but I tend to make a mess when I do. But I promise I'll clean everything up. You won't even know I was even in here baking. Do you like cookies? If you do, what kind? I can make almost any type of cookie that you like."

Joker couldn't hold his amusement in any longer, and he laughed. But she was still nervously rambling on.

"Clover..." he said calmly, but she kept going a mile a minute. He didn't even know she could string that many sentences together that fast. "I can make pecan. Or...Oh! I found this recipe for a banana—"

"Clover!" He repeated her name, this time a little louder, and it got her attention. Her eyes grew wide, and she pressed her lips together, peering up at him.

"Sorry. I also bake when I'm nervous. It helps ground me."

He smiled. "I don't care about the mess. Make it even messier."

He bent lower until he was at eye level with her. She stood perfectly still. She wasn't lying. She was nervous. He could see it in her body language—the way she shifted from one foot to the other, her habit of wringing her fingers, or the biggest known, biting those tasty lips of hers. He'd talk to her later about what had her worried. She was in her element right now, and he wouldn't ruin it. He leaned in and kissed her cheek.

"All I care about is keeping that smile on your face," he whispered close to her ear.

When he pulled away, she smiled, and he could see a light shade of blush creep into her cheeks.

"I think you'll be seeing this smile a lot more," she told him as she wrinkled her nose at him in a cute way.

He smiled and then cupped her cheek. "Good. Because you're even more beautiful when you smile."

Suddenly, it felt like time stood still between the two of them. Everything else around them was a blur as they stared deep into each other's eyes. She was everything he wanted in a partner for life. He now understood the meaning of the phrase; *good things come to those who wait*. He'd waited long enough, and it was time to show her that they belonged together.

He slid his hand around to the back of her neck, cupping it, and drew her closer as he leaned further in. Her hand came up between them, resting against his chest as her eyes slowly closed in anticipation of his lips meeting hers. He closed his eyes, feeling her warm breath as his lips hovered over hers.

Buzz…buzz…buzz…

Both their eyes popped open.

Buzz…buzz…buzz…

"Your phone," she told him.

"Shit…" he growled out, feeling frustrated.

The sound of his phone vibrating killed the moment. *Fuck!!*

"You better get that," she whispered, though her voice had taken on a husky tone that made Joker's cock harden beneath his pants.

He knew he had to take it, but he didn't want to. He would much rather get lost in kissing her.

He placed a kiss on her nose. "Later," he promised before running to grab his phone.

ଚ୭

Clover thought she would combust with all the heat and desire pooling between her legs. She knew that baking could be a hot job, but damn! That man was lethal on many levels. He could make her come with his low, deep voice as he whispered erotic words in her ear.

She turned and took one look at the mixing bowl and pushed it aside. Her brain was a pile of goo. She was hot, not because of the heat from the oven. She was hot for Joker. She reached for one of the dishcloths hanging on the oven door and used it to fan herself.

As she attempted to start cleaning up, all that kept going through her head was his promise of "later."

She couldn't take the heat any longer. She stepped over to the freezer, pulled open the drawer, and stuck her head between the chicken nuggets and frozen corn bags.

"Lord have mercy."

CHAPTER SEVENTEEN

It was getting close to dinner time, and Clover wondered how much longer Joker would be in the shower. He'd been in there for close to thirty minutes. *Didn't those guys take like two-minute showers?* She thought to herself.

She had already showered. Joker had teased her when she came out of the bathroom dressed in her pajama pants and a tank top with a zip-up hoodie. While she was in the shower, Joker had turned the air conditioner down to a temperature equivalent to Antarctica. She kept looking around, waiting for the polar bears and penguins to show up. When she complained about it being too cold, he told her she kept it too warm. They probably sounded like two little kids fighting over their milk and cookies. But in the end, he won out, and she agreed to let him have his way for tonight. Tomorrow she'd thaw out.

She reached behind her and pulled the soft taupe throw off the back of the sofa and draped it over her legs. Once she got comfortable under the cozy blanket, she leaned forward and plucked the tablet that had been packed for her off the coffee table.

Whoever bought it had downloaded some books for her, and Clover was pretty impressed with the selection. She enjoyed getting lost in a good romance book when she had the time. And since she had all the time in the world right now, after cleaning up her baking mess in the kitchen, she spent most of the day curled up on the couch reading some new-to-her-authors. *Kris Michaels, Reina Torres, Riley Edwards, and Susan Stoker* could write some out-of-this-world protector romance stories.

She glanced impatiently at the bathroom door again. She wanted to get on the internet, but she didn't have the WiFi password. Joker did, though. She knew she wasn't allowed to search or log in to anything associated with her name since someone could be monitoring it. All she wanted to do was check on Wally, her adopted seal. She fell in love with the flippered mammals while attending a week-long marine biology summer camp at Sea World in Orlando, Florida. During one of her conversations with a few of the trainers at the sea lion exhibit, she learned about the adoption opportunity. When she expressed interest in it, one of the trainers contacted one of the reputable wildlife organizations dedicated to bringing awareness to the animals. That was where she became linked with Wally. Since Wally was tagged, she could track him and see where he traveled to, which he mainly kept to the waters in the New England area. Now and then, the organization would send pictures to her. It was pretty cool.

"Finally." She mumbled under her breath as the knob to the bathroom jiggled right before it opened, releasing all the steam from Joker's hot shower.

Her heart did a little pitter-patter as she anxiously waited for him to emerge through the hovering warm mist. When the moment came, she wasn't the least bit disappointed. The whole scene played out like a sexy rock music video. She swallowed the moan making its way out of her mouth as she took in the sight of Joker standing there bare-chested in a pair of dark navy blue joggers that hung low on his hips. His black hair strands stuck up in all directions as if he'd just run his hand through the thick mane. It was messy, yet it looked sexy.

He ambled over to the sofa with a slight swagger and plopped down next to her. His soap's clean, fresh scent wrapped around her like a blanket, causing her to lean a wee bit toward him and inhale the divine aroma.

"Whatcha got there?" He asked, leaning into her personal space, heightening her body's awakening response to his closeness. His warm breath blew against her hair.

Trying hard to hide her arousal and appear unaffected, she shrugged her shoulders and focused on the tablet screen before her wandering eyes gave away what she was really thinking. It was a real struggle to maintain her composure and not give in to the sexual innuendos going through her mind, especially after watching him earlier as he worked out on the deck. He hadn't seen her drooling over him out of the small kitchen window as she attempted to clean the kitchen. It drove her crazy watching his muscles flex every time he pumped his arms doing push-ups, or his thick muscular thighs as he went through a series of squats. She finally had to turn away after she almost swallowed her tongue when he bent over to pick up his water bottle, and the fabric of his shorts stretched across his firm tushie. He was that tempting, and being locked inside the small house with him had her libido primed and ready.

"Can we get an internet connection here?" She asked him as she tapped the wireless connection icon on the screen.

When he didn't answer right away, she looked at him and found him staring at her. She gave her eyebrows a slight raise. "Well?"

He nodded toward the tablet lying in her lap. "You should know the answer yourself, considering all those romance books you downloaded on that thing."

"Ugh!" She gasped and pulled away slightly, pegging him with daggers through her narrowed eyes. "You were snooping on my tablet?" She accused.

He pulled the tablet from her lap, and she tried to snatch it back, but he threw his own glare her way, and she pulled her hand back quickly.

"Snooping, no. Doing my job, which is keeping you safe, yes."

"What does that even mean?" She countered.

"Searching the internet can be tracked, especially when searching for things specific to you. Like logging into an account belonging to you. Anybody who's watching can track the IP address back to your location."

"I may be blonde, and believe me, I've heard all the blonde jokes to offer…But I'm not that stupid."

"I never said you were. Many people don't realize how easy it is for a search to be traced back to them. That was all I was implying."

She licked her lips. Why did arguing with him arouse her? "Then why were you snooping on my tablet if you know I'm not stupid?"

He rolled his eyes. "I'm not going over this again," he mumbled before, pulling up the book app on the tablet and pointing to the downloaded fifty or so books. "You had to be connected to the internet to download these."

She cocked her eyebrow. "See, that's the thing. I didn't download these."

"Who did then? The book fairy?" He asked, trying to be funny.

"If you consider whoever bought the tablet to be a book fairy, then sure—the book fairy downloaded them."

"Funny. Anyway, let's get back to you and why you need the internet connection."

She sucked her bottom lip between her teeth. "Because I need to check something. I promise nobody can trace it back to me." She wasn't lying. She could check the general tracking chart and look for Wally's name on the list. It wouldn't give her all the details, but it would at least say when and where he last checked in.

"What is it that you *have* to check?" He questioned.

She slightly narrowed her eyes and gave him a hawkish stare, wondering why he gave her the third degree.

"I need to check on Wally."

"Who's Wally?"

She shrugged her shoulders. "Just a friend."

ॐ

Joker cocked his brow in surprise as he stared at Clover while she tapped away on the tablet screen as if she didn't just tell him that she needed to check on a guy. Who in the hell was Wally? Was it a boyfriend? There was no way. She would've said something. At least he hoped she would've, especially after the moment they shared earlier in the kitchen. He still damned that phone call. But Clover's safety was a priority, and the call had been from President Evans. He didn't have a lot of news mainly wanting to check on Clover. However, he did say that he'd call Monday morning with some information.

Joker cleared his throat as he tried his best to think of the best politically correct way of asking her who this Wally guy was, because the last thing he wanted to do was to come across as a jealous caveman. But then he asked himself, *when in the hell have I ever been politically correct?* He snorted a low laugh knowing the answer instantly—never. He would always be that person who spoke the truth whether anybody liked or didn't like what he had to say. It was just who he was, and he wasn't about to change his ways now.

"Is Wally your boyfriend or something?" He asked her flatly with a bite of snark.

She scrunched up her face, looking as if he had asked her an appalling question. However, in a matter of seconds, her lips turned upward, and she giggled.

"Wally is definitely not my boyfriend, but he is a Seal," she told him, still looking amused.

However, Joker didn't find it amusing at all. Truthfully it pissed him off that she was checking up on another guy—a SEAL, for that matter.

"What team is *Wally* on?" He asked.

"Team? Uhm...I don't think he's on a specific team, but he's on the East Coast."

Joker turned away from her for a moment, taking a deep breath to try and calm his jealous-induced temper. He tried to think through everyone he knew on the East Coast that wasn't assigned to a specific team, like office personnel and instructors. However, Wally's name wasn't ringing any bells, and he was sure he'd remember a *Wally*.

He turned back to her and caught her trying to suppress her laughter. That was when he had an inkling that he was being played.

Game on, sweetheart.

Acting completely unaffected by Clover's shenanigans, he bent over to reach into his bag, pulled out his personal phone, and scrolled through his contacts.

Clover's eyebrows bumped together as she watched him with her hawkish gaze. All the while, he was chuckling inside.

"What are you doing?" She asked, leaning toward him, trying to get a glimpse at his phone.

"I know who you're talking about. Wally is a sniper instructor at the base. The guys and I know him. Here it is," he said aloud and acted like he dialed the number.

Clover's eyes grew into giant balls of worry. "W-what are you doing?"

He put the phone up to his ear. "I'm calling Wally for you so you can talk to him."

Joker had never seen someone move so fast as Clover reached across him, snatched the phone out of his hand, and disconnected the call.

"What was that for?" He asked, trying to appear shocked at her abruptness.

"You really know a guy named Wally?" She inquired, and he had to hide his amusement, considering how serious she was.

"Yeah. As I said, he's an instructor." He then drew in his eyebrows. "Although, he's in his fifties. I didn't think you were into that much of an age gap."

Her mouth hung open. "Wally is a seal!" She yelled out.

He smiled. "I know. Wally is a SEAL."

She exhaled, shaking her head frantically like a maniac. "No! Wally is a real seal. A harbor seal. You know the kind with natural flippers, and he barks. He spends most of his time hanging out around Cape Cod."

Joker couldn't hold in his laughter anymore, especially when she clapped her hands together and barked like a seal. He held his stomach as he howled in laughter.

"I'm only messing with you." He managed to get out between laughs.

"You ass!" She scolded him. Well, she tried to, but it wasn't convincing because she too began to laugh along with him. They sat there chuckling for a good two or three minutes.

Clover wiped the tears from her eyes. "I seriously thought there really was a guy you knew named Wally. I can't believe you did that."

"Me?" He pointed to himself. "What about you? You were the one talking about Wally like he was your new side toy or something."

Her cheeks turned a light pink color right before she shook her head and adjusted her body's position, but slammed her eyes shut in pain. All the joking stopped as Joker became concerned. He scooted back over close to her and placed his hand on her knee.

"Clover, what is it?"

She took a few slow deep breaths before, opening her eyes. Her eyes were watery, and he could tell she was in a bit of pain.

"Sorry. I just moved the wrong way and tweaked my side. It's still a little sore," she explained, then offered a small smile. "I'll be okay. I promise," she told him and covered his hand with hers.

He looked into her eyes and could see there was more than just physical pain she was dealing with. It was time for Clover to tell her story.

"Clover, I know how hard it was for you to open up last night about what happened in the desert. And believe me, it makes me sad knowing how hard you're dealing with the consequences, and as I told you last night, I'll always be by your side to help you get through it." He paused for a moment and took a breath. "But there's also something I need to know."

"What's that?" She asked, tilting her head as if wondering what information he was seeking.

"What were you doing on a classified operation?"

೭ಾ

Clover blinked her eyes repeatedly to keep her tears at bay. Joker's concern for her deeply touched her, adding to his other fine qualities.

She knew this time would come. It was time to admit her role within the SCU.

"What did President Evans tell you when you arrived at the hotel?"

He tilted his head a bit. "He told me about the guy in the SCU who was helping move microchips with classified information and weapons, and how you were caught up in the middle of it. He mentioned you were injured, but he didn't go into great detail." He went on to further repeat everything that Evans had told him.

"So, he never said anything about me, specifically?"

He shook his head. "No. He said that you wanted to talk to me first and that he was honoring your request. So, I'm going to ask you the same question I asked him. What were you doing on a classified SCU operation?"

She cocked her head. "Why do you say it was classified?"

"Everyone knows the SCU is the elite squadron and closely guarded. They're the best of the best. Everything they do is hush, hush. I probably shouldn't be saying this, but your brothers and I have worked with them on many occasions."

She put her hand over her mouth to stifle her laugh. *Oh, I know quite a bit of what you and my brothers have been up to,* she thought to herself.

"Well, first. While it was an SCU operation, it wasn't classified. It was supposed to be a simple humanitarian supply aid drop, of which I'll get into the grim details in a minute. And second, I'm well aware of some of the rides you've partaken in, courtesy of the SCU."

"You do?" He asked, his eyebrows drawn inward.

She lifted his hand resting on her knee and linked her fingers with his.

"I've been keeping something from my family." She looked off to the side and then took a big breath. "Well, it's something I've been keeping from everyone."

Joker squeezed her hand, and when she looked back at him, he was staring at her intensely, but his eyes held an understanding that whatever she was about to tell him was difficult for her to admit.

"Clover, you know you can tell me anything, and I won't judge you."

She smiled softly. "I know that now."

She took another breath and exhaled.

"I'm not a helicopter mechanic."

He turned his body so that he was facing more of her.

"You're not?"

She shook her head and swallowed hard. "I'm one of the pilots," she admitted, and judging from the size of Joker's eyes, she had shocked him with that little tidbit.

"You're one of the pilots?"

She nodded. "I am."

His mouth opened and then closed without making a sound. Finally, after a few seconds, he was able to speak.

"Since when? How long have you been a part of that unit?"

"About four years."

Joker ran his fingers through his hair. Clover could tell his mind was spinning. Then suddenly, something clicked, and he looked into her eyes.

"Djibouti. You were there."

She grinned. "I was."

"Holy shit! It was you wasn't it? You're the pilot who flew us out of that mess in Eritrea. You're the pilot who everyone talks about. You're Clover. Lucky, like a four-leaf clover. You're Lucky!"

She nodded. "Guilty."

"I'm...I...I have no words right now," he admitted. But then his eyes fell to her right arm, and he reached for her bicep where the scar was from the stitches. "You were the injured pilot when the helo was hit?"

"Yeah. It wasn't anything big, just a nasty gash. Captain Mickens sewed me up. That's why I was sort of freaking out when Duke started talking about Captain Mickens while looking directly at me. I thought I was made."

He just stared at her for a few moments, studying her with piercing scrutiny. He showed no emotion, and Clover couldn't tell what he was thinking.

"I don't know what to say. Jesus Clover, you're like a freaking legend in the Special Forces community. How did you keep your identity hidden?"

"My team," she answered honestly. Our unit is pretty compact, and we all agreed, although I want it on the record that it was my choice. I knew how big the news would be if word got out that a woman was flying for the SCU. I'm not an attention seeker. Plus, if enemies found out, I'd have been a potential target because I was a woman."

He smiled and rubbed her leg. "I know you don't like attention. But seriously, Clover, nobody in your family knows? I know Bear doesn't, but not even your dad?"

Her eyes widened. "No."

"Why? What you've made of yourself is to be commended, and I think you should share it with your family."

"My dad probably would've kept it a secret, but I couldn't ask him to do that. That wouldn't be fair to him."

Joker leaned against the back of the couch but didn't remove his hand from her leg, which she was thankful for because his touch helped keep her grounded.

He shook his head in amazement and ran his hand over his scruffy jaw.

"All this time, I've wanted to meet the pilot who saved my ass on multiple occasions." He turned his head in her direction and cupped her cheek, letting his thumb caress her skin. "*She* was right under my nose, and I didn't even know it."

She covered his hand with hers.

"I was planning on telling my family this weekend since everyone would be there. Major Saunders and Captain Mickens talked me into it, though, deep down, I knew it was the right thing to do. I guess I was just afraid of their reactions. More so, my brothers than my dad's."

"Major Saunders, he was the other pilot?"

She nodded. "He covered for me. Anytime we flew, he was the one in communication with the teams." She snorted a small laugh. "Everyone thought he was Lucky."

"Was he with you the other night?" Joker asked, his hand still stroking her leg.

Her expression grew somber. "He was. I thought he was dead, but come to find out, he wasn't. However, he was in bad shape. Last I heard, President Evans said he hadn't woken up yet, but the doctors believed he'd make a full recovery."

"I take it you and the Major are pretty close."

She smiled. "Yeah, we are. He was really the only one I could be open with about my career and share my accomplishments."

Joker swallowed hard. "Did you and he ever…"

She smirked and shook her head. "No. Our relationship wasn't like that. It never even surfaced. We were just friendly coworkers. Or more like family. He's happily married to an amazing woman."

"How about the others within the unit? Weren't you close with them?"

"Not really. Our unit is separated by our small teams, which there aren't very many of, to begin with—sort of like your team. There's you and the other seven, but you guys make up a portion of a broader team, Team 2. Major Saunders and I stick together and keep our heads down. Well, there was also Sargent Hollis, the dickwad."

"He's the one who put you in this situation?"

"Yep. I never did like the guy. When he was assigned to our helicopter, something about his demeanor put me on edge. But I was always professional."

Joker shook his head again and chuckled. "I still can't believe you're Lucky. Damn. How many times have you worked in coordination with us?"

"A few, though not as many as you think."

"I wish it would've been you instead of some of the others we were paired with. What about your brothers, Justin, Ethan, and Zach?"

She grinned. "Same."

"Do you think your identity will be revealed after this?"

She let out a frustrated sigh. "I don't know how it could stay hidden. I planned on telling my family, but I'm sure it'll be public knowledge. But that's okay."

"You're amazing, Clover. And I'm sorry that I gave you such a hard time back in Djibouti."

"It's okay," she told him as she patted his hand.

He shook his head. "No, it's not okay. I acted like an ass. It was just…."

"Just what?" She asked.

He looked down at her. "Nothing."

He rose from the couch and turned to look at her. "What would you like for dinner? You have to be starving since you really haven't eaten in a few days."

He headed into the kitchen, but Clover wasn't accepting his answer of *anything*. He was going to say something else, but he hesitated. She wanted to know what it was.

When she walked into the kitchen, Joker was pulling a box of spaghetti noodles and a jar of sauce from the cabinet above the stove.

"What are you thinking about right now?"

He stopped, set the pot down on the stove, and looked at her.

"I can't stop wondering where you and I would be if things had gone differently that morning."

"Why didn't you ever call me?" She asked as she watched him dump the sauce into another pan.

꙳

Joker's eyebrows knitted in a frown as he met her eyes. *Was she joking right now?* He thought to himself.

"Call you? How was I supposed to call you?"

"With a phone, using the number I left you."

"Clover, I didn't get any phone number from you."

She appeared taken back. "I left it on the pillow next to where you were sleeping. My CO called early that morning, and I had to report to the base. I didn't want to wake you, though I'm surprised you didn't wake up when I got out of bed.

He shook his head slowly. "There was no note, Clover. I never got it."

"All this time, I thought that night didn't matter to you. I know we had a few drinks, but I was coherent and definitely aware of my actions."

He reached out, nudging her chin up. "Clover, look at me. Did you think that I purposely didn't call you?"

She nodded her head while keeping eye contact with him. "Yeah."

"Shit!"

"And I'm guessing you thought I just up and left."

"I did, and I'll be honest. I was fucking pissed when I woke up alone."

"I'm sorry."

Now it all made sense. How stupid! He ran his hand down his face. "Let's make dinner, and we can talk more about what we thought had happened. And then you can tell me a little more about your little 007 life you've been living under the radar."

She smirked. "As if. But only if you promise to tell me your secrets," she teased.

He stopped, turned around, and didn't even think before lifting her and setting her on the countertop. He pressed his body between her thighs and cupped her cheeks with his large hands.

"I only have one secret."

"What's that?" She asked with a breathy tone.

"It's only been you since that night."

"What do you mean?"

"I haven't been with another woman since you and I spent that night together."

"Landon…"

He shook his head as if he couldn't believe it himself, but it was the truth.

"Only you, Clover. I tried to get you out of my head, but you were stubborn up there," he pointed to his head, "just as you are stubborn here." He smiled to let her know he was only teasing.

"Well, since we're admitting secrets, I guess it's only fair that I tell you mine. It's only ever been you for me."

"What?" He studied her face. Her eyes were bright. "Clover, are you saying…."

She lowered her eyes as if she was embarrassed, but he tilted her face up towards him.

"Nobody else?"

"Only you. You kinda ruined sex for me with any other person." She gently wrapped her dainty little fingers around his wrists. "I felt a connection that night, and I never let it go. I still don't want to."

He licked his lower lip slowly as he listened to her words.

"What kind of connection did you have?"

"The same one I'm feeling right now. I feel the energy exploding between us. My heart is racing right now, and if I were standing, I'm sure my legs would feel weak. You do that to me."

She wasn't lying. Where his thumb rested against her neck, he could feel her pulse pounding.

He lowered his head slightly, and as if right on cue, she closed her eyes, and he covered her lips with his. He started out slow as he didn't want to maul her, but when he felt her arms slink around his waist and her hands grip the back of his t-shirt, he deepened the kiss, slipping his tongue between her teeth and exploring every inch of her that he could.

He released her plump lips when he felt her start to ease back, but not before giving her bottom lip a little nibble and tug, which drew a light gasp from her. And there was a lot more to her that he would love to nibble on.

☙

Clover's heart was in overdrive as she struggled to control her breathing. Only Joker could make her body come alive like it was.

She looked up into his green eyes and saw that familiar gleam. It was the same look he had the night that he walked her to her door and kissed her for the first time. The same night, she gave him her heart, body, and soul.

She ran her hands over his sculpted chest before looping them around his neck.

"I'm going to be completely honest with you."

"I want your honesty always. That's one thing I'll never get upset with you for doing. Honesty is an important part of a relationship, and it's a trait that I value."

She licked her lips nervously. What she wanted to tell him, she was afraid of his response or reaction. But she valued honesty too. It was ingrained in her and her brothers' brains growing up by their parents.

She looked him in the eye, because her mom had always told her that you could tell what someone was thinking with their eyes.

"Considering how things were left between the two of us after that night, what I have to tell you might seem unbelievable, at least by most people."

"Clover, I'm not most people. What is it?"

Damn, he was demanding. But sexy as hell when he was. It made her want him even more.

"That night meant so much to me. You allowed me to be me when we talked. I wasn't afraid to open up to you about my family or myself. We've known each other for a few years, but we've never really gotten personal until that night. When you kissed me at the door, I felt a spark that I never felt before when another guy kissed me."

He furrowed his eyebrows, and a small frown appeared on his face. He pulled her closer to where her crotch was pressed against his belly, and she instantly wrapped her legs around him.

"I don't want to think about other guys kissing you," he admitted, and a smile tugged the corners of her mouth.

"I haven't kissed anyone since you. After we made love and you held me in your arms, I felt something so deep inside me. I couldn't explain it at first. But then, as each day passed and I didn't hear from you, that feeling morphed into pain. It was then that I realized my heart held a special spot for you. It was a space I didn't want anyone else to have."

As she stared deep into his eyes, she noticed they had taken on a darker hue of green. She started to lower her eyes, but he wouldn't let her. He gripped her chin with his hand and made her keep eye contact with him.

"What are you trying to say, Clover?"

She swallowed hard. Her throat felt suddenly dry. She was on emotional overload.

"That feeling I had was love. It was love for you. I fell in love with you."

She held his gaze, waiting for any kind of reaction or confirmation that he might feel the same way, but all she got was silence and his intense expression. She actually squirmed a tad.

Suddenly, the hand he had on her chin slid around under her hair, cupping the base of her head as his other arm wrapped around her back. Before she could question him, his lips descended on hers. He didn't give her any leeway, and she relinquished all control to him as he smothered her moans.

She tried pulling him closer, but slowly he eased back.

"I want you so bad that it hurts," he admitted to her, causing her broken heart from before to mend even more.

"I want you too."

He went to lift her off the counter, but she stopped him.

"What about dinner?"

His eyes darkened. "Fuck dinner. I'm having dessert first."

She laughed but then sobered when she noticed something crossed Joker's eyes.

She gripped his forearms. "Joker, what's wrong?"

"Once we do this, I'm not letting you walk away again," he told her flatly.

She smiled and cupped his cheek.

"I never intended to walk away the first time." She held her hand out. "Give me your phone."

He looked at her funny, but then he reached into his pocket and pulled out the burner phone he was given and moved to hand it to her, but she shook her head.

"No. Not that one. Give me your personal phone."

He tilted his head to the side and gave her that sexy questionable look—the one where he lifted one eyebrow. But then he released her and walked over to his duffel bag that sat on the floor by the couch. She couldn't take her eyes off his backside as he bent over and rummaged through it before he stood back up. She remembered how firm those cheeks felt under her fingertips, and she wasn't reminiscing about the cheeks above his waist.

She was still fixed on his ass when he turned around, and immediately she knew she was busted for ogling his tush. The mischievous gleam in his eyes confirmed that.

"You keep staring at me like that, and I might say the hell with taking you to the bedroom and instead make use of this countertop."

Her eyes widened, and she felt the heat in her cheeks.

Trying to ignore his comment because what he suggested sounded hot and spontaneous, she snatched the phone from his hand. She opened his contacts, entered her name and phone number, and pressed save before handing it back.

"What's this?"

She cupped his cheek, and his sexy scruff shadowing his jaw chafed the palm of her hand. "Now you have my number *stored* in your phone. No excuses," she quipped with a wry smile.

He gave her that dazzling grin before leaning forward and pressing his warm lips against her forehead. She closed her eyes, absorbing the feel and emotions he poured into the simple yet intimate contact.

"So, what's the plan now?" She asked eagerly.

"The way I see it, since neither of us has any obligations to see to in the next twenty-four hours, my impromptu plan is to make sure you're well-loved."

"Oh…" She whispered, then slid her hands up his chest before gripping his shoulders. "Well, I'd very much like to reciprocate that loving."

His eyes darkened, and his tongue slipped out just enough to tease her as he wet his lips.

"Oh, don't worry, sweetheart. You'll have your opportunity. Now hang on," he ordered, and before she could ask what for, he slid his hands under her bottom and lifted her with ease off the counter. He walked the short distance to the bedroom and then set her down on her feet in front of the bed.

☙

Joker's body was shaking as if he was coming off an adrenalin high. As soon as he set her feet down on the rug in front of the bed, she reached for the waistband of his joggers, but he stopped her and shook his head.

She dropped her arms to her side and appeared a little jilted by his reprimand. But he was serious when he told her that tonight was all about her.

Stepping closer, he cupped her jaw. With her head tilted back, she stared into his eyes. He loved seeing her hazel orbs bright and full of anticipation. Her chest rose and fell with each breath she took, locked in step with her overactive pulse he could see beating on the side of her neck.

"You tempt me in ways that are unexplainable." He told her as his gaze moved over her messy hair and her one-size-too-big pajamas, before landing on her makeup-free face that even included a pimple, which actually made him smile. Not because she had a blemish, but that his woman wasn't afraid to show her faults.

Nobody was perfect. Everyone had faults, though some tended to think differently and would argue they were unfaultable. But not Clover. She wasn't afraid to be herself in front of others. And that was what first caught his eye about her that night in San Diego.

He'd hung out with her before when he attended family gatherings at her parents' house. But he'd never had the opportunity to spend any real quality time with her and get to know the person she was on the inside. He'd always known she had a tough exterior, but probably because of her upbringing and being who her dad and brothers were, she felt she needed to be that way. But it seemed that she kept a lot hidden inside, and he didn't want her to hide anything from him, especially when it came to the person she was.

He had been gifted the opportunity to show her that he was the man for her and wasn't about to blow it.

"I want you to relax and enjoy."

"But I want you to enjoy this as well," said said, her soft words filtering in the air.

He grinned. "Don't worry. I'm going to enjoy every single moment. Now turn around."

She quirked one of her eyebrows in question, but he gave a stern look, and she quickly turned her back to him.

Slowly, he ran his masculine hands down her arms as he pressed against her back and whispered into her ear.

"Close your eyes."

He slowly slid her hoodie off her shoulders, and the scar on her bicep came into view. He leaned down and pressed his lips against it. He felt her body shudder, and he grinned.

He gripped the hem of her tank top and peeled it up and over her head, letting his fingers brush against her ribs and then the sides of her breasts. It pleased him to see she wasn't wearing a bra, though he thought bras were sexy. And he knew Clover loved sexy bras.

He walked around and stood in front of her. She had gorgeous perky breasts. They weren't huge, but not too small either. They were perfect for his liking. He lowered his head and drew one of her tiny buds into his mouth. He closed his eyes as he swirled his tongue around her nipple. Suddenly, he felt her fingers in his hair and bit down on her bud with just enough force to give her a warning before he released it.

When he looked up, he found her staring back at him. Her eyes were the greenest he'd ever seen them. They were full of love, lust, and desire.

"You're killing me," she croaked out.

"You're killing me by not following directions and keeping me from my treat. Keep your arms by your side and keep your eyes closed."

She took a deep breath, and closed her eyes, releasing her grip on his hair, and moving her arms back to her side. He loved that she followed his orders in the bedroom. She had no idea how hard she had him right now. He was fighting his own desire not to throw her on the bed and fuck her relentlessly.

He hooked his fingers into the waistband of her pants and panties and pulled them down her legs.

"Lift your feet, sweetheart," he told her as he pulled them off completely and tossed them to the side.

Once she was completely naked in front of him, he was able to see all the bruises covering her body. It made him angry, knowing she had been used to help a traitorous monster and ended up paying the price for it.

He would give her nothing by pleasure, and he knew exactly where to start as his eyes locked onto her pussy. His mouth watered to taste her. He ran his hands gently up her silky thighs, and he lifted one leg then draped it over his shoulder, opening her up to his liking.

He heard her gasp and told her to hold onto his shoulders. Once he felt her hands on his shoulders, he dove in.

She thrust against his mouth as he sucked and licked. He felt her legs begin to quiver, and he knew she was close to exploding. Using his teeth, he gently bit down on her clit, and she screamed out her release.

He pulled away and wiped his face. "Fuck! I forgot how responsive you are."

He grabbed her around the waist as he stood up and turned her around to lay her on the bed. Once he got her situated, he stripped his clothes off, climbed onto the bed, and covered her body with his. He cupped her cheek.

"You're beautiful when you let go."

He bent his head and kissed her softly. She wrapped her arms around his neck.

"I love you."

Those words alone coming from Clover about did him in. She was the light of his life. He vowed from this moment on that she came first. She was his priority.

"I love you too, sweetheart. I'm just sorry it's taken this long for us to say it to one another."

"Let's forget the past and focus on the now," she whispered, and he couldn't agree more.

"I need to be inside you."

She smiled. "Then take me."

He kissed her again before lining up his cock at her entrance and nudging forward. He didn't want to go too fast since it had been a while for her. The last thing he wanted was to hurt her. He watched her face for any sign of pain, but when all he saw was her blissful expression and twinkle in her eyes, he began to push deeper until he was fully seated inside her.

"You okay?" He asked, and she nodded before that gorgeous smile spread across her face.

He shifted his hips as her fingertips dug into his back. He kissed her again, then pulled out and thrust into her hard. She moaned as her head tilted back and her back arched. His began to quicken his strokes, and he knew he wouldn't last long, especially with the way her tight vaginal walls gripped his cock and the way she chanted for him to move faster and harder. Jesus, the two of them together as one felt amazing.

Moments later, he felt the signs of her impending orgasm, and he began to thrust harder and quicker. He was there himself, but he promised her that this was all about her. As soon as he felt her tighten around him, he shoved once more into her.

"Fuck!" He roared as she moaned against his chest, muffling her cry. Then they both exploded as he emptied himself inside her.

They were both covered in sweat and breathing heavily. He collapsed on top of her, burying his face in the crook of her apple-scented neck. She wrapped her arms around his shoulders as if trying to pull him closer. But knowing he was probably crushing her, he rolled them to the side as he slid out of her.

He smiled when she immediately snuggled against him.

"That was amazing," she mumbled against his side, and Joker snickered as he ran his hand down her back, then gave her butt a little squeeze.

"It sure was. And I can't wait to do it again," he admitted, and she looked up at him and smiled.

"Me either. However, I need a bit of a reprieve."

He suddenly got serious and clutched her chin. "I didn't hurt you, did I?"

She kissed his jaw. "No. You didn't hurt me. It's just been a while, that's all. And those parts are sensitive."

He looked into her eyes.

"You said that I was your first and only?"

She nodded her head. "I was a virgin."

"Nobody else?" He whispered as he ran his thumb along her lower lip, avoiding the nasty cut near the corner.

She pressed her hand against his chest over his heart. "I don't want anybody else. I shared a lot with you that night. Stuff that I'd never tell anyone else. That night was special."

"Yeah, it was."

"I was pissed off when I woke up and saw you were gone. I tried to let work keep my mind occupied, but it never failed that something or someone would remind me of you."

"I never meant for you and me to sleep together that night. But I will admit that I don't regret it. What we shared was amazing. I was hurt when you never reached out, and it wasn't like I could call up my brother."

She heard him take a big breath, then he cupped her cheeks.

"You ruined me, Clover. Your compassion, demeanor, and the fact that you trusted me with the information you spoke about that night touched me."

"Well, I don't have anyone to compare to."

He scrunched his eyebrows together and thought back to that night. Yeah, she had been snug, but there was no barrier that he broke.

She took her thumb and rubbed the spot between his eyes. "I know what you're thinking."

"You do, huh?"

"You're wondering why my cherry didn't pop."

He rolled his eyes. "Jesus, Clover."

She snickered. "If it helps ease your wandering mind, when I was in middle school, I was riding one of my brother's bikes when I lost control and crashed. My legs and arms were bleeding, but my crotch hit the crossbar that runs horizontally. I hit it so hard it broke my hymen."

"It hurt like a mother." She started to laugh. "I was wearing white shorts, and I remember Bear screaming for my mom, telling her that I broke my vagina."

Joker couldn't hold back his laugh, especially knowing how serious of a person Bear was. He then became serious, wrapped his arms around Clover, and pulled her close. He stared into her eyes. She was mature yet appeared so youthful.

"I'm glad I was your first and your last."

She gave him a coy smile. "Me too."

༄

After another round of lovemaking, they were both exhausted. Neither wanted to get out of bed, so they cuddled and just cherished the time with each other, even in silence.

Joker could tell Clover was deep in thought as she lay on her side. Her eyes were closed, but he knew she wasn't asleep. He flipped onto his side, pressed his chest against her back, and rested his chin on her shoulder.

"What's on your mind, babe?" He asked, kissing her bare shoulder and neck.

She peered over her shoulder. "Why would you think I have something on my mind?"

He leaned in and met her lips for a quick kiss. He grinned. "Your foot."

She wrinkled her nose up, all cute. "My foot? What about my foot?"

"Whenever you get nervous or deep in thought, you bounce your foot."

She sat up slightly and glanced toward the bottom of the bed where her feet were. It was still bouncing.

"It's a habit," she admitted with a half-grin. "I've always done that. Half the time, I don't even realize I'm doing it."

She laid back down, and Joker could tell something was definitely on her mind.

"Talk to me, Clover."

She was silent for a few seconds. "What happens next?" She asked.

Joker scrunched his forehead. "What do you mean?"

"You and me? How is this supposed to work? My career and your career. You're based on the East Coast, and I'm on the West Coast."

That was simple. "I could transfer."

He felt her head move. "No. I couldn't let you do that."

She knew deep down she would sacrifice her career to be wherever he was. But she also knew she'd face an uphill battle.

Joker's arm around her tightened. "I already know what you're thinking, and I would never allow it, so get it out of your mind."

She peered up at him. "How do you even know what I was thinking? Do they teach mind reading in BUD/s training?"

"Whether you know it or not, your expressions and eyes give away a lot about you."

"Really?" She thought she had a good poker face when it warranted.

"Really. And I can't in good conscience let you give up something you've put so much hard work and dedication into. Flying is your life, Clover. It's what drives you. It's who you are." He grinned. "And you're fucking amazing when you're up in the air. I've flown with a fair amount of pilots in my career, and hands down, you're one of the best I've ever flown with. It's why we all get excited when we climb onto a helo and hear the name Lucky."

"Now you're being biased."

"Biased? No fucking way. If I asked everyone on my team who their favorite pilot is, their answer would be Lucky."

She sighed. "But then we're back to my original question. Where does this leave us? We also need to consider that we're breaking the rules."

She lifted up so she could look at him. Her hands rested on his chest, bracing her weight as she stared into his green eyes—eyes that were full of questions like her.

"I don't want to leave you, Landon. Not again. I don't think my heart could withstand us walking away from each other."

He cupped her cheeks, and his warm hand infused warmth into her body.

"I'm not suggesting that anyone walk away."

He moved his hand to the back of her neck before pulling her down on top of him. Her sensitive breasts pressed against his chest. She repositioned her body so that her legs bracketed his hips. She could feel his length getting harder, and it turned her on. Her tight nipples brushed against a little bit of his chest hair, and it aroused her even more.

There was no way she was walking away from this relationship, even if it meant having to give up her career. She accomplished what she had set out to do. She was a pilot for the elite team for the President of the United States. And not just any pilot. She was the first and only female ever selected for the SCU, though she hoped she wouldn't be the last. She knew without a doubt that there were others in her footsteps that craved what she had done, and she would make it her mission to assist any female to succeed in what they dreamed of being. But she would give it all up to be with Joker.

"Clover, don't try and overthink things. We'll make it work somehow." He brushed his thumb along her bottom lip, and she gazed down at him.

She believed him. The sincerity in his voice and words and his actions were believable, and knowing what she knew now about what happened two years ago, there was no way he'd walk away.

She rolled off him and curled into his side.

Changing the subject, he asked, "What made you become a helicopter pilot?"

She smiled, remembering the day that decided her future in helicopters.

"I was eight years old. It was the day of the big air show that was in town. I'd never been before, and I had always wanted to go, but something was always happening that day that prevented me from going. But not that year. I was so excited to spend the day with my dad and brothers and see all the different aircraft and even parachuters. Little did I know that my brothers had already mapped out our day."

Joker chuckled. "Of course, they did. It explains why they're good at what they do today."

She smiled. "You're probably right. Anyway, we had been there for a few hours and had watched the flight teams we wanted to see along with a few others, and the boys wanted to leave because they were hungry. Dad had promised that he'd take them to their favorite restaurant for dinner. Being only eight, I was short and couldn't see a lot around me with all the people in attendance. But by the grace of God, as we were walking toward the exit, there was a break in the wall of people just as I had turned my head toward the right, and there it sat—the most amazing piece of aircraft I'd seen all day." She looked up at Joker as she remembered that exact moment and how her eyes lit up like a sparkling Christmas tree. "And believe me, I had seen more than enough planes that day. But that UH-60 Black Hawk blew away those other fighter jets. My dad knew something had caught my eye. When he asked what I was looking at, I pointed to the helicopter sitting about fifty yards away. I was surprised when he asked me if I wanted to go see it."

Joker smiled. "You're daddy's little girl."

She furrowed her eyebrows, and Joker was quick to explain his comment.

"I didn't mean that in a bad way," he teased and tickled her side. He ran his hand down her arm before pulling her closer against him. "Anybody can see that you're the apple of your dad's eye. The love and pride that shines through his eyes when he talks about you is an amazing thing to watch. And that goes for your brothers as well."

She snapped her head up, unsure if she had heard him correctly. "My brothers?"

Joker nodded. "Your brothers have so much respect for you."

"But...but...they were the ones who blew a gasket when I informed my family I was planning on attending the NROTC program at Embry-Riddle." She sat up, leaning back against the headboard. Joker turned onto his side and placed his hand on her thigh. She shook her head, not understanding. "Remember when you walked me home that night on the beach?"

He offered her a soft smile. "Of course I do," he admitted as his hand slid up her bare thigh. She knew what he was insinuating. Of course, the first thing he thought about was them in bed together.

She smirked while shaking her head as she covered his hand, halting his advancement. She hid her smile when he stuck his bottom lip out in a pout. She loved being intimate with Joker, but she was seriously bothered by his remarks about her brothers and how he portrayed their feelings about her being in the service.

"I'm being serious right now," she half scolded him.

His eyebrows rose in response to her declaration.

"So am I. I remember every word you said to me that night. Mainly, how you felt that your family didn't take your career seriously." He cocked one of his eyebrows at her. "Even though they think you're a mechanic."

"I don't understand. Anytime I'm around them, they're always making comments about how many years I have left on my current enlistment agreement. They even try to offer suggestions on what job fields I should try to enter when I get out. Sometimes I feel like they think I don't belong in the military, or that I couldn't cut it. The first thing Justin asks me every time I see him is what my PRT scores were."

Joker sat up, mirroring Clover's position against the headboard, and took her hand. He caressed her knuckles.

"Believe me when I say your brothers have the utmost respect for you. And not only because you're their sister, but you wear that uniform with pride and dignity. As for their comments, did you ever stop and think that maybe they're also just concerned for their little sister? As for Justin's comment about your PRT scores, he's probably just making sure you haven't beat his numbers. You have to admit, all four of your brothers are competitive."

She considered his words, and he wasn't wrong. Her brothers were a very competitive group. No matter what they were doing when they were together, it always would end up as a competition of some sort. But it still didn't explain why they didn't act supportive.

"But—"

He put his finger against her lips.

"Let me finish. We're men, and we hear the way other men talk about women, especially those in the military. I'm not saying every man is like that, but there are some real assholes out there. When your brothers hear nonsense like that, I can guarantee that their first thought is you and the assholes you probably have to navigate just to do your job."

He took a deep breath. "For example, that douche over in Djibouti."

Clover sucked her bottom lip between her teeth, knowing precisely who he was referring to—Andrews.

Joker lifted his hand and pressed it against her cheek. "I know I didn't show it because I was giving you a hard time, but I was pissed seven ways to Sunday at that guy. Not only did I want to give him a piece of my mind, but I also wanted to rip his head off."

"I know. Bear read me the riot act about it."

"He wasn't the only one. The other guys felt the same way. We see things during missions that we wish we could erase from our minds. It often involves verbally and physically abused women, not to mention the manipulation we see that goes on. Those are the visuals we're left with, and what motivates us even more to protect those at home, especially the ones we love."

She tried to blink back the tears building in her eyes, but she had difficulty keeping her emotions hidden. She got it now. And it warmed her heart knowing the truth. If Joker hadn't explained in a way for her to understand, she'd continue to assume that her family didn't think that high of her as a soldier—as their equal.

He smiled softly, pulling her closer. He kissed her before he pressed his forehead against hers.

"So the next time one of your brothers starts talking shit or nonsense, just remember it's because they care about you. And as for me, you will always be my equal."

She wiped her eyes before she kissed him. "Thank you."

"Are you hungry?" He asked.

"Not really."

"How about I make pancakes for breakfast tomorrow?"

She shifted her body so she could see him better.

"You'll seriously make pancakes?"

A small smile formed on his lips.

"I'll make you whatever you want, sweetheart."

She gave him a cheeky grin. "Pancakes sound good."

He gently used his thumb and caressed her bruised cheek.

"We need to ice this in the morning."

"Okay," she agreed.

Joker laid back down and got himself situated before he helped Clover get herself comfortable. She curled into his side with her head pillowed on his chest, and her hand splayed across his rippled stomach.

"Landon?"

"Yeah."

"Thank you."

"For what?"

"For being you and not saying no when I chose you to help me."

His large hand slid down her bare back until it rested just above her butt. His touch sent a warm sensation flowing through her body and straight to her heart.

"I'd never say no to you, Clover."

She smiled and snuggled closer as she closed her eyes, and Joker hugged her close as if acting as a protective shield. For the first time since the ordeal began, she felt relaxed and fell fast asleep, knowing that Joker had her six.

CHAPTER EIGHTEEN

Joker stood in front of the stove, flipping pancakes and frying up some hash browns. He had woken up at his usual time—0430. It had been hard for him to get out of the bed, considering that Clover had her body pressed snugly against his. He wanted to go to bed and wake up with her next to him every day. Well, when he wasn't deployed, or her, for that matter.

He knew Clover was right when she said they were facing obstacles in being together, but he was serious too when he told her he wasn't walking away. They were meant to be together, and they'd somehow find a way to make it work.

He'd been able to get some things accomplished before he started breakfast, starting with getting in a good workout, though last night in bed with Clover could have qualified as a workout.

She was something else. He loved her inexperience, and he couldn't wait to open her up to more adventurous activities in the bedroom. She was passionate when she made love, and he loved that about her. She wanted to please him, just as much as he wanted to pleasure her. He couldn't wait to share more nights being with each other.

After his shower and before preparing breakfast, President Evans had called.

Evans wanted to give him an update on the investigation. And, in Joker's opinion, the FBI was making headway. They finally obtained a search warrant to search Hollis' apartment in San Diego and Perkins's townhome in Virginia.

During the search of Hollis' house, they recovered a journal that Hollis kept, detailing everything he'd been up to for the last year.

It included dates, locations, and specific instructions on how he was to carry out each drop. It gave the Feds more to go on in their investigation. Evans had told him that with everything Hollis had in place, it was apparent he was going to flee the country after he left the service. They discovered a small suitcase containing a few passports, each with different identities.

Evans told him that during the search of Perkins' house, they found evidence that Perkins was involved in the arms dealing not only for the money, but also to get back at Evans. Perkins had a vendetta against Evans, because Evans and some other soldiers testified against Perkins years ago when Perkins went rogue and didn't follow orders or protocol during a mission that resulted in U.S. troop casualties.

It pissed Joker off know that there were people who would undermine their own country for personal vendettas and greed. Hell, there were many people he couldn't stand inside the government and military, but he'd never break the law, especially commit treason like these assholes were doing.

Evans also gave him a heads up that he was calling in his cabinet and senior advisors to update them on the situation and inform them of Perkins' death. They were also using the meeting as an opportunity to see if anyone looked guilty.

Joker hadn't been surprised when Evans told him he'd recruited Tink, the owner of Rockwell Inc., to sit in on the meeting. Joker knew Tink personally. Tink was badass, as well as a former SEAL who served with Derek. But instead of moving into a more non-combat role within the teams, Tink got out and formed his own private security company, which was now considered one of the top security companies in the world.

Joker heard the shower shut off and knew Clover would be out momentarily. She was right on time because breakfast was almost ready. He thought maybe after they ate, they'd go for a walk or a jog, depending on how she felt along some of the many trails around Camp David. He had made sure that it was okay with Evans first, and he didn't see anything wrong with it, considering Camp David was pretty secluded.

Clover slowly blinked her eyes open, rolling onto her side. She felt a slight ache in her thighs, but she smiled, knowing why.

Last night had been incredible. She knew she and Joker still had some hurdles to overcome, but she was sure things would work out. Plus, she had already made up her mind, but she had to convince Joker that it was the right decision.

She slid out of bed and pulled on Joker's t-shirt lying near the bottom of the bed. She closed her eyes as the aroma of pancakes hit her nostrils, bringing a smile to her lips. Joker hadn't been kidding when he told her he'd make pancakes.

She needed a shower first. She grabbed one of the bags of clothes off the floor and rummaged through it, finding something to wear. She shook her head again when she saw the pink thong panties. She pulled them from the bag, but to wear them. She was going to put them in the trash.

She walked into the bathroom and could smell Joker's soap and shampoo. She wondered what time he had gotten up. She was surprised that she didn't wake when he did. Like her brothers, she was a pretty light sleeper. But considering what she and Joker had been up to last night, it was no wonder she was exhausted and feeling achy.

She started the shower and shed the t-shirt she was wearing. Once the water was just how she liked it—nice and hot, she stepped under the water spray. She closed her eyes, relaxed her muscles, and let the heated water pour over her. It felt so good on her sore muscles. She wished that the bathroom had a tub so she could soak. That was one stipulation when she had shopped around for apartments in San Diego. The bathroom had to have a soaking tub. She was also a bath bomb whore. She loved bath bombs.

Knowing Joker would probably have breakfast ready, she quickly washed up and dressed. Before leaving the bathroom, she threw the pink thong in the wastebasket. "Good riddance," she mumbled before opening the door and walking out to the kitchen.

When she turned the corner into the kitchen, she stopped midstride to take in the sight of Joker. He looked sexy wearing khaki cargo shorts, a fitted t-shirt, and a fitted ball cap which he wore backward. Not to mention, nothing looked sexier than seeing him at the stove flipping pancakes.

As if knowing she was ogling him, he turned around and threw a flirty wink her way. Feeling rejuvenated, she walked over to the stove and stood next to him. With the spatula in his left hand, he wrapped his right arm around her and drew her close for a kiss.

"Morning, beautiful," he told her as he released her lips.

She smiled. "Morning." She looked into the pan and then back at him. "You also made hash browns?"

The boyish grin on his face was to die for, and even added to his sexiness.

"I remember you told me how much you like them, so I figured I make pancakes and hash browns. Your two favorites."

"Thank you." She stood on her tiptoes and kissed his cheek.

She walked to the cabinet that held the dishes, and when she reached high above her, she yelped, feeling a sharp pinch to her side.

Joker was by her side in a flash.

"What's wrong?"

Holding her side, she breathed through the slight discomfort.

"Dammit! It's just my side again. It only bothers me when I move a certain way."

She could tell he was angry, not at her but at what happened to her.

"Go sit down. I'll grab everything," he told her.

She walked around the half wall and sat on a stool at the small breakfast bar. Joker grabbed two plates and silverware for them and set them down. She watched him go over to the refrigerator, pull a container of orange juice out, and pour each of them a glass.

"What time did you get up?" She asked, picking up the glass of juice he handed to her and taking a sip.

He moved back to the stove, scooped the shredded potatoes into a serving bowl, then piled the pancakes onto a plate and walked everything over to the breakfast bar.

"Around four-thirty. Evans called this morning too."

Clover raised her eyes and met Joker's gaze.

"Any news?" She probed, hoping for something good.

Joker nodded and explained everything that Evans had passed to him.

"Wow! That guy sounds like a real dick," she said, referring to Perkins.

"So I've heard. I've never met him in person, but several guys I've worked with have, and none of them had anything nice to say about him."

Clover dished out some food on each of their plates.

"I can't believe Hollis didn't tell any of us about his mom."

"Why does that surprise you?"

"Because even though he was a prick to everyone, we all still supported him while she went through her treatment."

She forked a few pancake pieces and shoved them in her mouth. She still couldn't believe that Perkins was the top guy they were focused on. But then she remembered something. She looked at Joker.

"When we're finished, can you pull up pictures of the President's cabinet and senior advisors on your computer?"

"Sure. Why?"

"I thought maybe if I see someone, something might jog my memory."

They talked a little more about what Evans relayed. Clover was feeling more nervous knowing that tomorrow her name would be revealed to members of the administration and possibly to the mastermind behind the operation.

She felt a slight nudge to her elbow and turned her head to the right. She met Joker's intense gaze. He covered her hand with his.

"Nothing will happen to you," he told her with such seriousness and conviction. And she believed him. As long as he was by her side, she knew without a doubt that he would protect her.

After eating, they cleaned up the kitchen, then went to the dining table, and Joker booted up his laptop.

"Here we are," Joker uttered, pointing to the screen.

Clover moved so she was standing next to him. She closely looked at each picture and then read their bio. When she got to the bottom of the page, she sighed. She'd been hoping to see something that caught her eye.

Joker's hands landed on her waist, pulling her onto his lap. When she looked at him, he was giving her a sexy smirk.

"You know you're pretty sexy when you go into detective mode."

She tried to slap him in the shoulder, but he was quicker, and he ended up restraining her arms behind her back.

She didn't let that stop her as she leaned in and kissed him.

"Mmmm," he mumbled with their lips pressed together.

He released her arms, and she moved her legs, straddling his thighs. He looked into her eyes.

"You're pretty smart. You know that?"

She smiled and looped her arms around his neck.

"It's one of my fine qualities."

His eyes traveled to her chest, and a sly grin formed on his face.

"You know what else are fine qualities?"

"What?"

"These." He gave her boobs a little squeeze.

Clover rolled her eyes. "I never figured you as a boob man."

"Oh, I love boobs. Your boobs, to be exact."

"They're just boobs."

"But they're beautiful boobs," he told her as he lifted her shirt and trailed his lips up her chest.

Clover grinned. "You know, every woman should feel beautiful about her body. Even her boobs."

Joker just nodded. He was too enthralled with her boobs and the pretty pink bra.

"I bet your mom has beautiful boobs, too."

Joker stopped kissing her, and he tucked the twins back into their carriers before he lowered her shirt. When he turned his face upward, she noticed his expression had taken on a sickly look.

"That was a low blow, Clover. Ewww. I never want to think of my mom like that. I don't want to talk about boobs anymore."

He lifted her off his lap and walked back into the kitchen to put away the last of the dishes.

Clover, of course, couldn't stop laughing.

⁂

A few hours later, Clover found herself immersed in nature as she and Joker jogged through the trails around Camp David.

She was thoroughly surprised when Joker told her that they were going out. She had been under the impression that she wasn't even allowed to open a window or a door. She was pleased that her body didn't give her any issues while running. In the beginning, Joker wanted her to just walk, but she ignored him and started to jog at a comfortable pace and didn't irritate any of her injuries.

It was a beautiful summer day, especially since the humidity was low, and the low eighty degrees temperature and cloudless sky made for perfect running weather.

She'd never been to Camp David before. It was beautiful, especially along the trails sandwiched between the lush forests.

They came to a fork in the trail, and Joker started to slow down, so Clover followed his lead. He wiped the sweat from his forehead before glancing at his watch.

Clover loved running and swimming. She was on both her high school and college swim and track teams.

Joker held his finger to his lips, telling her to be quiet. When she quirked her eyebrow, he pointed to a small clearing in the woods. She turned around, and when she saw what he had spotted, she thought her heart would melt seeing the Doe and baby deer munching on some berry bush.

Giving the mamma and her baby privacy, Joker and Clover continued on the path to the left, which would take them back toward their cottage.

Joker had been telling her about Virginia Beach when she didn't see the fallen branch, and she stumbled. She would've fallen on her ass, but Joker's quick reflexes saved her the embarrassment. He snagged her around the waist, keeping her upright.

They were both laughing, and Joker pulled her close and cupped her chin.

"I love you," he told her, and she smiled, feeling all giddy inside.

"I love you, too."

Sharing moments like this made her realize she wanted this full-time.

"Can we talk for a minute? About our future."

As if knowing where she would go with her statement, he said, "Clover, I thought we both agreed we wouldn't talk about this right now."

"But we need to."

Clover had already made up her mind that she wouldn't re-up. There were plenty of companies looking for helicopter pilots, and she shouldn't have difficulty landing one with her credentials. She fulfilled her dream and then some. But it wasn't every day when love was staring her in the face. Jobs come and go, just like people, but you only have one shot at true love. And Joker was her true love.

"What are you thinking about right now?" He asked

She swallowed hard under his intense gaze. Part of being in love was being honest with the person you have given your heart to.

She took his hand and interlinked their fingers. *Just rip the bandaid off,* she told herself.

"Joker, I already made my decision. I'm not re-upping when my enlistment ends."

He started to shake his head in frustration, and she could tell by the icy look on his face that he wasn't happy. But she needed him to hear her out.

She squeezed his hand. "Please don't be upset, and hear me out before you get your flippers in a twist."

He smirked. "My flippers in a twist?"

She tried not to laugh. "Yeah. You're a SEAL, and you use flippers."

"Cute."

"I thought so," she told him with a little sass, but then she got serious. "I just started my last year. In fact, I probably have an email or paperwork waiting for me inquiring if I intend to re-enlist. While I love flying and serving my country, I'm tired of jumping when told. I want to fly with minimal red tape. Who knows, maybe I can get a job with a good private company that dabbles in government contracts, and if I need a good adrenaline rush, I can maybe take on a mission. I love my team, and I love the Corps. But I love you more."

"Sounds like you've given this a lot of thought."

"I have. And also know that whether or not we had worked things out, I was thinking about this."

He released her hand and pulled her close, wrapping both arms around her.

"You are the most unselfish person I've ever met. How did I get so lucky?"

She gave him a cheeky grin. "Lucky is my call sign."

He bent his head and kissed her before taking her hand and continuing along the trail back to the cottage.

"Who gave you that call sign?"

"Colonel Jenkins, my CO."

"Let me guess, because Clover, like a four-leaf clover?"

"Actually, no. I got that name during that operation in Pakistan a few years ago." She looked up at him and grinned. "You know, the one where the pilot ran out of options to land the bird and ended up improvising."

Joker looked at her. "I'll never forget that. It was an amazing thing to witness, though, I'll be honest with you. The whole team, including myself, thought you were fucking crazy." He chuckled before turning his gaze back to her. "I've never seen anything like it since. The Corps is certainly going to miss you. Hell, my team and I are going to miss you."

She stopped walking. "But just think, you'll get to see me when you come home."

He smiled. "You'll be the best welcome home present I've ever had."

She lifted onto her tiptoes and kissed him. "I love you."

"I love you too, babe."

CHAPTER NINETEEN

Nick Russell, otherwise known as Tink to his friends, pulled open the door and walked into the main entrance of the White House. He beamed when he saw his good friend Agent Merrick standing inside the foyer awaiting his arrival.

"Tink. How's it going, man?" Merrick asked as he held out his hand.

"I can't complain. Life has been pretty good," Tink replied, shaking Merrick's hand.

"So, I hear. When's the big day?"

Tink smirked. "Damn. News travels fast, huh?"

Merrick chuckled. "News like that does. Hell, I remember sitting with you in a bar years ago and you saying how you weren't a family type of guy."

Tink ran a hand over his bald head. "I remember that." Then he shrugged his shoulder. "What can I say? Life threw me a curveball. But I think I hit this one out of the park with Mary Beth and Christian."

Tink knew early on in his career that he wasn't suited for family life. He loved his profession too much to want to settle down. But all that changed during an operation he was assisting in coordination with SEAL Team 2 – Alpha Team in the Philippines. He'd been completely blindsided when he locked gazes with Mary Beth and her young son, Christian. He couldn't explain it. It had been like a flip of a switch. At first, it had scared the shit out of him, but after some heavy thinking and getting to know Mary Beth and Christian more, he couldn't walk away from them.

Before he walked through the metal detector, Tink placed his bag on the conveyor belt to send it through the baggage scanner.

It annoyed him having to enter government buildings because he couldn't stand not being armed. Even though he was trained to improvise with what objects were at his disposal, he still preferred carrying his own weapon.

Once he was through security screening, Merrick walked him to the West Wing toward the Oval Office. Merrick gave him some updates they'd gotten from the FBI since Evans had last spoken to him.

Tink was still furious that someone in such a high position used government resources to commit treason.

Since Tink rarely slept, he worked all through the night scouring the dark web, searching for any information on any of the administration's top cabinet and senior advisors who the FBI hadn't ruled out as suspects. Even though nothing was revealed, he did find one particular market site where there was a mention of someone named "E," who claimed to have several microchips for sale, containing highly classified information on a western government body. Tink immediately knew the post was connected to the situation they were dealing with, and he took screenshots of the page. He also reached out to a contact he had who dabbled on both sides of the law. With a small incentive, the guy offered up a slew of information on the mysterious "E." If the information provided led to the person running the ship, then Tink would consider the investment well worth it because there was no place in America for scum like the people who seek to harm their own.

When they made it to the West Wing, a middle-aged woman with glasses stood up and greeted him.

"Hello, Mr. Russell. President Evans is expecting you. Please go on in."

Tink smiled and thanked her before Merrick opened the door leading into the Oval Office.

When Tink entered the room, he found Evans, Director Caruso, and Miles, the President's Chief of Staff, sitting on the sofas.

Tink wasn't concerned with Miles' presence since he'd been ruled out as a suspect last night.

Evans was the first to greet Tink with a handshake and man hug.

"Good to see you, man."

"Likewise," Tink responded before greeting the other two men.

Once everyone took their seats, Evans began their pre-meeting before they met with members of the President's cabinet, senior advisors, and agency heads.

"I want to get all of us on the same page before we go into the room with the larger group. I plan on keeping my comments brief. I'll provide an overview of where we stand in the investigation process before I open it up for questions."

"Will you be commenting about the status crew?" Caruso asked.

"I only will if I'm asked about it."

Tink nodded in agreement. "That's what I was going to suggest. What about the families of Captain Walker and Major Saunders? Are they being notified?"

"Yes. I have time set aside later this afternoon to call each one and give them the good news. I also received word today that Major Saunders has woken up, and he's not showing any signs of any permanent damage. He'll be sidelined a few months at the most."

"That's excellent news," Tink stated, but then another thought came to him. "What about their security?"

"What about it? Both Captain Walker and Major Saunders are under twenty-four-hour protection."

Tink shook his head. He had a bad feeling about this.

"I don't think that's good enough."

"What do you suggest?"

"I'd say bring in a team to provide an extra layer of defense. I could be wrong, and nothing happens, but something in my gut says things will get worse before they get better. Look at what these people have already tried to do to you," Tink said, looking at Evans. "Plus, knowing they killed Hollis, Perkins, and God knows who else, there's no doubt in my mind that they won't stop killing."

Evans tapped his pointer finger against his lips as he considered Tink's suggestion.

"I've briefed Lana on a little bit of what's been going on. The Walkers are very good friends of ours. This morning when I told her that Clover was safe and I was planning to call Ray and Jenelle, she asked if she and I could host the Walkers this weekend as they're reunited with their daughter."

"Then I'd definitely have a team in place. I have no doubt your protection detail could handle an attack, but it never hurts to have a back-up, especially when you don't know who or what you're up against."

"Who would you suggest?"

"I would offer a few members of my team, but most of them are preoccupied at the moment. Why not Joker's team? For one, there's no question of loyalty. And two, I personally know each of the men serving on that team. They're one of the best, alongside their sister team, Alpha team. Plus, keeping the whereabouts of Captain Walker contained to one group lessens the probability of her location being leaked.

"Alright. After the meeting, I'll speak with SECNAV Cornwall and have him contact Commander Connors, and then I'll call Joker and give him a heads up on the next step."

"Is there anything you're looking for me to focus on when we go into the meeting"

Evans grinned. "That's why I called you. You're one of the best I know who can read body language. Just keep your eyes peeled for anyone who may seem uncomfortable or guilty."

Tink smirked. "That I can do."

"Alright, gentlemen. I think we're about ready," Evans stated and started to stand, but Tink held up his hand, asking for a moment.

"There's one other thing."

"What's that?" Evans asked, retaking his seat.

"Last night, I did some investigating on the dark web. And I found a post referencing someone named "E," who claimed to have microchips for sale."

Evans' eyes widened. "More microchips."

Caruso spoke up. "'E' is a person of interest. Hollis referenced in his journal about receiving a note from a mystery person named 'E.' It occurred while he was in Djibouti a few weeks ago. But the person is like a ghost. We can't find anything on him."

Tink reached into his bag and pulled out printed screenshots he had taken from the computer. He handed each man a copy of the documents.

"'E' stands for Eyad Hakimi, though most intelligence agencies knew him by Baha' al-Din Nazari. He's very wealthy. Nobody knows exactly how much money he's worth, but sources say it runs in the billions. He makes his money by funneling other people's money for them. Sources say that it's almost impossible to track where the money comes from and goes, because he constantly changes his tactics. However, my source told me that Nazari likes to put his personal touch on his transactions."

"What the fuck does that mean?" Caruso asked, looking up from his notebook where he'd been taking notes.

"He apparently uses a seven-digit code on all his transactions."

"Holy shit. Why hasn't anyone caught him if he's such a popular man?"

"Because in 2009, Baha' al-Din Nazari was presumed dead when his luxury yacht exploded in the southern Indian Ocean about fifty miles north of Amsterdam Island," Tink explained everything he found on Nazari. "Sources think he's living in Cuba."

"I will pull in a couple of my forensic accountants and get them working on this."

Tink snickered, shaking his head. "Have your team contact my employee, Arianna Moretti."

Caruso stared at Tink with an unbelievable look on his face.

"Arianna! So, you were the lucky employer she went to work with."

Arianna had worked for the FBI as a Forensic Accountant until she ran into some trouble and decided the FBI wasn't for her. Tink wasn't about to let her talent go to waste and offered her a part-time job with his company.

"Yep. She's working part-time for me when she's not managing Bayside."

"That's great for her, but sucks for the FBI. We sure do miss her."

"I can believe that."

"Has she already started working on this?"

"Yeah. She took one of Sergeant Hollis' payments through a stock deal and started tracing it. So far, she's traced the money back through three banking institutions, and my source was right. There's a seven-digit number in the reference field on each transaction, though they're not the same. The first four digits are the same, but the last three are different."

Caruso just stared at Tink. "How in the hell did she get that far in such a short time?"

Tink laughed. "You said so yourself; she's that good."

"Fuck! I knew I should have offered her more incentives to stay with the bureau. I'll have my guys get with her."

"I'll let her know to be expecting the call."

"So, if we can trace these payments back to "E" or Nazari, or whatever the hell his name is, then eventually it should lead to who gave him the money to pay Hollis, correct?"

Tink nodded. "That's what we're hoping for."

"Jesus. This is one fucked up mess."

Tink couldn't agree more.

Evans glanced at his watch. "I guess we better get going. God forbid I keep some of our guests waiting."

As the five men walked out of the Oval Office and toward the stairs leading to the basement of the West Wing, a woman with long auburn hair caught Tink's attention. When she saw him and made eye contact, Tink thought she looked familiar, but then something flashed in her eyes. It was easy to miss, but Tink caught it. Before she could turn away, he clicked a button on his glasses, and it took a photo of her. He loved all of his spy gadgets, especially when they came in handy.

As they entered the room, Tink immediately sought out a few individuals he wanted to keep his eye on. He veered to the left to take one of the empty chairs at the opposite end of the table from Evans. Not being near the president gave him a better ability to access all who were inside the room.

As soon as Evans took his seat at the head of the table, he began with his remarks.

Forty-five minutes later, Tink stayed seated as everyone filed out of the room. After everyone was gone, Evans and Caruso walked over and sat down next to Tink.

"Well?" Evans asked.

"I'll be honest. I didn't see anyone who seemed suspicious."

"Really?"

"Afraid so."

For some reason, the woman he saw earlier popped back into his head.

"While we were walking here, there was a woman. She was tall and had long auburn hair."

Miles spoke up. "Oh! That was Carrie."

"Who's she?"

"She's Lana's Chief of Staff."

Tink thought about it for a moment. He then looked at Evans. "When you were doing your investigations, did you look at the First Lady's staff?"

From the deer in the headlights look he was getting from all three, Tink knew the answer. He looked at Caruso.

"You might want to look there as well. It's a perfect place to be. Far enough away, but close enough to strike.

છે

Carrie scrolled through her phone while waiting for the First Lady to show up to their meeting. She wasn't sure what it was about. She had just gotten a text from Lana saying she wanted to meet with her at this time.

She couldn't wait until Torres officially pulled the plug on the operation because then she could stop this whole charade of playing the part of the uppity Chief of Staff.

"Sorry, I'm late," Lana announced as she rushed inside the office and threw her bag on the sofa before taking a seat across from Carrie.

Carrie smiled. "That's quite all right. It gave me some time to reach out to the venue in Texas for your summit in the fall."

"Oh, how's everything coming along with that?"

Carrie spat off all the details that had been confirmed and what still needed to be done.

"Perfect."

"So, what did you want to see me about?"

"Rick and I are hosting some guests this weekend at Camp David."

"Oh," Carrie stated, clearly surprised at the last-minute schedule change.

"What about the dinner with the Nelsons you had planned for Thursday?"

"I had Courtney reschedule it. This trip is more important."

That raised Carrie's suspicions. What could be more important than hosting the Nelsons, who were large donors to the Evans campaign?

"What are the names of the guests? Just so I can get those to Agent Merrick to run all the proper background checks."

Lana chuckled. "That won't be needed. These are old friends."

"But we always clear everyone." Carrie pressed.

"Well, not this time."

"Should I have the staff at Camp David prepare rooms in the main house, or will your guests be staying at one of the cabins nearby?"

They'll need a cabin of their own. You can use any but the Eagle Cabin."

Carried frowned. "Why not the Eagle? It's the newest cottage with all the bells and whistles."

Lana hesitated, and Carrie picked up on it right away, which got her thinking deeper.

"Because the Eagle is undergoing some landscaping updates, and it's a mess."

Hmmm…. Carrie thought to herself as she jotted down notes in her folio.

They went over some other details such as the staff needed for the main house, and any special meals that needed to be planned.

"Is there anything else?"

Lana took a deep breath. "Not that I can think of, but I'll let you know if something comes to mind."

"Alright then. I'm going get started on this.

"Thank you, Carrie."

Carrie nodded and stepped out into the hallway, closing the door. Miles walked out of his office as she started to walk toward her office.

"Miles!" She called after him, and he turned toward her and smiled.

"Carrie. Hi. How are you?" He fumbled a bit through his words. God, she couldn't wait until this job was over so that she didn't have to be nice to people, especially Miles. He may seem like a nice guy, but he wasn't her type.

"Did you know the President and First Lady decided to take a last-minute trip to Camp David?"

The deer in the headlights look Miles gave her made her think one of two things. It was either a surprise to him, or he was well aware and was trying to think of a response. Boy, these people around the White House thought she was clueless.

He surprised her when he took her elbow and pulled her inside his office.

"Who told you about that?"

"Lana, of course. She needed me to help with a few things. I don't understand what all the secrecy around this trip is all about."

"What do you mean?"

"Well, for starters, she wouldn't even tell me who the guests were that she and Rick were entertaining. How strange is that?"

Miles looked as if he was debating something. Finally, after a few awkward moments, he said, "Look, you didn't hear this from me. You know the pilot who was involved in the incident last week?"

"Vaguely. I don't know her personally or anything."

"It's her parents that Rick and Lana are hosting."

"And that doesn't seem strange to you?"

"No, because the two families are very close."

"Oh. I see." She laughed dramatically. "Maybe Rick is surprising them."

Miles narrowed his eyes as if he was suspicious. "What do you mean?"

"Maybe he's planning on surprising them with something, like a happy reunion with their daughter. I mean, come on. Doesn't all the secrecy raise your suspicions?" She looked at him, and he didn't answer. He pressed his lips together tightly.

"Unless you know what's going on," she commented.

He relaxed his shoulders and exhaled. "Look, I'm sorry, but I can't say anything. And with everything else going on around here, the last thing I want is Rick to think my loyalty doesn't lie with him."

She smiled. Miles didn't have to say it out loud that Clover Walker was meeting her parents at Camp David. His body language told her all she needed to know.

"I understand, Miles, and I'm sure Rick appreciates that."

She started to leave when Miles called after her.

"Hey, do you want to go have a drink down at Red River?"

She smiled softly. "Thank you for the offer, and I wish I could, but I have a whole list of tasks I need to complete for Lana. Raincheck?"

He pushed his glasses up his nose. "Yeah. Sure."

"Goodnight, Miles."

"Night, Carrie."

Carrie stepped out into the hall and hurried back to her office. She pulled her phone out as she shut the door and hit the first name in her contacts.

The man picked up on the second ring.

"I hope you're calling with some news."

A slow savage smile spread across her lips.

"I think I found her."

CHAPTER TWENTY

"Mr. President, that is wonderful news. Clover is going to be ecstatic when I tell her."

Joker hung up with President Evans and tucked his phone into his back pocket. He couldn't wait to share the news with Clover that her parents were coming to Camp David at the end of the week. But the even better news was that Bear and the team would be arriving tomorrow.

He climbed the stairs to the front porch and unlocked the door. Once inside, he realized it was quiet—very quiet.

"Clover?" He called out but didn't get a response. When he checked the bedroom and bathroom, and she wasn't in there, he started to panic. But as he walked through the kitchen and into the living room, he spotted Clover through the back door carrying logs toward the fire pit.

He opened the door and stepped out on the deck. "Hey! You should have waited."

She smiled as she set the logs down next to the fire pit. "I think I can handle carrying a few logs."

He glanced at the table filled with graham crackers, chocolate bars, and a bag of marshmallows. It made him smile because earlier, Clover commented about making smores.

"What's all this?" He asked, walking over to her.

She picked up the zip lock bag containing the graham crackers and held it up. "I'm going to make smores. Want some?"

He smirked and sat down next to her. "You sure do know a way to a man's heart." He leaned over and kissed her on the lips.

"How was your call with Evans? Any breaking news?"

"It was good. In fact, I've got some news for you that I think you'll love."

"We're leaving?" She sounded so hopeful, and he wished he could give her that.

"Not quite." He hated seeing the disappointment on her face.

"Bear is coming tomorrow."

Her eyes got wide. "Here? Bear's coming here? Tomorrow?"

He grinned, seeing how fast her frown turned upside down.

"Yep. And so is the rest of the team."

He loved seeing that big smile on her face. He leaned over and kissed the side of her head.

"But that isn't the best news."

"It's not?"

"Nope."

"Well, don't keep me in suspense, Sr. Chief Davis."

Joker burst out laughing.

"What's so funny?"

It just hit me that you outrank me, Ma'am."

"Does that bother you?"

"Of course not. In fact, I find it sexy that I'm dating a Captain."

"Soon to be former Captain," she reminded him as he picked her up and placed her on his lap. He liked having her close.

Even though Joker knew she planned to retire at the end of her enlistment, he was still worried that she might regret it later.

Clover cleared her throat, and he looked at her.

"Are you okay?"

"Yeah, why?"

"I don't know, maybe because you suddenly got quiet and were staring at the fire as if it had you in a trance."

He cupped her chin before leaning in and kissing her deeply. As he released her lips and she gazed into his eyes, he smiled and winked.

"I promise, everything's good."

"If you say so." Joker knew she wasn't buying it, but he wasn't going to bring up his concerns.

"So, what's the other good news?"

"Your parents should be getting a phone call from Evans in the next hour or two."

He saw the happy tears building in her eyes.

"Really?"

He nodded. "I wouldn't lie about that," he told her with such seriousness. "But that's not all."

She looked at him.

"President Evans and Lana are also coming later this week for a visit." He watched as Clover's eyes lit up with joy.

"That's great. I'd love to see them."

"And this Saturday, Evans is bringing your parents here to see you."

"Seriously?"

"Yes."

She got so excited that she actually squealed. "Oh my gosh! That is the best news!" She leaned in and kissed him again. But when she pulled away, Joker could sense something was wrong.

Staring into her eyes, he asked, "What's wrong? I thought you'd be thrilled with all that. You get to see your family."

"I am. Believe me."

"Then what is it?"

She gave him a half-smile of sorts. "If my brother's coming, then we get to break the news to him—about us."

"Ugh! Don't remind me."

She started laughing. "He's going to be totally fine with it."

"You think so?"

"I know so."

Jesus. He hoped so.

He eyed the chocolate, marshmallows, and graham crackers.

"So, smores, huh?"

"Here." She handed him the stick with a marshmallow impaled on it, then set a paper plate with graham crackers and chocolate on her lap.

As he held the marshmallow over the crackling flame, he absorbed the feeling of holding Clover in his arms. So many nights over the last two years, he had laid alone in bed wishing she were snuggled next to him just like she was now, curled up and complacent on his lap.

Sensing eyes on him, he glanced down and found her greenish-brown eyes staring back at him. She tossed him a subtle wink, and he grinned before kissing the top of her head. She snuggled against him, and he beamed as an idea formed in his head.

"Close your eyes," he told her. At first, she gave him an odd look, but when he cocked an eyebrow at her, she smiled and shut her eyes.

Once the fluffy white marshmallow was warm and brown from roasting, he took a piece of the chocolate and laid it on top of the graham cracker. Then he placed the hot marshmallow on top of the chocolate. When he saw the chocolate melting, he swiped his finger through it, collecting a glob of the melted sweet.

Slowly he ran his finger down her neck, leaving a trail of the warm morsel. He noticed her breathing had increased, and a small smile dangled on the corner of her lips.

He moved his mouth close to her ear. "I would love to take a handful of this chocolate and let it melt down your body before I lick it off."

He lowered his mouth to her neck, where the sweet treat waited for him. Slowly he began to lick and suck the chocolate from her skin.

"Mmmm."

He heard her take a sharp breath, and he smiled against her skin.

Once he had removed every bit of chocolate, he moved to her mouth, kissing her deeply and passionately.

Needing to breathe, he pulled away. She slowly blinked her eyes open and met his gaze.

"That was amazing," she whispered.

"You liked it?"

"Like it? I love it! When women say they've orgasmed over chocolate, I think I now know why."

Joker burst out laughing.

After more smores, the two sat cuddled in front of the fire.

"How are your mom and dad?" She asked him.

"Okay, I guess."

"You guess? When's the last time you spoke with them?"

"It's been a while. You know how my mom is. I have to adhere to her schedule. And then you got my dad, who barely speaks a full sentence to me."

Clover snuggled closer. "No offense, but your family reminds me of a cactus."

"A cactus?"

"Yeah. It's full of pricks."

Joker couldn't hold back his laughter. He couldn't agree more with her perception. His family was—special.

"Well, that's why I have you, family," he told her.

"And we all love you."

֍

Bear walked into Bayside, a small hidden treasure along the beach that served up the best prime rib and drink specials in the Virginia Beach area. Paul, the owner, had opened the joint after retiring from the Marines. It was a place off the beaten path that not many tourists knew about. It was a place where service members like himself could go and enjoy a meal or a drink and not be haggled by tourists wanting to meet them. It was a place of solitude.

As he scanned the restaurant's interior, he met the eyes of two familiar faces. He walked between the tables until he got to the back table next to the doors leading to the patio deck.

Ace, Alpha team's leader, stood and greeted him with a handshake and slap on the back. Ace's new wife, Alex, who Bear admired, stood as well and gave him a big hug. And damn if he didn't need that hug. He kissed her cheek before releasing her.

He smiled down at her. "Congratulations on the wedding. Sorry, we couldn't be there."

Alex offered a sympathetic smile. "No apology necessary. I'm sorry to hear about your sister. Have your mom and dad received any more information?"

Bear shook his head. "No, and it gets harder every day that passes."

"How are your parents doing?"

Bear took a seat across from the couple. "Dad is handling it like I suspected he would. He shows the world his brave front, but I know he's hurting just as much as my mom is. She's having a difficult time processing that there may be a possibility that Clover may never come home."

Just saying those words left a bitter taste in Bear's mouth.

"Come on, man. Don't think like that," Ace told him.

A waitress approached, and Bear ordered a beer.

"If the government isn't giving up any information, then something major is going on."

"I fully agree, but how the hell do we find out?" Bear commented, clearly frustrated with the whole situation.

At that moment, Potter and Tenley appeared with their three daughters, Alejandra, Kensi, and Kelsey.

Bear shook Potter's hand and hugged Tenley. They also asked about Clover, and he gave them the same answer.

He looked over and noticed Alejandra had a slight pout on her face, and he wondered what was up with that. It was rare to see her without a smile gracing her beautiful face.

Bear glanced at Potter and nodded toward Alejandra.

"She okay?"

Potter looked at his daughter and sighed. Tenley chuckled.

"She's feeling lonely because Cody is at his Sea Cadet training for the week."

Bear nodded his head in understanding. Cody was Frost and Autumn's son. Frost was a member of Alpha team, serving alongside Ace and Potter. When Frost first met Autumn, he immediately formed a bond with Cody. Autumn's former husband, Cody's biological dad, was a Marine and killed in action while serving in Iraq. The day that Cody had been introduced to Alejandra was when those two kids had become inseparable. Everyone always joked that the pair would one day end up married. Well, everyone except for Potter. He was very protective of his girls, though Bear knew that Potter held a lot of respect for Cody. In fact, every member of Alpha and Bravo teams respected that kid. At twelve years old, he already exhibited the telltale signs of an alpha male. He had sacrificed himself on more than one occasion to help save someone else's life, including Alejandra and his mom, Autumn. Bear, along with the others had no doubts that Cody would fulfill his dream—to be a Navy SEAL.

But now, seeing how upset Alejandra was, he felt bad for her. He had no idea why but he pulled a twenty-dollar bill out of his wallet and handed it to her. Then he leaned over and whispered into her ear.

"Use this to buy something special for Cody when he gets home."

Seeing the smile on her face brought a bit of happiness to him.

He noticed Alex staring at him, grinning. "What?"

"I just didn't realize you had a soft side," Alex teased before taking a sip of water.

He smirked. "I have my moments. It just doesn't happen often."

He saw Alex's eyes light up as she looked past him towards the main entrance.

"Oh, look, Irish and Bailey are here," she announced.

Bear turned to look, and damn if they weren't. He then wondered if the rest of their team, Frost, Stitch, Dino, Skittles, and Diego, would show up. But as if reading his mind, Alex smiled and told him that they weren't expecting the others.

As soon as Irish sat down, Bear could tell that the sniper wasn't in the best of moods. He glanced at Bailey, Irish's wife.

"What's with him? He looks uptight."

Bailey tried to hide her laugh but didn't do a very good job because Irish gave her the stink eye. That only made her giggle louder.

"He's having a tough time getting over what Sienna told him in the car on the way here."

Bear could only imagine. He'd heard stories about the crazy but hilarious words that poured out of the spunky six-year-old's mouth. Biologically Sienna was Irish's niece, but after some family issues, he gained guardianship of her. Then when he met Bailey, and they got married, they decided to adopt Sienna.

The full-of-life little squirt appeared and jumped into Irish's lap as if right on cue.

"He's mad that my friend Robby told me that his wiener wanted to come out to play."

"Sienna..." Irish warned.

After nearly spitting his beer out, Bear tried unsuccessfully to hide his own laughter. He glanced over at Irish, who ran his hands down his face.

"Well, I'm sure your friend Robby has a very nice and maybe even playful wiener," Bear told her, knowing she was referring to Robby's dog.

Irish looked up and flipped the bird at him behind Sienna's head so she wouldn't see it.

"I can't wait until you're graced with a beautiful little girl who tortures you like this little nut here does with me," Irish said as he playfully tugged on Sienna's ponytail.

Bear shook his head vigorously before laughing off Irish's comment. However, Irish's words stung a little, because he wasn't sure he'd ever have kids. Not that he didn't want them, because he'd always believed he'd have a house full of kids and a wife by his side, just like the guys in his company now. It was hard to believe that just two and half years ago, the entire Alpha Team was where he was now—single. But seeing the joy that marriage and family brought to Ace, Potter, Frost, Irish, Stitch, Dino, Skittles, and Diego made him recognize what he could have had instead of letting his insecurities get the best of him.

He picked up his beer to take a drink but was interrupted when Alejandra appeared next to him. She had the prettiest brown eyes.

"Bear, why do you look sad?"

He took a deep breath and cleared his throat. "My little sister is missing, and I miss her very much."

"How?"

"Alejandra…" Potter said in a warning to his inquisitive daughter, but Bear was okay with her questioning him. She was a kid.

"It's okay, Potter."

He looked back at the little girl with the big brown eyes.

"My sister, Clover, is a Marine."

"Your sister is a soldier, too?"

"She is. She's a helicopter mechanic. Unfortunately, we don't have a lot of answers right now."

She took his hand and stared into his eyes.

"You're gonna find her, Mr. Bear."

"I am?"

"Uh-huh. But you have to believe it here," she said to him, placing her little hand over his heart. "When my mommy was missing, I told my daddy that she'd come home if we prayed. So, I'm going to say an extra prayer tonight for Clover."

Bear glanced up and met Tenley's glassy eyes. He remembered when Tenley was taken by a crazy Columbian drug lord.

Bear wiped the lone tear he felt about to slip out of his eye. Damn, He never thought he'd be brought to tears by a kid.

"That's very nice of you, sweetie, and I sure do appreciate it, and I know my sister will too."

"She'll find her way home. I just know it. Just like my mommy did."

"I don't like seeing you sad."

"Well, I don't like seeing you sad either."

"I miss Cody."

"Yeah, but he'll be home this weekend, right?"

"Yeah."

"I bet he'd love a welcome home party."

Her brown eyes widened. "Really?"

"Sure. All soldiers love a welcome home party."

He looked at Tenley and Potter and winked. Tenley mouthed thank you to him.

Alejandra looked at her mom. "Mommy, can we plan a party for Cody? He would love it."

Tenley smiled. "I'll call Autumn in the morning."

"Yes!" The little girl did a fist pump. "My boyfriend will love me!" She exclaimed, and right on cue, Potter spewed his beer all over the table.

The conversation had Bear thinking about the past. A past that he regretted now, but at the time, he thought he was doing the right thing. Now and then, he'd think about Joce and wonder what she was up to. With her looks, personality, and brilliance, it wouldn't surprise him if she was happily married with kids.

He picked up his beer, and before he could take a swig, he felt his phone vibrate. He closed his eyes for a second. *Can't a man just have a second for a beer?* He thought to himself as he plucked the phone from his pocket. Seeing Derek's name on the screen made him think he was being called in.

"Commander?"

"I need you here in my office. I've got the SECNAV on the way, and he specifically asked that you be here."

Bear set his beer down and fished his car keys from his pocket.

"Yes, sir. On my way."

As he disconnected the call, Ace raised an eyebrow at him.

"Going in?"

"Yeah, but I have no idea what for."

Alex got up and met him by his chair as he stood. She hugged him.

"I meant what I said. If we can help out in any way, please let us know."

He smiled and gave her another hug. "Thank you, Alex. We'll be fine. My gut is telling me that my sister is out there. She just needs some help finding her way back home."

With a nod toward Ace, Bear turned and walked out, wondering what type of situation would warrant a personal visit from the SECNAV.

CHAPTER TWENTY-ONE

Bear pulled the SUV up to the small but nicely decorated cottage tucked into a secluded spot inside Camp David. When he had met with the SECNAV last night and was told he and the team were being deployed, he hadn't expected to be operating inside the United States, much less at the President's country residence. Rarely did the teams operate in the country. It only occurred when the President approved of it.

"Are you sure we're at the right place?" Nails asked from the front passenger seat, leaning forward and scanning the property.

Bear looked at the large black numbers posted by the front door.

"92 National Court. That's the address the Commander gave me."

Bear had his hand on the handle when the front door to the cottage opened. He had to do a double-take the moment he saw Joker emerge through the doorway and walk out onto the small porch.

"I'll be damned," Duke commented from the back seat.

"You've got to be shitting me. You mean to tell me I had to go into the base over the weekend to clean out the equipment room because *he's* been enjoying life up here?" Snow grumbled as the team exited the vehicle.

"I don't know why you're complaining, Snow. You would've had to clean out the room anyway since Joker was supposed to be with Bear at his parents' house."

"Oh, yeah."

Bear laughed as he exited the vehicle and walked up the steps. He smirked as Joker stood there with his arms crossed.

"Funny meeting you up here?" Bear joked, although he was also intrigued by Joker's presence. It made him wonder what exactly their assignment entailed. All that Derek had told them was that the President specifically requested their team to assist with a protection detail.

Joker cracked a small smile and reached out to shake Bear's hand. "How was the drive?"

Bear shrugged his shoulders. "Wasn't too bad. Hit some traffic around the city, but other than that, it was pretty smooth."

Joker greeted the others as they all approached.

"Now, this is what I call heaven," Playboy commented as he looked around the area and towards the cottage's woods.

"Wait until you see the backyard. Come on in," Joker told them. Bear couldn't help but notice how Joker appeared on guard and kept looking around the area. Because of the training instilled in them, they were always well aware of their surroundings and constantly looking over their shoulders. However, Joker appeared on heightened alert, as if he was expecting something to happen at any given moment.

As the team filed inside and set their gear down, a familiar scent attacked Bear's nose—apples, just like the lotion and sprays that Clover wore. Clover loved anything that smelled like apples. He gave his head a slight shake, reminding himself that he was working. Of course, his sister's situation was on his mind twenty-four-seven, but he couldn't afford to lose focus while on a job.

He had spoken with Derek about his concern about not being on top of his game, but Derek had assured him that he had all the confidence in him to perform his duties to the best of his ability.

Playboy, Duke, and Snow plopped down on the sofa, stretching their legs out.

"So, considering you're already here and the President sent us here, I assume you know what's going on?" Bear asked Joker with his eyebrows raised.

Joker nodded and went to speak, but Nails interrupted him.

"Before we get down to business, what's for dinner because I'm fucking starving."

"We were planning on making pizza. We just weren't sure what time you were getting here."

Bear pinned Joker with a curious look. "We?" He asked, wondering if Joker had a mouse in his pocket.

"Yes, we."

Bear didn't need to turn around to see who was there. It was a voice he thought he'd never hear again. Judging from the wide eyes and gaping mouths of the others staring at the woman behind him, he knew he wasn't wrong.

Slowly turning around, he found his sister standing in the doorway, a big smile planted on her face. The sight of her nearly made his legs go weak, and for a brief moment, he thought they'd buckle under him.

"Bear—" Before she could finish her sentence, he was across the room in two long strides, sweeping her up into a big hug. His mind was reeling with questions, but more importantly, Clover was alive.

Tears stung his eyes as she wrapped her small arms around his neck. He wasn't the least bit embarrassed about crying in front of the team. They were all family, and had all experienced a situation that affected them deeply at one time or another.

"Bear, you're crushing me," Clover whispered as he hugged her tight. He snickered as he pulled back a smidge and looked into her eyes. Suddenly, the muscles in his face tightened upon seeing the purplish bruise covering the right side of her cheek.

He set her back onto her feet and gently cupped her injured cheek.

"What happened to you?"

She took a step back and peered over her shoulder at Joker, who smiled and winked at her, which Bear thought was odd.

Clover cleared her throat and wiped away a few tears of her own.

"Why don't we go sit down and talk," she offered, and Bear couldn't agree more. He was more than curious to hear what had been going down the last few days since they were told she was missing.

Playboy, Duke, and Snow got up so Clover could sit. They, along with Aussie, grabbed the chairs from the kitchen table and brought them over. Nails took the recliner while Jay Bird leaned against the wall with his arms crossed.

Bear followed Clover and Joker to the couch, but he couldn't take his eyes off their interaction. Joker had his hand pressed against the small of Clover's back as he guided her to the sofa before taking the seat next to her.

Bear took the spot on the other side of Clover, but he looked at Joker first.

"Was this why you left my parents' house? The call from Derek? Did you know?"

Joker shook his head. "At the time, I didn't know anything. I wasn't told anything until I arrived in D.C. and met Evans at a hotel. That's when he filled me in on what was going on."

Clover took Bear's hand into hers. "Bear, don't be angry with Joker. I'm the one who asked that he come to Washington."

Bear cocked his head, not understanding a goddamn thing about what was going on.

Clover took a deep breath. "I guess I should start from the beginning, considering there's a lot to tell."

Bear thought that was a great idea.

"Okay."

She licked her nervously, instinctively beginning to play with her fingers.

"First, I lied to you." Bear knew he didn't hide his shock at her admission. Her statement caught him off guard, knowing that Clover was one of the most trustworthy people he knew.

"About what?" He asked.

"I didn't just lie to you. I lied to everyone, including Mom, Dad, Justin, Ethan, and Zach."

She paused a moment, and Joker reached over and squeezed her leg. When their eyes met, anyone watching could see something pass between them. Bear thought it was interesting, considering the last time the two of them had been in his presence, they were about to take each other's heads off.

When Clover turned her attention back to Bear, Bear saw something in her eyes—guilt, maybe? She took a deep breath.

"I lied about what I do for a living—for the Corps. I'm not a helicopter mechanic." Bear's eyebrows rose, but he didn't say anything and let her continue. "I'm a pilot for the Situational Combat Unit assigned under the President."

Bear sat there for a moment, letting her words soak in. At first, he wanted to laugh and say, "you got me," thinking this was all some big joke or prank, and he was the butt of it. But from the solemnity pouring off her and the shakiness in her voice, he knew it wasn't a laughing matter. He knew she was telling him the truth.

"You're not kidding," he said honestly, and she shook her head.

Bear wasn't sure what to think or how he even felt about that bombshell. His baby sister was a member of the SCU, and nobody in his family knew.

"Mom and Dad didn't know?" He asked, just to confirm.

"No. I knew none of you would accept me being in a position like that."

She wasn't wrong there. None of them had been thrilled when she told them all she was joining the Marines. But over time, they all came to accept it and loved knowing that she still got to enjoy being around helicopters, even though they all knew she'd much rather be behind the controls of one.

Once he had a little time to digest what he was hearing, he released her hand and stood up. He began pacing the small room—a few steps to the right, then back to the left. He repeated his movement several times and pinched the bridge of his nose when it hit him. And boy did it hit him hard—like a freight train running at full steam.

He turned to face his sister, who looked slightly frightened as he pinned her with his piercing gray eyes.

"It was you, wasn't it? In Djibouti."

Clover nodded as if knowing what he was asking.

"Jesus Christ!" He exclaimed, running his hands over his face in disbelief. But then another thought hit him, and he turned toward the others.

"Did you guys know?"

Not knowing what Bear was talking about, Duke spoke for the group.

"Know what?"

"That Clover was the pilot who extracted us that night in Eritrea."

Several mumbles echoed the small space, but the small voice that followed shocked him.

"And I'd do it again if I had to," Clover announced, and Bear turned to look at her. Her attitude and demeanor had changed in seconds. The frightened look she had just moments ago had been replaced by a woman full of confidence as she jutted her chin and held his firey gaze.

Suddenly, Nails stood up from his chair and walked over to Clover. He reached for her hand and pulled her onto her feet. Before Bear could ask, Nails had her wrapped up in his arms, hugging her.

Shocked at Nails' reaction, Bear looked to Joker, who appeared the same, but Bear saw something else in his best friend's eyes—fire and jealousy. That was interesting, Bear thought.

Joker with his hands on hips glared at Nails as he held Clover close.

"What in the hell are you doing?" Bear finally asked his teammate.

He saw Nails whisper something to Clover and swore Clover said, "you're welcome," before he released her, and she sat back down.

Nails then looked at him. "I'm thanking the pilot who saved our asses on more than one occasion." Nails turned back toward Clover. "I meant what I said. Never in the nine years that I've been serving in the Navy have I met a more talented and badass pilot than you. You're truly fucking amazing."

"So amazing that the government should look into cloning you," Aussie added and winked.

"Fucking unbelievable," Snow chimed in, grinning in Clover's direction.

"You're a remarkable and talented person," Duke told Clover.

"Don't forget to add beautiful and kind," Playboy added.

Bear glanced over at Jay Bird, who'd been quiet. "Do you want to add anything?"

Jay Bird looked at Clover. "I'd take you on my team any day, sweetheart."

Bear couldn't believe it. His sister—his baby sister, had just dropped a fucking bombshell, and his teammates were fawning all over her. Was he the only one pissed that she had lied to her family and put herself in danger?

Clover stood up and walked over to him. She took his hands into hers as she stared up into his eyes.

"I know you're upset, but you don't understand."

"Explain it then."

"Ever since I was old enough, I've wanted to join the Marines. I wanted to be just like you, Dad, Justin, Ethan, and Zach. I wanted to make you guys proud. When I watched all of you join the service and get selected for Special Forces, I knew I had my work cut out for me. I wanted to be a Special Forces operator. I wanted that journey just like you guys.

I busted my ass at college and flight school. I had expectations to live up to, but that isn't what drove me to succeed. It was my determination. And, you know what? It all paid off. I went through the same intense training as you did. There weren't any lower standards I had to meet to become one of the top elite soldiers. And not only was I selected over hundreds of other applicants to be a part of an amazing unit, but I also got to do what I loved. And that was flying. I was proud to work under the direction of the President of the United States. But in the end, all I wanted was to be an equal in your eyes and the others. My god, do you know how many missions I've been a part of? Hell, I've pulled all your asses out of the fire on numerous occasions, but you just didn't know it."

"Don't remind me," he said, gritting his teeth. He was pissed, but she was trying to make a point. But in a stunning turn of events, he found himself softening his gaze and stance as he looked into her eyes—the eyes of a true warrior. His sister was truly amazing.

"Clover, I never intended to make you feel that way. None of us did. I wasn't trying to undermine your abilities. You don't have to prove your bravery and courage to any of us. We knew all along that you were going to make a great soldier. I, well, we all just obviously didn't realize how great you were, considering what I know now."

He cupped her cheek. "We all just care about you, Clover. You're our little sister, and it's our instinct to want to protect you. But now that I look at the big picture, it seems your big brothers needed some protection too."

He smiled, and when she smiled back, he knew things would be okay between them. But he wasn't sure how she would fair with his dad or brothers.

"Now that we've gotten that out of the way, how about you tell us why we're really here?"

He watched Clover swallow hard as her smile vanished completely—she looked as if she were about to be sick.

రు

Bear sat next to Clover as she finished explaining everything. He was pissed, and if she hadn't already killed those men, he'd see to it that they died a slow death.

"So, how did you get out of there? Who found you?"

"The Colonel and Evans knew something was wrong when the signal to the transponder went out. Evans called for back-up."

"Who?"

"Oz and his friends," She told him.

Bear wrinkled his forehead. "Oz?"

She gave him a cheeky grin. "My new Delta Force friends. Oh! They told me to tell you hello, and Oz said you still owe him a beer and a new watch."

Bear grinned, realizing who she was talking about. Oz and his unit were a powerhouse, and one that he'd be happy to partner with any time. They had embarked on a few joint missions together when the operation called for a mix of elements from both teams.

"I'll have to thank Oz the next time I see him."

For the next several hours, they all sat around discussing the situation as well as the upcoming retreat that President Evans was planning at Camp David. It was going to be a happy reunion for the Walker family. But, it was also going to be tense and nerve-wracking, as bringing Clover out into the open and announcing the investigation into top administration officials was bound to put a target on her back.

He looked toward the kitchen where Joker and Clover were making pizzas for everyone. He noticed how attentive Joker had been towards Clover earlier when she was talking to them. He found it rather interesting how they acted affectionate toward one another, considering the last time the two were seen together, they were practically trying to bite each other's heads off.

Right at that moment, Joker glanced up, and Bear met his gaze. Bear raised an eyebrow, but Joker shook his head, indicating that now wasn't the time to talk. That was fine with Bear. He'd move it to the back burner for now, but it was still simmering, and eventually, it would come to a boil again.

ಞ

After dinner, Joker went looking for Bear. Bear and Jay Bird had stayed behind while the others went up to the main lodge to scope out the place before Evans and his wife arrived.

Joker spoke with Clover, and they both agreed that they needed to be honest with Bear and tell him about their relationship. Clover wanted to be there when Bear found out, but Joker thought it was best if Bear heard it from him first. Clover finally agreed. So, while she was showering, Joker decided to talk to him.

As he walked through the living room, he caught Jay Bird's eye, and as if knowing who he was looking for, Jay Bird nodded toward the back door.

He walked over to the French doors and saw Bear leaning against the railing, looking out towards the woods.

He opened the door and walked out. It was a beautiful summer night—not too hot and not too cool. Bear turned around, and from the look in his eye, Joker had a feeling that Bear might be thinking about the same thing he was coming to talk to him about.

"You got a minute? There's something I want to talk to you about," Joker said, motioning toward the chairs sitting around the fire pit.

Bear nodded and followed Joker over to the chairs. Once they were settled, Joker started.

"I know you're wondering what's going on between Clover and me."

Bear arched his eyebrows. "What makes you think that?"

"Come on, man. I saw the way you were looking at us."

"Alright. Yeah. It did catch my attention, especially since the last time I saw you two together, you wanted to kill each other."

"Well, that's true. Granted, there was a reason behind it, which I'm not getting into with you because it's private between Clover and me."

He could see Bear was biting the inside of his cheek, and Joker prayed that his and Clover's relationship wouldn't harm him and Bear's friendship or working relationship.

"What I will tell you, is that Clover and I have gotten to know each other very well over the years. She's someone who I have the utmost respect for. She's also someone who I care about deeply."

"So, are you saying that she and you are…"

"Dating? Yeah. And before you think that this has been going on for a while behind your back, it hasn't." Joker tried to think of how he wanted to word the next part. "Remember that night when we met Clover for dinner in San Diego?" Bear nodded. "Well, she and I connected that night. We shared a lot in conversation. I know I've known her for years, but that night she opened up to me about things that made me see who she really was."

"Who is she, really?" Bear asked, seeming a little put off by Joker's comment. But Joker didn't mean it in the way that Bear was probably thinking.

"I don't mean that she's a different person, and you don't know who she is. She loves and respects you and your brothers so much. But for me, it's different. She's the woman I've waited my entire life to meet. She's who I want by my side. She's my equal."

"Wow..."

"Are you mad?"

"Not mad, but disappointed that neither of you told me. I wouldn't have cared. Hell, Joker, you're my best friend. You're the one person I'd never question if you had feelings for Clover.

Joker shoved his hands into his front pockets. "It's more than just feelings, man. I love her."

Judging from Bear's wide eyes, Joker knew he'd surprised him.

"You love her?"

Joker grinned. "I do, and don't ask me how I could since she and I haven't spoken in two years, but I can assure you that I have nothing but good intentions. She's it for me."

Bear rubbed his hand along the scruff on his jaw.

"Jesus. You both must be trying to send me to an early grave. First, I find out my sister is some super pilot, and now my best friend is telling me that he loves her."

Before Joker could respond, the door opened, and Clover emerged.

"Everything okay out here?" She asked, worrying her bottom lip.

Joker looked at Bear and waited for him to answer since the ball was in his court. He either accepted the fact that he and Clover were together, or he didn't. And if it were the latter and meant him leaving the team, then that was what he would do, because the one thing he wouldn't do was leave Clover.

Bear smiled at his sister. "Yeah. Everything's good, sis."

She walked over and hugged Bear. "Good, because I would hate it if things weren't," she told him, and Joker closed his eyes, feeling like an elephant had been lifted off his shoulders.

CHAPTER TWENTY-TWO

A few days later, Clover walked into the sunroom at the main lodge. It was in the evening, and the sun was starting to set. President Evans and Lana had arrived earlier and invited everyone to dinner at their place.

Her mom, dad, and brothers were due to arrive the following day. She was so excited to see them.

She had spoken with Evans earlier, and he had told her that they still hadn't figured out who Perkins and Hollis had been working for. She felt a little disappointed, because she still wasn't safe or free to live a normal life. He had assured her that the FBI was working around the clock to smoke out the person, but it was going to take a little longer.

He did, however, inform her that with the help of a security firm, Rockwell Inc., the FBI, along with other foreign law enforcement agencies, were able to track down a man, Baha' al-Din Nazari, a.k.a. Eyad Hakimi, who they believed was the middle person hosting the auction sites that the weapons lists were posted on, along with funneling the money between the person in charge and the people like Perkins and Hollis who were doing the work. He had been taken into custody in London when he was trying to board a plane headed for Cuba.

Clover took the seat next to Joker on the sofa. She felt a migraine coming on, and she rubbed her temples, hoping the little massage would help.

Joker leaned over. "Hey, are you okay?"

She squinted at him. The lighting was making the headache even worse.

"I've got a migraine."

He cupped her cheek. "You've been through a lot in the last few days. Maybe you should lay down for a little bit."

"What's wrong?" President Evans asked from across the room.

"She has a migraine," Joker told him, and even Evans advised that she go lay down.

She would love to lay down, but they were all discussing security around the base and how they planned to sneak the family in without anyone knowing since the person they'd been looking for could be watching.

"I'd rather stay to hear everything."

"Clover, go rest. We can update you later," Bear told her.

"Come on. I'll go back to the cottage with you," Joker said, and he started to stand.

Just at that moment, Jocelyn walked into the room, and Clover couldn't help but notice the way Bear's body tensed up next to her, which she found very interesting.

Jocelyn Thomspon worked for Lana on her clean water initiative, but she was also an old family friend of the Walkers. In fact, Jocelyn and Bear grew up together and were best friends throughout school until they went their separate ways after graduating high school. Since then, she had never heard her brother even bring her name up.

"I can walk her to the cottage and stay with her," Jocelyn offered.

Clover could tell that Joker wasn't a fan of that idea, but she knew that he would want to hear everything, even though his team could update him.

Clover placed her hand on Joker's arm. "I'm good with Jocelyn coming with me."

"I already have men stationed at the cottage," Merrick informed them. "They'll be protected."

The indecisive look on Joker's face was telling.

"Joker. I'll be fine. Merrick's men can be trusted."

After a few moments, he finally relented.

"Alright. I'll come up as soon as we're finished."

She smiled. "Okay."

He kissed her cheek before she and Jocelyn left.

As Clover and Jocelyn stepped out into the cool, mountain summer air, a sudden feeling of doom settled upon her. She wasn't sure why. Maybe it was just her nerves. And, of course, the headache could be messing with her mind. Either way, she'd heed the warning and stay alert.

CHAPTER TWENTY-THREE

Joker couldn't stop fidgeting as he tried to concentrate on the discussion at hand. Merrick explained how Clover's family would be flown via a private charter from Tri-Cities Regional Airport to Dulles International Airport in Virginia, and then flown via helicopter into Camp David.

Bear nudged his elbow, and Joker looked at him.

"What in the hell is the matter with you? I've never seen you act this nervous."

Joker couldn't put his finger on it. But something in his gut told him that danger was close by, and he wasn't comfortable having Clover out of his sight.

"I just have a bad feeling."

Bear's expression turned serious. "What do you mean?"

Joker explained to Bear the only way he knew his team leader would understand.

"You know the feeling we get when we're out in the field, and something isn't right?" Bear nodded. "That's the feeling I have right now. I don't know why, but I just do."

Before Bear could respond, one of the secret service agents burst into the room, and from the worried look on his face, Joker was about to find out why he had that feeling.

"What's wrong, Agent Lloyd?" Merrick asked, standing up.

"Sir, we've been trying to call the agents at the cottage where Captain Walker and Ms. Thompson are, but we can't get a response from them."

Just then, the President's phone rang, and he answered. "This is Evans."

In seconds, Joker watched Evans' expression go from concerned to downright pissed off. But all he could do was listen to the one-sided conversation.

"He did?"

"Are you positive?"

"Fuck!"

"Alright, I let Merrick know. I'll see you in a few minutes."

Evans disconnected the call and looked at Merrick.

"Lock down the entire base right now. Nobody leaves, and nobody enters."

Joker felt the adrenalin already building, and he didn't even know what the hell was happening. But it was a strong indication that whoever they were hunting was close by.

Merrick was already on the phone barking orders when Evans faced Joker and the rest of the team.

"That was Caruso. He received a call from Tink a few minutes ago. When Tink was at the White House the other day, he saw a woman that looked familiar. Something in his gut didn't sit right with her familiarity, so he took a picture of her. He pulled up her picture this morning and started running it through facial recognition, and he got a hit."

"Who is she?" Joker asked.

"It was Carrie. She's Lana's Chief of Staff."

"What did Tink find out about her?"

"Her name isn't Carrie. Her name is Rose Woodland. She's an ex-operative who worked years ago with not only Perkins, but Blanyard too. Two of the men who were killed last Friday. She's the one who's been forging my name. With her close relationship with Lana and other key figures on my staff, she had access to a lot of information and resources."

"Holy shit!" Bear exclaimed.

But Joker started thinking. "Since you're locking the base down, does that mean Tink and Caruso think she's coming here?"

Evans shook his head. "No. Caruso's team already has her in custody, and she already admitted who she was working for."

"Who?"

"Vice President Torres. When Caruso's team got to his house, he was gone. He apparently gave his protection detail team the slip."

"Where do they think he went?" One of the other guys asked.

"I don't know for sure, but Carrie—or Rose, told Caruso that Torres knows where Clover is, and that he has plans for her."

"Fuck!" Joker blurted out. "He could be headed here right now."

"Or he could already be here," Bear said grimly.

"Shit! Clover and Jocelyn are at the cottage," Joker said aloud, before turning to Merrick. "Have you gotten a response back from the agents at the cottage?"

"No."

"Fuck! We need to warn them."

"How can you get a hold of her?"

"I gave her the burner phone before she and Jocelyn left."

"Call her, Joker. Tell her what's going on and to stay put, we're on our way," Bear ordered as they ran out of the house toward the cottage. Joker just prayed they weren't too late.

੭

Clover's eyes popped wide open. She hadn't been in a deep sleep. She was in that stage where her subconscious could still hear things going on around her.

She thought she heard a noise, almost like a heavy thump. She sat up and let her eyes adjust to the dark room. When she didn't see Jocelyn, she wondered where she had gone. Maybe she got hungry or thirsty and went to the kitchen for something.

But everything was quiet—too quiet, Clover thought to herself. She had to pee anyway, so she pushed the blanket off her and slid out of bed. Just as she was about to open the door, she glanced at the alarm clock on the table next to the bed and noticed it wasn't lit. She then looked at the phone next to the clock and saw it wasn't charging, even though it was plugged in.

The power was off.

A sudden chill raced down her spine. She reached for the phone before going to search for Jocelyn.

As she made her way down the hallway, she saw Jocelyn face down on the floor near the front door. Blood was oozing from the side of her head.

"Oh God, Joce!" She yelled, racing to her side.

At that moment, the phone rang, and she answered it as she felt a pulse in Jocelyn. "Thank God," she whispered to herself.

"Hello?!" She said frantically on the phone.

"Clover! Thank God. Listen to me. Vice President Torres is the one behind everything. They think he's on his way to Camp David," Joker told her.

Clover saw a shadow move quickly across the room toward her.

"Unless you're inside the house, he's already here," she yelled quickly before the phone was knocked from her hand.

She could hear Joker cursing through the phone. She screamed as her attacker smacked her across the face, but she fought back with some self-defense moves. She could hear Torres breathing heavily, even though she could barely see him. They went back and forth, trading kicks and punches, until suddenly, bullets sprayed the wall behind her. A few narrowly missed her head as she dove to the floor for cover behind the recliner.

She waited a few seconds. All was silent until a hand grabbed her. She screamed in surprise as Torres gripped her shirt and lifted her off the floor, but she managed to swing her arm around and knock the gun from his hand. She heard it land somewhere across the room. He grabbed her arm, yanking it behind her before slamming her face into the wall.

"Face it, Clover. You're no match for me and my abilities. The sooner you give yourself up, the less painful your death will be."

She wanted to ask him how he planned on killing her since he no longer had his gun, but her question was answered when she felt the cold metal blade at her throat. It was then she knew there was nothing more she could do. She didn't move a muscle until she spoke.

"What do you want?" She asked him. She could hear the fear in her voice.

He pressed the knife harder against her skin. "You're my ticket out of here. Let's go," he said, pulling her away from the wall and toward the door. Before they went outside, he threw a pair of handcuffs at her.

"Put those on."

She didn't argue and clicked them around her wrists. He grabbed her as soon as she had them on and moved them out the door. As they exited the cottage and the metal front door closed behind them, the entire area suddenly lit up like someone flipped all the lights on.

Men and women with weapons poured out of the woods. They were all screaming at Torres to let her go.

Torres grabbed her around the waist and moved her in front of him. He cursed and tried to move them back into the house, but the door was locked. She probably would've laughed at him if she weren't in the position she was in.

There were people everywhere, aiming their weapons at them. Torres' arm tightened around her neck. He was a strong man, and being former military, she knew he was capable of snapping it.

"Just give up, Torres. There's nowhere for you to go," she tried pleading with him.

"Shut the fuck up!" He growled loudly in her ear and increased the pressure on her neck, making her gasp for air.

Bear and Nails both stepped forward, their rifles still aimed in Torres' direction.

"She's right, Torres. There's no other way out of this. Just do everyone a favor and surrender before anybody else gets hurt."

Torres didn't say anything, and Clover knew their words had fallen on deaf ears. There was no way Torres was going to wave the white flag. She looked around frantically for Joker. Her eyes filled with tears when she couldn't see him.

She looked back toward her brother. His face was red and full of rage.

Clover knew someone had Torres in the crosshairs of their rifle, waiting for that perfect shot to open up. But Torres wasn't stupid. He was too well trained and knew the drill. But she also knew that if he was killed, he was possibly taking her with him. Even if someone could get a clean shot off, it was still possible he could slice her throat.

As they all stood there playing the waiting game, Clover was trying to figure out a way where she could come out of the situation wounded but not dead.

She tried her hardest to appear brave, but fear was taking over on the inside. Time was running out.

Think, Clover, think!

She glanced around at all the guys with their weapons aimed in her direction. Then an idea hit her, and even though it was the last thing she wanted, it was the only option, because it was clear that Torres wasn't going to end this voluntarily.

She closed her eyes and concentrated on where Torres' body was positioned against her back.

If she could shift her body to the left a few inches, a sniper could easily shoot through her shoulder area and hit him in the chest. Again, there was no guarantee it would work. However, it was the only option they had if they wanted to end this standoff with a chance of her surviving.

She was scared as hell knowing this could be the end, but she was willing to make the ultimate sacrifice to save the world from one evil son of a bitch.

With her decision made, she opened her eyes and found her brother, and the moment they locked eyes, she swallowed hard as the tears filled her eyes. He squinted his eyes as she moved her upper body slightly toward the left. She started communicating with her eyes, praying someone would understand.

༄

Joker hadn't taken his eye off the scope of his rifle. He and two snipers from the secret service were in an overwatch about one hundred yards from where Clover and Torres stood.

All he needed was that perfect shot, and he'd take Torres out. Playboy laid beside him, peering through his binoculars.

"What is she doing with her eyes?" Playboy asked out loud.

Curious, Joker moved the rifle slightly to his left. She was doing some weird blinking thing.

"I have no idea, but it has to mean something."

"Holy shit. It's Morse code," Playboy exclaimed.

"Morse code?"

Joker knew Morse code. He focused on Clover's eyes. He'd seen this before. Eyes closed for one second equals a dot. Eyes closed for two seconds equals a dash.

He cursed, knowing he missed the first part of it. He pulled a small notepad he kept in his rifle case and handed it to Playboy.

"Write down what I tell you."

He waited until he knew Clover had started over.

"Dot, dot, dot. Dot, dot, dot, dot. Dash, dash, dash. Dash, dash, dash. Dash. Dash, dash. Dot."

He waited, and when she just stared at her brother, he assumed she had finished the message. He glanced down at Playboy.

"Anything?"

Playboy peered up at him with a confused look.

"It says shoot me."

"What?"

He radioed to Bear through their comms system.

"Bear, she's doing Morse code with her eyes."

"Do you know what she's saying?"

"If we relayed it correctly, she's asking that we shoot her."

"What?" Bear came back with the exact same reaction. "What does that mean?"

Joker kept repeating the words in his head. *Shoot me. Shoot me. What are you trying to tell us?* Suddenly, it dawned on him. He understood the message, and he suddenly became nauseous.

"She wants us to shoot through her to hit him," he said aloud and knew Bear could still hear him.

"Fuck! That explains the look she gave me right before she shifted her body. Goddammit!"

"We don't have a lot of time. Torres is getting antsy," Caruso voiced through the communication device.

"This may be the only way that they come out of the situation alive."

"Who has a shot?"

Joker took the binoculars from Playboy and held them up to his eyes. The moment Joker saw blood start to trickle down Clover's neck, he didn't waver. The man holding her hostage wasn't going to take her with him. And he wasn't going to put her life in anyone else's hands.

"I've got the shot," Joker announced.

"Joker?" Bear questioned, and Joker understood why. He would have to put a bullet in the woman he loved in order to stop Torres.

"I've got the shot," Joker repeated, his voice firmer, leaving no room for argument.

There was a pause, and Joker thought Bear might try to argue, but Joker was serious, and it sounded ridiculous even to his own ears. Nobody but him was going to pull the trigger of a gun aimed at Clover.

Instead of Bear's voice, Caruso's came back over the comms.

"Sector three has a shot. I repeat, sector three has a shot."

As they stood there on the roof of the building, Playboy looked at Joker. "You sure about this, man?"

Joker inhaled sharply. "Honestly? No. But I'm not about to put Clover's life in anyone else's hands."

"Alright then. Let's do this," Playboy stated, dropping to one knee.

Joker followed, then pulled a green bandana from his pocket. He removed his ball cap and wiped the sweat from his forehead before wiping his hands. He lowered himself to the ground onto his stomach, turned his hat around backward, and took position behind his rifle.

In a prone position with his legs spread out behind him and his cheek pressed firmly against the rifle's stock, he zeroed in on the target as Playboy recalculated the distance and wind.

Once Joker was locked onto the target, he began his firing sequence. He started breathing out slowly, taking up slack in the trigger.

Everything fell onto this moment. He blocked everything from his mind, but ensured that Clover would come out of this alive and that the son of a bitch holding a knife to her neck wouldn't live to take another breath.

There was silence all around, except for the thumping sound of his heartbeat. He drew in a deep breath with his finger steady on the trigger.

"Ready!" He announced, and Playboy returned in two seconds, giving him the go.

"Please forgive me," he whispered before pulling the trigger. As the gun fired, Joker exhaled, releasing all the air trapped inside him.

~

Clover stood perfectly still, wondering if they got her message. But then her brother, who was talking to someone through his mic, met her gaze.

"Everything'll be alright," he assured her, although Clover knew he was letting her know that her message was received. But he wasn't happy. In fact, none of them were. It wasn't the outcome they wanted. But it was the only way to end all of it.

She took an oath to defend her country and its citizens, and she intended to, even if it meant sacrificing herself.

She took one last look at her brother, and she almost lost it when he lifted his hand and wiped his eyes.

Before she changed her mind, she closed her eyes and tried her best to relax her body, considering she had just put her life in someone else's hands. Not knowing what the next few moments would bring, she used the precious time to send up a small prayer before reflecting on the life she'd gotten to share with her family and the man she loved with all her heart.

A lone tear slipped out of her eye as she took a deep breath and waited. As the seconds passed, the anticipation intensified. Before she even heard the gun firing, a numb feeling swept over her body as she was pulled to the ground.

Moments later, the situation became chaotic, and confusion soon clouded Clover's mental state. The first person she saw when she opened her eyes was Bear. His mouth was moving, but she couldn't hear a damn thing he was saying.

Without any warning, the numbness in her chest gave way to a hot, blistering pain, tearing through her body. Her breathing became rapid, and she started gasping for air. She struggled to breathe, the tightness in her chest becoming more and more painful with every attempt. Joker appeared above her as the blackness took hold of her and began to pull her under. She tried to reach out to him, but she couldn't move. A coldness set in, and she began to shake violently as the fight inside her started to diminish. The struggle was too painful, and the frightened look on Joker's face as he stared into her eyes was too much to bear.

She was so scared. She didn't want to die. She still had so much she wanted to experience in life. She wanted to become a wife and, hopefully, one day, a mom. She wanted to grow old with the man she loved. She wanted to live. But she soon realized the heavens above might have other plans for her.

She gazed into Joker's eyes as he caressed her forehead. The tears falling from his eyes did her in.

"I love you," she told him, though she wasn't sure if he heard. The last thing she felt before being sucked into darkness was Joker's warm lips pressed against her forehead.

ತ

Joker didn't even wait around to see if his shot was on target. As soon as he felt the bullet exit the gun barrel, he was on his feet and heading toward Clover.

Bear, Duke, and the paramedics were already working on her by the time he reached her. They had her shirt cut open and were working vigorously to try and stop the bleeding, but it seemed endless. Everything was covered in red—Clover's blood.

He dropped to his knees by her head, making sure he stayed out of the way of the paramedics. Her body was shaking as she struggled to breathe.

But that wasn't what put a knife through his heart. It was the panic and fear he saw while staring into her eyes. She was scared, and so was he. For the first time in his career, he didn't know what to do. Both he and Bear kept talking to her to try and keep her calm.

She looked up at him, and he could tell she was losing focus as if she was going in and out of consciousness. The tears hit his eyes.

She struggled to stay with him, and Joker knew from the dull look in her usually bright eyes that she was losing the fight.

"You hang in there, sweetheart. Do you hear me? You fight, dammit!"

"I...l-love...y-you," she rasped out before closing her eyes for the last time. He squeezed his eyes shut, trying to stop the flow of tears. He leaned down and kissed her forehead. "I love you, baby."

Seconds later, he was pushed out of the way by the paramedics as they loaded her on a stretcher and hurried toward the ambulance. Joker and Bear followed, watching as they worked frantically on her.

Once they had her loaded in the back of the ambulance, the doors slammed closed, and they took off.

Joker was left standing there, watching the ambulance drive away. When it registered that he may have lost her, he dropped to his knees and covered his face with his hands. It was then that he let the tears flow. Moments later, he felt a set of arms come around him. He knew it was Bear, and they both embraced one another, crying and praying that they hadn't lost a woman they both loved.

CHAPTER TWENTY-FOUR

Bear was pacing the waiting room when he heard the door open. He saw his mom, dad, and three brothers as they rushed inside. As soon as he met his parents' eyes, he nearly lost it seeing them upset.

"Tripp." His mom exclaimed and rushed to his side. "How is she?" She asked as she tried to hold back the tears, but Bear could tell she had already been crying.

He swallowed hard and glanced at Joker, who had bloodstains on his shirt, hands, and arms. Clover's blood. His sister that he may never get to talk to again because he gave an order to shoot her. *Jesus.* How was he going to tell his family that Clover was fighting for her life because he gave the order?

One look at his dad and brothers, and they understood his silence. But he had to be strong for his mom right now. The worst part was that he had to be honest with them.

He cleared his throat and got his emotions in check before he spoke. "She's alive, but her injuries are severe."

"What happened?" His dad asked as he put his arm around his wife as if he needed support. His dad wasn't stupid. He knew the situation was dire.

"She took a bullet to her lung." He ran his hand down his face as he recalled all the blood and heard her struggle to breathe. He glanced over at Joker and only saw his back as he retreated from the room.

"What's with him?" Justin asked as if he was annoyed that Joker had left the room.

Bear didn't answer right away. He looked at his family. "Why don't we sit, and I can explain everything."

Bear watched his family's expressions while describing the timeline of events leading up to where they were right now. When he got to the part where he had ordered Joker to shoot Clover, he paused for a brief moment, as his emotions literally stole his voice. No matter how hard he tried to speak around the tightness in his throat brought on by his feelings, he couldn't find his voice. It didn't help that, at the same time, hot tears burned his eyes, threatening to spill over his lids. He hung his head in defeat and squeezed his eyes shut. But even that wasn't enough. As soon as the first teardrop slipped out, he couldn't stop the flow of tears that followed. Surprisingly, it wasn't his mom or dad who came to his side to comfort him. All three of his brothers were there.

అ

A little while later, Bear and his dad and brothers were sitting and waiting.

"What's with Joker?" Justin asked.

"He blames himself."

"He knows it isn't his fault, right?" Zach asked.

Bear shook his head. "Try telling him that." Bear was worried about Joker. He knew that his friend and teammate cared about Clover more than a kid-sister way. He saw the love as Joker held Clover in his arms. He saw the fear on Joker's face knowing that they could lose her.

"I don't understand any of this. How long has she been moonlighting as a fucking special ops helicopter pilot? How did we not know? She lied to us. She shouldn't have even been in that situation to begin with."

"That's enough!" Ray gritted through his teeth.

"What? Dad, how can you sit here and say that you aren't disappointed?"

Bear watched as his dad leveled his eyes with each of them. "Disappointed? Hell no. I'm fucking proud of my baby girl."

"Did you know?"

Ray ran his hand across his jaw, and for the first time, Bear saw a fault in his dad's expression. It was clear as day—guilt.

"Officially? No. But I sensed something was up with her."

"Do you guys know that she pulled my team out?" Zach said, and they all looked at him.

"She did? How do you know?" Ethan asked.

"Lucky. It's her call sign. I've ridden with a Lucky before, and if that were her, I'd be the first to say that she's one fucking amazing pilot."

"As dad said, I'm fucking proud. But I'm also sorry that she felt she had to hide this from her own family. She has accomplished so much, and the sad part is that she couldn't even celebrate those feats with us." Bear stated.

"Justin, sweetheart, what's wrong?" His mom asked.

"A few months ago, a platoon from my unit was pinned down. There was a rescue mission that took place. The helo pilot took on enemy fire, but got those Marines out. Back at the base, I remember those same group of guys talking about the kickass pilot who did unimaginable things up in the air." He looked at everyone. "The pilot's name was Lucky."

"She has to be good to be handpicked by the President," Ray interjected.

Bear looked at his dad. "What happens now?"

"What do you mean?"

"Her career. An injury like this has ramifications."

His dad gave everyone a dire expression. "Let's cross that road when we come to it. Right now, we need all the prayers we can muster to make sure your sister makes it through this."

૱

The air outside the hospital was hot and humid. In other words, it was miserable. Just how Joker felt.

He took a seat on a bench just outside of the emergency entrance. He looked down at his hands. They were stained with Clover's blood. He bowed his head. He'd been all over the world and had seen some of the nastiest things—blood and body parts, but when someone was faced with it while tending to one of their own, it was a game-changer. Completely different. They were trained to be desensitized. But not when a loved one was lying in your arms while you tried to stop blood from pouring out of her body or listening to her struggle and fight for every goddamn breath of air she could get.

He heard the automatic door open and assumed it was Bear or one of his brothers. He was shocked when Jenelle took the open seat next to him on the bench.

She didn't say anything. Instead, she took his hand into hers, and they sat like that until she spoke.

"You know, my little girl is strong and stubborn." He still didn't say anything. "She's also a protector just like my husband, my sons, and yourself." She turned her head and met his gaze. "She cares for you very much. She always has."

Before he could question her, she continued. "I always saw that spark in her eyes as soon as you would walk into a room."

He gave her a half-smile. "You did?"

She gave his hand a gentle squeeze. "A mom notices these things." She winked, which drew a small laugh from him.

"I can't lie to you, Jenelle. I love your daughter with all my heart. But I can't get past the fact that I feel like I failed her."

"How can you say that?"

He shook his head in frustration. "She's in surgery fighting for her life right now, because she never should have been put in the situation she was in, to begin with."

"Landon, look at me," she commanded sternly.

He slowly turned and met her gaze, and she lifted her hand to cup his cheek.

"There was no way any of you knew that Torres was the person behind this. He fooled everyone. That isn't your fault."

He blew out a frustrated breath, knowing she was right. None of them picked up on Torres' part in the whole situation. But it still didn't sit well with him that Clover was put in harm's way.

"I still feel responsible, because I'm the one who pulled the trigger."

"But shouldn't Clover be partially responsible?" She asked, and the question surprised Joker. When he didn't respond, she continued. "As I said before, my daughter is just as much of a protector as you and my sons are. And she sacrificed herself doing just that—protecting those she loved."

Jenelle was trying to re-enforce her take on the situation, and Joker understood what she was saying, but it still bothered him.

He was going to respond when he spotted Zach walking out the door. He lifted his hand, and Zach saw him and walked over.

"What's going on?" Zach asked, eyeing his mom and Joker.

Jenelle gave her youngest son a soft smile. "Landon and I were having a nice talk." She turned her head and winked at Joker, who grinned.

"Okay," Zach replied. But the knowing look on his face told Joker that Zach had an idea of what he and Jenelle were talking about.

"Did you need something, son?" Jenelle asked Zach.

"The nurse just came in. Clover's out of surgery. She said the doctor would be in to speak with us in about fifteen minutes."

Jenelle turned toward Joker, and a huge smile graced her face. She retook Joker's hand and squeezed it.

"Did you hear that? She's out of surgery."

It was positive news.

She stood up and smoothened out her dress pants. Jenelle Walker was always a woman who was well put together. Before she walked back inside, she leaned down and hugged Joker.

"Come on now. My baby girl needs you."

༒

Beep-beep-beep...the sound was becoming annoying to Clover's ears. That, mixed with the humming sound and the constricting feeling around her upper right arm, was enough to drive her crazy.

She looked around, but it was dark. So dark she couldn't see a thing. She strained her eyes as she attempted to peer further into the distance when suddenly, a sliver of a golden glow of light illuminated before her, reminding her of the first rays of the morning sunshine.

"Clover, honey..."

Mom?
"We're all here with you, baby."
Dad?
You're so close, Clover. I know you can hear us."
Ethan?
"Come on, sis, fight like I know you can."
Zach?
"Stubborn Marine…" The next voice said with a hint of amusement.
Justin…
"Come back to us, Lucky. You've got a lot more in life to prove. I'm so proud of you, baby sis." She'd know that voice anywhere—*Bear.*

"I can hear you, but I can't see you." She called out. But all she got in return was silence, until that darn beeping, and humming sound started up again.

Suddenly something warm pressed against her forehead, followed by a light warm breeze caressing the skin by her neck and ear.

"You're the bravest woman I know." The voice whispered softly into her ear. "I promise that I'll never fail you again. Please come back to me, sweetheart. I love you." The voice was sincere and familiar, but different at the same time. A moment later, the warmth that had encompassed her was gone, leaving her chilled and feeling lost in his words, and she slipped back into the darkness.

❧

Clover pulled into the marina not far from the hotel she'd been staying in for the last two days.

After getting discharged from the hospital a few weeks ago, she had spent the following two weeks recovering at her apartment in San Diego. Her mom and dad had stayed with her, which had been a blessing since she had been limited in what she could do physically.

During her hospital stay, talking with Joker before he and her brother had to leave for deployment and during the time she was recovering at home, she had thought long and hard about her future. She realized her initial choice had been the right one.

On one of the days when she felt up to it, her dad accompanied her to the base to meet with Colonel Jenkins. When she arrived at his office, she was surprised to see President Evans sitting in the office.

Come to find out, her dad had given Jenkins and Evans a heads up as to why she wanted to meet, and Evans had told her that he wanted to be there.

When she broke the news to them that she had decided not to re-up, they both understood and respected her decision, though they were both extremely disappointed they would be losing one of the best pilots in SCU history.

Because of the time it would take for her to recover from the injury fully, her time in the Corps would have expired before she could climb back into a Black Hawk. So, the Corps had been trying to get her medically discharged. When Jenkins found out, he went straight to Evans, who made a call, and the entire case was thrown out.

Knowing that she planned to move to the East Coast upon her exit from the Corps, Jenkins and Evans had made a few other calls and surprised her by pushing up her moving date.

So, until she left the Corps, she'd be working as a Recruiter out of the Virginia Beach office for the next few months. Yeah, it was a desk job, but it was only temporary. And she'd love to share her success stories with high school and college students who might be on the fence about joining the Marines.

She still hadn't heard from either Joker or Bear, so she hadn't been able to share the good news with them yet. Her mom and dad told her that they'd handle all the moving logistics for her. She was due to report to the Recruiting office early next week, so she got into town a few days earlier. Plus, she had an interview the day before for a job she hoped to secure once she no longer wore the uniform.

She had received a text late last night from her mom, telling her that she needed to be at this specific marina at 0700. She was a bit leery, but her mother assured her that everything was fine.

She got out of her rental car and walked toward the main dock when she spotted a familiar face. She smiled at Bear as he leaned against his truck, staring out at the water. She followed his line of sight and the gorgeous view made her smile grow. The view of the sun welcoming another summer day as it rose in the cloudless sky was beautiful. The few rays of light made the calm ocean surface sparkle like it was filled with diamonds.

As if sensing her presence, Bear turned his head and grinned when he saw her. She smiled back as she walked over to him.

He immediately pulled her in for a hug, and she hugged him back.

"I'm so happy to see you," he told her.

"Likewise. But how did you know I was even here?" She asked curiously.

"Mom texted me."

"Oh. When did you get back?"

"Yesterday. I was surprised when she told me that you were here. I'm even more surprised that Dad let you come out alone."

She laughed. "I think I was on the phone with him the entire trip, except when I stopped to sleep."

Bear smirked. "Of course you were. You're his favorite."

She laughed. "Hey, Mom and Dad never played favorites. I believe I got my ass whipped just as many times as you, Justin, Ethan, and Zach." She scrunched her nose up. "Actually, now that I think about it, I probably endured more spankings than the four of you."

"No way," he argued playfully.

"After you all left for the service, I didn't have anyone who I could shift the blame to." She said with a sarcastic smirk.

Bear put his arm around her shoulders and pulled her to his side. She heard him take a deep breath.

"How are you doing? And be honest."

She inhaled a deep, calming breath, then exhaled. She was still dealing with the effects of her injury. "Physically, I'm doing good. There are still times that my lungs remind me that I need to slow down, but for the most part, I feel good."

"I don't think I've ever seen Justin, Ethan, or Zach as scared as they were when we thought we lost you. Hell, I know I was a basket case."

She looked up at him. "Really?"

He pinned her with his grey eyes. "Really, Clover. Growing up, you may have been a pain in our ass, but that never stopped us from loving you. The thought of losing you made us all realize exactly what we could have lost."

"Like what? I was your annoying little sister."

He turned her around so she was facing him.

"You are so much more Clover, and I can't wait to see what lies ahead for you."

She squinted her eyes at him. "Did Mom or Dad already tell you?" She was referring to her move to Virginia Beach.

He gave her a wry grin. "Maybe."

You didn't tell Joker, did you?"

He shook his head. "No. But Mom did text him to let him know that you were in town."

Why did Clover think that her mom was up to something?

Bear took her hand and looked into her eyes. "You and Joker are two of my favorite people. I can't tell you how happy I am for the both of you."

He leaned down and kissed her cheek. "Turn around," he whispered.

Clover gave her brother a suspicious look before acting on his order. She saw a nice-sized boat with a center console pulling up to the dock when she turned. She looked closer as the man behind the wheel looked awfully familiar, but the glare of the bright sun made it difficult for her to see clearly.

She took a few steps forward as the guy was tying up the boat to dock, and when he looked up, and they locked eyes, she knew exactly who it was. She started toward him as fast as her recovering body would allow. As soon as she made it to the boat, she didn't even wait for Joker to get off as she hopped into the boat and threw herself into his arms.

☙

Joker had been a nervous wreck ever since Clover's mom called him last night and told him that she was in town and had some good news for him. It was perfect timing, because he had news for her too.

As he pulled up to the dock where he told Bear to have Clover, he saw her. She looked so beautiful. The way she had her hand above her eyes, shielding the sun's glare, made him believe she wasn't sure who he was.

As he tied the boat to the dock, she walked closer, and when he looked up and met her sparkling eyes and bright smile, he knew she realized who it was. However, he hadn't expected her to take off the way she had and make it to the dock before he finished tying it down. He had just gotten the last rope tied when she leaped into the boat, and he caught her.

As soon as he had her secured in his arms, he buried his face in the crook of her neck and hugged her tight.

"God, I've missed you," he told her as he pulled back and kissed her on the lips.

She was smiling and even crying.

"I missed you, too."

She looked around and then back toward the parking lot where Bear's truck was pulling out of the parking lot.

"I feel like this was a set-up."

He grinned. "I won't lie. It was."

She looked around the boat as he set her down on her feet. "Do you have room for one more?"

Pulling her against his chest and clutching her chin, he said, "I always have room for you."

☙

Clover and Joker sat next to each other, staring out at the water as the boat bobbed up and down over the gentle sea.

After they left the dock, he drove them a ways out where they sat and talked before driving them into a little secluded cove with a few homes lining the shore where they currently sat.

He reached over and took her hand into his much larger one. He tugged on it, pulling her off her seat and onto his lap. He ran his fingers through her windblown hair and stared at her lips as she licked them subconsciously. God, he wanted her.

"Why else did you come all of the way out here?"

She smiled. "To finish off my career, and for a job interview."

"What? Are you transferring?" He asked, seeming surprised.

"For a little bit. But I've had my fun playing James Bond."

"But you're interviewing for a job here in town or—"

"Here, locally." She slid her arms around his neck. "It just so happens that a top-notch security firm in the area is in need of an experienced kick-ass helicopter pilot."

"Are you talking about Rockwell? Tink's firm?"

"The one and only."

"When's your interview?"

"It was yesterday."

"And…"

"Well, I have to start looking for a place to live since it looks like I'm going to be staying for a while, and I'm hoping that the man I'm madly in love with would be so kind as to let me stay with him."

"Is that right?"

"Mmm…hmmm."

She cupped his cheeks and looked him in the eyes.

"I love you, Landon."

He smiled. "I love you, too."

She leaned in and kissed him. She was in an awkward spot, so she moved her legs around and straddled him. His phone started to vibrate, and she released his lips.

"I can't reach my phone. Can you grab it out of my side pocket?" He asked her.

She reached inside, and when she pulled the phone out, a pair of hot pink thong panties came out along with it, and her eyes widened as her tempter began to rise, but then she looked closer.

Son of a bitch!

"You did not steal my panties!"

The smirk on his face was adorable and totally gave away his guilt. He looked at her as if she had just caught his hand in the cookie jar.

"Stole? No. Took? Yes," he told her in a calm and steady voice.

"That's still stealing!"

"Not if the object was in the trash."

"Ugh!" She snatched them from his hand and put them in her pocket. "I'm not wearing those."

He wrapped one arm around her waist, slipped his other hand under her hair, and cupped her neck, bringing her face closer to his. His expression was now full of amusement.

"You can have those because I have a drawer full of all different colored ones for you at our house."

She started to roll her eyes, but then his words sunk in. *Our house?* She pulled back a smidge and looked into his eyes that sparkled like diamonds.

"Our house?" She repeated.

He bit his lip, then slowly nodded his head.

"When the hospital let us see you for the first time after your surgery, and I saw you laying there with tubes and wires connected to your body, I couldn't stomach it." He paused for a moment, and Clover saw his eyes flood with tears. She reached up and wiped them away before they could fall. "You had sacrificed so much that I knew I had to do something," he told her.

"When Bear and I got that call from Derek while you were still in the hospital telling us that we had to get back because we were being called out, it was the first time in my career that I wanted to say no to a direct order. It killed me having to leave you alone there."

His words warmed Clover's heart, making the love she had for him grow even more.

"I'm glad you chose to do the right thing and listen to your commander."

He pulled her closer. "Before the team and I headed out, I met with an attorney and had them draw up papers, adding you to the deed of the house I just bought for us."

She smiled as her eyes filled with tears. "You bought us a house?"

"I did. I only want you, Clover. And one day I'm going to ask you to marry me."

"And that day, I'll say yes."

Joker smiled and kissed her before starting up the boat and driving toward their new home on the water's edge in the city she now called home—Virginia Beach.

EPILOGUE

Bear sat on the porch swing. He wasn't in the best mood, so he thought it was best he isolated himself from the partygoers. His parents were throwing a barbeque, and they had invited everyone.

"Hey. What are you doing out here? The party is out back," Clover stated as she came from around the side of the house. She climbed the steps and joined him on the porch.

"Just thinking," he told her as he gazed out toward the mountains in the distance.

Clover walked over and took the seat next to him. She nudged her foot against the deck, sending the swing into motion.

"You being out here and non-sociable doesn't have anything to with Jocelyn, now does it?" She asked, and Bear looked at her.

"What makes you think that?"

"Oh, I don't know, maybe because you haven't taken your eyes off her since she arrived."

He shook his head. He wasn't about to jump down that rabbit hole.

"Bear, what happened between you and Jocelyn? Y'all used to be so close."

He wasn't going to get into his problems with his sister. Plus, it wasn't worth pouring salt into old wounds. He had to man up and admit that he fucked up and had assumed something instead of being the mature one.

Luckily for him, his phone rang and saved him from an incoming interrogation from his sister.

When he looked at the screen, his gut clenched. It was the lawyer's office. He excused himself and walked to the other end of the porch.

"Hello?"

"Hi, Mr. Walker?"

"Speaking."

"Hi, Mr. Walker. This is Glenice Waters from Waters and Bates. I was returning your call from last week."

"Yes. Ms. Waters."

"I do apologize for the delay in getting back to you. It took me a while to locate your file, as my dad was in the process of moving his paper files to electronic."

"No worries. I can understand."

"You have no idea."

"I moved around a lot, and now that I've settled somewhat, I started unpacking, and that's when I realized I never got a signed copy of my divorce papers when they were finalized."

He heard a faint sigh on the other end of the line.

"Well, there seems to be a slight problem," she told him, but Bear didn't understand.

"Problem?"

She sighed. And it was one of those sighs where the person was going to tell you something you weren't going to like. How bad could the problem be? Maybe the file was just lost, and they would have to get a new copy from the courts?

"Mr. Walker, I'm quite embarrassed to say this, but after reviewing your case file, it appears that your papers were never submitted to the courts."

Bear gave his head a slight shake, hoping he had misunderstood Ms. Waters. "I'm sorry. Can you please repeat that? I thought I heard you say that my papers were never submitted."

"You heard me correctly."

"I don't understand. What does that mean?"

Another sigh. *What the fuck is with all the sighing?*

It means, Mr. Walker, that you and Ms. Thompson are still legally married.

Bear and Jocelyn's story is coming soon!

BOOK LIST

The Trident Series
ACE
POTTER
FROST
IRISH
STITCH
DINO
SKITTLES
DIEGO
A TRIDENT WEDDING

The Trident Series II
BRAVO Team
JOKER
BEAR
DUKE *(2023)*
PLAYBOY *(2023)*
AUSSIE *(2023)*
SNOW *(TBD)*
NAILS *(TBD)*
JAY BIRD *(TBD)*

ABOUT THE AUTHOR

Jaime Lewis, a *USA TODAY* bestselling author, entered the indie author world in June 2020 with ACE, the first book in the Trident Series.

Coming from a military family, she describes as very patriotic; it's no surprise that her books are known for their accurate portrayal of life in the service.

Passionate in her support of the military, veterans, and first responders, Jaime volunteers with the Daytona Division of the US Naval Sea Cadet Corps, a non-profit youth leadership development program sponsored by the U.S. Navy. Together with her son, she also manages a charity organization that supports military personnel and their families, along with veterans and first responders.

Born and raised in Edgewater, Maryland, Jaime now resides in Ormond Beach, Florida with her husband and two very active boys.

Between writing and her two boys, she doesn't have a heap of spare time, but if she does, you'll find her somewhere in the outdoors. Jaime is also an avid sports fan.

Follow Jaime:

Facebook Author Page: https://www.facebook.com/jaime.lewis.58152
Jaime's Convoy: https://www.facebook.com/groups/349178512953776
Bookbub: https://www.bookbub.com/profile/jaime-lewis
Goodreads: https://www.goodreads.com/author/show/17048191.Jaime_Lewis

Made in the USA
Monee, IL
21 June 2023